$\mathcal{H}$e tried not to notice how the collar of her blouse gaped open to reveal the erratic pulse beating at the base of her throat, because it looked altogether too tempting, and because he doubted she'd be interested in anything other than peeling the skin off his hide with a blunt instrument.

"Mr. Gallagher, I know for a fact that just a short time ago you were writing sports columns, not critiquing restaurants. You should stick with what you're good at."

There was a compliment in there somewhere, Dan was positive.

"I've got a pretty discriminating palate, and I can judge a good meal from a poor one."

Her spine stiffened. "Says who? I think your palate stinks, and so does your review."

Turning on her heel, she headed for the door, then stopped abruptly and looked back. "And another thing: my chocolate cannolis are innovative and delicious. Fabulous, even!"

The door slammed shut before Dan could respond. Damn, but the woman had fire in her soul!

THE
TROUBLE
WITH MARY

Millie Criswell

IVY BOOKS • NEW YORK

This book contains an excerpt from the forthcoming paperback edition of *What To Do About Annie* by Millie Criswell. This excerpt has been set for this edition only and may not reflect the final content of the forthcoming edition.

An Ivy Book
Published by The Ballantine Publishing Group
Copyright © 2000 by Millie Criswell

Excerpt from *What To Do About Annie* by Millie Criswell © 2000 by Millie Criswell

www.randomhouse.com/BB/

Library of Congress Catalog Card Number: 00-109181

ISBN 978-0-345-48481-9

146673257

To my sister, Nina Cahouette, and brother, Frank Arcuri, who shared many of the memories found in this book, and the joys of growing up in a dysfunctional—who knew it wasn't normal?—Italian family. I love you both!

ACKNOWLEDGMENT

I would like to single out some very wonderful ladies who helped me tremendously in the writing of this book.

First, and most especially, my brilliant agent, Meg Ruley, who prodded, tweaked, and encouraged, always with grace and humor. Also, the folks at Jane Rotrosen, who are such a pleasure to work with.

My editor, Shauna Summers, who saw something special in this book and had the marvelous insight to buy it. And for her invaluable help during the editing process. Thank you!

Fellow authors Christiane Heggan and Leanne Banks, my telephone lifelines to sanity, and the best friends a neurotic writer could have.

I feel truly blessed to be surrounded by such extraordinary people!

THE TROUBLE WITH MARY

Cannoli del Cioccolato

Chocolate Cannoli Shells

1 cup flour
1 $\frac{1}{2}$ tbsp. cocoa powder
1 cup butter, melted and cooled
$\frac{1}{2}$ cup sugar
1 tbsp. vanilla extract
4 egg whites

Mix ingredients and pour into cannoli form molds and bake in 325° oven, 8–10 minutes. Cool. Packaged shells can be used.

Ricotta Filling

2 cups ricotta cheese
$\frac{1}{4}$ cup confectioners' sugar
$\frac{1}{2}$ cup cocoa powder
2 cups heavy cream
1 tsp. vanilla

Prepare filling and spoon into cooled shells or fill with pastry bag.

Chocolate Sauce:

$\frac{1}{3}$ cup sugar
2 tbsp. cocoa powder
$\frac{1}{4}-\frac{1}{2}$ cup water
3 oz. semisweet chocolate

In saucepan combine sugar and cocoa powder. Add water and stir until blended. Add semisweet chocolate and melt over low heat, stirring to blend. Cool. Pour cooled chocolate sauce over ricotta-filled shells. Dust with ¼ cup confectioners' sugar, if desired. Serves 8, 2 cannolis per person.

CHAPTER ONE

On any given day Mary Russo could usually find a compelling reason to eat chocolate. Maybe the sun was shining too brightly, or perhaps the cloud cover was too thickly depressing, and there was always the possibility that her cat, Morty, had coughed up more than his usual share of hair balls.

But on this fairly cloudless, not too terribly sunny day, as Mary bit into a luscious, palate-pleasing chocolate cannoli oozing with chocolate ricotta filling and covered with the most fabulous chocolate sauce she'd ever invented, she had an even better reason to indulge, to eat herself into oblivion, and to feel totally crappy about life in general, much crappier than she usually did.

Luigi Marconi was dead.

Luigi's death might not have come as a shock to most people who knew him. The restauranteur had been dreadfully overweight, suffered from diabetes for years, and he'd been unusually depressed for the past four months. But no one, including Mary, who'd worked for the owner of Luigi's Pizza Palace for the past ten years as head cook and bookkeeper, had expected him to put a gun to his head, say *arrivederci*, and check out.

Boom! Just like that. One shot. One lethal, impulsive bang, and Mary had lost not only a dear friend, a man whom she'd come to adore like an uncle, but her job as well.

And finding another job at her age was not going to be—no pun intended—a piece of cannoli.

"If you have one more bite of that cannoli, you're going to gain another ten pounds. The trouble with you, Mary, is that you've got no willpower. You haven't lost the last ten you gained after breaking up with that nice Marc Forentini. And that was two years ago!" Sophia Russo's mouth pinched tight as she gazed disapprovingly at her daughter. "Men don't like fat."

Mary looked up, chocolate smearing her lips. Her mother never failed to comment on just what it was that was wrong with her. If it wasn't her weight, it was Mary's choice of men, or clothes, or friends. Mary's self-esteem was somewhere at basement level—*low* didn't even come close. There was no pleasing Sophia, and Mary had given up trying long ago.

"I thought you said they don't like bones." Sophia was always telling Mary's younger sister that, because Connie had escaped the curse of the Russo hips and thighs, even after having three children. She was skinny, fashionably skinny, and Mary envied her that.

Just the ability to put on a pair of jeans and zip them up without having to lie prone on the bed sucking in your breath for all you were worth was Mary's idea of pure heaven. She didn't have to be bones, she just had to be zipper-proof. And she knew she wasn't going to get there by eating cannolis—even if they were her latest delicious recipe—but at the moment she just didn't care.

"*Lascia la bambina solo.* Leave the *bambina* alone, Sophia," Mary's grandmother said with undisguised hostility toward her daughter-in-law. "She suffers a terrible loss. Whatsa matter? You no gotta heart for such tings?" And to Mary: "You wanta some nicea creama, *bambina*?"

Mary didn't usually enter into the ongoing hostilities between her mother and grandmother. It was the classic in-law

dislike that had plagued dysfunctional families for genera-
tions. Mary suspected it had started the moment the love of
Flora Russo's life, her son, Frank, had brought Sophia home
to meet his mama.

No woman would have ever been good enough for Flora's
Frank, that was a given, so Sophia took the criticism in
stride, though she didn't take it lying down.

Sophia knew in her heart of hearts, though she'd deny it
to her dying breath, that no woman would have ever been
good enough for her Joe, either. Fortunately Mary's older
brother had become a priest, so whoever the unsuspecting
future daughter-in-law of Sophia's might have been, she had
escaped a fate worse than death.

Besides, who in their right mind would enter into a family
that made Vito Corleone's look normal?

Though Mary disliked her mother and grandmother's constant bickering, she did appreciate her grandma taking her
side in the numerous disagreements she had with her mother.
They were allies, of sorts, and Grandma Flora had been there
for her more times than not over the years.

For an eighty-three-year-old woman who walked with the
help of a cane, employed two-inch-thick lenses while she cro-
cheted, and wore tentlike undergarments she referred to as
bloomers, Grandma Flora could hold her own with Sophia,
which was no easy feat.

Sophia Russo had an opinion on just about everything, especially when it came to one of her children. Though Mary
loved the woman dearly, there was no denying they didn't see
eye to eye on anything, including Mary's penchant for exper-
imenting with traditional Italian recipes. Except perhaps the
amount of time it took to cook pasta; both liked theirs al
dente.

Winking at the old lady, Mary replied, "Thanks, but no
thanks, *Nonna,*" then she smiled somewhat spitefully at her
mother before grabbing another cannoli off the plate and
shoving half of it into her mouth, knowing she'd be sorry

tomorrow when the scale tilted into overdrive, but needing the comfort that would not be forthcoming from her mother.

What Sophia lacked in compassion she made up for in conviction. "Luigi Marconi was a stupid, selfish man. Killing yourself is against God's law. He broke a commandment and now his poor wife will suffer because he was a coward and took the easy way out." She crossed herself, as if poor Luigi's indiscretion against God might come back to haunt her.

Mary didn't understand why Luigi had decided to kill himself, but she, unlike her mother, could empathize with his need to take the easy way out. After the realization had hit her that she was out of a job, and that her miserable existence had just gotten a whole lot more miserable, she'd considered doing the very same thing, for about five seconds.

She came by her morbid obsession with death legitimately. Like any good Italian girl, she was raised on the belief that judgment day was just around the corner. Both her mother and grandmother implied with unrelenting certainty that their demise was imminent, ending most of their sentences with *"if I should live so long."* Which was usually proceeded by *"Only God knows how much longer I'll be on this earth,"* and *"Your grandmother* (or mother) *is driving me to an early grave."*

However, Mary would never have considered a gun as the ultimate method of suicide. Too messy. She could still recall the gruesome sight of Luigi's brains splattered over the stainless steel stove and Sub-Zero refrigerator when she'd showed up for work that fateful Friday morning two weeks ago and had discovered his body lying on the kitchen floor. The memory made her cringe. At the time, it had made her barf.

In her opinion, a swan dive off Baltimore's Francis Scott Key Bridge would have been far more preferable. And she had briefly entertained the idea until she remembered how awful the traffic was on the bridge at any time of the day or night, how she hated to drive anyway, and how death by chocolate seemed a far better way to end it all.

"You always take her side, so I think you should just keep quiet, old woman," Sophia told her mother-in-law, who kept on crocheting and glaring. "Mary's been depressed and wallowing in her grief for too long. She needs to get over it and go out and find a new job. It's not healthy for her to be sitting around, stuffing herself with cannoli. Whoever heard of chocolate cannoli anyway? That's not Italian!"

As if the matter was already settled, Sophia nodded to herself, adding, "I'm going to call Father Joseph to come over and counsel her."

At the suggestion, Mary swallowed the remaining half of her pastry, licked the chocolate sauce off her lips, and grinned. "Joe'll just tell me to say three Hail Marys and call him in the morning, Ma. And why do you keep referring to your own son as Father Joseph, for God's sake?"

Not that she minded talking to Joe. She and her older brother were very close, and she loved him. But he would always be Joe to her, not Father Joseph, and she wasn't about to go sit in some confessional and pour out her guts to the poor guy. She was positive he got a daily dose of some pretty hideous stuff.

Besides, Joe already knew all her terrible secrets, like about her addiction to chocolate, and how when she'd been twelve she had read all of the dirty parts of the Bible, underlining them with a yellow marking pen.

Unfortunately—or fortunately, depending on how you looked at it, because it could have been her mother—Joe had been the one to catch her alone in the closet doing her thing. But he'd never told anyone, and for that reason alone she would always adore him.

Growing up a Russo hadn't been easy; all three of Sophia and Frank's children wore battle scars from their upbringing.

Connie had chosen to escape their domineering mother by marrying right out of high school. Of course, to Sophia, who considered marriage the end-all to the world's problems, this had been a blessing.

Not as big a blessing, however, as when Joe had announced his intention to enter the priesthood shortly after graduation from college. He'd been at loose ends and very unhappy and had sought to lose himself in the church.

Mary blamed her parents, mostly her mother—though her father bore some responsibility for allowing Sophia to ride roughshod over him—for her sister and brother's flight from the family. They'd never been encouraged to have goals or aspirations, never been told to live up to their potential. And that was especially true in Mary's case.

As the middle child, Mary had always felt somewhat ignored. She wasn't as smart as Joe or as pretty as baby Connie. She was just, well, rather ordinary. She'd gotten average grades in school, had never been encouraged to think beyond getting married and having kids. She'd been programmed from birth to be just average.

So when she didn't graduate from college, no one was surprised or angry, just disappointed. And when she'd ended up working in a dead-end job, no one really said anything.

Living at home had become safe. Nothing was expected of her, and she, in turn, expected nothing of herself. To sum up her life in a nutshell, Mary had taken the easy way out. Just like Luigi. Only she wasn't dead, just living a dead existence.

Cupping her hands, Sophia raised them to the heavens, shaking to and fro. *"Mama mia!* Do not take the Lord's name in vain." She crossed herself again, and even Grandma Flora nodded in agreement this time. Then they both turned in unison to look at the gold crucifix hanging over the mahogany sideboard, which rested against the outdated pink-and-brown floral wallpaper in the dining room. The cross was centered beteen two photographs of Sophia's parents—a solemn duo who looked like the Italian version of *American Gothic.* Both women mouthed silent prayers that Mary would be spared His disapproval.

With her daughter's fate once more secure, Sophia continued without breaking her stride. "You know, I was thinking that it would be nice if you could find a job where you might meet some professional men—doctors, lawyers. Carl Andretti is a very good podiatrist, a good catch now that he's widowed. He might need a secretary.

"The trouble with you, Mary, is that you haven't set your sights high enough."

Mary rolled her eyes and tried not to gag. It was bad enough that Connie had allowed their mother to push her into marriage with a proctologist—a butt doctor, for chrissake! Okay, so Eddie was a really nice guy, but he still looked at people's butts for a living. And now she wanted Mary to enter into a relationship with someone who spent all day touching smelly feet.

I don't think so!

Just the thought of hangnails and athlete's foot was enough to back up her cannoli.

"I'm flattered you think I'm capable of being someone's secretary, Ma," she said with no small amount of sarcasm, wondering why that exalted opinion hadn't been voiced years ago. "I mean, wouldn't Betty Friedan or Gloria Steinem be excited if they knew?"

Sophia pushed herself up from the table and shook her head. "A lot you know. Those women are lesbians. They're not interested in finding a man.

"And what's wrong with being a secretary? It's respectable work. It's how I met your father at the electrician's local. And we're married almost forty-three years now."

Mary had the uncharitable thought that her father deserved a medal, but swallowed it before replying, "I'm not saying there's anything wrong with it, Ma. I'm saying that I don't want to be a secretary. I'm not sure what it is I'll be doing with the rest of my life, but I know it won't include filing and typing." She'd been the only student in Miss Lafferty's tenth-grade typing class that hadn't memorized the keyboard and still looked down at her fingers when she typed, utilizing the hunt-and-peck method.

Despite her mother's belief, Mary was not executive assistant material. All of her business teachers had told her that she lacked the necessary skills for secretarial work. The fact that she'd landed a job that had included bookkeeping would have given them all a stroke.

Mary had felt lucky when Luigi Marconi had taken a chance and hired her. She'd known her limitations and hadn't wanted to try something at which she might fail. But though she'd succeeded at bookkeeping, she still hadn't been convinced that she was smart enough or clever enough to go beyond that.

Failure had always been her biggest fear.

"All those men who eat at pizza parlors are blue-collar slobs and lowlifes. How are you going to meet a nice man, settle down, and have a family if you won't listen? The trouble with you, Mary, is that you're thick." Sophia thumped her head to make her point. "You've got to stop being thick and use your head."

Mary licked the confectioners' sugar from her fingers and countered, "Pa was an electrician before he retired, Ma. You don't get much more blue-collar than that."

Showing more animation than she'd displayed in weeks, Grandma Flora's brown eyes suddenly flashed fire, her lips slashing into a thin dry line. "My Frank's a saint! He's been a good provider for you, Sophia Graziano, so don't you be a calling him no lowlifa slob." She flicked the back of her right hand under her chin and gave the traditional Italian salute of displeasure. *"Vaffunculo,"* she cursed, and Sophia's face reddened.

"You crazy old woman! How dare you talk to me like that after I've put a roof over your head and taken care of you all these years? This disrespect is how you repay me?"

Respect was very big among Italians. Being dissed was—

well, a person could end up wearing cement pantyhose if they showed disrespect to the wrong person.

Not that Mary's mother would ever consider—make that *carry out*—retribution against her mother-in-law, but she often implied that her brother, Alfredo, had ties to the Teflon man himself. But then, what self-respecting Italian didn't lay claim to being in the bosom of the Mafia?

Of course, Mary knew it was all a lie, but it seemed a harmless enough pretense, and it made her mother and uncle happy—they believed it gave the family stature—so she went along with it.

"Puttana! Sie la figlia del diavalo."

Grandma Flora had more to say about Sophia's relationship to the devil, but Mary tuned the two women out. She'd heard it all before. Many, many times before. In fact, Mary had thought *puttana* was an endearment until her aunt Angie explained that the word meant "whore."

Pushing away the plate containing the three remaining cannolis, she glanced up at the crucifix and wondered just how long it would be before she started sounding exactly like her mother and grandmother.

After all, she was almost thirty-five, or would be in two years. She had little to show for her existence up until now. She hated to admit it, even to herself, but maybe her mother was right. Maybe it was time to stop wallowing and do something constructive to change things.

Life was too short, and she didn't want to spend the rest of hers living in her mother's house and listening to the two old women battle it out.

It was time to get her act together, take a few chances, make a few mistakes. She'd lived her entire life believing that she was a failure and taking the safe route. And so what if she tried something new and it didn't work out? She was older now, more mature. She could handle it.

A wonderful idea suddenly squeezed through the gray matter of Mary's brain, and she smiled at its utter brilliance.

The trouble with you, Mary, she told herself, is that you really are thick. The answer to your problem has been right before you all along and you never even knew it.

"Ma!" she shouted to be heard above the din. "I've decided to take your advice. I'm going to open my own restaurant."

The crucifix crashed to the floor.

It was not a good sign.

Dan Gallagher paced the confines of his office at *The Baltimore Sun*, wondering why the editor-in-chief, Walter Beyerly, had asked to see him, and why he was at this very moment on his way to Dan's office instead of the other way around.

There'd been persistent rumors floating about that changes were going to be implemented at the newspaper, and Dan hoped his promised promotion to editor of the Sports section was in the offing. It would mean less travel and more money, and now that he was solely responsible for Matthew, both would come in handy.

He wasn't worried that he would be canned. He'd been at the paper for fifteen years, always met his deadlines, hadn't missed a day of work in the last five years, and his sports column, "The Sporting Life," was one of the most popular at the paper. The promotion was definitely in the bag.

He straightened the collar of his white polo shirt and flicked the lint off his navy sports jacket, which he'd just yanked off the back of his swivel chair and decided to don. Dan never wore a tie, which was one of the many advantages of covering the sports world. Only pussies wore ties in a locker room. Pussies and TV broadcasters. Besides, ties with Levi's always seemed a bit over the top.

The door opened and Walter strolled in, a too-bright smile plastered on his very bronzed face, a sure indication that he'd recently visited his favorite tanning salon. The actor George Hamilton was Beyerly's personal god, and he tried to emulate that Southern California image of health and vitality, though he was a two-pack-a-day smoker and probably ashen as hell under the reddish hue. He, of course, wore a tie. Red with tiny blue fishes that matched the three-piece Armani suit his wife had no doubt purchased at Saks or Neiman's.

Mathilda Beyerly's family owned *The Sun* and the woman had some serious bucks. Walter had always been one to heed what he referred to as his wife's *suggestions*, though in reality they were orders. No one would ever come right out and say it, but the woman had the power to fire his ass if she so chose.

"Dan, my boy, how the heck are you? Loved that last column you wrote on Cal Ripken, Jr. It had a nice personal touch. Very nice. Very nice indeed."

Having been in the newspaper profession long enough, Dan grew immediately wary. Walter's effusive comments, though nice, were just a bit, well, too effusive. The man usually grunted his approval over most things. Walter was not a touchy-feely kind of guy.

Dan could think of only one reason Walter was being so nice to him, and it turned his stomach sour. Dan's stomach was touchy at the best of times, and he kept several rolls of antacids handy in his desk and the pocket of his jeans. Just in case.

"I'm not getting the promotion, am I?" Even beneath the tan Dan could see his boss's face redden, and the acid churned, refluxing like crazy. He needed that promotion. Not just because he deserved it, but because he had more responsibilities now.

"That's what I came here to talk to you about, son."

Son. Oh, damn! He was screwed all to hell now, Dan thought, bracing for the worst. Maybe he was getting fired after all.

"Have a seat," he said, offering his boss a chair in front of the desk and taking the one behind it.

"I don't know quite how to begin, Dan, except to just

come right out with it. Mathilda's nephew is moving to town, and she's insisting I give the little weasel the Sports editor position." Dan opened his mouth to object, but Walter held up his hand. "I know how unfair it is. We've talked in the past about your getting the job. And you will. But not immediately."

"What the hell's that supposed to mean, Walter? I've waited fifteen years to be promoted to that position, how much longer do you think I'll wait?"

Dan was pissed, and he didn't give a shit who he offended at the moment. The editor's job had been promised to him. The Sports section needed a younger man's slant and every-one knew it. When Fletch Cooper finally retired two months ago, Walt had all but said the job was Dan's. And now this.

"You've got every right to be upset, Dan. I don't blame you. I know we've been dangling that position in front of you for years. God knows the Sports section needs resusci-tation. But my hands are tied." Those very hands were at the moment rubbing sweaty palms on thighs.

"You know Mathilda's got a say in what happens here at *The Sun*. Her stupid nephew Bradley's been a thorn in my backside ever since the little bastard was born. But he's family, and there's nothing much I can do about it. I'm go-ing to have to give him a trial period. After that I can dismiss him and put you in the position that rightfully should be yours."

Leaning back in his chair, Dan heaved a sigh and asked the question uppermost on his mind. "How long?"

"Six months, at most. After that, we'll get rid of Bradley. The man's got no background when it comes to sports. Shit! His sport of choice in college was backgammon. Backgam-mon, for chrissake, Dan! Are you hearing me? And she wants me to put that asshole in charge of my Sports section. I just pray we won't be ruined before I can fire his ass."

"And what about me, Walt? Am I supposed to just sit

back and take orders from Bradley, allowing him to make editorial decisions he knows nothing about?" Being a man used to taking control, Dan didn't like that prospect one little bit.

The older man shook his head. "No. I wouldn't think of asking you to work under my nephew. I intend to offer you an interim position, something that's just opened up. It's another editorial position. You'll be head of the department."

That bit of news took Dan by surprise, and his eyes widened a fraction, though he was still a bit wary. "No strings attached" wasn't a concept Beyerly usually subscribed to. "Is that a fact? And what about my salary? Do I still get an increase?" He had years of Matt's upbringing to think about, as well as sending him to college. "Because I can tell you flat out—"

"Yes," Walt answered quickly. Dan was one of his top staff reporters, and he didn't want to lose him. "A slight one now, which will be increased when you move back to Sports. You deserve it after all the sweat and hard work you've put into this newspaper."

Well, that was something anyway. Not much, but something. "So which department do you have in mind? Travel? Real Estate? Business?" He guessed he could live with one of those for six months.

Walt cleared his throat, looking a little uncomfortable. "I suppose you've heard that Rosemary Flores is going on maternity leave?"

"Yeah, so what?" Rosemary was on her sixth little Flores. The woman had obviously been successful in combining a career with marriage—something he wasn't totally in favor of—though she may have taken that "go forth and multiply" thing a bit too seriously. Well, more power to her, Dan thought, grateful it wasn't him that had to deal with six kids. Matthew was more than enough to handle at the moment.

When realization finally dawned, Dan got this horribly sick Rolaids-can't-touch-this feeling in the pit of his stomach.

"No. No way. Rosemary is the Food editor and restaurant critic. You're not suggesting . . . ? Come on, Walter, that's one step above working the obits."

"Now, Dan, you're not looking at this sensibly. You've got the right background to handle the Food section. You're a gourmet cook, a lover of fine wines, and you've got a sophisticated palate. What better credentials do you need for writing restaurant reviews?

"And it's only going to be for six months. By then, Rosemary will be back from leave, I'll have canned Bradley, and you can take over the Sports section as editor."

Walt made it sound so simple, but Dan knew better. If it weren't for the fact that he'd just been tossed a curve by his ex-wife, he'd have told Beyerly to stick it.

The humiliation factor was tremendous. The only thing more demeaning than writing restaurant reviews was describing how some octogenarian had choked on a piece of meat, gone into cardiac arrest, and would be planted according to his wishes the following Tuesday evening during a full moon.

But Dan had his son to think about. Sharon, who'd fought him tooth and nail for custody of their child four years ago, had dropped Matt off two weeks before, after deciding that she was no longer cut out for motherhood, and had left town with her aerobics instructor, a guy ten years her junior.

Dan was still trying to deal with his traumatized son, who seemed to resent him almost as much as he now resented his mother.

With Matt to consider, he just couldn't afford to make a rash decision and quit.

But he sure as hell wanted to!

Though he had difficulty pulling the words out past the bile in his throat, he finally asked, "Six months, you're sure?"

Walt had that look a contented predator gets right after

swallowing his prey, whole. He didn't even bother to burp. "Six months," he said, then flashed that George Hamilton ul- trawhite smile of his.

Dan reached frantically for his Rolaids.

Grandma Flora's Fig Cookies

Dough

4 $\frac{1}{2}$ lbs. flour
$\frac{1}{2}$ box Softasilk Cake Flour
3 lbs. Crisco shortening
4 oz. bottle vanilla
2 tsp. baking powder
1 cup water, boiled then cooled
pinch of salt
2 lbs. sugar
5 eggs

Mix flour and cake flour together. Cut in shortening. Add baking powder. Add remaining ingredients and mix well to form a soft dough.

Filling

3 1-lb. pkgs. dried figs
1 16-oz. container candied fruit
2 8-oz. pkgs. walnuts
2 6-oz. pkgs. almonds
1 19-oz. jar honey
2 tsp. cinnamon
rind of 1 lemon, 1 orange, grated
pinch of cloves
2 small boxes of raisins

Prepare filling by grinding the dried fruit very fine and adding the other ingredients. Make dough, and cut into approximately 4" x 6" rectangles. Place filling on dough, and pinch ends together. Gently form into horseshoe shape or circle. Bake at 350°, 10–15 minutes, or until brown. Makes 3–4 dozen cookies.

CHAPTER
TWO

"Is it true? Did Lou Santini really give your mother a discount on veal cutlets?"

Annie Goldman flashed an irrepressible smile—a smile that had cost her father "a shitload of money," as he so colorfully put it whenever the topic of teeth came up, but that her mother assured him would secure her future, maybe with a dentist.

Two bright spots of color dotted Mary's cheeks, making Annie laugh. With her olive skin and big brown eyes, Mary was a knockout, and she didn't even know it. "I'm impressed. What did Sophia promise him? Your virginity?"

Mary rolled her eyes and shook her head. She and Annie had been best friends since first grade, and there wasn't much the outspoken woman could say that would shock her. Though she tried her hardest.

Annie had arrived on Mary's doorstep promptly at ten that morning to help her unpack and arrange the furniture she had just purchased for her new apartment. Annie's hair, which had been dyed bright orange, was in keeping with the young woman's philosophy that hair color should match one's mood. Since Annie's moods were mercurial, she changed the hue almost as often as she changed men.

Mary wasn't sure what the orange signified. The woman had died it purple once as a show of support for Barney, whom she felt had been getting a bad rap in all the newspapers. So, it could have been just another protest against society's treatment of dinosaurs—Annie was very good at objecting to things—or it might have had something to do with the alignment of the planets—her friend was into astrology in a big way, too.

Annie never rode the fence like Mary was inclined to do. She had definite ideas and opinions on just about every subject, not unlike Sophia, and she expressed them fervently, whether or not they were popular or you wanted to listen. Mary would much rather listen to Annie than Sophia.

Annie was steadfast and loyal. If she liked you, she took up your cause and remained your friend for life. But if you got on her bad side, she'd usually warn that she was half-Jewish and half-Italian, and that her Italian side didn't get mad, it got even.

Anyone familiar with Italians knew to steer clear when they were in a foul mood. An Italian woman out for revenge or upset about something was far more dangerous than PMS in its most lethal form. Usually men were at a loss as to how to deal with them, like in the Alan Alda movie *The Four Seasons*, when Rita Moreno's husband, frustrated with his wife's behavior, stuck his head out the window and yelled at the top of his lungs, "My wife's Italian!" as if that could explain it all.

Mary thought it probably could.

Unpacking another carton of books, she placed several hardcover novels in her new hunter-green pine bookcases, making sure the pretty, slick, colorful jackets were lined up just so, then sat back on her haunches to admire how great they looked.

New bookcases. New apartment. New life.

Even Annie's outrageous comments couldn't put a damper on her mood today. She had moved into her own apartment. Away from Grandma Flora's bloomers hanging over the curtain rod, away from the madness that was normalcy in the Russo household, and away from her mother's smothering advice.

"The trouble with you, Mary," her mother had told her when she found out she was leaving, *"is that you're too independent. Men don't want to marry Miss Know-It-All—a woman who runs her own business. They want someone who can take care of them, iron their clothes, clip their toenails. They want a wife!"*

Well, men might want a wife, but Mary had finally gotten a *life*, and she intended to keep it. And her new apartment, which she loved almost as much as her freedom.

The four-room flat wasn't really new. But it was hers. And as her landlady, Mrs. Foragi, a two-hundred-plus-pound widow with an attitude, had judiciously pointed out between bites of her dripping calzone, it was conveniently located above Mary's new restaurant, which was scheduled to open in just a few weeks—maybe sooner, if she could get the rest of her suppliers lined up.

So far, the liquor distributor hadn't been totally cooperative. She had taken over the former restaurant owner's license, only to discover that he had been cited several times for serving alcohol to minors. Mary'd been working diligently with the Maryland Alcohol and Beverage Commission to clear up the matter so Mama Sophia's could open on time.

Mama Sophia's. The name had started out as a joke between Mary and her sister. From the onset, her mother had been adamantly opposed to the restaurant, which is why, Mary supposed, she'd come up with the idea of naming it after her. Of course, Sophia had turned the tables on her and was now taking credit for the idea, as if she hadn't bucked Mary every step of the way.

"You're going to be sorry, Mary. It'll never work, Mary."

It would work. Mary intended to see that it did. If only to prove Sophia wrong.

"Veal always has a price, Mary *mia*," Annie said, bringing Mary back to the here and now. "You don't get a discount from Santini's Butcher Shop without putting out for it. Mrs.

Santini is not as anxious to get rid of Lou as Lou is to get into your pants. I hear he's got a big Italian sausage he's dying to share with you." Though she tried not to encourage Annie's ribald comments, Mary couldn't keep from laughing.

Her friend always said the most outrageous things, and Mary often wished she could be just as outspoken and say whatever was on her mind. "You're bad!"

"So tell me, has he asked you out yet?"

Mary hated it when Annie was right about things, which was most of the time. The woman was too worldly and intelligent for her own good. She had a degree in social work, but found the profession too draining and depressing, and had quit several years back. Since then, she'd wandered from job to job—sales clerk, waitress, receptionist. She'd even answered phone calls for one of those sex hotlines, claiming it was very stimulating work and that it had improved her salacious vocabulary tenfold.

And now Annie was going to work for Mama Sophia's as manager and hostess, and Mary couldn't be happier. *"The dynamic duo together at last,"* Annie had said when Mary offered her the job.

She and Annie had done everything together as children: sleepovers, spelling bees, lemonade stands—only instead of lemonade they had sold Annie's father's supply of Manischewitz, along with Grandma Flora's fig cookies. Business had been brisk, until Sid Goldman discovered three gallons of his favorite concord wine missing from his basement.

In high school Mary had run for junior class president, at Annie's urging, but had lost by a narrow margin, which had only reinforced her fear of trying something new and failing. Annie, on the other hand, had been elected homecoming queen by an overwhelming majority. She had gone to the dance with Mary's brother, Joe, who'd graduated two years before.

Joe had reluctantly agreed to take her as a favor to Mrs. Goldman, if Annie promised to wear something sedate. The young woman's flamboyance had started at an early age and been somewhat legendary at the high school they attended.

Not one to be dictated to, Annie had shown up at her door wearing a strapless black velvet evening gown, three-inch spiked heels, and long black gloves, à la Rita Hayworth in *Gilda*, which happened to be her favorite movie at the time. Her hair had been long and red back then, so she'd pulled off the look to perfection.

To say Joe had not been pleased would have been an understatement. Pinning on the rose corsage he'd bought had been out of the question, and he'd spent the entire evening fighting off Annie's many male admirers, earning himself a cut lip and a black eye for his trouble.

"Are you going to tell me or not?" Annie prodded, drawing Mary's attention back to the present.

"Lou asked me this morning," she admitted, adding, "No need to look so smug. It's only a first date. And I'd never put out for veal. I'm holding out for at least a beef tenderloin."

"You'll be so senile by the time you finally get around to having sex you won't remember what that convenient little opening you have is for."

"At least I won't need retreads after fifty thousand f—" Mary caught herself just in time, feeling her cheeks warm, but Annie wasn't at all offended. In fact, she threw back her head and laughed, which displayed her very straight white teeth.

Mary envied Annie's teeth, for her own were slightly crooked in the front, making her feel self-conscious whenever she smiled.

Frank Russo hadn't subscribed to the orthodonture route as Sid Goldman had, in spite of Sophia's constant assertions that Mary would go through life in pain and suffering because her father was too cheap to pay for braces.

"The trouble with Mary," Sophia would say, *"is that she's*

got an overbite. Not a big one, mind you. But she needs some metal in that mouth of hers."

"Very good, Mary *mia*," Annie said, her eyes still twinkling. "I see that living alone has given a boost to your sarcastic wit. Now if it would only heighten your libido . . ."

"Quit nagging, will you? I'll get around to it one of these days. I'm in no hurry."

"Get real, Mary! You're nearly thirty-four and you still think an orgasm is something that grows in a petri dish. Get a life. And get laid, for chrissake! Despite what Sophia's been telling you, you are not going to burn in hell for sleeping with a man. If that were the case, I'd be roasting in those white-hot flames for all eternity."

Her best friend's lectures always produced a thirst, so Mary headed into the compact kitchen, grateful she rarely had to cook in it, and returned a few minutes later clasping an open bottle of chardonnay under her arm and two long-stemmed wine glasses.

Pouring the golden wine, she handed Annie a glass, then plopped down next to her on the sofa. Morty jumped up on her lap and promptly went to sleep. "I haven't met anyone I'm interested in sleeping with yet," she said, tugging hard on the hem of her gray University of Maryland sweatshirt—a nervous habit she employed whenever she found herself lying, which wasn't all that often in the great scheme of things.

The truth was, she had desperately wanted to sleep with Marc Forentini. The man had been a hunk carved out of granite, and he'd treated her with equal amounts of respect and adoration. The perfect male specimen come to life.

But when the time had come, and Marc had not, because she'd refused to have sex with him, on religious grounds, she'd insisted, he'd ended their relationship.

Mary wondered to this day if she had refused because she'd been too cowardly, too self-conscious about her body—she wasn't fat, but she wasn't Calvin Klein jeans thin, either—and had used the religious thing as a convenient escape.

It wasn't any great mystery why successful relationships with men continued to elude her. Her Catholic upbringing—translation: guilt Italian-style—combined with her mother's dire warnings about men not wanting the cow when they got the milk for free had been too much to overcome.

Mary feared intimacy, but wasn't entirely sure why. Although she suspected it was because getting close to someone, putting herself on the line, would set her up for rejection, and ultimate failure if things didn't work out.

She rarely lived up to anyone's expectations, including her own. And did she really want to make her mother happy by getting married and having a bunch of kids, so she could hear her say: *"See, Mary, this is what you're cut out for. You don't need to work, to be independent. Let some man take care of you."*

Okay, sure, the psychological stuff was definitely part of it, but that cellulite issue and her less-than-perfect body also played a big part.

The thought of exposing herself to a man, both inside and out, terrified her.

"Oy vey! You know damn well Marc dumped you because you wouldn't put out. The man had six months of dinners invested in you. He wanted a return on the money he'd spent."

"You sleep with every guy you meet, and you're not any happier than I am."

Annie shrugged, then sipped her wine thoughtfully. She had been happy once, deliriously so, but that had been a long time ago, a lifetime ago. Hiding her pain behind a flip remark, as she so often did, she replied, "Maybe not overall. But I do get thirty- to sixty-minute stretches of pure unadulterated heaven from time to time. Which makes me very happy."

"Well, I hope you're being careful and using protection."

"Listen to yourself, will you? You sound just like your

mother." Annie raised her hands prayerfully toward the ceiling, and in her best imitation of Sophia made the sign of the cross and said, "Protect Mary, dear God. She's contemplating a life of sin and degradation."

Mary grinned in spite of herself. "At least I'm not in danger of dying from some sexually transmitted disease."

"That's for sure. You'll die of *eff*ing boredom first." At Mary's sigh, Annie said, "I hate to be blunt, but you need to make some major adjustments in your life, *cara*. You don't have to subscribe to the till-death-do-us-part theory, but 'Like a Virgin' went the way of disco."

"Disco's back. Retro's in. The Bee Gees are making a comeback." Mary's smile was smug.

Annie scrunched her nose, saying, "You're kidding, right?" then added, "Well, at least you didn't pick out any of that 70's crap for your apartment. I like the red leather couch and painted pine tables. Country is very in." She smoothed her hand over the leather material. "It feels so sensuous."

"I thought it was homey. My mother was pushing for olive-green tweed. Scotchguarded, of course." The couch her mother had picked out looked almost exactly like the one garnishing Sophia's own parlor—a green-and-orange floral design. It was hideous. Of course, when you have orange shag carpeting beneath it . . .

"I overruled her." And it had taken every bit of her self-control and persuasive powers to convince Sophia that she wasn't taking her suggestion.

Once her mother made up her mind about something, it took an act of Congress to dissuade her. The woman could have single-handedly negotiated the Camp David accords. She could have probably nagged Saddam Hussein into converting to Catholicism, she was that determined. And most of the time it was just easier to give in than argue with her, but Mary decided this time she'd have it her way or not at all.

"You took Sophia shopping with you? You are brave, *cara*.

Well, at least she didn't talk you into any of those religious pictures or crucifixes, like she's got hanging up all over her house. They give me the creeps." When Mary didn't respond right away, Annie's eyes widened. "Oh, shit! Please tell me it ain't so."

"Don't go into the bedroom," Mary warned. "There's a statue of the Virgin on the dresser. It was a housewarming gift from Grandma Flora."

Religious icons were as important to the Russo family as attending mass on Sunday. Aside from the comfort and protection they supposedly provided, Mary thought they were really used to display the family's excessive religious devotion, so friends and relatives would be suitably impressed. The same theory applied to those weekly visits her mother and grandmother made to the cemetery to visit Grandpa Russo and Sophia's parents. The dead people certainly didn't get any benefit from them.

Annie rolled her big blue eyes—a throwback to her father's side of the family. "Hand me that chardonnay, will you? One glass of wine will definitely not be enough to handle this latest depressing disclosure."

After refilling Mary's glass, then her own, she added, "Maybe you ought to consider moving it into the bathroom, *cara*. Two virgins in one bedroom is too much to ask of any healthy, heterosexual male."

Staring down at the recipes spread out on the desk before him, Dan couldn't believe how low he'd sunk. The paper was running a contest for the best-tasting ground beef recipe, and he was in charge of choosing a winner from 887 entries.

Rosemary's brainchild "The Many *Mooooo*ds of Beef" had been put into place before the woman had left on maternity leave, but Dan was the one stuck with giving birth to the stupid idea, which was definitely putting him in a bad *mooooo*d.

In his opinion, ground beef was a meat that deserved to be used strictly for hamburgers or tacos. And then only because they were considered American institutions, like apple pie and pizza. It did not deserve to have a contest named after it, where it would try to pass itself off as a culinary equal to veal or chicken.

No self-respecting gourmet would lower him- or herself to prepare one of these 887 vile concoctions, which had names like "Maxine's Hamburger Heaven Casserole," and "Jeanne's Humdinger Noodle Bake"—the humdinger apparently the grated cheddar cheese and jalapenos scattered on the top of the unappetizing mess. To Dan, it sounded like someone had eaten a large amount of Mexican food, thrown it back up, and named it.

"You're supposed to prepare each of those recipes before choosing a winner," Rosemary's secretary, and now his, Linda Fox, informed him, taking the whole matter quite seriously. She was a short woman with graying dark hair and a pointy chin and nose, and she sort of resembled the animal she was named for.

"Rosemary usually spent a full week trying out the entries on her family before she decided which one she liked best."

Dan tried not to smirk. There was no way he was going to waste his time preparing ground-beef recipes. If it became public knowledge that he'd been dabbling in ground round, he might lose his subscriptions to *Bon Appetit* and *Gourmet*. "Some people are just naturally lucky, I guess."

"Actually, Rosemary was lucky," Linda pointed out, "because the newspaper paid for all of the ingredients, so she got to cook all those meals for free and store the leftovers in the freezer. Guess when you've got as many kids as Rosie, you need to use all the angles."

Free food? Maybe he'd been too hasty. Dan's grocery bill had skyrocketed since Matt had come to live with him. The kid was a bottomless pit, though he craved mostly junk food, which Dan abhorred with a passion.

The amount of fat grams and carbs in a Double Whopper with Cheese was enough to make a grown man cry. Or send him into cardiac arrest.

Mulling over an idea that could save him a lot of grief, Dan finally said, "Linda, how would you like to help me choose the winner of the contest? I'll let you write up the copy and present the winner with—" He glanced down at the mess of papers on his desk and riffled through them. "What is it they win?"

"A year's supply of hamburger."

"Right. You could take half of the entries to judge and I'll take the other half. Once we've narrowed them down, we can declare a winner. What d'ya say?"

Linda removed her tortoiseshell glasses and set them carefully on her desk while she contemplated the offer. Dan couldn't help but notice that she had rather nice blue eyes, and her legs weren't half-bad either, except that she wore those mannish Doc Marten shoes and heavy-duty support hose.

What the hell am I thinking!

Linda Fox had ten years on him, maybe fifteen. If he was suddenly finding her attractive, then it was time for him to get laid. And fast.

Not that Linda wasn't a very nice woman, because she was. Hell, she was probably somebody's mother or grandmother, even if she was divorced. But Dan had a strict policy of never dating anyone he worked with. He'd done that once, with disastrous results.

For two long, interminable weeks he had dated Dolores Murray from the accounting department. It hadn't taken Dan long to figure out that he and Dolores were not going make it, in bed or otherwise. In addition to the fact that she was a big fan of Hamburger Helper—he repressed a shudder—they had absolutely nothing in common.

After their breakup, which he'd initiated, the vengeful woman had deleted all of the computer files from his hard drive, and Dan hadn't been proficient enough to retrieve them. He also hadn't had the foresight to make any disk copies, which had resulted in his spending weeks redoing everything, popping Rolaids like candy, and swearing that he'd never date another *Baltimore Sun* employee ever again, no matter how desperate he got.

And he was pretty damn desperate! Four years' worth of desperate, in fact. He hadn't made love to a woman since his divorce. Not that he wasn't interested in climbing between the sheets—he was definitely interested—he just couldn't find anyone that he wanted to make love with.

In Dan's opinion, making love was like drinking fine wine. All the right elements had to be there or it wasn't going to be any good. And women tended to equate lovemaking with marriage. Dan didn't intend to go that route again. Not, at least, until he found a woman who was content to stay at home and be a wife and mother. A woman whose career wasn't more important than her marriage.

Been there, done that, he thought.

"I'm not sure Rosemary would approve of that, Mr. Gallagher. I've never helped with the contest before."

Refocusing his attention on the matter at hand, he picked up what looked to be about half of the 887 entries and dropped them in front of her, ignoring her wide-eyed expression. "Rosemary's off having a baby and I'm in charge in the meantime, so I don't think we need to worry about what she thinks or doesn't think.

"But—"

"Besides, I thought you told me yesterday that you wanted to do more than just secretarial stuff. Here's your chance."

Contemplating the opportunity, Linda's uncertainty started to dissolve. "I do have a degree in English. And I'm also a very good cook. I guess I could do it." Then she got a look of determination on her face. "No!" she declared emphatically, her voice filling with resolve. "I know I can do it."

"That's the spirit."

"If you're sure this could lead to something, Mr. Gallagher. Rosemary is always promising to promote me, but I've been in this department for ten years and I'm still doing the grunt work."

"Trust me, Linda," he said with a sigh, "I know exactly how you feel." And he did. In spades.

Dan's life was about to take another turn for the worse, if that was possible. At this point, it was hard for him to imagine it could get any lousier, but it just had.

His first assignment as restaurant critic was to review an up-and-coming Italian eatery that had just opened.

Unfortunately, Dan hated Italian food.

Mama Sophia's Lasagna

Tomato Sauce

2 28-oz. cans crushed tomatoes with puree
2 28-oz. cans tomato puree
2 8-oz. cans tomato sauce
2 12-oz. cans tomato paste
2 lbs. ground round
4 cloves of garlic and 1 large onion (chopped)
basil, oregano, salt, and pepper to taste

Sautè onion and garlic, add ground round, and brown. Add tomatoes, puree, sauce, and paste. Add basil, oregano, salt, and pepper. Simmer until thick, about 6 hours.

Lasagna

3 lbs. lasagna noodles, cooked
2–3 lbs. ricotta
3 lbs. mozzarella
Parmesan cheese

Cook noodles according to package directions in water to which a teaspoon of olive oil has been added. Drain. In a large lasagna pan, ladle tomato sauce on bottom. Layer noodles, overlapping a bit. Add sauce, ricotta, mozzarella, and Parmesan. Repeat layers until you reach top of pan. Finish final layer with sauce, ricotta, Parmesan, and a generous helping of mozzarella. Bake in 350° oven for 1 hour, or until cheese is melted and lasagna is heated through. Let stand 30 minutes before serving. Serves 8–10.

CHAPTER
THREE

"*Bastardo!* I spit on your mother's grave!"

Mary had just entered the restaurant when she heard her chef's loud tirade, followed by a gross spitting sound. She cringed, wondering if he'd actually made good and dirtied the Saltillo-tiled floor, which had been designed to look like red bricks. The health department had very stringent guidelines about spitting and clean floors, and she'd stayed well past closing the previous night to mop it.

Marco was apparently very unhappy about something. And when Marco Valenti was unhappy, everyone was unhappy. Or soon would be.

He was a brilliant chef—his Saltimbocca à la Valenti was fabulous—even if he was her mother's cousin once removed, and so Mary was inclined to put up with his frequent emotional outbursts.

"*A man of Marco's talent must be humored,*" her mother had explained upon recommending him. "*The trouble with you, Mary, is that you have no eye for genius. He's short— his parents were like pigmies—but he's very big on ability.*"

Mary should have known then and there that Marco Valenti was in league with the devil. Only this devil didn't wear horns: Sophia wore polyester.

And Mary should have pointed out that at five-foot-three Sophia wasn't exactly of supermodel stature. None of the Russos were. Shortness plagued the entire family, except for

Joe, who'd been lucky enough to take after his maternal grandfather and was well over six feet.

Mary consoled herself with the fact that she wasn't fat, just short for her weight. After all, what was life without rationalizations?

She hurried across the main dining room, which had been decorated with an alfresco, garden theme. Determined to avoid the traditional red-and-white-checked tablecloth mentality, she had seized upon the idea of bringing the outdoors in by using painted murals of the Italian countryside, wooden trellises on the walls and ceiling, and terra-cotta urns filled with ferns and other greenery.

Fresh flowers dotted the center of every mosaic-tiled table. Today's bouquet was baby's breath, stephanotis, and red carnations. The green, white, and red tables designed to look like the flag of Italy had been Annie's brilliant idea and had already saved Mary a ton of money on laundering tablecloths.

Mary thought the entire effect was very appealing and restful, unlike her chef, who was waving a newspaper over his head and cursing.

"*L'uomo é diabolico.* Stupid. *Ha* shit *per i cervelli.*"

Apparently some man was evil, stupid, and had shit for brains, as near as she could translate. Fortunately, growing up a Russo gave her insight into the most colorful expletives of the Italian language. She was pretty certain her first spoken word had been *puttana*, or maybe *bastardo*.

"What is it, Marco? What's wrong? Has one of the suppliers failed to deliver something again?" Their opening night had been a near-disaster when her food service supplier had shorted her on several cases of tomato products and olive oil, and then the produce man failed to deliver the additional crates of lettuce she had ordered.

They'd run out of Chianti, Diet Coke, and cheesecake. And to make matters worse, the toilets had backed up, making the food shortages seem trivial by comparison. But they had survived until closing, thanks to everyone who had pitched in to help, including members of her family. Even Mrs. Foragi had assisted by folding napkins, asking to be compensated for her time with food rather than salary.

Mary had concluded that it would have been cheaper to pay the woman rather than feed her. Donatella Foragi could pack it in when she put her mind to it.

"What's the problem?" she asked again.

His face a mask of outrage, Marco shook his head, then his fist, which still clutched the newspaper, drawing himself up to his full five-foot, four-inch height.

There was something disconcerting about being at the same eye level with a man, Mary decided. Dressed in his white chef's coat, his thick wavy hair nearly the same color as his hat, Marco reminded her of the Pillsbury Dough Boy. His protruding belly just begged to be poked, though she would never be brave enough to do it. She wasn't sure what Marco's sexual orientation was, because he seemed to hold men and women in equal disdain.

"*Madonna mia, disgrazia!* We have been reviewed. I have been insulted to the heavens." He pointed in that direction. "I cannot work under such conditions."

Mary fought the urge to roll her eyes. The man had taken drama lessons from Sophia, she was sure of it. "Calm down, please, and hand me the paper." He did, slapped his forehead, then stormed back to the kitchen, cursing and shouting with every step he took, and banging the swinging door separating the two rooms before disappearing through it.

At that moment, Annie strolled in, looking like a million bucks in a short, tight, black skirt; simple white knit tank top; and black cardigan. The outfit was understated for the eccentric woman. But Mary had convinced her flamboyant friend that the manager of Mama Sophia's could not look like a hooker when greeting customers.

"Hey, kiddo! What's happening? Guess you saw the lousy review in this morning's *Sun*, huh?"

The comment drew Mary's attention away from Annie's green-and-red Salute to Italy hair-color combination to the newspaper clutched in her hand. Turning to the Food section, she read:

> Baltimore needs another Italian restaurant like the Chesapeake Bay needs Pfiesteria. Enter Mama Sophia's, the newest addition to the dining scene in Little Italy. Newest, but certainly not the best, by any stretch of the palate.
>
> One must give the owner, Mary Russo, points for trying, but her endeavor falls short.

Gasping in outrage, Mary looked at her friend, who was shaking her head in commiseration, then read on:

> If one rates lasagna by the pound, then I guess Mama Sophia's would get five stars. The layered, heavy concoction weighs more than this country's national debt. What is the chef hiding amongst all that ricotta, Parmesan, and mozzarella, I wonder? Certainly not taste!
>
> In contrast, the marinara seemed almost nonexistent. It was painfully thin and rather bland, as were many of the pasta dishes. Dull and uninspiring, to say the least.

There was more, but Mary had read enough. At any rate, it was difficult seeing through a red haze.

"He liked the pizza, even compared it to Pizza Hut's," Annie pointed out, wondering if her usually composed and always-in-control friend was going to lose it this time. Mary's face was flushing much more efficiently than the restaurant's toilets.

Mary scrutinized the name of the reviewer and the accompanying photo, which showed a handsome man in his mid-to-late thirties. Dropping the paper on the table as if it were contaminated, and with murder glittering in her eyes, she said, "Who does Daniel Gallagher think he is? How dare he write such things! Marco was right. He does have shit for brains!"

Unlike Annie, Mary rarely used profanities, so the woman knew her friend was totally and irrevocably pissed. "He dares because he's a restaurant critic, *cara*. And everyone knows restaurant critics are scum. Those guys in New York City are the worst."

"But he's not! Daniel Gallagher's no more a restaurant critic than you or I. He's a sportswriter. Or was. I've read his column dozens of times. I used to respect his opinion, but not anymore. He's not qualified to come in here, taste my food, and make disparaging remarks for all the world to see."

"Uh, he already did."

"Well, we'll just see about that."

The phone rang then, and Mary sighed. She'd just gotten up a full head of steam and didn't want anything or anyone to diffuse her anger. Not before she had a chance to take it out on that poor excuse for a newspaper man.

"It's your mother," Annie said, holding the phone out as if she were dangling a dead mouse, and made a face of distaste. "She's seen the review."

Mary nodded, resigned to the fact that no diffusion was likely to take place any time soon.

Thirty minutes later, the irate restauranteur found herself seated on the infamous green-and-orange sofa in her parents' parlor, surrounded by members of her family, who were just as outraged by the review as she and Annie. Someone had just raked the shag rug, because the nap was all going in the same direction.

"I intend to call your uncle about this. Alfredo will know how to handle Daniel Gallagher." Sophia's lips thinned in disgust as she paced, flailing her hands like a whirligig. "An Irishman. Wouldn't you know? Those Irish have no taste. They eat boiled potatoes and meat. *Mama mia!* How can a man who eats like that have the gall to write something like this?"

Sophia had never been a big fan of the Irish and made no bones about it. They drank to excess, ate bland food, and, in her opinion, had too much attention paid to them on St. Patrick's Day. Italians had their Columbus Day, but it wasn't given the same importance or respect.

Even with her mother's dislike of the Irish, Mary hadn't expected Sophia to take her side against the reviewer quite so vehemently, especially since he had merely reaffirmed Sophia's own opinions. "You should be gloating, Ma. The reviewer thinks the menu is uninspired and my chocolate cannoli untraditional." That had hurt. She'd spent hours and hours perfecting the cannoli recipe, and she knew it was outstanding, incredible even. She had the extra pounds to prove it! "I guess Daniel Gallagher must have agreed with you."

"I tried to tell you not to put pizza on the menu. It attracts blue-collar, beer-guzzling lowlifes. But would you listen?

"And it's true—I had my doubts about the cannoli. We should uphold our Italian traditions. They're what make us who we are. Why mess with a good thing?"

"So you agree with the reviewer that my food is bad?"

Mary's mother looked toward the ceiling for divine intervention. When none was forthcoming, she shook her head. "No. The food is very good. But you should listen to your mother."

"If I'd listened to you, I would never have opened the restaurant in the first place." Or moved out. But she wasn't going to open up that can of worms again. Her mother had viewed her move as a defection, taking it as a personal affront.

"Mary's right," Connie stated, moving closer to wrap a diamond-braceleted arm around her sister's shoulders in a show of support. "You didn't like the idea from the beginning, so you shouldn't have an opinion now."

"Your mother not have an opinion?" Frank Russo threw back his head and laughed, and twenty-five pounds of excess weight jiggled. "That's a good one. Just try and shut her up. I've spent forty-three years trying and I haven't succeeded yet. *Forgetaboutit!*" Shades of Frank's Brooklyn upbringing crept into his speech, as did the eloquent way he used his hands, like a conductor before a symphony.

In fact, most of the Russos expressed themselves in similar fashion. It was widely thought that if Italians were forced to sit on their hands while talking, they'd be rendered mute.

"You should worry about your mother's light-fingered habits, not my opinions," Sophia told her husband with a look that promised retribution later.

It was doubtful she was holding sex over his head. Mary was pretty certain her parents didn't indulge anymore. But whether they did or not, she tried not to dwell on the image of them doing the procreational mambo.

Sophia had always been reticent to discuss anything having to do with the birds and bees. Mary had found out about menstruation from the girls at school, but only after believing she was bleeding to death.

And the one time she'd gotten the courage to ask her mother about the sexual act itself, she'd been told that a wife had a duty and must submit to her husband. She'd talked in code about cherries, nuts, and balls, and it was only later that Mary discovered those were euphemisms for male and female body parts. After that discussion she had never broached the subject again.

"Where's your mother?" Sophia asked. "I don't dare take my eyes off that crazy old woman. I swear she's turning my hair gray."

"Mama's napping," Frank informed his wife, eyes twinkling. "And your hair's already gray, *il mio amore*. You just put that red dye on to hide it."

Sophia had been putting henna on her hair since Lucille Ball had popularized it back in the 50's. Though there were times when the color came out looking more like Bozo than Ball. Still, for a woman in her sixties, Mary thought her mother had held up very well, all things considered. It gave Mary hope for the future.

Glaring at the grinning man, Sophia said, "Don't you have something to do in the basement, Frank?" From the annoyance on her face, it was obvious she wanted to get rid of him. "Aren't you working on one of your harebrained inventions?"

Taking the less-than-subtle hint, Frank winked at his daughters and stood up. "I know when I'm not wanted. I'm going down to the park to play a little bocci, drink a little *vino*. See you later, girls." He blew them a kiss before disappearing out the door.

"Your father is driving me to an early grave. I will not survive his retirement," Sophia stated. "First, it's those crazy things he's always making, and now bocci. Everything is bocci, bocci, bocci! The man is obsessed with the game. Do you know he keeps the balls in a velvet-lined box on a shelf in the closet, next to his autographed picture of Eddie Fisher?" She screwed up her face, clearly disgusted.

Their mother's complaints about their father were all-too-familiar to the sisters, and Mary and Connie exchanged knowing looks, before Mary said, "You're too hard on Pa. You're lucky to have him. He loves you like crazy, Ma."

"So? I can get the same devotion from my dog. And I don't have to listen to insults about my hair."

The three women took seats at the long kitchen table, which was covered with a yellow-and-white-checked oil-cloth that matched the egg yolk–colored walls. Sunlight spilled in through the double-hung windows, muted only by the stiffly starched curtains of the same yellow color, to land on the black-and-white linoleum tiles, which were so spotless you could eat off them.

Sophia was meticulous, if not obsessive, about keeping her house clean. You'd be hard-pressed to find a glob of grease in the oven, and her bathrooms would impress even the Tidy Bowl man.

Fortunately—because Mary hated picking up after herself and loathed housework—she had not taken after her mother in the spic-and-span department. In fact, now that she was living on her own she purposely left dirty dishes in her kitchen sink, just because she could. Mary considered her bathroom to be clean, but she wouldn't recommend eating off the floor. Not that anyone would want to.

While Sophia filled rose-patterned china cups with coffee strong enough to stand a spoon in—she claimed Mary's coffee was weak and tasted like piss water—Connie passed around a plate of biscotti her mother had bought earlier that morning from Fiorelli's Bakery/Cafe.

"So, how's the butt business these days?" Mary asked her sister between bites of the cookie, trying to hide a teasing smile. "Has Eddie looked at any really interesting rear ends lately?"

"Mary! Such a topic at the table, and while we're eating."

Connie was quick to ignore her mother's objection, and replied, "I'm not supposed to say, because it's a breech of ethics"—of course, that didn't stop her; Connie thrived on gossip—"but Mrs. Santini came in for her regular monthly sigmoidoscopy the other day. I think she gets off on having it done, because Eddie says there's nothing wrong with her. He says her colon's so clean she could hold dinner parties in it."

"Ha! That woman's been full of shit for years," Mary's mother stated. "Though it was sweet of Lou to give me a discount on the veal. I doubt his mother knew. She's cheap, that one." Sophia's dislike of Nina Santini began years ago, when the butcher's wife had overcharged Sophia fifty-eight cents on six lamb chops.

Holding a grudge—some liked to call it a vendetta—was very Italian, and few people did it better than Sophia.

"You are going out with him, aren't you?" her mother asked, looking pointedly at Mary.

"Heaven forbid you should have to pay full price, Ma."

"You and Lou Santini?" Connie's dark eyes widened, then she began to giggle. On anyone else the childish sound would have seemed affected, but Mary's sister was like a perfect porcelain doll. In a word: adorable. And sweet. That was two words, but when it came to Connie it was hard to choose.

It was also hard not to adore her sister, even if Connie was her mother's favorite daughter, owing to the fact that she was happily married and had presented Sophia with three grandchildren to dote on.

If Connie had a flaw it would have to be her hair. Big hair, Mary called it. Sprayed, teased, and moussed. Priscilla Presley during the Elvis years had nothing on Connie's do. But Eddie liked it poofy, had said it made his wife look taller, so Connie kept it big.

"Guess you won't be able to tease me about Eddie's job any longer," her sister added. "Not if you marry Lou, the butcher boy."

"Lou's a nice man." Sophia made warning eyes at her younger daughter, trying to shut her up. "Mary could do a lot worse."

"We're only going out on a date, Ma, so don't book the church yet." The restaurant was closed on Mondays, and Mary had made a date to go out with Lou this coming week. She had put him off for two weeks because of the restaurant's opening, but now, as Annie would say, it was time to "put out." Only she had no intention of swapping body fluids with Lou Santini, despite her friend's urging to the contrary.

Pleased by the news, and pacified for the moment, Sophia grunted her approval. "That's good. So what are you going to do about the newspaper man? Do you want me to write a letter to the paper and complain? Or better yet, I can call, give them a piece of my mind."

Imagining Sophia in the role of self-appointed avenger was enough to break Mary out in hives. Shaking her head, she pushed back her chair. "I'm going down there. I needed to cool off a bit first, but now that I'm not so emotional, I'll pay Mr. Gallagher a visit and let him know exactly what I think of his review." And shove a few of her meatballs where the sun didn't shine. She'd give him Eddie's card afterward.

"I can call Uncle Alfredo. He's . . ." a meaningful pause ensued, and Mary would have laughed if her mother hadn't looked so serious, ". . . connected, you know."

"I don't need hit men to take care of my problems, Ma. I'm Italian, remember? I don't get mad. I get even."

Uncle Luigi's Pizza

Pizza Dough

2 $\frac{1}{4}$ cups flour
1 tsp. yeast
1 tsp. sugar
$\frac{3}{4}$ cup warm water
1 tbsp. olive oil
1 tsp. salt

Tomato Sauce

2 28-oz. cans crushed tomatoes with puree
2 28-oz. cans tomato puree
2 8-oz. cans tomato sauce
2 12-oz. cans tomato paste
garlic, onion (chopped) to taste
basil, oregano, salt, and pepper to taste

Prepare dough by dissolving yeast and sugar in warm water. Add oil and salt, then flour. Blend well, then knead. Cover with cloth, let rise. Meanwhile, prepare sauce by sautéing garlic and onion in olive oil. Add tomato sauce, paste, puree, and crushed tomatoes. Season with basil, oregano, salt, and pepper to taste. Simmer 4–6 hours.

After the dough has doubled, turn out on floured board and knead. Using your hands or a rolling pin, stretch dough to cover large pizza pan. Ladle sauce over crust, add mozzarella, Parmesan, or Romano cheeses, and toppings of your choice. Bake at 375°, for 15–20 minutes, until cheese is melted and crust is browned. Serves 8.

CHAPTER FOUR

Dan gazed out the plate-glass window of his office, to the bustling street below. The traffic was heavy and congested at this time of the afternoon. Horns honked, irate commuters shouted, pedestrians in crosswalks hurried to avoid being hit by overzealous truckers intent on finishing their deliveries. But he was too busy concentrating on the emotional scene that had taken place that morning between him and his son to notice any of it.

Matt hated his new school, hated living in a condo, and Dan was afraid that before long he'd grow to hate Dan, too.

"Why did Mom have to leave?" his son had wanted to know. *"Doesn't she love me anymore?"*

Dan had hated Sharon at that moment for putting Matt through so much agony and heartache. Didn't the woman realize what damage she'd caused by her defection? Didn't she care?

"Why can't you live in a regular house, instead of this stupid one with no backyard? Fluffy doesn't like it here."

Curled up on the back of Dan's expensive whiskey-colored leather sofa, Fluffy the cat didn't seem to mind that Dan's condo had a small, enclosed brick patio that faced the water of the Inner Harbor, a postage-stamp-sized patch of grass that was brown and nearly dead—because Dan never remembered to water it—and a flowering crabapple tree that blossomed when it damn well felt like it, which wasn't very often, because Dan never remembered to fertilize that, either.

Fluffy didn't mind, because Fluffy crapped in a plastic litter box, ate expensive cat food, and slept most of the day,
contributing very little to the Gallagher household, as far as
Dan was concerned.

Dogs at least earned their keep. They were loyal compan-
ions who gave unconditional love, asking only an occasional
pat on the head in return. But when he'd tried to point that
out to his son, even offering to buy him the canine of his
choice, his suggestion had been met with cold resistance
and an emphatic *"Dogs smell!"*

Dan was oftentimes at a loss as to what to say to his son.
Though the child was obviously devastated by his mother's de-
sertion, he wouldn't give in to his tears. And Dan wasn't sure
who Matt hated more: his mother, for leaving like she did, or
Dan, for taking him in and providing a home he didn't want.

*"Your mom still loves you, Matt. I don't know why she ran
off with her aerobics instructor."*

Though he had a pretty good idea. The guy was a good ten
years younger than Sharon and had muscles that didn't bear
thinking about. Other than an occasional jog, Dan wasn't
into physical torture. Fortunately, he'd been blessed with a
Road Runner metabolism and didn't worry about gaining
weight.

*"I guess she fell in love with him. It happens. But that
doesn't mean she doesn't love you, too. I know she does, just
like I do."*

*"Then why'd she leave? Moms aren't supposed to run
away from their kids. It's supposed to be the other way
around."*

Wise deductive reasoning coming from an eight-year-old.
Unfortunately, Dan had no logical explanation to give him.

*"Only she can answer that. But I'm glad you're living
with me full-time now. I've missed having you around. And
now that we're together again we can do all kinds of
things—things we didn't always get a chance to do before."*

His job as a sports journalist had kept him on the road a

great deal of the time he and Sharon had been married, which had contributed, among other things, to their divorce.

Though he loved covering Orioles baseball, and hanging out in the Baltimore Ravens locker room with the football players, he regretted the time he'd spent away from his family. Which is why he'd always made the extra effort when home to spend quality time with his son, help him with school projects, or just take long walks in the park.

"I know you miss your mom, son, but we're going to have a great time together, you'll see. It'll be just like before."

Shaking his head, Matt stomped his foot. *"I hate it here! My school sucks. And so do my teachers. And you're always in the kitchen cooking stupid stuff."*

Stupid *gourmet* stuff, Dan wanted to amend, but didn't. *"I don't think you're giving things a fair chance, Matt. It's only been a couple of months. In time—"*

"No! I'll never like living here with you. I want my mom. I want her to come back and take me home. I want things to be like before you and Mom got divorced."

The lump in Dan's throat suddenly felt as large as the one that had formed this morning when Matt had uttered those hurtful words before slamming out the door to wait on the porch for the school bus. It was important to Dan to have a successful relationship with his son, unlike the one he'd had with his own father.

Drew Gallagher had been a hard man, a stern taskmaster. He'd been away a lot when Dan was growing up, working on the road as a salesman for Encyclopedia Brittanica. He'd never made time for them to attend ball games together. He'd never once come to watch Dan play Little League ball. His father always had an excuse. He was too busy, too tired, but Dan suspected it was really because he just wasn't interested in being a father or a family man.

His mother had suffered as much or more from his old man's indifference. She'd been lonely and had grown embittered, withdrawing into herself over the years. His parents' marriage had not been a happy one, by any stretch of the imagination.

When his father had died unexpectedly of a heart attack while Dan was still in his teens, Dan had resented the hell out of him for the final act of abandonment, though in his heart he knew his father had absented himself long before.

Dan intended to be there for his son, whether or not Matt wanted him. The child needed him. Dan just had to figure out a way to reach him.

The phone buzzed, breaking into Dan's disquieting thoughts. Turning back to his desk littered with piles of helpful kitchen hints, food-freezer favorites, and an assortment of yet-to-be-written columns, he picked up the receiver. "Yeah, Linda, what is it?" He must have sounded short, because there was a definite lull of uncertainty before she spoke. Smart woman, Dan decided, hating life at the moment.

"There's someone here to see you, Mr. Gallagher. She says it's important."

What now? He had no time for chitchats with ladies this afternoon, especially those intent on dropping off recipes for the contest, even though the deadline had long since passed and they knew it. Some had even brought bribes in the way of prepared dishes to circumvent that fact. But all had been made from hamburger, and he hadn't been the least bit inclined to make an exception.

"I'm busy. I've got two more reviews to type up and an article to write on the 'wonderful world of asparagus' before tomorrow's edition." Hell, he didn't even know asparagus had their own world. "Try and get rid of her, will you?"

There was a weighty pause, some muffled conversation, then Linda came back on the line. "I don't think you can put this lady off, Mr. Gallagher. Mary Russo is here about the review you wrote on her restaurant. She's—well, I just think you might want to talk to her."

Mama Sophia's. Not one of his more favorable reviews.

Dan swallowed. No doubt the woman was here to rip him a new asshole.

He remembered Mary Russo from the restaurant. She was short, fat, had hideous red hair, and a mouth on her that had more velocity than his '97 Ford Explorer. She could have given General Patton a run for his money in the orders department.

"Show her in," he said finally, falling into his chair. "And make sure she's not armed."

"Sir?"

"Never mind." He slammed down the phone, brushed impatient fingers through his hair, and steeled himself for an unpleasant confrontation.

Damn, but he wished he'd worn his bullet-proof vest today! He had a feeling he was going to need it.

Mary paced the confines of the outer office, which sported walls of celery green, three mismatched vinyl chairs, all in terrible condition, and not much else, unless you counted a couple of hideous oil paintings that had probably been purchased at one of those starving artists' shows. It reminded her of the waiting room at the VA Hospital—depressing and totally tacky.

Daniel Gallagher was obviously well-connected at the paper, because most reporters did not get their own offices— let alone their own waiting areas—even if that area was ugly and encouraged thoughts of suicide. Newspaper people usually worked in tiny cubicles that were part of a much larger newsroom that somewhat resembled a rat's maze.

Rats. Reporters. That fit.

Her adrenaline had been pumping like a narcotic since leaving her mother's house. The more she thought about the nasty review the man had written, the more she wanted to give Daniel Gallagher a close encounter with a cattle prod.

Unlike her mother, who usually vented about every little thing that annoyed her, Mary tended to internalize her feelings. She guessed it was a self-defense mechanism against all the shouting and cursing that went on in the Russo household.

Not that her family was abusive or anything. They were just nuts!

The murderous rage she was now experiencing and needed to express was totally uncharacteristic, but definitely a part of her heritage. Italians were known to be demonstrative, and they tended to speak their minds, loudly and succinctly. She certainly intended to speak hers.

"Mr. Gallagher will see you now, Miss Russo."

Mary spun on her heel and faced the secretary, who had been kind enough to insist the reviewer see her. Maybe she didn't agree with the man's nasty review, either. Thanking the older woman, she marched in to meet the enemy on his own turf.

"You're Mary Russo?"

Dan's eyes widened, and he could hardly keep them from bulging out of their sockets as he stared at the pretty woman. Though short, this Mary Russo was far from fat, had long black hair that curled riotously around an arresting face, and she didn't resemble General Patton in the least.

In fact, she was a knockout, if you didn't count that spit-in-your-face, *Exorcist*-looking, unnatural light shining in her chocolate eyes. Still, she didn't appear quite as fierce as the redheaded harridan he remembered.

He was about to breathe a sigh of relief when she advanced on his desk, hands fisted at her sides, and looked him squarely in the eye. Her nostrils flared, and he half expected smoke to emanate from them.

Oh, yeah! The woman was pissed off.

"Of course I'm Mary Russo. And I'm not happy to make your acquaintance, Mr. Gallagher, so let's cut to the chase, shall we? I'm sure you've figured out by now that I'm here about the nasty, obnoxious review you wrote about my restaurant. It's as plain as the nose on your"—*very handsome*—"face that you know zip about Italian food."

On the contrary, Dan knew a great deal about Italian food and its preparation, he just detested it—a little problem that went back to his childhood. But he wasn't about to admit that to this avenging angel.

"Hey, I'm entitled to my opinion. And reviews are subjective, at any rate, Miss Russo," he said with a surprising amount of calm, considering how much he hated having to explain himself to anyone, especially irate restauranteurs. "I call 'em like I see 'em. I gave my opinion of the food, service, and surroundings at Mama Sophia's as honestly as I could. I'm sorry you were offended, but it's my job to be honest with my readers. And I believe I was."

She rolled her eyes, leaning slightly over the paper-littered, gray-metal desk, and Dan had the feeling she was about to hurdle it. He tried not to notice how the collar of her blouse gaped open to reveal the erratic pulse beating at the base of her throat, because it looked altogether too tempting, and because he doubted she'd be interested in anything other than peeling the skin off his hide with a blunt instrument.

Pushing Draculian thoughts aside, he focused instead on her full, cherry-red lips. Big mistake!

"I'm one of those readers, Mr. Gallagher, and I know for a fact that just a short time ago you were writing sports columns, not critiquing restaurants. You should stick with what you're good at."

There was a compliment in there somewhere, Dan was positive.

The woman's cheeks were stained pink, and damn if that didn't make her look all the more attractive. Even though her choice of clothing—a shapeless brown corduroy jumper and beige blouse—did nothing to enhance her image.

With her dark coloring she should be wearing red. Vibrant, heart-stopping red. Which also happened to be his favorite color.

"That's true. But my position as sports columnist has nothing to do with my qualifications as a reviewer. I've got a pretty discriminating palate, and I can judge a good meal from a poor one."

Her spine stiffened. "Says who? I think your palate stinks, and so does your review.

"I've worked hard to make Mama Sophia's into a fine-dining establishment. I admit, we had some start-up problems the first few days we were open. But I won't allow your insulting comments to ruin my restaurant's reputation before it has a chance to establish itself." Turning on her heel, she headed for the door, then stopped abruptly and looked back.

"And another thing, my chocolate cannolis are innovative and delicious. Fabulous, even! If you had an ounce of sweetness in your soul, you'd have recognized that."

The door slammed shut before Dan could respond. He leaned back in his chair, grateful he'd been sitting down. Mary Russo's verbal tirade had taken the wind right out of him.

And then he grinned.

Damn, but the woman had fire in her soul! Not to mention a sharp tongue. He felt for his rear to make sure his butt hadn't been chewed off entirely.

God must have taken exception to Mary's behavior, because instead of taking her straight back to her apartment as was her original plan, He had detoured her to St. Francis of Assisi's Catholic Church.

Mary considered herself to be a card-carrying Catholic. Not as devout as her mother or grandmother, but she attended mass regularly, went to confession when forced—she tried to be entertaining when Joe was on the other side of the screen—and she didn't use birth control, because unfortunately, and as everyone apparently already knew, she'd never had sex.

One of these days she was going to open up her medicine cabinet and find a twelve-month supply of Ortho Novum inside.

Goals were important.

All in all, Mary was pretty sure God was pleased with her behavior, religious and otherwise. Okay, maybe not today. But that didn't mean she had any intention of repenting for delivering a well-deserved rebuke.

Even though she found him irritating beyond belief, Mary hadn't expected Daniel Gallagher to be quite so good-looking. The photo in the newspaper hadn't done him justice.

His eyes were actually green!

Yeah, well, so was snot, she reminded herself.

And what else would they be? He was Irish.

She had, however, expected him to be offensive and arrogant, which he most definitely was. And smug. She hated smug. All the more reason to dislike him, as if she really needed another. The review was quite enough.

At this time of the afternoon Mary knew where she'd find her brother and exactly what he'd be doing.

His office was located in the rectory next door to the brick church, which had stood on Eastern Avenue for as long as she could remember and had served as the Russos' parish for a lot longer than that. Sophia and Frank had exchanged their wedding vows at St. Francis's almost forty-three years ago. All three of their children and grandchildren had been baptized and received their first communion there.

Mary entered the large, sunlit room without bothering to knock. She found her brother just where she'd expected: behind his desk, working on next Sunday's sermon. He was dressed casually in jeans, and a black T-shirt that stated in bold white letters THOU SHALL ATTEND CHURCH. I'M NOT KIDDING! GOD, belying the prevailing opinion that God had no sense of humor. A brown bomber-jacket hung over the back of his chair.

Glancing up from his papers, Joe smiled when he saw who had entered. "Hey, peanut!" He came around the walnut desk to envelop her in a bear hug, then tipped up her chin with his forefinger, eyeing her speculatively.

Most sisters would probably have objected to having their

brothers call them *peanut.* Peanuts were, after all, short, rather unattractive, and had begun life in the dirt. But they were also Joe's favorite snack, which, Mary had deduced long ago, made her his favorite sister. She'd never shared this conclusion with Connie, however.

"Why the long face? You look troubled. You haven't been fighting with Mom again, have you?"

"We don't fight, we merely argue loudly," she explained. "And no, it isn't Ma this time. I've just come from *The Baltimore Sun,* where I behaved in a very un-Christian-like way, and I'm not the least bit sorry for it."

He cocked a disbelieving brow. "So you're here to confess?"

"Get real. I'm not about to tell you all my deep, dark sins." Not that she had any. And Joe knew her well enough to realize that spilling her guts just wasn't her thing, no matter how good it was for the soul. Mary firmly believed that confession was designed to relieve a guilty conscience. If you didn't have one . . .

"I just chewed out the reviewer who blasted Mama Sophia's. Told him what I thought of his nasty comments."

"That's it? No adultery? No mass murder? Not even a little white lie? I'm very disappointed."

Noting that her brother was trying hard not to smile, she finally did. "I knew you would be." She could always count on Joe to tease her out of a bad mood. It was what made him such a good priest. He combined compassion and understanding with large doses of humor. Problems never seemed quite so dire after talking them over with her big brother.

"So, have you saved any souls today?" She sat down on the lumpy black Naugahyde sofa, which also doubled as a hide-a-bed. Her brother was prone to taking in strays. "How's the Gennaro kid doing? Is he still walking the straight and narrow?"

Joe had taken Nick Gennaro under his wing after the fatherless teenager had been arrested for possession of cocaine.

The boy's mother had been at wit's end about what to do and had come to her parish priest for help.

Lena Gennaro was one of those women who dumped all of her problems in the lap of the Lord and expected him to come up with a home-run solution.

Joe was God's designated hitter.

The judge assigned to the case had a reputation for taking a hard stand on drug-related incidents and had been about to throw the book at Nick. But Joe, a friend of Murray Abrahms since grade school, had convinced the magistrate to release Nick into his custody.

After enrolling the troubled teenager in a rehab program at Johns Hopkins, Joe had counseled Nick himself, giving him the time and attention that had been missing from his life.

No one knew better than Mary what a wonderful big brother Joe made.

"Nick's a good kid. He's off drugs now and has cleaned up his act. He just got in with the wrong crowd at school. You know how tough peer pressure can be."

Did she ever. Mary recalled the one time she had succumbed to peer pressure had been in high school, when she'd allowed Annie to dare her into doing something totally asinine and quite against her nature. Looking back on it now, it brought a smile to her lips, but she hadn't always thought it so amusing.

She and Annie had gone to a Friday night football game at their high school—Lombard High, which had since been turned into a junior high school. Neither was all that interested in watching the game, just the muscular guys who played it. Afterward they had indulged in a fifth of vodka judiciously appropriated from Annie's father's liquor cabinet.

After becoming drunk as sailors on shore leave they got giggly and reckless, and Annie had dared Mary to pull down her pants and join her in mooning the star quarterback of the football team. Unfortunately, the person they'd exposed themselves to turned out to be Mrs. Merriam, the school principal, who'd promptly contacted their parents and subsequently suspended them from school for two weeks.

Annie had nearly been stripped of her homecoming queen status, but Mrs. Goldman had made such a scene, threatening to sue the school district, that Mrs. Merriam had finally backed down. Mary hadn't been quite as lucky.

When Sophia and Frank learned what their daughter had done, Mary had been grounded for an additional month and forced to attend mass every day to pray for forgiveness. Her knees still had calluses from the ordeal.

Pushing the memory aside, she finally told her brother, "Nick's lucky to have you on his side."

He shrugged, uncomfortable with the praise. "I got him a part-time job at Santini's. Lou's going to get him into weight lifting. I think it'll be good for Nick."

"You're a good man, Joe. Guess that's why you became a priest. And why Ma loves you best." If Sophia had her way, Joe would be canonized and given sainthood. Or at least be elected pope.

"Mom gets to brag to all her friends about me." Her brother's smile was suffering. "It's better than having a movie star in the family. I'm real, they can come gawk at me every week for free, and she can take all the credit."

"Ma's still rating your performance, you know. She puts a little gold star in the Sunday missal every week after you give the benediction."

"Another crack like that and I'll drag you into the confessional myself."

"Then I'll be forced to sic Annie on you. You know how protective she is of me."

At the mention of the woman with whom he had shared a past relationship, a strange look crossed his face. "How's Annie doing? I was surprised when I heard she was working at the restaurant. Rather a sedate profession, considering all the others she's tried, isn't it?"

"Why don't you come over and see for yourself? I won't even charge you for dinner."

He smiled, displaying two big dimples. Mary thought it a crime for a man of God to look so hunky, even one who happened to be her brother. A major waste. Gay men and priests had no right to be handsome, she decided. It wasn't fair to the female population at large.

"I just might. My own cooking stinks. And if I remember correctly, you make a mean lasagna."

"Yeah? Well tell that to Daniel Gallagher, the bozo who disparaged it. Didn't you read the nasty review he wrote on Mama Sophia's?"

Joe shook his head. "I don't take the newspaper. It's too depressing. Besides, what I hear in the confessional is far more entertaining than anything I could read in the paper or watch on the tube."

"Unfortunately for those of us who have inquiring minds, you're not like dear sister Connie. You don't share all the sordid details." His devilish grin told her he had plenty to share.

"Lucky for you I don't."

"Oh, yeah. Like I have anything remotely interesting to tell. I should be so lucky."

"Connie says you're going out on a date with Lou. Maybe you'll have something to confess after that." Her brother's teasing was nothing new. She'd been his favorite target since they were children; he knew she could give as good as she got. Joe would never pick on a weakling.

Mary knocked him playfully on the arm. "Connie's mouth is faster than a 56k modem. Is there anyone who doesn't know about my upcoming date with Lou Santini? Even my landlady congratulated me the other day. It's embarrassing. It's not as if I haven't gone out on a date before or been in a relationship."

"Mom says it's been a while. She's worried you might decide to enter a convent."

Mary laughed at the ridiculous notion. Deprivation wasn't one of her strong suits, especially as it pertained to eating. "They don't serve chocolates or pizza to the novitiates. I'd starve."

"I remember when you worked for Luigi, you used to always bring over those big pies on Friday evening after work and we'd pig out."

Mary's eyes filled with pain at the memory. "I miss him, Joe. Luigi was a kind man, a wonderful boss. He always remembered my birthday, always sent food home with the employees each evening, especially if he knew they were short on cash or having a tough time. And he never forgot the vets over at the VA Hospital.

Her brother nodded. "Luigi was a good guy. There's no denying that."

"I still don't understand what motivated him to take his own life. And in such a gruesome way. I know he wasn't in the best of health, which might have caused him to become depressed, but to have killed himself over it."

She shrugged. "Guess we'll never know why some people fall into such despair. If only he'd reached out to me. Maybe I could have helped." That's what plagued her most. How could she not have noticed his depression? And why hadn't he come to her, confided in her? They'd had that kind of close relationship. How could she have failed him?

Joe took her hand and squeezed it. "You mustn't blame yourself, Mary. I know better than anyone that it's not possible to help everyone who needs it. Luigi obviously had demons that no one knew about. And now that he's dead, we'll probably never know the truth. I admit it's frustrating and hard on the ego, but that's life."

"Do you ever miss your old life, Joe? Do you ever wonder what it would have been like . . ." If you and Annie had married, she wanted to finish, but didn't. Joe's relationship with Annie had ended a long time ago. It was pointless to dredge up the past, especially now, when there was nothing he could do about it.

But Mary couldn't help wondering what had happened between them. What had caused their breakup? Neither Annie nor Joe would talk about it.

"I'm sorry. I shouldn't have brought it up. I know it's all behind you now." His eyes filled with uncertainty, which gave her pause. "Is everything all right? You seem distracted."

"I . . ." Joe looked as if he wanted to confide something but then thought better of it. Finally, he shook his head. "It's nothing."

But Mary couldn't help feeling that her brother wasn't being totally honest. And that wasn't like him. Something was bothering Joe. She could feel it in her bones. And somehow, someway, she intended to find out what.

Stuffed Artichokes à la Marco

6 large artichokes
2 cups Italian-seasoned bread crumbs
2 eggs
³/₄ cup Parmesan cheese
¹/₄ cup chopped parlsey
¹/₂ cup olive oil
¹/₄ cup chopped garlic
salt and pepper to taste

Wash the artichokes in cold water. Cut bottom of artichokes, so they are flat. Then cut off about ½ inch at the top. Spread leaves apart to hold stuffing.

In a bowl, combine bread crumbs, parsley, Parmesan cheese, garlic, salt, pepper, and olive oil. Stuff each artichoke to the top, and drizzle with 1 tbsp. of olive oil.

Place artichokes in a large pot to which you have added about ¼ cup of water. Bring water to boil, then simmer for about 45 minutes, depending on the size of the artichokes. Serve hot. Serves 6.

CHAPTER
FIVE

Later that day, Mary walked into the restaurant to find Annie with the phone pressed to her ear, waving frantically as she motioned her forward. The woman looked frazzled, which was a rarity in itself for Annie, who put ice cubes to shame in the coolness department.

"You won't believe how many reservations I've taken today," she said, cupping her hand over the mouthpiece so the caller couldn't hear their conversation. "They're crawling out of the woodwork! That nasty review has actually helped business."

Mary's jaw unhinged. "I don't believe you. It can't be true." But she hoped it was. She had invested all of her life savings into Mama Sophia's. But more important than the money, she had invested a great deal of herself, because she had something to prove.

Mama Sophia's meant more than just a way to make a living. For Mary, it symbolized her declaration of independence.

For the first time in her life she had only herself to answer to. If the business succeeded, she would take full credit. Failure would be hers, too, but she wasn't going to allow that to happen.

Having failed at too many things in the past—college and men, for starters—Mary was determined that history wouldn't repeat itself. She'd taken the easy way out for far too long, placed too much emphasis on the opinions of others, instead of having the confidence to believe in herself. And she'd only exerted herself when she felt in danger of being swallowed up by her mother's overwhelming, controlling personality.

She didn't blame Sophia for steamrollering over her, because she'd allowed it to happen. But Mary wasn't about to give her mother the chance to say *I told you so*. Not this time.

Perched on the wooden stool next to the reception desk, she waited for Annie to complete her call, then said, "Tell me you're not just putting me on."

"Would I lie?"

Eyes rolled heavenward, Mary retorted with a no-brainer. "Is my mother opinionated?" Of course Annie lied, but only when it suited her purposes; like most people, and she never did it maliciously.

"It's true, Mary *mia*. Cross my heart and hope to score with Mike, the hunky waiter I just hired." She licked her lips, anticipating. "I'm just beginning to discover the benefits of my managerial position. But don't worry, I won't sexually harass him unless he really wants me to."

"Annie . . ." A wealth of warning came in that one word.

"*Oy vey*. Lighten up, will you? I was only kidding. Geez. What happened to your sense of humor?"

"It went down the toilet when the plumbing backed up and cost me three-hundred-and-fifty dollars." And meeting Daniel Gallagher hadn't helped, either.

It was difficult to hate a man who turned your insides to mush and made your mouth water. Every time Mary closed her eyes she could picture Dan Gallagher as she'd last seen him, seated behind his desk, and damn if it didn't make her hot all over.

Nodding in sympathetic understanding—for what woman couldn't relate to money, especially as it pertained to something as wasteful as toilet repair?—Annie explained, "One customer who read the review said the lasagna sounded fabulous. Said he hates it when there's no filling, and yours sounded absolutely mouthwatering, just like his 'sainted mama' used to make. I'm quoting here. Then he booked a party of eight for Friday evening."

"Well, I guess I should go back and apologize to Daniel Gallagher. I pretty much flayed his hide over the review."

"Apologize!" Not usually the gullible sort, Annie's jaw dropped just the same. "You're kidding, right?"

Mary flashed her friend an Are-you-out-of-your-mind? look. "Of course I'm kidding." She might find Gallagher devastatingly handsome, might even admit to being attracted to the man. But apologize?

I don't think so!

"We're just lucky most people have better sense than to believe restaurant critics. I mean, do you ever judge a movie by what you read in the paper or hear on those morning talk shows? I'd have missed a lot of good flicks if I'd allowed someone else's opinion to sway me."

Tapping a number-two pencil against the reservation book, Mary's manager frowned as she counted the reservations. "Do you think we need to hire more help? I hope this won't leave us shorthanded."

"I can wait tables and so can you, if push comes to shove. We can't afford to hire anyone else right now. We'll just have to make do."

"So tell me about your meeting with Daniel Gallagher. Is he as good-looking as his photo?" Annie asked.

Mary nodded reluctantly. "Even better. He's got green eyes, brownish hair, and, from what I could tell, because he was sitting down, a pretty decent body." Sinewy forearms. Muscular chest. And, she was sure, buns of steel.

A woman with a tush like a cream puff could appreciate such things about a man.

"Not that I'm interested," she added quickly, refusing to supply Annie with any ammunition.

"You sound interested."

"Well, I'm not! As my mother is fond of saying: 'When you lie down with dogs you get fleas.' "

"Or a juicy bone." Annie's grin was downright lascivious, and Mary heaved a sigh of frustration.

"I think you worked at that sex hotline too long."

"No need to get testy. And anyway, you owe me big-time. I had to placate that nutty chef of yours all by myself. The man should be committed to an institution for the criminally insane. He's a few slices short of a loaf, if you get my drift."

"And you did nothing to upset him?" Mary found that hard to believe. Annie was definitely a "chop-buster." If she couldn't get your goat one way, she'd try another.

"I merely tasted one itty bitty fingerful of the lemon meringue pie filling he was making, and he threatened to maim me with a butcher knife. The guy's scary."

Marco and Annie didn't get along too well. Annie thought he was pompous and egotistical, which he was. But Mary needed her chef, warts and all, and she didn't intend to encourage Annie's animosity toward him. Besides, his weirdness was starting to grow on her. "Marco's a chef, an *artiste.* He's supposed to be eccentric. And you're hardly one to talk when it comes to eccentricities."

Unable to argue that point, Annie dropped the subject and moved on to another. "So, why are you so late, if you weren't playing hide the hot dog with the reviewer?" She grinned at Mary's long-suffering expression.

"I stopped by the rectory to visit Joe."

Brow raised, Annie remarked, "Oh?" trying to mask her interest by appearing nonchalant. "And how is Father Joseph the Anointed these days?"

"As handsome as ever. And he's coming to dinner one evening soon, so you'd better be on your best behavior."

"Joe and I get along just fine, as long as he doesn't preach to me about my lifestyle, the clothes I wear, or the men I choose to sleep with."

Mary didn't miss the hurt flaring briefly in those bright blue eyes, and wondered if there were still unresolved issues between the couple. For all her tough exterior, Annie was sensitive about certain matters—Joe being one of them—though she'd deny it if pressed. "You and Joe have a history. He worries about you."

She made a face. "Yeah? Well he ought to worry about his celibate state instead. It can't be good for him. His plumbing must be backed up by now."

Mary knew Annie was being anything but honest with herself. "You worry too much about everyone's sex life, or lack thereof. You shouldn't. Joe and I will handle things our own way."

Annie's ribald laughter had several of the waiters turning to stare in their direction. Mike the hunk smiled and winked. Mary gave them all an imperious glare that had them scrambling back to their work stations.

The dinner crowd would start arriving around five P.M., and there were still plenty of napkins to fold, silverware to polish, and glasses to inspect for spots. Mary might not be a neatnik when it came to her own house, but she was a stickler about the restaurant and the place settings.

"Joe's *handling* things is what worries me, *cara*." Annie tucked her tongue in her cheek. "It might make him go blind."

Knowing there was no reasoning with her friend when she was in one of her playful moods, Mary eased off the stool and clasped Annie's hand. "Come on. Let's go taste some of Marco's specials. He's making Stuffed Artichokes à la Marco this evening, and I'm starving."

Annie rolled her eyes. "So what else is new?"

"I'm afraid Matthew is very disruptive in class, Mr. Gallagher. He's not attempting to make any friends, and his attitude toward learning is worrisome. And there's also the matter of his language."

Dan returned Miss Osborne's worried look with one of his own. Matt's third-grade teacher had summoned him to the school to discuss his son's unruly behavior, as if it were somehow Dan's fault that Matt had cursed and flipped off a couple of his classmates during a playground disagreement.

He'd been called out of an editorial meeting—not that he minded missing Walt's critique of the Food section—by an urgent phone call. At first, he'd thought something terrible had happened to Matt, and he'd panicked. But when he'd found out the reason for the call, that fear had turned into a slow burn. Matthew was in deep doo-doo as far as he was concerned.

Dan couldn't really blame Miss Osborne for alerting him to the situation. Apparently the woman subscribed to The-buck-stops-here approach to parenting.

Knees banging the underside of the midget-sized table they were seated at, Dan adjusted his long legs, trying desperately not to fall off the chair. "I'm doing the best I can, Miss Osborne. It's been difficult for Matt to adjust to his new surroundings." And for Dan to adjust to being both a mother and father. "He's upset about his mother leaving, and I'm trying hard to help him through a very difficult time. And it's not helping matters that my son blames me for what happened. The kid resents and thwarts me at every turn."

Matt had made it clear he wanted nothing whatsoever to do with sports. That had really hurt. Sports were, after all, Dan's life. Not to mention his bread and butter. His son was far more content to sit around all day, surfing the net on his computer or reading. The last book Dan read cover to cover had been *Joy of Cooking*. And his ineptness on the computer was laughable. Finding common ground was proving difficult.

Miss O. flashed her baby blues in his direction and smiled compassionately. She was young—he guessed about twenty-five—honey blond, and very attractive. Dan wouldn't have minded switching places with Matt for a while. The kid didn't know how good he had it. When Dan was in school, all of his teachers looked like Attila the Hun or Quasimodo.

"I'm aware of the circumstances that brought Matthew to you, Mr. Gallagher. His guidance counselor, Mr. Simms, and I have discussed his problems at length. And although I empathize with your plight, I can't allow your son to disrupt the class. That wouldn't be fair to the other children.

"Plus, his swearing cannot be tolerated. We have very strict rules here at Marymount about such things."

"I'll talk to him again. See what I can do." Wash his mouth out with soap! That's what Dan's mother had done to him when she'd caught him swearing, and it sure as hell had been an effective deterrent. At least he'd learned not to swear in front of her.

Matt's teacher stood and held out her hand, and he noticed she wasn't wearing a wedding ring. Figures, he thought. She's good at giving advice about child-rearing and probably doesn't have a kid of her own.

"Matt's down at the front office waiting for you. Perhaps on the way home you can have a heart-to-heart, explain what's expected of him."

As if that would do any good. He'd already talked to the kid until he was blue in the face, with no results. Dan smiled politely. "I'll do that. And thanks for your time."

"You're welcome. And by the way, Mr. Gallagher, I read your review of Mama Sophia's in the newspaper the other day."

"Oh, yeah?" Dan's chest puffed up with self-importance. "What d'ya think?"

"I must say that I don't agree with your assessment at all. My sister and I dined there just the other evening, and found the food to be extraordinary."

With a strained smile, Dan mumbled a suitable response

and departed quickly, thinking how appropriate that old adage was: Opinions are like assholes. Everybody has one.

But as restaurant critic, his was the only one that mattered.

Dan's thoughts were still on Miss Osborne's comments when he entered the Shopper's Paradise Market a short time later.

Thinking about what the teacher had said about his review of Mama Sophia's brought Mary Russo to mind. Again. He'd been thinking about her a lot since she'd stormed into his life a few days ago. There was something about her, some indefinable quality he found intriguing.

A spark had ignited between them that day. One she wasn't likely to acknowledge. He was the enemy, after all, but he'd seen the heightened color in her cheeks when he'd looked into her eyes, noted the way those big brown orbs had riveted on his lips. She'd looked interested, and he didn't think he was imagining things.

So when he pushed his cart around the corner of the cleaning supplies aisle, in search of fresh vegetables for tonight's dinner, he was stunned and very pleased to find the object of his musings standing before a mound of strawberries, inspecting each one carefully before dropping them into a plastic bag.

"Miss Russo, fancy meeting you here. I thought all you restaurant types only frequented the produce market." As lines went, that one was pretty original—original but lame, he decided.

Mary glanced up, and her heart caught in her throat. Daniel Gallagher was grinning at her, and she was— dammit!—reacting to those devilish dimples, those sparkling green eyes. She tried desperately to keep the unwelcome re-action to his nearness out of her voice.

"Strawberries aren't always easy to find this time of year," she explained. "The store manager, Mr. Gillati, always calls when he gets in a good batch. We're featuring strawberry shortcake on the menu tonight, not that you'd be interested." She forced a smile.

"You'd be surprised what I'm interested in, Miss Russo." He took the berry from her hand and sucked it, and the erotic gesture went straight to her . . . Good grief! She was actually becoming aroused.

"These are very sweet and juicy." He stared at her lips, licking his as if savoring the thought. "I have a real weakness for things sweet and juicy."

"How . . . how nice." My God! The man was making her stammer. "Well, if you'll excuse me, I've got to get back to work."

"Maybe we'll see each other again. I've been known to shop here."

"I rather doubt our paths will ever cross again, Mr. Gallagher." Not if she could help it, anyway.

"Why's that? Don't you like shopping here?"

She heaved a sigh, wondering if the man was obtuse. "Because, Mr. Gallagher, even though I like shopping here, I don't like you. I hate to be blunt, but you did ask." Your venial sins are piling up, Mary, she told herself, knowing she'd told him a bald-faced lie.

"Reviewers, as well as sportswriters, are used to being maligned and misunderstood, Miss Russo. I know we got off on the wrong foot, but—"

"Good-bye, Mr. Gallagher," Mary said, pushing her cart farther down the aisle, not giving him the chance to weaken her resolve. Gorgeous men were not necessarily pretty on the inside, she thought, forcing herself to keep walking, even though he called out to her.

"We'll definitely see each other again, Mary Russo. You can count on it."

Concentrate on your date with Lou, Mary told herself the entire way home. But it wasn't Lou's smile she kept imagining, and it wasn't Lou's musky cologne teasing her senses. It was Daniel Gallagher's.

* * *

"Zing went the strings of my heart."

Well, that's how the song went anyway. But as she sat watching Lou Santini stuff his face with moo shoo pork and listening to him expound on muscle mass and the benefits of exercise and proper diet—cruel, considering the amount of pork fried rice she'd just tucked away—Mary was pretty certain Lou wasn't going to make a good zing candidate.

So far, she hadn't felt so much as a bing, boom, or boing!

She'd decided late last night, while staring up at the flaking paint on her ceiling during a *Jay Leno* commercial break, that she was going to have an uncomplicated affair with someone.

Now that she had her freedom she needed to add a little "zing" to go along with it. Annie had been right about the depressing state of her social life, aka her sex life, aka nonexistent. And after her chance meeting with Daniel Gallagher and her combustible reaction to him . . . well, she knew it was time to confront those issues head-on.

What she wanted and needed right now was an affair.

Uncomplicated. Passionate. No strings attached.

She'd hoped it would be Lou who would rock her world. She liked Lou. He was a nice, caring man, even if he still lived with his mother. (How did he bring women home?) But nice didn't necessarily mean exciting.

And Mary really needed a little excitement.

Dan Gallagher—now, he was exciting.

Quit thinking about him, Mary. He's the enemy, and he's out of your league.

Besides, exciting was probably overrated. What she really needed was a little *release*. She'd built up a lot of *tension* over the last thirty-three years, and just about any man, even Lou, could provide her with . . . well, release.

"Did you like the fried rice, Mary?" Lou dumped a generous amount of soy sauce over his steamed dumplings as he asked the question, seemingly unconcerned about the amount of sodium he was about to ingest.

Of course, Lou didn't have to worry about stomach bloating, boob inflation, and all the other wonderful things that went along with water retention, because Lou was a man, and men didn't have to put up with the injustices of female physiology.

Water retention ranked right up there, with menstruation, yeast infections, sagging breasts, and cellulite.

"I highly recommend the sweet and sour pork or the sesame chicken to go along with the rice. Both are good."

Caught up in her reverie, Mary suddenly realized that she hadn't replied. Heat crawled up her cheeks, and she grabbed for the cup of steaming oolong tea, eager to have an excuse for her heightened color. "Everything's delicious. Thanks for inviting me out tonight. I needed a break from the restaurant."

"How's it going? My mama said you got a lousy review from *The Sun*."

She frowned, thinking back to her encounter with Daniel Gallagher. And the fact that he had dimples. She'd always been a sucker for dimples. "I dimp—I did. But it hasn't hurt business. If anything, it's helped. We've been packed every night."

"That's good to hear." He smiled, as if he really meant it. Lou was a nice man, unlike some others she could think of. "Maybe some evening after you close I could come over and see your new apartment."

Mary found it difficult to muster up much enthusiasm for his suggestion. By midnight she was too tired to do anything but fall into bed and zone out. Sometimes she watched Leno or read a steamy novel—it was hell living vicariously through the pages of a book!—but usually she just fell asleep. Alone.

Of course, confessing that to Lou would make her appear pathetic.

She should probably invite him over tonight. It's what he

was obviously hinting at. But what would she do with him once she got him there? Their conversation thus far hadn't been all that scintillating.

The density of bone and muscle mass was just not her thing. And she feared Lou would suggest she try weight lifting to firm up her flab. Mary had a real allergy to exercise and sweat. She'd practically convulsed once during an aerobics class!

"The trouble with you, Mary, is that you don't keep an open mind. Lou's a nice man, a good provider."

But was he a good kisser?

Remembering her mother's words made her feel somewhat guilty, as they'd been designed to. She guessed there was only one way to find out about Lou. And she really couldn't rule him out as a possible candidate until he'd been thoroughly tested—well, not too thoroughly, but a kiss wouldn't hurt.

Swallowing her nervousness, she heard herself say, "Why not come over this evening? We can have some cappuccino, listen to Pavarotti. Do you like opera?"

"Mama likes it. She's still got a bunch of old 78 LPs of Enrico Caruso and Mario Lanza."

"Really? How does she play them? I mean, I didn't think you could even buy needles, let alone a record player anymore."

"She's got an old Victorola," he said, taking a bite of his egg roll and talking around it. "It still works good. Mama never throws out anything."

Sophia had said Nina Santini's apartment looked like a museum, it had so much junk in it, but she may have been exaggerating. Her mother liked stretching the truth.

Mary had believed for years—because Sophia spewed it forth as if it were Gospel—that if she walked around barefoot or went outside with her hair wet that she would catch a cold. And though everyone knew that colds and flu were caused by viruses, damn if she didn't get sick just the same if she ignored the woman's warnings.

"Do you like living with your mother?" she asked, then wondered why, because no one in their right mind liked living with their mother. She'd done it only because it had been easier than being an adult and facing the real world.

He shrugged, as if the matter was inconsequential. "Mama's a good cook. She needs me. And after she dies I'll inherit the butcher shop and apartment, so I can't complain."

His answer had her eyes widening a fraction. "But it must make it rather difficult for you to . . . to entertain."

First he smiled, and she realized he was quite good-looking, in an Alec Baldwin kind of way—before Alec entered into marital bliss with Kim Basinger and gained all that weight—but then when her question finally sank in he looked at her as if she'd just broken commandment number eleven: Thou shalt not fornicate in your mama's house.

"There are hotels for that sort of thing. I would never bring a woman home to . . ." He looked affronted. "It wouldn't be right. It wouldn't show the proper respect, for a son to do such a thing to his mama. You understand?"

"Not to mention it could get rather crowded," she said, grinning. Her attempt at levity dropped like a two-hundred-pound dead marlin. She tried desperately to recover. "Well, I'm just so—"

Reaching across the table, an unfathomable light shining in his eyes, Lou laid his catcher's-mitt-sized hand over her smaller one, and she never got the chance to tell him what she'd started to—that she was so full, her stomach was about to explode. From here on out she was buying slacks with elasticized waistbands.

"We'll go back to your place," he said with a squeeze that would have made Mr. Whipple cringe. "Take care of matters there."

"Matters?"

"Lou's got a big Italian sausage he's dying to share with you."

Remembering Annie's earlier comment made her swallow the grapefruit-sized lump in her throat. "What kind of matters?" Maybe he wanted to be reimbursed for the veal.

But Lou the butcher boy with the big sausage only smiled, making her think that wasn't it at all.

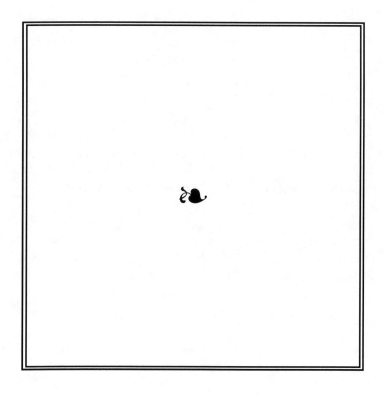

Aunt Emilia's Cheesecake

1 lb. cream cheese
¼ lb. butter
1 lb. ricotta cheese
1 pint sour cream
4 eggs
3 tbsp. lemon juice
3 tbsp. vanilla
1 ½ cups sugar
3 tbsp. cornstarch
3 tbsp. flour

Double graham cracker crust recipe on graham cracker crumbs box (I used Honey Maid). Mix: 2 ½ cups graham cracker crumbs, ½ cup sugar, ⅔ cup melted butter. Mix and press in bottom and sides of a 10-inch springform pan. Mix cream cheese, sour cream, eggs, and other ingredients, and pour into crust-lined pan.

Bake at 350° for 1 to 1½ hours. Leave in oven additional hour, with door ajar. Cool in refrigerator overnight before serving. Serves 10–12.

CHAPTER SIX

"Those are not cockroaches, Matt. They're shiitake mush-rooms," Dan explained as patiently as he could, despite the fact that the kid was making him nuts. "Expensive, tasty, and a great accompaniment to the veal medallions." He gulped rather than sipped his cabernet, needing all of the fortification he could get.

Full-time fatherhood was a lot tougher than he'd expected. He could only equate his experience thus far with being up at bat, having the bases loaded, and laying a goose egg—a big, fat zero.

Dan wasn't used to striking out. Up until now he'd always considered himself a winner. Funny how an eight-year-old kid could change all that by making a perfectly self-assured, reasonably well-adjusted male feel like a failure.

The child screwed up his face in disgust, and Dan gripped the stem of his wineglass, bracing for another encounter and empathizing with mothers everywhere who relied on Valium to get them through the day.

"Yeah, well, they're named right, because they taste like shi—"

"Watch it!" Approaching irate, Dan shot his son a no-nonsense look. "You've already been warned about using bad language. And if you think I'm kidding, I've got a bar of soap with your name on it. I don't believe in spankings, Matt, but in this case I can make an exception." Though he was trying his best to be reasonable, Dan had no intention of allowing his son to ride roughshod over him. He'd seen the results of parental permissiveness at the ball games he attended. Spoiled brats, he'd called them then; he didn't intend to raise one of his own.

Dan's condo, located in the trendy area of Baltimore's Inner Harbor, was within spitting distance of the water. He enjoyed watching the boats sail by from his kitchen window while he cooked. There was always a cool breeze blowing in off the Patapsco River, like the one presently ruffling his son's hair as he sat making fork trails through his pureed carrots.

Matt brushed absently at his unruly hair, missing the stubborn cowlick that refused to flatten, no matter how many swipes he took at it. "I've been beat before," he retorted, casting his father a mutinous look. "Mom spanked me lotsa times, but it never hurt." He uttered the last as if in challenge.

Dan had a difficult time believing his ex-wife had ever raised a hand to their son. If anything, she'd spoiled him rotten. But then, there were a lot of things he hadn't known about Sharon—like, for instance, her preference for younger men. Studmuffins, he believed they were called.

Sometimes he wondered if he'd really ever known her at all.

"I'm stronger than your mom, and a lot more determined. If I decide to spank you, it's definitely going to hurt. So I wouldn't push your luck." He doubted the kid believed him; Dan had never spanked his son.

Matt squirmed in his seat, digesting his father's threat along with the veal medallions. He might be stubborn, but he wasn't stupid. "How come we never get nothing good to eat? I hate all the fancy stuff you make. The kids at school get frozen dinners and Kentucky Fried Chicken. Why can't we ever have good stuff like that?"

Because it tasted like cardboard and had no nutritional value. Dan wasn't the food police, or Martha Stewart, for that matter. He was just a guy who happened to like good food.

Gazing at his son was like looking at a reflection of himself in the mirror, only Matt had a touch of red in his hair. Like his dad, Matt's eyes were green, and Dan knew the kid took after him in the stubborn and opinionated departments, too.

If only he could find a way to break through the barrier Matt had erected. They'd always had a great relationship, but this situation with Sharon had put a strain on it. "So, is pizza still your favorite thing to eat?" he asked, even though he knew what the answer would be. Since he'd been old enough to chew, the kid had been nuts about pizza.

Matt brightened like an incandescent lightbulb. "Yeah! Pizza! Pizza!" he replied, mimicking the TV commercial. "I love it. I could eat it three times a day, every day of the week."

At least pizza covered most of the basic food groups. Dan refilled his son's glass with more milk, earning himself another frown. "So let's compromise, okay? I'll take you out for pizza on Friday nights, and you humor me the rest of the week about what I cook. What d'ya say?" He hoped Matt agreed, because he was not buying KFC, or Hungry Man dinners. The next thing you knew, the kid would be asking for hamburgers and hot dogs. Dan ate hot dogs at ball games, but only when he was desperate.

Though Matt was somewhat appeased by the suggestion, Dan could see his mind working as he tried to figure out a way around eating the foods he didn't like.

"Can we get rid of the mushrooms? They're gross."

"Only the shiitake. I can't cook many of the dishes I like without using mushrooms. Besides, I happen to love them. But you can pick them out if you want."

"And what about those cornball hens? I hate 'em."

"You mean Cornish game hens?" Dan's eyes widened. "Even glazed with a delicate mandarin-orange sauce?" he added, waiting hopefully and feeling crushed when the boy nodded.

Why doesn't the kid just rip out my heart?

Dan heaved a sigh. "I guess we can compromise on some of the dishes. Maybe you can look at the cookbooks and magazines with me, help me decide on the menus for the week. Would you like that?" Though the boy shrugged, Dan could tell he'd hit on something that interested him.

"I can probably do a search on the Internet," Matt said. "There's a bunch of stuff on the Web. Lots of food sites."

Matt was a master when it came to the computer and the Internet. Dan preferred getting his information the old-fashioned way—out of books. Still, if the Internet could bring them closer together, it was worth a shot.

"Go ahead and see what you can find. It'll be fun working together on this and finding meals we'll both be happy with."

The kid didn't look at all convinced, but he nodded just the same. "Where we going for pizza? How about Pizza Hut?"

"Pizza Hut's good." But Dan knew just where they'd go to find pizza, and maybe a whole lot more. "I was thinking about trying a new place I reviewed recently. An Italian restaurant that serves pizza. How's that sound?"

Matt hid his disappointment with a shrug. "Okay, I guess. What's it called? Maybe they've got a Web site."

Visions of dark brown eyes, creamy skin, and a full figure came to mind. "Mama Sophia's," he replied. "It's called Mama Sophia's."

The restaurant was packed when Dan and his son entered the following Friday evening. Dan could hardly contain his surprise when informed that it would be at least a forty-five-minute wait for a table.

"Man, this place must be good!" Matt said, peering wide-eyed through the throng of waiting customers, to see into the main dining room buzzing with activity.

Tuxedo-attired waiters and waitresses darted between tables, carrying large trays laden with delicious-smelling dishes. The scents of garlic and tomato sauce perfumed the air. Glasses clanked, and the sound of laughter and conversation hummed steadily. Behind the swinging doors leading to the kitchen, the chef could be heard shouting out orders like Mussolini on a rampage.

"Gosh, this place sure smells good." Matt's stomach rumbled, making his father smile. "I've never seen so many people in a pizza place before."

"Oh, it is good," a tall, thin woman in a lime-green wool coat, standing next to Matt, said. "We've eaten here three times since it opened; each time's been excellent. And they have much more on their menu than pizza, young man."

Matt looked up at his father, not saying a word.

"The lasagna's made just like my mama's," an older, white-haired gentleman chimed in, leaning heavily on his cane. "I bring my whole family." He gestured to the large group of people, both young and old, standing behind him. "We're here to celebrate my niece's engagement. The food is supposed to be as wonderful as my Stephanie." He winked at the smiling young woman adjacent to him. "I don't think that is possible, but an old man can hope."

"That's good to hear," Dan responded, praying none of the customers waiting in the vestibule recognized him from his newspaper photo.

Matt tugged his father's shirtsleeve, his eyes filled with confusion. "Whatta ya mean? I thought you—"

Dan yanked him forward. "Let's take a trip to the rest room, son." He smiled apologetically at the throng of hungry patrons, who made room for the young boy to pass. The green-coated woman cast Dan a suspicious look.

"Dad, why'd you act like you hadn't eaten here before?" Matt asked when they were a safe distance away. "I thought you reviewed the place."

"It's a long story. Let's not talk about it right now, okay?"

The child's expression grew knowing. "Oh, I get it. This

must be what Miss Osborne was talking about in class the other day when she told us we shouldn't believe everything we read in newspapers."

Sure, now *the kid paid attention to what Miss Osborne said.*

"Look!" Matt grew more animated by the minute. "Man, that is so cool! They've got grapes growing on the ceiling." He pointed at the vines and clusters of plastic purple grapes entwined on the trellis. "Wow! Do you think they're real?"

He looked like he was actually enjoying himself, and though Dan felt like skulking out, he didn't want to disappoint him by leaving.

Dan also wanted to taste the food again. He couldn't believe all the wonderful comments he was overhearing about the various Italian dishes. Could he have been so off base? Had his palate become somewhat jaded?

If so, it was probably the result of all those damn hamburger recipes Linda insisted he try. His taste buds had been tainted by "*Bad* Cow disease."

During their confrontational meeting, Mary Russo had confided that there'd been some problems right after Mama Sophia's opened, which was not at all uncommon in the restaurant business. Larger, more prestigious dining establishments than hers had suffered the same fate.

Maybe it had been an off night. Hell, even ball players had off nights. Maybe he'd been too hasty in his judgment. Maybe he should have waited, given the place more time to establish itself. After all, he didn't like Italian food, and that might have colored his opinion somewhat.

Damn, what if he'd been wrong?

Dan took his job as a journalist and food critic seriously, and he wanted to be fair. As a sportswriter, he reported the facts and stats as he saw them, never embellishing to favor one team or player over another.

So why, then, had he been so hard on Mama Sophia's?

Because he was opinionated and liked being right, because he'd probably been in a bad mood that day and had taken it out on the restaurant, and because he was a sports-writer, not a damn restaurant critic!

While in the midst of berating himself, Dan's name was called. He and Matt were shown, by an exotic-looking young woman with short, spiky hair the color of Kool-Aid, to a small, tiled table adjacent to the front window. The enigmatic smile the woman cast him made him feel as if she knew something he didn't. It was very unsettling.

Seating himself, he picked up one of the red leather-jacketed menus she'd left on the table, and that's when he noticed Mary Russo standing across the room. His gut started churning, and he was suddenly grateful for the Rolaids stuffed in his pants pocket. Too bad they hadn't invented a similar remedy for lust, though he doubted it would have been strong enough to cure what he was feeling at the moment.

The sexy woman was talking to some of her customers, gesturing wildly with her hands, laughing at something they said. The sound of her laughter sent a shiver of awareness tripping down his spine, which went straight to his crotch. His breath caught in his throat, his heart hammered in his chest, and he felt as if he were having an anxiety attack—the kind he always experienced before stepping on a plane.

Crash and burn. An apt description of his last two en-counters with Mary Russo. Well, at least he was batting a thousand, he thought.

Dan hadn't been able to stop thinking about Mary, which was the real reason he'd wanted to come to the restaurant this evening. No matter that she still detested him, he was deter-mined to see if that impossible emotion that had plagued him at their first meeting and at the grocery store was still there. Something much stronger, much more powerful than anger flowed between them, he was sure of it. And he knew damn well that she felt it, too.

As she did every evening, Mary was making the rounds of the tables, chatting with several new customers, recognizing familiar faces, and was delighted to find that she was already establishing a list of regulars.

Repeat business was what would make Mama Sophia's a resounding success.

"Don't forget to try the cheesecake tonight, Mrs. Heggan," she told the blonde with the pronounced sweet tooth and distinctive French accent. "It's my aunt Emilia's recipe, and it's absolutely scrumptious. You won't be disappointed, I promise you that."

The woman's eyes lit. "And will you also promise me, Mary, that I won't gain any weight?"

"But, of course, *mon ami,*" she replied, eyes twinkling. "All our desserts and pastas are calorie free. That's how I keep my trim"—*I wish*—"figure."

With a wink, she moved on, nodding and smiling at the anniversary couple who were celebrating twenty-five years of marital bliss with a bottle of Dom Perignon and the special almond cake Marco had prepared just for them.

Mary was about to cross the room when she spotted her archenemy seated at a table by the window. She sucked in her breath, trying to stem her rising emotions and murderous intent.

How dare Daniel Gallagher show his face in here again!

"We'll definitely see each other again, Mary Russo. You can count on it."

The reminder made her eyes narrow as she took in the small boy seated next to him. He looked like a miniature version of the man, only instead of well-worn jeans, a blue polo shirt, and docksiders, the kid wore baggy denims, a *Star Wars: The Phantom Menace* T-shirt, and high-top sneakers.

His son, Mary concluded, though she'd never really thought about Gallagher as being married. Not that she thought much about him at all, she lied to herself. But he just didn't seem to have that settled, married look about him.

He looked up from his menu, gazed directly at her, and smiled a hundred-watt smile that had her palms and soles itching. There was no way she could avoid going over to greet him without appearing small and vindictive.

At least that's what she told herself.

"Mr. Gallagher, what a surprise! You're the last person I expected to find willing to eat my 'heavy, tasteless food,' I think was how you put it." She forced a smile, but it came out looking like a grimace.

He ignored the jibe, concentrating instead on her delectable mouth, which at the moment was pursed tighter than a clamshell. Should he mention how fond he was of clams? He thought not. "I brought my son in to try the pizza. Matt's a big fan of pizza."

The boy smiled, revealing two slightly crooked front teeth, and Mary identified with him instantly. Even though she disliked his father, she would not be rude to the child. After all, she knew all too well that one could not choose their relatives, though she doubted she'd trade in any of hers.

Normal just didn't compute anymore.

She returned the boy's smile. "Hi, Matt! Welcome to Mama Sophia's. So you're a huge pizza fan, huh? What kind do you like? I'll have my chef make one up special for you."

"Wow!" The child practically launched himself off the chair. "Did you hear that, Dad? Can I have one with everything on it? Except mushrooms. I hate mushrooms. And . . ."

Gallagher smiled indulgently at his son, and Mary felt her heart warm, but she cast the feeling off to the sausage and peppers she'd eaten earlier that day, unwilling to believe it could be anything else.

I will not be attracted to this man. I will not!

While Mary listened to the child's excited recitation of everything he wanted on his pie, she studied his father as unobtrusively as she could beneath lowered lashes.

Daniel Gallagher was what Annie referred to as "a hotty, a hunk, a walking orgasm." Damn him! Those green eyes were sparkling as he listened to his son wax poetic over the pizza—his fringe of long lashes, thick; his smile, oh-so-sexy—when he looked up at her and said, "I'll try the eggplant parmesan special and a glass of Chianti." His voice was deep, rich, and smooth, like satin sliding over bare skin, hot fudge oozing over ice cream, a mocha latte with extra whipped cream to tickle your tongue.

Boiiiiingg!!!

Why couldn't she have felt that spark of excitement when Lou kissed her the other night? Not that it hadn't been a very nice kiss, because it had. It just hadn't knocked her socks off. Her toes hadn't curled. Her hair hadn't singed. There'd been absolutely no zing whatsoever. And there certainly hadn't been a *boing*!

Studying Daniel Gallagher's mouth, she knew whomever this reporter kissed would definitely feel something beyond "nice."

Despite her best efforts not to, she was getting a little *siss! boom! bah!* in her lower extremities. Damn, what was wrong with her? How could she feel the least bit attracted to a man who had trashed her restaurant? Who held all she worked for in disdain? Who'd tried to deprive her of a livelihood? Not to mention a man whose taste buds suffered from paralysis!

She couldn't. She wouldn't. End of story.

Mary assumed a professional demeanor. "I'll get your waitress. Loretta will be serving you this evening." Loretta Pazzoli was the least pleasant of all her wait staff, which was why, she was sure, Annie had chosen her to wait on Gallagher's table. Though excellent at her job, the woman had the personality of a piranha. And the good part was—she hated men, especially the good-looking ones who reminded the new divorcée of her faithless ex-husband.

"I'll make sure Loretta brings the wine and pizza right over," Mary said, smiling at the boy. "Enjoy your dinner, Matt."

Dan watched Mary walk directly over to the wild-haired woman and engage her in conversation. They looked over in his direction, turning away quickly when he smiled, making him feel something akin to regret.

Mary Russo hated him. He could see it in her eyes, hear it in her voice. Damn!

"She's nice," Matt said, fidgeting with his silverware. "I like this place."

"Yeah, me, too." And he had no intention of giving up.

It ain't over till it's over.

Having been around baseball most of his life, Dan was quite familiar with the adage.

And as far as he was concerned, it wasn't over yet.

Uncle Alfredo's Fettucini

6 tbsp. butter
1 ½ cups whipping cream
3–4 cups cooked and drained fettucini noodles
1 cup shredded Parmesan or Romano cheese
salt and pepper to taste
freshly grated nutmeg to taste

In a chafing dish or frying pan over high heat, melt butter until lightly browned. Add ½ cup of the whipping cream, and boil rapidly until large shiny bubbles form. Stir occasionally. (This part can be made early in the day.) Reduce heat to medium and add cooked noodles. Toss vigorously with two forks, and pour in the cheese and remaining cream, a little bit at a time. The noodles should be moist, but not too liquid. Season with salt and pepper. Add grated nutmeg to taste. Serve immediately. 4–6 servings.

CHAPTER
SEVEN

When the women of the Russo family got together, as they did that Monday afternoon, several topics of discussion were usually covered: Grandma Flora's hemorrhoidal flare-ups; Sophia's disgust with Frank's inventions, or her delight with Father Joe's performance at mass, depending on her mood; Connie's frustration with the amount of hours her husband-doctor worked; and Mary's many shortcomings.

The latter usually being the most popular.

"The trouble with you, Mary," Sophia said, twirling the fettucini noodles around her fork and shoveling another bite of the Alfredo into her mouth—Mary's uncle thought the dish had been named after him—"is that you're not willing to take a chance. Lou's a good catch. He'd make an excellent husband. Trust me, I know what I'm talking about."

Here it comes, Mary thought, bracing herself for the worst. Sophia was like a racehorse with an eye on the finish line, and she had no intention of allowing anyone, least of all her "ungrateful" daughter, to keep her from reaching her goal.

"Ma, I'm not going to marry Lou. He's nice. I like him. But only as a friend. And I'm well aware he's become your latest choice for a husband"—the veal cutlets had apparently done their work—"but there's no spark between us, no zing when I kiss him." They'd had three dates, three make-out sessions on her sofa, and afterward—nothing. She'd felt as if she'd been kissing her brother. Not that she'd ever locked lips with Joe!

"Like Betty Everett sings: 'It's in his kiss.' Well, it's not in Lou's." Her smile was borderline spiteful. "Trust me, I know what I'm talking about." No one, especially her mother, was going to push her into getting married.

Sophia rolled her eyes, looked over at her mother-in-law, who was at the moment stuffing a piece of bread down her throat with two fingers. Grandma Flora had a problem with her false teeth coming loose at inopportune moments. No matter which denture adhesive she tried, she couldn't just fix it and forget it. Her teeth clacked like castanets as she made short work of the doughy bread.

"You see, Flora? You see how it is with these young people? Mary is throwing away a good man. A hardworking man."

A good, hardworking man who lived with his mother, Mary wanted to point out, but didn't. Because to her family's outdated way of thinking, there was nothing wrong with a grown man in his early forties living with his mother. Why that was acceptable, she wasn't certain. She just knew it was.

" 'Zing!' What kind of talk is that?" her mother wanted to know. "The only zing you should worry about is when the cash register rings at Santini's to tell you how much money the man is making. Do you know what they're charging for a standing rib roast these days? Not prime, not even choice, but select. They should be ashamed of themselves."

"Money isn't everything, Ma," Connie stated, a forlorn expression on her face, making Mary wonder if there was trouble in proctology paradise. She knew her sister resented the long hours her husband sometimes worked, but she also knew Connie was crazy about Dr. Eddie Falcone. Twelve years of marriage hadn't changed that.

And Connie liked spending the money he made. The teal-blue designer pantsuit she wore had no doubt cost more than a year's supply of food for a third-world country.

A lot of butts had gone into that pantsuit!

Mary glanced down at her J.C. Penney ensemble and grimaced. Fashion was not her forte. While food was a necessity of life, clothing was merely a necessary evil. She hated shopping for clothes, mostly because garments that looked great on the rack and mannequins looked like hell on her body. And she was fairly certain all clothing stores used trick mirrors, because when she did buy dresses that looked good in the store, they sure as heck didn't when she got home.

"Thatsa enough, Sophia!" Grandma Flora had finally swallowed and was now voicing her opinion. "The *bambina* is talking about *passione. Amore.* The heart knows these tings. Whatsa matter, you no gotta heart? Mary musta decide for herself who she marries. Itsa her right." Satisfied that her point had been made, she grunted, dipped another piece of bread in the garlic-flavored olive oil, and stuffed it into her mouth.

Mary had the distinct feeling she would like to have stuffed it into Sophia's. Or maybe that was just wishful thinking on her part.

Sophia glared at her mother-in-law, as if the old woman had just committed high treason. To her way of thinking, she had. There was apparently some little known, unwritten law that older people had to take sides against their children, no matter if they were right or not.

It was the same way with families in general. You were either in, going along with the game plan, never taking sides against your family, or on the outs, which meant no one would talk to you.

At the moment Sophia's sister Angie was on the outs, because she had said something derogatory about Aunt Josephine's overweight daughter. Even though it was true that Sally weighed just slightly less than a baby elephant, no one but her mother was supposed to criticize her.

"Why, Flora?" her mother asked, clearly annoyed. "You married Sal when you were only fourteen. Your parents arranged it. Mary's thirty-three. She needs to find a husband and have children before her eggs dry up."

"Bah! Such talk. Whatsa matter wid you? Mary has the heart and blood of a Russo, not a Graziano. She feels tings deeply. I was lucky. My Salvatore was a good, honorable man. But the old ways are not always the best. You should know that better than anyone, Sophia. Frank went against my wishes to marry you. You're happy, no, that he didn't listen to his mama?" Eyes and fist raised heavenward, Grandma Flora cursed the fates that had conspired against her.

Sophia's face reddened, even as her eyes narrowed. She twirled her finger round and round beside her ear, indicating the old woman had lost her mind. "*Sie pazzesca nella testa!* You're crazy in the head!"

Mary and Connie exchanged surprised looks. They'd always suspected what lay at the root of the problem between their mother and grandmother, but until now it had never been confirmed.

It was no wonder Sophia bore such animosity toward her mother-in-law. And why hadn't *Nonna* wanted her parents to marry? They seemed well suited. Frank loved to eat, Sophia loved to cook. Frank had the patience of Job, Sophia the temperament of a fishwife. It was a match made in heaven, as far as Mary was concerned.

Never one to concede an argument before she had exhausted all possibilities, Mary's mother tried another tack. "That Annie Goldman is the one who puts these crazy ideas in Mary's head. The girl is wild, always has been. And such a trial to poor Mrs. Goldman. The woman is a saint for putting up with her." She pinched her fingers together and gave the five-finger shake. "Mark my words, she'll come to no good one of these days."

Sophia had been saying that about Annie off and on since first grade, especially after the mooning incident at the high school. Thus far, it hadn't come to pass.

"Leave Annie out of this, Ma." Mary shot her a warning

look. "She's got nothing to do with my decision to quit dating Lou. If Annie had her way, I'd be—" *Horizontal by now.* "Just leave her out of it, okay?"

Sipping her coffee, the older woman studied her daughter thoughtfully for several moments, then set her cup down on the table, careful to use a coaster, while she tried to find the right words to express what had been bothering her of late. "You've changed, Mary, since you opened the restaurant. Are you sure you're not . . . you're not doing drugs?"

From across the small living room of Mary's apartment, Connie, who'd been listening with half an ear to the conversation and the other half to her favorite soap, suddenly burst out laughing. "Mary on drugs? Ha! She gets sick taking aspirin.

"But I've noticed a change in Mary, too. That glow she's wearing is either new makeup or she's having a torrid love affair with someone other than the butcher boy."

Gasping at the idea that a child of hers would have sex out of wedlock—it was the "buying the cow" thing again—Mary's mother said accusingly to her younger daughter, "You never liked Lou!"

"Ma, he lives with his mother," Connie pointed out, throwing her hands up in the air in frustration. "Even if he were to bring a woman home, what would he do with her? Teach her how to stuff a pork loin?"

Mary couldn't contain her laughter, even though her mother was staring daggers at her. Thank God for Connie, and Grandma Flora, too, because if Sophia had her way, Mary would be Mrs. Butcher Boy faster than you could stuff a pork loin, or a cannoli.

"Ma, I'm not doing drugs. I'm not having an affair." *Yet.* "And I'm not desperate to get married. I know you won't understand this, but I'm content for the time being. I'm enjoying my life as a single, independent woman."

"A woman needs a man to make her whole. Being single

isn't natural. That's how come those women become les-bians. Isn't that right, Flora?" Sophia looked once again to Frank's mother for confirmation, but the old woman ignored her and began rolling and rerolling her heavy-duty support hose around blue elastic garters.

Mary wondered, not for the first time, why Grandma Flora's circulation wasn't cut off by the round elastic. She also found it somewhat amusing that the garters, which rested at the top of the old woman's knees, always stuck out below the hem of her dress when she sat down. Apparently fashion wasn't her grandmother's forte, either.

Noting that her mother was waiting for a response, Mary heaved a sigh and said finally, "I'm already whole, and I don't need a man." *Okay, maybe just for sex.* "Let's just drop it, Ma."

Someday maybe she would get married, but Mary had nei-ther the desire nor the self-confidence to do so now. When she felt ready to make such an important commitment, when she could rely on her judgment not to steer her wrong, when she had the trust to open herself up to a man, to share her innermost thoughts and desires, then, and only then, would she get married. And only if she was positive that she wouldn't fail. Based on past experience, she wasn't holding her breath.

Smart enough to realize that this was one argument she wasn't likely to win at the moment, Sophia moved on to the next subject. "Your father burned the hell out of my fanny the other night. I've got blisters." She lifted sideways off the chair and pointed.

"Kinky!" Connie winked at her sister, who swallowed a smile. Her mother, however, found nothing humorous about it.

"*Madonna mia, disgrazia!* He invented a heated toilet seat. I sat down and got shocked. It's a wonder I wasn't elec-trocuted to death." She harrumphed. "Some electrician. The man's getting senile."

"My Frank's a smart man," Flora said, but didn't elaborate. Mary thought she detected a twinkle in the old woman's eye.

"Yeah? Well, if he's so smart, how come I got blisters on my ass? Tell me that, old woman."

"All right, who wants zabaglione?" Mary butted in before things got too heated. Another argument between the two old ladies would definitely create indigestion. "The custard is nice and light. Just right for finishing off a heavy meal."

"I shouldn't. I'm getting so fat."

"Please, Connie," her mother said, shaking her head. "You eat like a bird. Men don't like bones."

Satisfied that everything was now back to normal, Mary fetched the dessert.

A light rain was falling by the time Mary parked her reliable but ugly brown 1991 Ford Escort in an adjacent parking lot and hurried into *The Baltimore Sun* building. The imposing structure located at the corner of Calvert and Center Streets had been part of the city's landscape for decades.

"Solidly built in the 1950's and designed to stand the test of time," her father had said of the old building many times.

Of course, Frank thought anything built in the 1950's, like their postwar-era, three-bedroom brick house, was an engineering marvel. Copper pipes, even corroded, were unquestionably the best thing invented since bocci balls, in his opinion.

The advertising department was located on the seventh floor of the tall building. She hurried toward the elevator, hoping to catch it before the doors slammed shut.

The beige-leather, Coach portfolio—a recent gift from Connie—clutched to her chest was stuffed with photos of the restaurant, both interior and exterior, and a sample of the menus, which changed daily, thanks to Marco's insistence that no specialty would be repeated within a four-week period.

Mary planned to purchase a series of ads to acquaint the city with Mama Sophia's. She'd received nice reviews from the *Washington Post* and *Washington Star* newspapers, and hoped their comments would offset the negative one from *The Sun*. Not because business wasn't good, but because she just couldn't stand to give that odious man the last word.

She hadn't seen Daniel Gallagher since that night at the restaurant a few weeks back, though she'd thought about him more than she cared to admit—especially at night while lying in her big empty bed, pondering her pathetic love life . . . but she didn't want to go there.

The man was one complication she didn't need right now, and she hoped she wouldn't see him today. She had enough on her mind at the moment—her parents' upcoming anniversary party, for one. Grandma Flora was insisting on helping with the preparations, though only God knew why, and He wasn't talking.

Forty-five minutes later, having completed her consultation with the ad designer, who'd promised Mary she'd be delighted with the results—she'd better be for the amount of money it was costing her!—Mary was making her way down the hallway, peering over her shoulder to keep a watchful eye out for the enemy.

As luck would have it, Gallagher's office was located on the same floor as the advertising department, and she had to pass by it to reach the elevator. She encountered a few newspaper employees along the way, but fortunately none had been the obnoxious reviewer.

Arriving at her destination without incident, she breathed a sigh of relief and waited, watching the lighted numbers above the double doors flash as the elevator descended from the twenty-first floor.

Searching her purse for her car keys, she looked up and stepped forward when the bell rang and the elevator doors slid open. At exactly the same time, Daniel Gallagher emerged from the elevator's confines, holding a cell phone to his ear. He was so absorbed in conversation he didn't see her until it was too late, and collided into her with the force of a football lineman, making her grunt and lose her balance.

Mary's portfolio went flying, as did her purse, keys, and left shoe; she tried desperately to balance herself.

Dan's eyes widened in shock when he realized what he'd done—and who he'd done it to—and he grabbed on to her before she fell. "Jesus! I'm sorry!"

She righted herself, extricating herself from his hold, straightening her spine and her clothing. "Well, you should be. You weren't watching where you were going, and—"

He arched a brow. "And you were? Let's play fair, Miss Russo. You weren't paying attention, either." He handed her the black leather flat and she put it back on.

Even though he spoke the truth, she wasn't about to agree. She scrambled for the items strewn all over the floor, hoping she reached the tampons before he did.

She didn't.

He stared at them, then at her, dropping them quickly into her purse without comment.

"Thanks." She forced the word out of her mouth with great effort.

He grinned good-naturedly. "My pleasure. How nice that we keep running into each other. Were you coming to see me again? My butt's still intact, even though I thought for sure you'd chewed it off that first day we met."

And an attractive butt it was! The front wasn't bad, either, she noticed, despite her best efforts not to. Clothes might make the man, but Daniel Gallagher definitely made his jeans.

Reining in her lustful observations, she ignored his attempt at humor, though she secretly found the comment amusing, in a perverse sort of way. "I've got to get back to work. Business is booming, in spite of your caustic review."

Her hackles were still up, he noted with regret. "I've been meaning to stop by again. I've just been busy."

"No doubt decimating unsuspecting restaurants."

He swallowed his smile. "Matt loves your pizza."

"Just goes to show you bad taste isn't hereditary." The elevator door opened and she disappeared into the car, leaving Dan holding something far worse than the proverbial bag.

Stepping out of the office and into the hallway at that moment, his secretary asked, "Is there something you'd like to tell me, Mr. Gallagher?" She focused on his hand, eyes wide behind the tortoiseshell rims, a hint of a teasing smile on her lips.

Dan looked down to find he was still clutching one of the tampons, and felt his face turn red. "I was just— Never mind! Don't you have something to do?" He looked around for a trash can, and when he found none, stuffed the offending hygiene item into his pants pocket.

Linda shook her head. "I'm on my break. Are you saving that for any particular reason?"

"Yeah. I'm thinking about adding glitter to it and hanging it on my Christmas tree this year. Satisfied?"

Cheeks pink, she said, "Well, you might want to dispose of it before entering your office. Mr. Beyerly's in there, and he's brought his nephew Bradley with him."

Bradley the ass-kissing moron who knew bupkis about sports. As far as Dan could tell, the only thing Bradley Forrester knew anything about was how to piss off the reporters working under him. A few of Dan's disgruntled Sports department coworkers had filled him in on the man's ineptness and unwillingness to listen to their seasoned advice. He was on a power trip, heading for a major collision.

Dan cursed his bad luck. "On second thought, I can think of something else to do with it." He didn't elaborate.

"Don't look now, *cara,* but the man of your wet dreams is back. Damn, but he's good to look at!"

Mary had been folding napkins into attractive triangular shapes while talking to Annie, who had taken a break. She turned to follow her friend's gaze, and her pulse rate quickened. Like a recurring nightmare, Dan Gallagher kept coming back. The man was even more dense than she'd previously given him credit for.

As usual, Annie's remark hit too close for comfort. Those nighttime musings of hers were getting a little X-rated of late. The little ice cream fantasy she'd had going a couple of nights back certainly seemed real. Chocolate Häagen Dazs had never tasted so good. That would teach her to eat ice cream in bed while reading torrid novels!

"What's he doing here again?" Mary asked. "I know his son likes the pizza, but there are plenty of other pizza places in town. I wish he'd go find one."

"Isn't it obvious? Daniel Gallagher's coming here to see you. He sure as hell doesn't like the food."

Her face as red as the napkin she twisted nervously between her fingers, Mary swallowed, though the idea generated tingles in her lower extremities. "Don't be ridiculous! We can't stand each other. If there were ever two different types of people . . ." She began tugging the bottom of her sweater.

Annie laughed at the protestation. "You two generate enough electricity when you're in the same room to run this restaurant's entire heating and air-conditioning system, so quit lying to yourself. Why fight it? Some things are just meant to be."

Mary shot her friend an annoyed look. "Get a grip. I'm not interested in pursuing a relationship with a man who has such lousy taste in food."

"Me thinks he's got pretty good taste when it comes to women," Annie retorted with a wink, ducking before Mary's arm could connect, then made her way back to the front reception area to resume her duties.

"Annie's right, Mary," Loretta said, coming up behind her harried boss to fill two glasses with ice water. "I recognize that guy from the last time I waited on him. He couldn't keep his eyes off you. Men are scum. You want me to dump something in his lap, like this water? It could cool him off."

Unsure whether she should laugh, cry, or merely run screaming into the night, Mary opted for the first option and forced a strained smile. "No thanks, Loretta, but I appreciate the offer. I don't think it's a good idea to douse the paying customers. It might give people the wrong impression of our hospitality."

The waitress glanced toward the Gallaghers' table, where father and son had their heads bent close together while they discussed the menu. "That kid of his is awfully cute. He kept telling me the last time he was here how much he loved the pizza, thanking me over and over again, saying 'yes, ma'am' and 'no, ma'am,' like I was someone special. Shows his father taught him right."

Or his mother, Mary thought, wondering why Mrs. Annoying Sportswriter was never with them when they dined.

It was one thing to tingle over a single man/enemy but quite another to have impure thoughts over a married one. *Impure thoughts!* God! Annie was right. She was starting to sound like her mother.

"You'd better go take their order. They look impatient. The boy must be hungry."

Loretta disappeared, as did Mary into the kitchen. There was no way she was going to make small talk with Daniel Gallagher tonight. Not if she could help it.

Mary had been in the kitchen for about half an hour, helping Marco chop vegetables for the minestrone, when a bloodcurdling scream erupted, causing her chef to curse and her to drop her knife.

"*Dio mio!* What the hell isa going on?" Marco's face flushed angrily. "I can't create with these crazy people screaming." Her chef fancied himself the Steven Spielberg of the kitchen. Every last detail had to go according to plan, and noisy commotions didn't play a part.

Mary left the reply to the kitchen staff, who were just as perplexed as she and not at all pleased by her defection, and rushed through the swinging doors into the dining room, wiping her hands on her apron. There she found a small crowd gathered around the Gallaghers' table. "What now?" she mumbled, not really wanting to find out.

By the time she reached their table, Matthew Gallagher's face was purple with the exertion of his screams, while his father's appeared white as Elmer's Glue. The child was clutching his belly, writhing with pain, and yelling at the top of his voice.

"That kid's got some set of lungs," Loretta pointed out to no one in particular.

"He's been poisoned!" Dan accused, gathering his son into his arms to comfort him while staring at Mary, who shook her head in disbelief and denial. "The cheese must have been tainted. Why else would Matt have gotten sick so quickly? He was fine before we came here."

"I—I don't know." He looked furious; she felt ill. "Call an ambulance," she instructed Loretta, who was beginning to pale a bit herself. "This child needs to be taken to the hospital immediately."

Customers were staring in their direction. A few got up to leave, their looks uncertain. But Mary was too upset about the boy's condition to worry over a loss of business.

"There's nothing wrong with the cheese, Mr. Gallagher," she assured the distraught man. "My chef makes his own mozzarella. I don't know why your son took ill, but I can assure you it's not the food."

Mary had taken every precaution to guard against food contamination. E-coli and salmonella were very dangerous forms of bacteria. Because of that, perishables were kept only a few days, and employees had been instructed to wash their hands frequently. She'd even posted a sign in the bathroom to that effect.

But it was obvious from the nasty sneer on Daniel Gallagher's face that he didn't believe a word she said.

"I don't have time to discuss this now. But if my son's illness turns out to be your fault, Miss Russo, you'll be hearing from my lawyer."

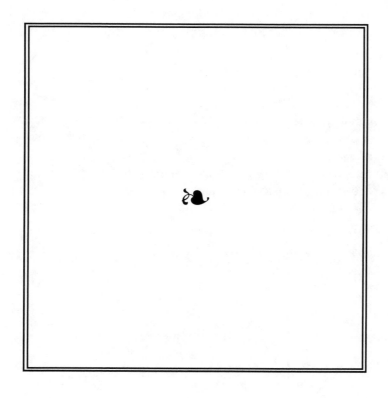

Dan's Roasted Chicken

1 5-lb. whole chicken
2–3 cloves of garlic, sliced
2 tbsp. parsley, bunched and chopped
1 tsp. tarragon or rosemary
(1 tsp. oregano and basil, if desired)
3–4 lemon slices
salt and pepper to taste

Wash and pat dry the chicken. Slice the garlic thin, and place several pieces under the skin of the chicken. In the cavity, place the remaining garlic, lemon slices, and bunched parsley. Brush olive oil on the skin of the chicken, and place the chicken in a roasting pan. Sprinkle with salt, pepper, tarragon, and chopped parsley.

Roast in a 350° oven for 1 hour, or until juices run clear. Serves 4.

CHAPTER
EIGHT

Mary burst through the double doors of the pediatric unit at Mercy Hospital, marching with purposeful strides down the long corridor.

She should have been furious at the way Daniel Gallagher had spoken to her, blamed her for his son's illness—anyone in their right mind would be—but she just couldn't muster up any anger against the man. He'd been crazed, and for good reason. If the same thing had happened to her, she probably would have reacted just as irrationally. Well, maybe not quite as mean, nasty, and ill-tempered, but she would have been upset.

Inquiring at the nurses' station about Matthew's condition, she was told he was still in surgery.

Surgery! His father must be beside himself with worry, she thought, quickening her steps to the pediatric surgical waiting room, where the duty nurse said she would find Daniel Gallagher.

He was seated on a royal-blue vinyl sofa, head in hands, looking for all the world like he'd lost his very best friend. Behind him Bugs Bunny and Daffy Duck frolicked on the brightly painted red walls, oblivious to his agony.

Her heart ached for him. She wouldn't even think about the other organs that were responding to the sight of 190 pounds of male vulnerability.

"Mr. Gallagher," she said softly, and he looked up, surprised at seeing her there. "I hope I'm not intruding. I . . .

How's Matt doing? I've been worried sick since the ambulance left. I left work early to come see for myself how he is."

A mixture of embarrassment and gratitude crossed his face, and he smiled ruefully, motioning her forward and patting the space next to him on the sofa. "I'm glad you're here." It was not the greeting she'd been expecting.

They were alone in the waiting area, and Mary was tempted to keep her distance, for all kinds of reasons, not the least of which was the strange attraction between them. But he looked as if he needed a friend, so she removed her jacket and sat down.

"Thanks for coming. I was going to call and apologize. I acted like an ass. I'm sorry. I hope you'll forgive me."

Mary had changed into black wool slacks and a lightweight red cashmere sweater before leaving for the hospital, but even with the warm clothes she felt a shiver slip down her spine at Dan's apology.

Forgiveness wasn't taken lightly in the Russo family, nor was it dispensed too frequently. But the man seemed genuinely sincere and full of remorse, so she decided to make an exception. "Apology accepted. So I gather it wasn't food poisoning that caused your son's illness?"

He shook his head. "Acute appendicitis. They're operating on him now. The doctor says it's pretty common, that I shouldn't worry, but I'm terrified something will go wrong. He's so small, so helpless." If anything happened to Matt . . . He couldn't bear even to think about the possibility.

Reaching out, she placed her hand over his. "Nothing will go wrong. Kids are resilient. They bounce back from these kind of things, you'll see. My nephew Tony had his tonsils out a few months ago and was back in school within a week." What she neglected to mention was that her mother and grandmother had lit enough candles at church to illuminate the entire city of Baltimore in order to ensure his recovery.

"Matt will be eating pizza again in no time. In fact, as soon as he's well, I'll bring him one from the restaurant."

"I hope you're right. I'm not very good at these kind of things. Matt hasn't lived with me very long, and I'm not up to par on childhood illnesses. Apparently he had all the classic symptoms of appendicitis—abdominal pain, nausea, fever—but I wasn't smart enough to figure it out. Sharon, my ex-wife, would have known what to do, but she's out of the picture now."

His revelation surprised her. "You're divorced?" Unable to squelch the relief she felt, Mary chided herself for being foolish.

He nodded. "Four years. But Matt only came to live with me a few months ago, when my ex-wife came to the conclusion that she didn't find motherhood all that fulfilling and decided to run off with her aerobics instructor."

"Get out!" Mary's jaw dropped, then she snapped it shut with such force her teeth clacked. "I can't believe a mother would walk away from her own child." What kind of a woman was Sharon Gallagher? Sophia would have called her a heartless *puttana*, and Mary would have agreed.

He screwed up his face. "Yeah, me neither. Matt's devastated over it. Wonders what he did wrong to make his mother leave like she did. Of course, he blames me most of all. Somehow Matt's convinced that her leaving must be my fault."

"I'm sure he's just frustrated. He'll come around eventually." She squeezed his hand, trying to offer what comfort she could. The man was in a tough, no-win situation. He couldn't defend himself without maligning the boy's mother, who was the real villain in all of this.

He squeezed back, and Mary's toes did a little tap dance that rocketed all the way to her groin. "I know he's frustrated and hurt," Dan said, "but it's damn hard to put up with. I didn't want the divorce to change things between me and my son, but it has. I feel like such a failure at times. I love Matt. I've always tried to be there for him, but now . . ." He shook his head. "I just don't know what to do.

"I was on the road a great deal of the time when Matt was younger. Maybe things would be different now if I hadn't been so selfish then. I should have stayed home, been a better father."

"That was your career. How could you have done any differently? Quit blaming yourself. It's your ex-wife who should be ashamed of the way she's treated that innocent child."

Her vehemence made him smile. "You sure are pretty when you're angry, which seems to be most of the time, at least with me."

His compliment had her face flaming. "Italians are known for their temper. It's because of our hot blood, or so my grandmother says." Mary used to think she was in need of a transfusion. Not anymore.

"Did you always want to own a restaurant?" he asked, grateful for the conversation and the opportunity to focus on something other than his son's illness for a few minutes.

Matt's attack had thrown him for a loop. He'd felt so useless, so helpless and alone. It wasn't a good feeling for a man who was supposed to be in control of things, who was expected to know all the answers. Who wasn't supposed to show fear. But he was afraid. Very afraid of losing his son.

She shrugged. "Not really. I never followed through on anything, never had any lofty ambitions. I guess I've always been afraid of failing, of not being good enough." Of disappointing my mother, she realized now.

"I dropped out of college after my second year and went to work for Luigi Marconi at Uncle Luigi's Pizza Palace. That's where I learned about the restaurant business."

"Tough break, him killing himself like he did." The man's death had been in all the newspapers, but no motive, other than depression, had been given for his suicide.

Rising to her feet, Mary moved to look out the window. It

was dark, but the lights from the parking lot cast a pinkish hue over the black macadam. "My mother was after me to get on with my life after Luigi's death, and I finally realized that life was passing me by, and if I didn't do something to change things, I'd end up like . . ." *My mother.* But she didn't say it. "Anyway, I decided to open my own business, and it was the best decision I ever made."

"Until I came along to mess things up?"

She spun around, but the anger he expected wasn't there. He was both relieved and glad. He truly liked Mary Russo. She was compassionate, intelligent, and he found her frankness refreshing.

"You're entitled to your opinions, not that I agree with them, of course. I doubt we'd agree on much of anything. I bet you don't like listening to opera or watching old movies." Why do you care? she asked herself. But she did.

"You're right. At least about the opera. I never understood what the big deal was about." The only fat lady Dan wanted to hear sing was the one at the ballpark. "But I love the old black-and-white films and those corny MGM musicals."

Her eyes lit. "Really? I used to dream about dancing at Radio City with the Rockettes, after watching Ann Miller and Eleanor Powell tap dance in all those movies." Annie had gotten her hooked on old flicks. They used to perform all the Ginger Rogers–Fred Astaire dance numbers, taking turns at being Ginger by wearing Mrs. Goldman's yellow chiffon gown and matching satin pumps. Sometimes when Mr. Goldman had had a few too many, he would don his tuxedo and play the Fred Astaire part, but not very often.

"Why didn't you?" he asked, drawing her back to the present.

"As my mother is fond of saying," Mary transformed her voice, doing her best imitation of Sophia, " 'Two left feet should never be stuffed into a pair of patent-leather tap shoes. The trouble with Mary is she's got no rhythm.' "

He threw back his head and laughed. "Your mother sounds very opinionated."

Is the Pope . . . ? Yeah, right! Mary plopped back down on the sofa. "You know what they say about opinions."

"I don't suppose you like sports?"

"Are you kidding? I'm a huge Orioles fan, but I don't go to the games as often as I'd like. You must have really great seats since you're a sportswriter."

"I've been temporarily transferred. Just for six months, until the regular Food editor returns from maternity leave. Then I'm going back to the Sports section."

That'll be a happy day for restauranteurs everywhere, she was tempted to say, but opted not to. They were getting along well. Why spoil things? Besides, the review was a thing of the past. And Daniel Gallagher didn't seem to be the Antichrist after all. He was actually quite nice and very charming.

"I bet you're looking forward to that," she said.

"Yeah. I love to cook, but there's nothing like sports to get a man's adrenaline pumping." Well, maybe one thing, he amended silently. But it had been so long since he'd done *that*, he'd probably forgotten how.

"So, what do you like to cook?"

"I make a mean roasted chicken, if I say so myself. I use lots of garlic, rosemary, and fresh parsley. Maybe you could come over to dinner next week and try it. I'll even let you do a review, then you'll see the job's not all it's cracked up to be."

He was asking her out on a date! Surprisingly, Mary found herself eager to accept. "I'd like that. The restaurant's closed on Mondays. Is that a good day for you?"

His smile had her blood heating to the boiling point. "Perfect. As soon as I'm sure Matt's going to be okay, we'll firm it up," he said, adding, "Guess you're happy my stint as reviewer is only for six months, huh?"

"Ecstatic is more like it," she admitted. Dan threw back

his head and laughed, and Mary's heart did twelve bars of "I've Got Rhythm."

"Hey, it hasn't been all bad. Because of that review, we got to meet each other." The rough pads of his fingers moved gently over her knuckles, making the hairs at her nape stand on end. "I consider that very fortunate," he added, his voice dipping low.

Boing! Boing! Boing!
Zing! Zing! Zing!

What was fortunate was that the doctor chose that moment to enter the waiting room, otherwise Mary may have been tempted to do something totally un-Mary-like, like offer herself up as a virginal sacrifice.

The surgeon was wearing soiled blue surgical scrubs and a very confident smile. Mary knew the news was good, and relief washed over her.

"Mr. Gallagher, I'm Doctor Peterson. Matt's surgery went just fine. He's in recovery. You'll be able to see him just as soon as the anesthetic wears off."

Dan breathed a sigh of relief and pumped the man's hand, then turned and drew a startled Mary into his arms, hugging her tightly to his chest.

If he lifted her off the ground, she was going to propose, Mary decided. Before now, only chocolate had had such a stimulating effect on her.

"He's going to be all right. Matt's going to be okay!"

He smelled of Polo aftershave and the musky scent of man. Mary thought she'd died and gone to heaven. Afraid she was going to start hyperventilating at any moment, she took a deep breath. "I know. I heard. I'm so happy for you, and for Matt." She hoped her cheeks weren't as flushed as they felt.

"I'm glad you finally got here, Mrs. Gallagher," the doctor said, mistaking her identity and holding out his hand. "I'm sure Matt will be anxious to see you once he awakens."

"I'm . . . I'm not Matt's mother, Dr. Peterson, just a

concerned friend. But I do plan to visit him, if that's all right with"—she turned to Dan—"Mr. Gallagher," and was relieved when the doctor mumbled an embarrassed apology and quit the room.

"Call me Dan. And of course it's all right. Anyone bearing pizza will be welcomed by Matt with open arms."

"I'd like to bring my grandma Flora with me, if that's okay. *Nonna*'s fantastic with kids, and I think she and Matt will get along great. I sensed he could use a friend or two."

"That'd be great."

She gathered up her purse and jacket. "Well, I'd better get back to the restaurant. Now that you know Matt's going to be okay, you should go home and get some sleep." Sleeping was about the furthest thing from Mary's mind, though her thoughts did stray to bedtime activities.

"Thanks for coming tonight, Mary. I really appreciated your being here. It made waiting and worrying a whole lot easier. And I'm glad we had a chance to talk, get to know each other better. Do you still want to get together Monday night?"

Mary, who'd never had a man cook dinner for her before, nodded, knowing the experience was going to be interesting on all sorts of levels. They decided on seven, which would give Dan time to visit Matthew before cooking dinner, and he gave her directions to his condo.

Dan's eyes filled with warmth. "You're a nice lady, Mary Russo."

His compliment warmed her. "Can I have that in writing so I can show my mother?" With a grin, she waved good-bye, and walked out the door, anticipating the time when she would see him again.

Mary had dressed carefully for her dinner with Dan. The black wool pantsuit was casual, yet dressy enough for a dinner at home, and the bonus was, it was slimming.

Knowing Dan had to visit Matt at the hospital before going home, Mary had offered to drive the short distance herself.

As she pulled into the condo's driveway, butterflies flapped nervously in her stomach. A quick glance in the rearview mirror told her that her command of makeup left a lot to be desired. Pressing a tissue between her red-stained lips, she took a deep breath and made her way to the door.

Waiting anxiously for Dan to answer her knock, she fidgeted nervously with the hem of her jacket. When the door finally opened and she saw the startled expression on his face, her meager supply of confidence rapidly dissipated.

Dan didn't look thrilled to see her, not at all.

"Mary! Oh shit! We were supposed to have dinner tonight, weren't we?"

The classical brush-off, she thought, trying hard not to be disappointed. But it was difficult. She'd really looked forward to their date. "Well, you did say Monday, unless I was mistaken."

He motioned for her to stay put. "Wait one sec while I grab my coat. We'll go out and grab something to eat. I've had the worst day."

Dan left her standing outside on the porch, and Mary decided that either his apartment was a mess—it didn't look messy from where she was standing—or he was hiding a dead body inside.

Suddenly she felt foolish and embarrassed. "I'll go. You're busy."

"No!" he shouted emphatically, grabbing his sports coat off the newel post and putting it on. "Do you like Mexican?" he asked as he slammed the front door behind him. "I know a great place just around the corner. It's not fancy, but the food's good."

So much for Dan's roasted chicken. "You really shouldn't feel obligated to take me out, Dan. I understand, and—"

"We're going out," he insisted, grabbing hold of her arm

and tugging her along to the car, not giving her the chance to protest further.

Once inside the car, his smile was full of apology. "I had a horrible day at work. My assistant called in sick, and I barely made deadline. Matt was in a sh—sour mood when I reached the hospital, then I ran out of gas on the way home. To top it off, I completely forgot about our dinner date and neglected to take the chicken out of the freezer.

"Can you ever forgive me? I'm not usually this spaced out."

His look was entreating, his smile apologetic, so Mary decided to let him off the hook. "No problem. I'm a big fan of Mexican food."

Pulling into the parking lot of Señor Pancho's, he shut off the engine and turned to face her. "I want to get to know you better, Mary. I know we didn't get off to a very good start, but I'd like to rectify that."

Her cheeks warmed, and she found herself saying, "Me, too," rather horrified that she actually believed it.

Over frozen margaritas, toasted chips, and salsa, they talked, and Mary found herself relaxing in Dan's company. He told her a bit about what his job as Food editor entailed, some of the problems he'd been having with his son, but nothing about his family background or the breakup of his marriage.

She felt compelled to ask. "At the hospital you mentioned your ex-wife. Had you been married long?"

"Sharon and I married right out of college. And things were good for a while. But her career became more important than our marriage. After Matt was born the problems only intensified. She wasn't happy being a stay-at-home wife and mother and things just sorta fell apart."

"Let me get this straight. Are you saying that to have a successful marriage a woman must give up her career and stay at home? That hardly seems fair." Mary had never before considered herself a feminist, but Dan's opinion had made every feminist gene in her body stand at attention.

He shrugged, then reached for a handful of chips. "That's not exactly what I'm saying. But after what I've been through, I don't think it's asking too much. This business about juggling a career with marriage and family just doesn't wash with me anymore. I learned the hard way that it just doesn't work."

She stared openmouthed, wondering if he'd been attending marriage and family lectures from the Sophia Russo School of Matrimonial Bliss. "I'd expect to hear such views from someone of my mom's generation, but from you it sounds archaic and, well, selfish."

"Since I don't plan to marry again I don't see it as a problem."

Relief washed over and through her. A man who didn't want to get married! Now, here was someone she could get interested in. Dan Gallagher was quickly becoming an excellent zing candidate. If she chose him, she wouldn't have to worry about complicating their relationship with commitment.

"On that we both agree, Dan. I'm not interested in marriage, either. At least not right now. My mother keeps hoping I'll get married, but for the first time I'm enjoying my life, my freedom, and I don't want to tie myself down to anyone."

His brows rose at her admission. "I take it you were involved in an unhappy relationship?"

She was embarrassed by the question, but decided to be honest. "I was involved with taking the easy way out, burying my head in the sand, and allowing others to live my life for me. I'd been living at home, playing the role of dutiful daughter and granddaughter, trying to please my family, and living the status quo. It was safe. I didn't have to take chances, didn't have to put myself up for failure."

"But something happened to change your mind?"

"Luigi Marconi shot himself in the head. His death was the catalyst I needed to begin living my life. And so I am."

Her candor was refreshing. But he'd already discovered that Mary Russo wasn't a woman who liked beating around the bush. "And are you enjoying your new life?"

She smiled, and her face lit up like a sunrise. Dan felt the warmth all the way down to his toes. "Yes. I feel useful, moderately successful, and I've set goals for myself." She wouldn't mention the Ortho Novum.

"Good for you."

One of the goals I've set is to have a no-strings, passionate affair, she wanted to say, and you've been selected as the most promising candidate.

But, of course, she didn't.

Instead, she nibbled her chip, sipped her margarita, and decided she had made an excellent choice.

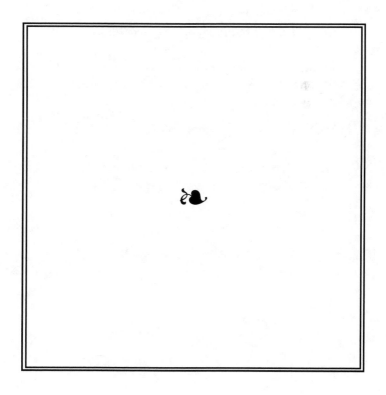

Mary's Love Potion

(Flavored Olive Oil)

1 16-oz. bottle extra virgin olive oil
6 cloves roasted garlic
3–4 sprigs of fresh rosemary
1 dried red pepper, chopped small

Add ingredients to olive oil, and let sit for several days. When flavors have blended, serve atop warm Italian bread or on pasta.

CHAPTER NINE

Grandma Flora banged her cane on the car's floorboard for emphasis. "I cannot go empty-handed! Whatsa matter wid you?"

Mary let loose a sigh that any Russo woman would have been proud to claim—she came from a long line of suffering sighers—and pulled the car to a halt on Albemarle Street in front of Antonio Moressi's drugstore.

The sandstone, brick-faced store, like its owner, was tired, old, and had seen better days, but still sold most of what the bigger superstores did, if you could find it. Organization was not the pharmacist's strong suit. But Mary had known the old man since she was a kid, her mother and grandmother refused to buy their drugs and cosmetics anywhere else, and she had a hard time saying no to *Nonna*, at any rate.

Driving anywhere was a chore for Mary, and having to make an unscheduled stop fell into the nightmare category. Parallel parking should have been an Olympic sport!

She'd decided that when, not if, she won the Maryland Lotto she was going to buy herself a black limousine and hire a driver to haul her around: Sven, the Nordic prince. He would be blond and look like Brad Pitt. Not because she wanted to put on airs, but because she hated to drive!

"Matthew doesn't expect anything, *Nonna*. Your company will be enough."

The old woman shook her head and the tight gray curls moved not an inch. Neither, unfortunately, did Grandma

Flora. "No! I will not go to see the *bambino* with no gift. It is not the Russo way."

"I thought your social-security check didn't arrive until the first of the month." As a young woman, Flora Russo had worked in New York City's garment district as a sewing-machine operator. But her stint among fashion's finest hadn't translated into any kind of style awareness. Grandma wore unrelenting black like a professional mourner.

When her grandmother refused to answer, Mary got a bad feeling in the pit of her stomach. This time the sigh she heaved was Oscar-worthy. "All right. I'll wait in the car. But be careful. The sidewalk is slick from this morning's rain shower. On second thought, maybe I should come with you." She reached for the door handle.

"Bah! I am old, not stupid. I know how to walk. I will be right back."

Leaning her head against the seat's headrest, Mary wondered if her idea to bring Grandma Flora to visit Matt was such a wise one. The Gallaghers were no doubt ignorant of the idiosyncrasies pertaining to short, stubborn, Italian grandmothers. The child would probably find her broken English difficult to understand, might not comprehend that *Nonna*'s bluntness was just her way, and he could become a bit frightened by the smothering kisses and hugs of affection she was sure to bestow on him.

To *Nonna* every child was fair game for hugs and kisses, and an occasional pinch on the cheek. She also tugged ear-lobes, rapped knuckles, and pulled hair. But only if you ticked her off.

But even with all that strangeness, Mary figured Matt would welcome the additional company, no matter what.

Mary had been to the hospital a few times to visit the boy since his surgery. He seemed to welcome her visits with open arms. They laughed at the silly jokes she told, played checkers and various other board games, and she read to him if there was time. His favorite children's book, and hers, was *The Velveteen Rabbit*.

But mostly they just talked. The boy seemed starved for female companionship, for his mother. And though Mary knew little about being a mother, she knew a lot about being a friend.

Sometimes Dan would be there when she arrived, and he always seemed happy to see her. She felt very comfortable with him, and the animosity she'd once harbored was now a thing of the past.

Dan had started coming to the restaurant for lunch every day, and more often than not, she found herself looking up at the clock and waiting anxiously for his arrival. He usually came toward the end of the shift, when the crowd had thinned.

Sometimes they had a glass of wine, accompanied by bread and flavored olive oil—which Annie insisted was a love potion—and talked of inconsequential things, and sometimes they spoke of their families and backgrounds.

Though he hadn't admitted as much, she sensed Dan's childhood had been somewhat unhappy; he was still reluctant to talk much about it. She'd found out through persistent questioning that he'd grown up in Gaithersburg, Maryland, and that his father had died when he was a teenager. But other than that, she knew very little about his innermost feelings, while he knew a great deal about hers. For some reason she couldn't explain, she'd confided in him, probably more than she should. But he was easy to talk to and seemed interested in what she had to say.

The previous afternoon Dan had accompanied her to the produce market. She never knew buying produce could be such fun, or such an erotic experience. Just thinking about it made her tingle all over, and she doubted she'd ever go there again without thinking of him.

"Did you know tomatoes were considered an aphrodisiac at one time?" Dan asked, holding up a fat, juicy one for her inspection. "I think they were called love apples." A mischievous glint entered his eyes as he dropped several into her shopping bag, then took a bite out of a particularly ripe one.

Without thinking, Mary reached out with her finger and wiped the juice dribbling down his chin, soon realizing what a provocative gesture she'd made. The intensity in Dan's eyes made her heart start to pound. Then he grabbed her hand and started sucking her fingers, one by one, and she almost lost it, right there in the middle of the produce market.

"I—I didn't know," she said breathlessly, and he grinned. The man was sex personified.

"You're awfully cute. But I guess you know that."

Her hand still in his, they moved farther down the aisle, unmindful of the sawdust covering their shoes. Dan stopped before the cantaloupes.

"Tomatoes are great, but give me a melon any day." He placed her hand on top of the melon, covering it with his own. "Feel how firm it is. Can you imagine how sweet and juicy it would be to run your lips over the soft flesh?"

Hell, yes! she wanted to shout, because she could definitely imagine. Gooseflesh broke out over her arms and neck when his warm breath tickled her nape, making her swallow with a great deal of difficulty. "I like melons."

"Me, too." His gaze dropped to her breasts. "Ripe, full melons. There's nothing like 'em. I think I could eat them all day."

Oh, my God! Hang on, Mary! she told herself. But her nipples were hard as rocks, and she had the funniest feeling between her legs. It was obvious Dan was coming on to her, making sexual advances, but she didn't exactly know what she was supposed to do about it. If only there'd been a book to advise her. Oh sure, she'd read Helen Gurley Brown's *Sex and the Single Girl* from cover to cover, but Helen had neglected to include a chapter on sex at the produce market!

"Except for grapes," Dan said, drawing her attention

back. "I love grapes, don't you?" When she nodded, he took a large purple one and placed it between her lips. "Suck it slowly, Mary," he urged. "Draw all the juice out." Her cheeks flamed when she accidentally sucked too hard and got hold of his finger.

"Hmmm. I like that."

So had she. A little too well. And Mary knew she had to be careful. Dan Gallagher was a lot more experienced than she could ever hope to be, and she was likely to get herself into a heap of trouble with such a sexy, appealing man.

The evening they'd spent in the hospital waiting room had somehow wiped away all the unpleasantness standing between them and had served as a new beginning for a friendship. Their subsequent dinners and lunches had only cemented their growing attraction for each other.

Daniel Gallagher was the man she had chosen for her no-strings-attached affair. He was handsome, intelligent, and he presented no problem in the zing department. In fact, she was pretty certain his *zinger* was quite up to the challenge.

Her erotic musings had her squirming restlessly, and she glanced at her watch, noting with concern that fifteen minutes had elapsed since her grandmother's departure. Visiting hours would be over by the time they finally got to the hospital if they didn't get a move on.

She pulled open the glass door and entered the pharmacy, but didn't see anyone, including her grandmother or Mr. Moressi. The store was eerily quiet. She was about to call out when she heard the telltale click of her grandmother's pocketbook snapping closed.

It shattered the silence with the same finality as a jail cell door slamming shut.

Uh, oh! *Nonna* was obviously availing herself of some of Mr. Moressi's goods without paying for them. Grandma Flora had the unfortunate habit and reputation of being a little light-fingered.

"Nonna?" she called out. "Are you ready to go?"

"*Si. Si.* I come." Cane in hand, her grandmother rounded the toy and magazine aisle, looking not the least bit guilty that she had just swiped something and stuffed it into her huge pocketbook. Only hookers had bigger purses than Grandma Flora. Of course, Mary had no proof of anything, and it wasn't as if she could accuse her own grandmother of a crime anyway.

Everyone in the family knew of the old woman's predisposition to stealing, but no one, including Sophia, ever made mention of it to her directly. It was talked about in a roundabout fashion but never really addressed, and Mary had no intention of bringing it up now.

"We're going to miss visiting hours if we don't hurry. Did you find everything you need? Do you need some money to pay for it?"

The old lady shook her head. "I tell Antonio to put it on my account."

"You don't have an account. The Moressis haven't had accounts here since 1966." Her grandmother obviously considered that a minor detail.

"He makes an exception. I am a good customer."

"Where is Mr. Moressi? I didn't see him when I came in."

"He suffers from gas. Must be the onions. Onions can give you terrible gas. He's in the bathroom."

Mary wasn't about to touch that explanation with a ten-foot pole. She would come back later and pay Mr. Moressi what was owed. She would claim her grandmother was getting senile and had forgotten, which was sort of the truth, although *Nonna* seemed pretty shrewd to her.

After Mary escorted the old woman back to the car, they headed to the hospital.

"How come you're pacing back and forth, Dad? You sure look nervous. Is something wrong at the paper?"

Dan glanced at his watch again, then up at the TV screen,

which was broadcasting the Orioles game. "Oh, man! They struck out Albert Belle."

He looked over at his son and asked, "Shouldn't Mary have been here by now? I hope nothing's happened to detain her." He was anxious to see her again, hear her voice, inhale the heady fragrance of her perfume.

Mary was like a narcotic, and he needed a fix!

Matt sat up straighter, adjusting the pillows behind his back, and pushed the stack of comic books off his lap. "She's bringing her grandma with her today. That might have slowed her down."

"Ah. That's right. I forgot." He breathed a sigh of relief, frowning when Ripken was called out at first. "Blind bastard umpire," he cursed beneath his breath, hoping Matt hadn't heard him.

"I hope she brings another pizza. I sure am hungry for pizza."

Dan was hungry for a little Italian delicacy, too, but pizza wasn't what he craved.

The better he got to know her, the more he liked Mary Russo, and the more he wanted her. She was a fever in his blood, and damned if he didn't get hot every time she walked into a room. He hadn't felt this way about a woman in a long time, maybe never.

His and Sharon's initial attraction had burned hot and fast, but over a period of time indifference and complacency had replaced passion. Dan had been focused on building a journalistic career, and Sharon—a lobbyist by profession— had never really settled into a suburban lifestyle, missing the frenetic challenges of her job and the social whirl of the nation's capital. The only thing that had kept them together the last few years of their marriage had been Matt.

Dan glanced at his son, and his heart filled with love and pride. Since the operation they'd grown closer. Matt was beginning to accept the likelihood that his mother wasn't coming back. And he'd told Dan just last evening that he wanted to get a dog. Dan took it as a sign that things were finally starting to get back to normal.

Mary was partly responsible for his son's attitude adjustment. She was great with Matt. The woman had the patience of Job. She knew just what to say to cheer him up, had all kinds of stories with which to amuse him, and the young boy lapped up the attention like a starving puppy.

It was hard not to be jealous of their burgeoning relationship. Matt adored Mary. She had a nurturing, mother-earth quality that had Dan wishing she'd look at him, smile at him, with the same high regard as she did his son.

Dan's mother had not been a particularly warm individual. She'd been unhappy in her marriage. His father had been as indifferent to her as he'd been to Dan. She had loved him, and that had made her pain all the worse.

Loneliness had consumed him as a child, and Dan had promised himself that if he ever had a son, he would not treat him in the same detached manner that his father had treated him. And though his work had separated them at times, Dan had done his best to make Matt feel loved and an important part of his life.

It wasn't surprising Mary had touched a longing deep within Dan. Desire. That's what he felt for Mary Russo. Desire so keen, so all-consuming, he found himself thinking about her during the day, when he should have been working, and while lying in bed at night, when he should have been sleeping.

He'd made love to her in his mind dozens of times.

Now he wanted to do it for real.

As if conjured up by his thoughts, the door opened and Mary and her grandmother walked in. The old woman took one look at Dan, sizing him up as only an eighty-three-year-old woman can do, nodded perfunctorily, then hurried over to the bed, pulling a brown stuffed bear out of her pocketbook, the price tag still firmly attached.

Grandma Flora needed no introduction. *"Osserva quanto dolce è! Mi ricordo del tuo fratello a questa èta."*

Mary smiled at Dan's questioning look. "Roughly translated: 'Look how sweet! He reminds me of your brother at this age.' My brother's the apple of both my grandmother and mother's eyes, so you should feel honored."

"Are you fluent in Italian?" He'd flunked Spanish and French in high school and was impressed by her bilingual ability.

"Mostly I just know the swear words, but I picked up a few phrases along the way. I know when to duck and when to get out of Dodge." In the Russo family those were good things to know, especially if you didn't want the back of your head used as a target. Love taps, her parents called them.

He smiled, then glanced at his son, warmed by the rapture he saw on his face. "Whatever your grandmother's saying to Matt has him spellbound. He's hanging on to her every word."

"Probably because he can't understand her. But she's a good storyteller, and she's always eager to relate the adventure of how she came to America at the age of fourteen."

"With her family?"

She shook her head. "No, with her husband. People married young back then. Guess I'd be considered a spinster by those standards."

"It's better to wait," he said, taking her hand and leading her to one of the chrome and turquoise vinyl chairs lining the wall. His hand was warm and comforting, hers embarrassingly clammy. "Finding the right man's important."

"If you're looking for one, I guess it is."

"Sometimes you find something important when you're not looking," he said, his voice low, his gaze holding hers spellbound. "Sometimes you get sucker-punched without even realizing it, and sometimes you meet someone and *bam*! lightning strikes, and you're done for."

Mary swallowed, wondering if he was referring to himself,

to them. The possibility excited and, at the same time, terrified her.

Mary wasn't absolutely positive, but she was pretty darn certain that her mother led the field in the annoying habits category, followed closely by Aunt Josephine, who sniffed everything she came into contact with, including Uncle Jimmy's socks.

Seated across from her at Fiorelli's Bakery/Cafe Sophia was stirring packets of sugar into her coffee, clanging the spoon against the sides of the cup, until Mary wanted to scream and run out of the restaurant. "Ma, I think the sugar's sufficiently dissolved. You can set your spoon down now."

"What's so important you made me come out in the middle of the day and miss my soap opera? You haven't changed your mind about Lou, have you?" There was a note of hope in her voice that said: Let me show you the error of your ways.

"The trouble with you, Mary, is that you're fickle. You take forever to make up your mind, and—"

"Ma!" she interrupted. "It's not about Lou. I asked you to meet me so I could break the news in person that I've accepted Daniel Gallagher's dinner invitation. He came to the restaurant last evening and asked me out." Mary hadn't bothered to tell her mother about their other meetings, because she already knew what Sophia would say. She wasn't wrong.

Her mother clutched her chest. "*Dio mio!* Save me! The Irish reviewer? You want to go out with a man who disgraced you in the papers?" She dumped two more packets of sugar into her cup and began stirring again. "Are you nuts? Have you no shame?"

Mary gritted her teeth, then explained, "I've spent time with Dan at the hospital and I know him better now. He's actually very nice, and . . ." How did one tell their mother that a man made her feel hot all over? She didn't.

"Nice? Nice! Ted Bundy was nice, but he still murdered

all those women. How do you know the man isn't a homicidal killer? A serial rapist? You know nothing about him. And he's not Italian! Holy Mary, mother of God. An Irishman!"

That wasn't even the worst of it. Dan had admitted that he didn't practice Catholicism, that he didn't even believe in organized religion. Good thing they weren't contemplating a serious relationship, Mary thought, because something like that would have really sent her mother over the edge. Not that she wasn't teetering at the moment.

"Have you lost your mind?" her mother asked.

Mary eyed the eclairs in the refrigerated case and sighed. She needed a chocolate fix. And soon. "*Nonna* likes him. Dan reminds her of Grandpa Sal."

Sophia slapped her forehead with her palm. "Your grandmother is sick in the head. You can't rely on what she says."

"I'm not relying on Grandma's opinion," Mary said, sipping her latte. "I'm relying on my gut instinct, and it's telling me to go out with Daniel Gallagher."

"Is this about sex?" her mother asked, and Mary's face flushed guiltily. Damn, Sophia was good!

"You think I don't know what you young girls do nowadays? Lust, not love, rules the world. It's a disgrace. Your friend Annie sleeps around. You think word doesn't get out about women like that? Once your reputation is gone, that's it. No decent man will want you for a wife. They don't buy the cow when they get the milk for free."

So Sophia had said, a hundred times or more. Mary had lost count. Crossing her fingers beneath the table, she smiled, presenting the picture of innocence. "I'm not talking about sex, Ma. I'm talking about chemistry. There's attraction between Dan and me, and I want to see if our relationship is going anywhere." That was mostly the truth. Sort of.

"Chemistry. Zing. For this I missed Susan Lucci?" She threw up her hands. "You're going to die an old maid, Mary. I'll never have any grandchildren of yours to spoil."

"Even if I don't get married, I can still have a baby. You

don't even need a man anymore. I can go to a sperm bank and make a withdrawal." Mary grinned at her mother's look of outrage. "Just kidding."

"Why can't you be more like Connie? She's settled, happy in her marriage to Eddie. They're thinking about having another child. Did she tell you?"

Mary's eyes widened at the news, and she shook her head. "No! But she's already got three kids. Why would she want more?" More importantly, why would she want to risk losing her shapely figure?

"Because she's a good Catholic girl, that's why. The church favors procreation."

"That's because the church doesn't have to feed and clothe all the little babies who come into the world. Babies who grow into big strapping teens, and who demand hundred-dollar Nikes, and Calvin Klein jeans."

Spine stiffening against the back of the chair, Sophia stared aghast, stunned by her daughter's comments. "That's blasphemy!" She quickly made the sign of the cross, then for added protection tugged at the small gold one resting at the base of her throat. "I will speak to Father Joseph about this, Mary. You will have to confess and do penance.

"*Mama Mia.* What did I do wrong?"

"Actually, Ma, you did everything right, even though we didn't know it at the time. I'm turning into a strong, independent woman, and I have you to thank for it. You were a good role model."

Sophia's mouth fell open. "Wha—!"

It was obvious from her mother's shocked expression that she didn't know whether or not to be flattered. But Mary meant every word. It had taken her thirty-three years to finally realize that her mother's strong-willed nature was very much a part of her. Sophia was a woman of the new millennium and didn't even know it.

"I love you, Ma." She covered the older woman's hand with her own. "You worry about me, and I appreciate that."

Not! "But I'm a grown woman and I have to make my own mistakes. Sounds like you bucked the system when you married Pa, and now I'm going to take a page from your book and do the same."

Misty-eyed, Sophia heaved a sigh of despair. "Of course I worry about you, Mary. You're breaking your mother's heart. I'm an old woman. I don't know how much longer I'll live."

Forever, no doubt, for Mary knew her mother's expertise was in aging others. "You shouldn't worry, Ma. As you're so fond of telling me, I'm thirty-three years old. I can take care of myself."

Nodding in resignation, her mother issued a silent prayer and said finally, "He's going to knock you up. Those Irish don't shoot any blanks."

Sophia had always been good at having the last word.

Sophia's Banana Bread

½ cup butter
1 tsp. vanilla
1 ½ cups sugar
2 eggs

Using mixer, cream above ingredients until smooth, and set aside.
  Mix together:

2 cups all-purpose flour
¾ tsp. baking soda
½ tsp. baking powder
¼ tsp. salt

Add dry ingredients to butter mixture.
  Mash 3 very ripe bananas and blend. To this, add ½ cup sour milk (milk to which 2 tbsp. lemon juice have been added).
  Blend banana mixture into rest of batter and mix well. Add 1 cup chopped walnuts or pecans, if desired. Pour into large greased and floured loaf pan, and bake at 350° for about 1 hour and 15 minutes. Cool on rack. Serve plain or with cream cheese.

CHAPTER TEN

Cruising down the Patapsco River on *The Bay Lady* as it navigated the Inner Harbor, Mary enjoyed the soft breeze that brushed her cheeks. She felt wildly alive. The night sky glittered with diamondlike clusters, the water slapped soothingly against the hull, and the man standing at the rail beside her had her hormones in an uproar.

It should have been a crime for anyone to look as good as Dan did in his charcoal-gray sports jacket and yellow oxford shirt, which had been left open at the collar because he was tieless. She detected a sprinkling of hairs, which added to his appeal.

Mary had a thing for hairy-chested men, as long as the hairs didn't extend to the shoulders and back, where it would then enter into the gorilla/Neanderthal category. She'd seen Carmine Delvechio once in his bathing trunks and had never gotten over it. The man looked like King Kong without the height.

"Thanks for dinner. It was delicious," she told Dan. They'd dined on succulent roasted duck glazed with a bing-cherry sauce; parsley new potatoes; and asparagus with hollandaise. "Hard to believe, but I've lived here all my life and have never taken one of these cruises."

His smile was downright sexy, and a shiver slipped down her spine. "Cold?" he asked, wrapping his arm about her shoulders and hugging her close to his side.

"A little," she lied, feeling as if she were a volcano ready to erupt.

"I'm glad I'm the first to introduce you to the delights of nighttime cruising."

She hoped he'd be the first to introduce her to something a little more provocative. Tonight was the night. Mary could feel it. Tonight Dan would kiss her, make mad passionate love to her, and she would let him. Fear tingled her spine at the thought, and she swallowed.

Would she be able to go through with it? Surrender her virginity and form an intimate relationship with Dan?

She was still consumed by worries that he wouldn't find her attractive enough, that her lack of experience would be humiliating for both of them.

But dammit! she couldn't remain a virgin forever. That was even more humiliating.

"It's so quiet out here," she said finally. "I feel like we're the only people on this boat."

"We very nearly are. It's Monday. They don't do much business during the week, except during the height of tourist season. Then every night's packed." He pointed across the black water to a building in the distance. "There's my condo."

She followed his gaze to the set of newly built brick buildings situated near the water's edge. Given their proximity to the nearby shops and restaurants, they were pricey. Mary could only hope that one day she'd be able to afford something as nice. "The perfect bachelor pad, huh?"

"Not anymore. Matt's put a definite crimp in my social life."

Good for Matt! she found herself thinking. At this point in their relationship she didn't need any competition. "Who'd you find to baby-sit Matt tonight?" she asked.

"My friends the Griers. Alan and Helen wanted Matt to visit their kids. Ted and Grace are about the same age as Matt and they've invited a few kids to join them. Helen thought it might be good if he made some new friends. I should have thought of it myself."

She could tell he was mentally beating himself up. Being a good father was very important to Dan. "Pretty soon that'll all become second nature, you'll see." His expression remained skeptical.

Dan was trying hard with Matt, and his son hadn't made things easy for him. Though Mary sensed that the boy was starting to come around. They'd had some long talks about his mother and father, about their divorce, and the child was finally beginning to see that Dan hadn't been entirely to blame for the breakup, or responsible for Sharon's leaving.

"I know you said you didn't want to get married, but don't you want to have children someday?" he asked, surprising Mary. Men didn't usually broach such ticklish subjects.

"Maybe someday. But I'm not in any hurry, though my mother continues to harp on me about it. I think I've disgraced the Russo name. My cousin got married recently, and I'm the last holdout."

"The trouble with you, Mary, is that Josie's fat Sally married that skinny malink, Carmine Delvechio, and you're still single." Sophia had a way with words.

He grinned. "The typical Italian way of thinking, right?"

"You don't know the half of it."

The boat pulled into its mooring, and a few minutes later Dan and Mary stepped onto the pier. She could see the lights of McCormick & Schmick's Seafood Restaurant and wondered how the food was. Annie had said it was quite good, but it wouldn't hurt to check out the competition herself.

"How about we stroll over to The Cheesecake Factory and have some dessert? I'm a sucker for their chocolate turtle-praline cheesecake."

Her heart quickened, and this time the man standing next to her had nothing to do with it. "Say no more. You've just uttered the magic word."

"Cheesecake?"

She shook her head. "Chocolate."

They pulled up in front of her apartment a little after ten. Mary pondered whether or not to invite Dan up for a drink. They hadn't kissed yet, and she was more than a little disappointed. How were they supposed to have a torrid affair if they didn't kiss? And she desperately wanted to kiss him, to feel his lips pressed against her own.

Now that she'd convinced herself to go through with the affair, she'd been conjuring up all kinds of erotic images. Nothing like a little moonlight and water to get a woman's imagination fired up. Not that hers hadn't been in overdrive since the produce incident.

"I had a great time tonight," he said, hands still gripping the leather-encased steering wheel. "Let's do this again soon."

"I'd like that," she said, wondering why he wasn't wrapping his arms around her and kissing her passionately. Boldly, she leaned toward him, anticipating, but he reached for the door handle, exited the car, and came around to open her door, leaving her lips cold and her ego in a nearby gutter.

Disappointment reared its ugly head at his gentlemanly behavior. A woman had a right to expect a little debauchery on a date. And this wasn't even their first date!

When they reached the door to her building, Mary decided to take matters into her own hands. Nothing ventured, nothing gained had just become her new motto. "Would you like to come up for a drink or some coffee?"

She read hesitation on his face, uncertainty, and her heart sank. "Thanks, but I've got an early editorial meeting tomorrow at the paper. And I've still got to pick up Matt at the Griers'."

Forcing a smile, she said, "Another time, then," trying not to let her frustration show.

He leaned forward and pecked her chastely on the cheek. "Definitely."

A handshake instead of a kiss! Wasn't that what the commercial said about bad breath? Well, that miserly peck could not be construed in any way, shape, or form as a kiss. Her father put more oomph into his hellos and good-byes, for godsake!

Humiliated, Mary hurried into her apartment, not knowing what to think. Dan had been all over her at the produce market, had intimated his feelings for her at the hospital, and now this! Talk about mixed signals.

Holding her hand in front of her face, she exhaled, then sniffed. It wasn't her breath. The minty fresh mouthwash was still working as promised.

The only conclusion she could draw was that Dan hadn't found her attractive enough to kiss, though he'd spent much of the evening complimenting her looks and apparel.

And they called women fickle!

When she reached the small bedroom that housed a queen-size brass bed, an oak nightstand, and her Barbie collection, she stood in front of the full-length cheval mirror and took a good look at herself. She'd lost about five pounds, so the dress she wore looked okay. But the whole effect was nothing to write home about.

She'd chosen a black jersey-knit with a cowl neck and a flowing skirt to minimize her waist and hips. It was conservative, but classy in an understated way. The faux pearls and matching earrings added a touch of elegance, or so she thought.

"Who are you kidding, Mary?" she told her reflection, wrinkling her nose in distaste. "You look like a schoolmarm. And a spinsterish one at that!"

And her hair! The wind had blown it every which way, making her look like Medusa on speed.

No mystery about Dan's lack of passionate response.

She'd scared him off. And to think she'd actually thought they might make love tonight.

Unhappy that she was destined to remain a virgin, Mary heaved a dispirited sigh. She hadn't come across as a sexy, worldly woman. Dan was probably used to dating women with more experience, more savoir faire. More bosom.

"I can do that! I can become sexy and worldly. I can look hot and make men want to kiss and ravish me."

I can buy a Wonderbra.

She could, but she needed help. And she knew just who to ask for it. Reaching for the phone by the bed, she dialed Annie's number.

Dan cursed as he maneuvered the Explorer into traffic, calling himself all kinds of names, not the least of which was stupid. Why hadn't he kissed Mary tonight? He knew she wanted him to. He'd read it in her eyes, heard it in her voice when she extended the invitation for coffee.

"Dumb-ass fool!"

But he'd wanted to take things slow, hadn't wanted to screw up their date by behaving like a macho jerk, and he didn't want to scare her off, especially after coming on so strong that day at the produce market.

He'd read in one of those women's magazines Linda always left lying around that women were looking for sensitive, considerate men. They didn't want to be mauled or manhandled. They wanted respect. And they wanted romance.

Well, Dan was prepared to give Mary all the respect and romance she could handle. She had just about forgiven him for the review, and the unjust accusation regarding his son's illness. He didn't want to ruin things by messing up again.

Mary Russo was a woman worth waiting for.

But Dan had already waited four years, and he just wasn't certain how much longer he could wait without doing physical damage to himself.

*   *   *

"You look like the poster child for Playtex."

Annie's criticism made Mary want to cover herself. "So what if I don't shop at Victoria's Secret like everyone else? There's something to be said for a good, sturdy foundation."

"Foundations are for buildings, not breasts. You, *cara,* are in need of some major renovation." Annie circled her half-naked friend, tapping her chin, then shaking her head, not looking at all pleased with her findings.

"What? What are you staring at? Is it that bad?"

"That depends on how much you want to sleep with Gallagher. Obviously you do, or we wouldn't be having this conversation."

Mary's cheeks reddened. Having to confide to her best friend about her unrequited lust had been nothing short of humiliating. Sex was as natural to Annie as breathing; Mary, on the other hand, was in dire need of an oxygen tank.

"Underwear should make a certain statement about a woman. Yours, Mary *mia,* cries out 'Virgin, don't touch me, proceed with caution.' Those white cotton briefs you're wearing are an insult to women everywhere. You certainly don't need a chastity belt when you're wearing those ugly things!" Annie pulled her T-shirt up and over her head, then removed her jogging shorts, revealing her fabulous body.

So that's what sit-ups and push-ups can do, Mary thought, shaking her head and sighing. It wasn't worth it.

"Here's what my underwear looks like," Annie said, standing proudly before her. Her bra and panties were fire-engine red, satin with lace edges, and the smallest scraps of material Mary had ever seen.

"You expect that little bit of nothing to hold me up and in?" She had goose bumps bigger than those underpants.

"It's small but mighty. No offense, *cara,* but my boobs are bigger than yours. And this bra is doing a fine job of keeping them in place. Plus, it has a front clasp that makes for easy removal."

Mary had never thought about underwear doing double

duty. "I'd have to wax if I wore underpants like that." She cringed, thinking of the pain. She'd waxed her upper lip once and nearly fainted.

"Waxing's part of the whole package, kiddo. You don't want unsightly hairs sticking out when your big moment comes, especially if you're wearing a thong."

"A thong! Why wear underpants at all if your butt cheeks are going to hang out? If I wanted hemorrhoids, I could lift heavy objects."

Annie shot her an impatient look. "I know what I'm talking about."

Mary sighed. "I suppose. What else?"

Annie plopped down on the bed, reaching for another slice of banana bread. She gave her friend another measuring look while taking a bite. "Mmmm. This is really good. I wish your mother would give me the recipe."

Mary wished Annie would gain weight like normal people when she ate fattening foods. It would only be fair. "You can't cook worth beans, and you know Ma doesn't like to share." Sophia only shared recipes with her daughters, no one else. But she had made a few exceptions, allowing Mary to use one or two at the restaurant, saying that Mama Sophia's couldn't be Mama Sophia's without Sophia's recipes. The banana bread, however, remained a family secret.

"I think your hair could use a good cut," Annie said, licking her fingers. "Nothing too drastic, but maybe shoulder-length, and we could take out a bit of the curl. The color's good. No gray yet in that dark-brown mop of yours."

"*Yet* being the operative word." She expected to look like Grandma Flora when all this was said and done. "Mrs. Brucetti always does my hair." Brucetti's Beauty Parlor, which had just changed its name to Curl Up and Dye because Bertha Brucetti wanted to give her shop a more modern-sounding name and had read this one in a romance novel, was frequented by the entire family. With the exception of Frank, who visited Max the barber for his haircuts and had for as long as

Mary could remember, even though Max Pollesini was slightly arthritic and nearly blind now.

"Mrs. Brucetti does your mother's and grandmother's hair. She's also a butcher. Did you see what she did to poor Sylvia Greenburg? Mrs. Brucetti was talking and eating at the same time she was cutting that woman's hair. Sylvia now has two bald spots on the top of her head. She could nest with the eagles, she looks so bald.

"You'll go to my hairdresser, Mr. Roy. He can work wonders with split ends. And he's a superb colorist. Do you like this new color I just had done? It's called Silverado." The sunlight streaming in through the window glinted off the short, shiny locks, making it look as if Annie's hair was wrapped in aluminum foil. If Mr. Roy had been responsible for that, Mary wanted no part of him.

"Silverado, huh? Where'd you leave Tonto?"

"Very funny. Now get dressed. We need to get to the mall. We've got hours of work ahead of us. You know," Annie added, giving her friend another once-over. "You've got fabulous legs. Very long and shapely. Most women would kill for legs like yours. You should show them off more."

Mary shook her head adamantly. "No leather, no fishnet stockings. I don't want to look like a hooker."

"The secret is to look like a hooker without being one, *cara*. It drives men wild."

A mental image of Dan going over the edge suddenly surfaced, making Mary's heart beat faster. "Okay, maybe leather, but definitely no fishnet."

Alan Grier had been Dan's best friend forever. They'd grown up in the same neighborhood, gone to school together, and had been roommates at the University of Maryland, both graduating with a degree in journalism.

While Dan set his sights on the sports world, Alan had been drawn into the covert world of investigative journalism and was now considered one of the best in the business, his name often mentioned in the same breath as Woodward and Bernstein.

"I heard through the office grapevine that the mystery woman you've been dating is Mary Russo. Is that the same Mary Russo who used to work for Luigi Marconi?" Alan asked, wondering why Dan hadn't confided in him as yet; they had few secrets between them.

Smiling at his friend, Dan sipped his beer and grabbed a handful of peanuts. He and Alan met after work at least three times a week at The Rusty Rudder, a little pub in Fell's Point overlooking the water. It had a nautical theme, with lots of dark paneling and highly polished brass. It was the kind of bar a man could hang out at and not feel like he was on the make. Though there was plenty of opportunity, if one were looking for it.

Alan had been married to Helen for almost eleven years, so appearances did make a difference to him. Plus, women were just naturally drawn to Alan's brooding dark looks and light blue eyes, or so Dan's friend was fond of telling him.

Grier was a one-woman man who didn't want to give off mixed signals. He had a nose like a bloodhound when it came to ferreting out information and a penchant for asking questions that were usually none of his business. Like now.

"Can't a man date someone without it becoming public knowledge? I find it extremely annoying that everyone at the damn newspaper knows my business. Don't they have anything better to do than gossip?"

Alan grinned. "Heard about the tampon episode."

Heat rose up Dan's neck, despite his best efforts to ignore his friend's teasing. "Shit! I was just trying to help the woman pick up her purse." Damn Linda's big mouth! No doubt every department at the newspaper had gotten wind of the incident, thanks to her.

"No need to explain, sport. I'm married, remember? Tampons and hair remover are staples in my bathroom."

Another good reason to remain single, Dan decided.

"Thanks for looking after Matt the other evening. I hope he wasn't too much trouble for you and Helen."

"Not at all. Ted and Gracie can't wait till he comes over again. So if you're going to be needing some privacy . . ."

It wasn't difficult to discern Alan's meaning. The shit-eating grin on his face said everything. "This is the reason I didn't tell you anything, Alan. I knew you'd start asking all sorts of questions that are none of your business. Do I ask you about your sex life with Helen?"

The reporter arched a dark brow. "She's special, is she?"

"It's too early to tell what's going to happen between Mary and me. I like her, she seems to like me. But we haven't taken things to the next level, if you get my drift. I want to take things slow. A woman like Mary doesn't come along very often." Once in a lifetime, if you're lucky. But he wasn't looking for a lifetime. Was he? Damn, he felt so conflicted where she was concerned.

Alan's brow shot up. "So this could be serious?"

Glass lifted halfway to his lips, Dan was about to take a sip when he paused to answer. "Neither of us are looking for anything serious at the moment."

"So it's just sex?"

"Dammit, Alan! I said this is none of your damn business. Now quit pushing. What is this, the Spanish Inquisition? I have a few dates with a woman, and you feel the need to grill me on it."

"No need to get touchy, sport. I'm just curious, that's all. Since your breakup with Sharon, you haven't dated that much. In fact, you've been living the life of a monk. I'm happy, that's all, that you've decided to enter the world of the living again."

"I like Mary, okay? Matt likes her. But I'm just not sure what's going to happen between us."

"Sounds to me like you're already pretty far gone, buddy. I hope things work out the way you want. I'd hate to see you get hurt."

Dan's feelings for Mary were muddled. He wasn't sure how

he felt about her, only that he wanted to be with her. Wanted her. She filled a void, made him happy and less lonely. He hadn't felt such a longing for a woman in a very long time.

"I'll take my chances. As you know only too well, Alan, ol' buddy, life without risk is boring as hell."

The waitress came over with a fresh bowl of peanuts and took their drink reorder. The crowd had increased, as had the noise level. The steady hum of conversation, laughter, and clanking glassware permeated the large room.

Dan had never been a big fan of the bar scene. Too many lonely people just like him who were looking for something that didn't seem to exist. Single women with marriage on their minds flocked to bars, hoping the men who approached them had something more on theirs than sex. They rarely did.

"Helen's thinking about going back to work," Alan said with a scowl, changing the subject.

Dan arched a brow. "I thought you two had pretty much decided after Grace was born that she'd be a stay-at-home mom." Alan was a pretty traditional guy, and Dan doubted he was pleased by his wife's decision to return to the workplace. Not that Dan could blame him.

"She's itching to get back into real estate. Helen's still got her broker's license and wants to start her own business. I'm not in favor of it."

"Well, it would mean more money for your kids' college education. Helen was an ace agent before you guys got married."

"That sounds strange coming from you, Dan. You've said Sharon's career was the main reason your marriage failed. Besides, the kids are still a long way from college, and I'd like them to be raised in a two-parent home where the mother doesn't work. It's not like Helen has to. We don't need the money.

"And I don't want Ted and Gracie becoming those

'latchkey' kids you read about in the paper. My mom was always home when I came home from school."

Dan shook his head. "Women nowadays have this thing about independence. Christ, look at Sharon. Who would have thought?"

"Yeah," Alan agreed with a nod. "You got a bum rap, that's for sure. Which just reinforces my theory that too much independence in a woman isn't good for a marriage. Sharon's job was high-profile. She got used to the fast-paced life. Marriage became too humdrum for her. She grew discontented being just a wife and mother."

There was no way Dan could dispute Alan's words, for they mirrored his own thoughts on the dissolution of his marriage: Sharon had grown bored with him, their marriage, and their child. It wasn't a flattering assessment, but it was the truth.

No matter how attracted he was to Mary, Dan wasn't looking to enter into another relationship with a woman whose career came first. He'd been there, done that. It hadn't worked out. There was no reason for him to think it ever would.

Mary's Chocolate Tiramisu

$\frac{1}{2}$ cup cream
1 $\frac{1}{3}$ cups marsala wine or brandy
24 ladyfingers, split lengthwise
6 eggs, separated into yolks and whites
$\frac{3}{4}$ cup expresso coffee, cooled
6 tbsp. sugar
14 oz. mascarpone cheese (room temperature)
8 oz. bittersweet chocolate, chopped or grated

Make custard filling by beating egg yolks and sugar in top of double boiler over boiling water until light in color. Add ⅓ cup of the liquor, and whisk until thick. Let cool. Stir coffee into mascarpone. In separate bowls, whip the cream, and beat the egg whites until stiff. Fold both into custard mixture.

Place ladyfingers on cookie sheet and lightly toast in a 375° oven for 5–7 minutes. Cool, then dip in remaining liquor and arrange in a single layer in a rectangular serving dish. Spread half the custard over the ladyfingers, then sprinkle with half the chocolate. Repeat layers of ladyfingers, custard, and chocolate. Cover and refigerate for several hours before serving. Serves 8–10.

CHAPTER
ELEVEN

"Man, you look hot!"

Mary blushed to the roots of her newly cut, shoulder-length, fairly straight swing of hair; noted the same sentiment mirrored in Dan's eyes; and smiled.

Being described in such a way was usually reserved for women like Annie, who had the body and the attitude to go along with the clothes. Mary thought of herself as more the clean, neatly dressed type. She wasn't hot; *lukewarm* was probably the better adjective.

"Why, thank you, Matthew," she told the grinning child as the threesome entered the gates of Camden Yards. She had left work early, a rarity for a Saturday, and had arranged to meet Dan and Matt at the baseball stadium. The Yard was a short drive from the restaurant, but the traffic had been nightmarishly heavy and she'd arrived late.

Dan had scored tickets for an Orioles home game against Cleveland, and this was the first time she'd seen him since the "makeover from hell," as she now referred to Annie's intervention.

Her underwear—a few pieces of black lace held together with satin strings—was horribly uncomfortable, the slinky, form-fitting dress she wore barely covered her thighs—for the first time in her life she'd actually received catcalls while walking across the parking lot!—and her high heels were totally inappropriate for a ball game. But the lust in Daniel

Gallagher's eyes, the look of appreciation on his face, made every moment of her torture worthwhile.

As he followed Mary up the bleachers, Dan resisted the urge to place his hand over his son's eyes to block the vision of her in that tight, black, next-to-nothing dress. He, on the other hand, couldn't keep his eyes off her sweet, softly rounded derriere and impossibly sexy legs, even though he was supposedly old enough to exert self-control. Supposedly.

Matt had been right. Mary was definitely hot! And so the heck was he. Hot and bothered. And wishing he could do something about it.

They settled themselves on the bleachers located behind first base. Matt sat between them, disappointing Dan, who wasn't able to scoot closer to the gorgeous woman. The need to touch Mary was overwhelming. His gaze traveled up her stockinged thighs and he wondered what, if anything, she had on beneath her dress. Nothing, he ventured, crossing his left ankle over his right knee.

Shooting a quick glance at his son, Dan was relieved to find Matt still absorbed in the pregame festivities as he watched the players warm up on the field. It didn't seem right to have such lurid thoughts in front of an eight-year-old boy, but he just couldn't help himself.

Mary offered him the container of popcorn she'd just purchased. "Want some? I'm starving. I didn't have time to eat before I left."

He wanted some, all— Stop it! he told himself. Smiling, Dan reached into the bag, and their hands met. Something akin to an electric current shot through him. Mary must have felt it, too, because she pulled her hand back suddenly and her cheeks grew flushed.

"Thanks," he said. "I'll get us some hot dogs as soon as the vendor comes around."

"And nachos," Matt insisted. "With lots of that cheese stuff on 'em."

"Don't stuff yourself, Matt," Mary cautioned. "I've made a special dessert for after the game. So save room, okay?"

"At the restaurant? Not that cheesecake stuff again, is it?" Matt was definitely not the adventurous type when it came to food.

"Nope, not cheesecake, and not at the restaurant. I've made my own special recipe for tiramisu. We'll have it at my apartment. You're going to love it. I promise."

His brows furrowed at the strange-sounding name. "If you say so. I like pretty much everything you cook. My dad makes all kinds of fancy stuff for us to eat."

"I bet he's a good cook."

"Yeah, I guess. But I'd rather have hamburgers and hot dogs than chicken kinda blue."

Mary giggled at the mispronunciation. "You mean Chicken Cordon Bleu, don't you?"

The child nodded and made a face. "Yeah, that's it. I hate it."

"Now, Matt," she chastised gently, "that's not a very nice thing to say. You might hurt your dad's feelings. And you should be happy he's such a good cook. There's a big difference between eating and dining. When you get a little older, you'll realize that."

"I guess," he said with a shrug, turning his attention back to the playing field, which was a lot more interesting than talking about food. The Orioles had taken the field and the crowd was screaming its approval as Mike Mussina claimed the pitcher's mound.

"Matt's not a big fan of my cooking," Dan admitted, painful though it was, reaching once again for the popcorn when the boy leaned forward to talk to the kid in front of him.

"He's just being a typical eight-year-old. I'm sure when you were his age you didn't like your mom's cooking, either." In that, she'd been fortunate. Sophia was a master in the kitchen.

"I didn't. But then, my mom's a terrible cook." He winced

at the memory of all those burned and tasteless dishes. "She tries hard, though. You gotta give her credit for that." His mother's gastronomic failures were what had propelled him to learn how to cook in the first place. In the beginning it had been for self-preservation, but then he found that he enjoyed the process, especially the eating part. Food, he'd discovered, was actually good.

Not being able to cook was a totally foreign concept to Mary. She knew there were people like Annie, who couldn't boil water to save their soul or cook a hard-boiled egg without turning it to rubber, but she didn't understand why. And now Dan was telling her that his mother was the same way. Of course, remembering his unkind comments about her own cooking skills, it was highly likely that he was stretching the truth a bit.

"You're exaggerating, right?"

"Nope. Mom's crazy about Italian food. She cooks it at least three or four times a week. I dreaded those dinners. Still do."

He waited for her to assimilate the statement and when she did, she finally said, "And now because of that you hate Italian food?"

He smiled ruefully. "Something like that." Dan spent every trip home to Gaithersburg praying his mother wouldn't have one of her Italian experimentation dishes waiting for him to eat. So far, the vegetable lasagna had been the worst. She'd used okra, cauliflower, and zucchini between layers of noodles, and had topped the whole concoction off with Gouda cheese. Dan had almost given it up that time.

"I should smack you," she said, but she was smiling when she said it. There was some comfort in knowing that Dan's horrendous opinion of Mama Sophia's had been the result of personal prejudice, rather than a lack of skill on her or Marco's part. She intended to ask for a retraction or a second review, just to make certain that point was made clear.

"Probably," he replied with a naughty smile. "But I get to choose where you smack me."

Color rose to her cheeks, and his eyes settled on the full blush of her lips for a moment, then traveled upward. "You look terrific. You cut your hair. I like it."

"I did. And thanks. Annie thought it was getting too long and suggested I try her hairdresser." Mr. Roy had been a unique experience. He'd called her Mademoiselle Mary and insisted on massaging her feet before he began to work on her hair, subscribing to the theory that blood had to circulate from the toes to the scalp before the hair roots could be fully nourished. She'd made certain, however, that Mr. Roy washed his hands before beginning her beauty treatment.

"My mom's going to hate my new look. She likes my hair long, and she's not used to seeing me wear much makeup." Mary knew Sophia would blame Annie, who she considered Satan's handmaiden, for the transformation.

He studied her intently from top to bottom, then flashed a sexy, heart-stopping grin that made her pulse quicken and her toes curl down. "Matt was right on target when he said you looked hot. I wouldn't worry about what your mom thinks. Not that you didn't look pretty before, because you did, but you look absolutely incredible now." And he wanted her, as he'd never wanted any other woman.

Feeling nothing less than euphoric, Mary silently thanked Satan's handmaiden.

"Hey, Dad! Quit being mushy and watch the game. The Cleveland Indians' pitcher just struck out Brady Anderson."

Dan grinned, not giving a hoot about the game. A first for a man who ate, slept, and dreamed sports. But now he had other, more important things to think about, like how Mary's cheeks had gone from soft pink to red at the boy's comment.

Mary was special. He knew it, and so did Matt. The kid had done a real turnaround since meeting Mary and her grandmother. Whatever those two had said to the boy had apparently worked, because the animosity he'd shown before had all but disappeared.

"Wise guy!" He ruffled his son's hair. "Just wait till you start dating."

Matt made a face. "Ugh! Gross!"

The sound of Mary's laughter tightened Dan's gut. Reaching behind his son, he clasped her neck and pulled her toward him. Wonder and confusion filled her eyes. Determination filled his. "I'm looking forward to sampling dessert later," he whispered.

Pulling up in front of her building on High Street, Mary shifted the car into park and set the emergency brake. The turn-of-the-century street lamps gave off a golden hue as they illuminated the surrounding area, and a soft breeze ruffled the leaves of the poplars lining the broad street, which was congested, due to the number of restaurants in the vicinity.

Though she'd driven home, Mary could have just as easily flown from the park on her own power. Her feet hadn't touched the ground since Dan's dessert comment. Of course, he could have just been talking about the tiramisu, but she didn't think so.

Dan had a way of making her feel special. The compliments were nice, but it was more than that. He was attentive without being fawning, as if every word she put forth was a gem, as if their being together brought him great happiness. There was no doubt she felt the same way about him.

A glance in the rearview mirror told her he was parking his car right behind hers, and a thrill of anticipation at what might lay ahead coursed through her. Looking toward the restaurant, which was still packed and doing a brisk business, she smiled happily to herself. Everything was working out, for a change, not only for her business, but with her personal life, as well.

And it was about time!

Dan came around to the driver's side and opened the door. "Matt's asleep. I don't know if I should wake him."

She wasn't about to let him escape this time. Tonight she was determined to get that kiss, no matter what she had to do. "Matt had a busy day. Don't wake him. Just carry him upstairs. We can put him down on my bed, while we have . . . dessert."

His eyes darkened. With a sleeping Matt in his arms, Dan followed her up the stairs, waiting while she fumbled in her purse for the key. "Do you need some help?" The impatience in his voice mirrored her own.

Shaking her head, she cast a puzzled look upward. The porch light had been replaced only last week and it seemed odd that it had burned out so quickly. "The light's out. I'm having difficulty seeing, that's all."

She was finally able to fit the key into the lock and pushed open the door. What greeted her had her gasping for air, and she clutched her stomach as waves of nausea rolled up her throat. "Oh! Oh, my God!"

The apartment was a shambles. Books had been yanked off shelves and strewn all over the floor, cabinet drawers pulled open and emptied, and much of the new furniture upended.

Her safe little world had been totally compromised, and Mary felt physically violated.

She looked around frantically, shouting, "Morty! Morty!" relieved a moment later when the orange tabby sprang from his hiding place beneath the sofa and into her arms, purring loudly like a well-tuned carburetor. She hugged him fiercely to her chest, kissing the top of his head. "Thank goodness you're okay!" He nuzzled her neck, obviously thinking the same thing.

Dan stepped around her, eyes widening at the mess, and anger tore through him like a Teflon-coated bullet. Setting his still-sleeping son down on the sofa, he reached for Mary's arm, dodged a hiss and swat from the cat's paw, and pulled her back when she went to straighten one of the end tables.

"Don't touch anything. It looks like you've been burglarized. We've gotta call the police. They need to dust for prints."

"But how? Why? This has always been a very safe building. No one in this neighborhood has been bothered for years. I can't believe this has happened."

Kids and drugs. It was an old story. Unfortunately, no one was safe anymore. "It's probably kids out for some mischief, or looking for money to buy drugs." He tried to reassure her, hating the look of panic and fear on her face.

"I just can't believe this has happened. You read about stuff like this, but until it happens to you . . ."

Her face was pale and she was shaking, so Dan took matters into his own hands, wishing he could throttle whoever had done this. "I'll call the cops. Where's the phone?"

Mary pointed toward the bedroom, praying silently that she'd made her bed. It was a stupid thing to think about at a time like this, she realized. "You can take Matt in there and lay him on the bed. I don't think he'll wake up, but the sight of the police might scare him if he does."

Even with all her troubles, Mary still took the time to consider his son's welfare. Dan was touched and grateful. Most of the women he knew wouldn't have spared a thought for a young boy.

But then, Mary wasn't most women.

Dan had a friend on the police force, and he intended to contact him and ask that he keep an eye on her apartment building and restaurant. Whoever had broken into Mary's apartment might come back, though he doubted it. This was a random break-in, he'd bet money on it, though he didn't want to take any chances. Better safe than sorry.

The police arrived a few minutes later and performed a thorough search of the premises, both inside and out, dusting for prints, but finding none. Finally satisfied that nothing had been stolen, they departed, offering little encouragement that this type of thing wouldn't happen again.

Restaurants were often a prime target, they had explained. And Mary being the owner, and living above her establishment, needed to take extra precautions. They recommended that she install a security system, which seemed an excellent idea to her.

"Are you all right?" Dan moved to sit beside her on the sofa. She looked fragile and exhausted, and just a little bit scared. A well of protectiveness rose up within him. It had been a long time since he'd worried about a woman, and he found he liked the feeling, too darn much.

"You still look pale. Can I get you something? A glass of wine? Coffee?" He could use something a bit stronger, like a Maker's Mark.

Taking a deep, halting breath, she shook her head. "I'm fine. It's just—I've never been a victim before. It's scary. To think someone was actually in my apartment, going through my things." What if she'd come home alone and surprised them? She shuddered at the thought, rubbing her arms against the chill.

He wrapped his arm about her and drew her to his chest. "I'm sorry this happened, Mary. Fortunately nothing appears to be stolen, and your furniture and possessions were not destroyed."

Apparently whoever had broken in had found nothing worth taking. She almost felt insulted.

"It could have been worse," Dan added.

"Yeah. I could have been here when they broke in." Nestling against him, she welcomed the warmth and protection of his arms, the way his lips pressed against the top of her head, the way his heart beat steadily, comfortingly beneath her ear. She heaved a deep sigh of longing, then looked up.

Their eyes locked. Their lips met. And in that moment Mary forgot about everything else except the touch of Dan's mouth on her own. There were no words to describe the feeling of utter joy. *Boing* and *zing* didn't even come close.

The kiss was slow and thoughtful, his searching tongue sending shards of desire racing through her. She wrapped her arms around his neck, pressed her body into him, and matched him stroke for delicious stroke, wishing the kiss would never end. She would be quite content, she realized, to spend the remainder of her days in Dan's arms.

Mary had just formed that disturbing thought when the front door burst open and Sophia rushed in, Frank following close on her heels. Mary's mother took one look at the embracing couple on the couch, crossed herself, then began shouting. "Rapist! Defiler of women! Frank, do something. That man is attacking our daughter."

Mary and Dan broke apart.

Dan's mouth unhinged at the sight of the avenging couple, and his ardor, which had pretty much peaked to Mount McKinley status, deflated immediately.

Mary was so stunned that she remained motionless for a moment, until she saw her father, murder flashing in his eyes, bearing down on Dan, holding something in his hand.

"Ma! Pa!" she called out to thwart their attack. "Stop! Wait! What are you doing here?" Her father had a white sauce-stained napkin tied around his neck, and the threatening object he held appeared to be nothing more than a piece of garlic bread. She breathed a sigh of relief before cursing inwardly.

"We were having dinner. I looked out the window and saw the police," Sophia explained, casting Dan the evil eye.

The evil eye was nothing to fool around with. It was tantamount to a curse being leveled on your head, and it supposedly brought destruction down on whomever it had been bestowed upon. Sophia had the squinty-eye glare down pat, though Grandma Flora insisted that only she had the power to exact evil-eye revenge on her enemies. It was a seniority thing apparently.

Dan was safe for the moment, Mary thought.

"Is this the Irishman?" her mother asked, her words venom-laced. "The one who trashed your restaurant?"

Then again, maybe not, she reconsidered.

Dan forced a smile. "I'm Dan Gallagher. Nice to meet you, Mrs. Russo," he said, not realizing how close he'd come to being reduced to a eunuch. He held out his hand, which she refused to take. Fortunately Mary's father wasn't as rude.

"My wife thought you were a rapist," Frank explained with a shrug, as if that were a commonplace occurrence. "You know how women are. They get these ideas in their head."

There was no way Dan was going to agree with Frank Russo that his wife was nuts, especially when she was glaring at him, though he had a pretty good suspicion she might be.

"Of course he doesn't know how women are! Especially women like Ma. This is all so humiliating." Mary wished she would just dissolve into the floor. "I can't believe you two would come barging in here—"

"We saw the police." Sophia's chin jutted out, and she crossed her arms, assuming a defensive posture. "Most daughters would be grateful," she added, then looked around and shook her head, not bothering to hide her disgust.

"The trouble with you, Mary, is that you were never much of a housekeeper. Look at this place. It's a sty. And with—" she paused meaningfully "—company here." She might as well have said "a piece-of-shit-Irishman," because that's what she meant.

The younger woman heaved a sigh. No one should have to put up with a burglar and their mother all on the same evening. "My apartment was broken into tonight, Ma."

"I knew it." The older woman crossed herself again, then did a quick recitation of the rosary. Mary didn't need to see the prayer beads to know they were in her mother's dress pocket. Like the American Express Card, Sophia never left home without them.

"See, Frank, I told you Mary was in danger. I felt it here."
She pressed a hand to her breast. "A mother knows these
things."

Dan felt like laughing, but he wasn't sure why. Red-faced,
Mary was biting her lower lip and looking as if she were
ready to spit nails. He merely felt like a teenager who'd been
caught in the girl's locker room with his pants down.

"The would-be burglars messed up the place, Mrs. Russo.
They tossed Mary's apartment pretty thoroughly, I'm
afraid."

"Was anything stolen?" her father asked, looking around
at the new furnishings and nodding approvingly to himself.
"Business is good, no?" There was pride in his voice.

"Frank, what kind of question is that to ask? Your daughter's been robbed. Of what, we can't be certain." She stared
accusingly at Dan, alleged violator of women, who smiled
innocently in return.

"Did you check your CD player, Mary?" Frank asked to
appease the bossy woman. "Those are very popular items for
thieves to take." He disappeared into the kitchen, then declared a few moments later, "Tiramisu! Can I have some?"

"Madonna mia!" Sophia slapped her forehead.

Dan gave Mary an encouraging wink, then headed into
the kitchen after him. "Why don't I make some coffee, Mr.
Russo," she heard him suggest, and her heart gave a funny
little flutter. Most people usually ignored her father—he
tended to recede into the background when Sophia was in
the room—and the fact that Dan didn't said a lot about the
kind of man he was.

"I'd like some of that dessert, too," Dan said.

"Good. Then you can tell me about the Orioles. I love
baseball. Do you get free tickets? And what about bocci?
Ever seen a tournament? Now, there's some excitement."

"Humph! Now the reporter is claiming he likes Italian
food. I think he likes Italian women, not food." Mary's mother
flashed her husband the you-traitor! look.

"*Ssh,* Ma! Dan'll hear you." Not that Sophia hadn't already insulted the poor man to the high heavens. No doubt this would be her last date with him. The thought made her sad, but she had to be realistic. What man with an ounce of sense would want to put up with a crazed, overprotective mother when he didn't have to?

Sophia eyed her daughter up one side and down the other, and her frown deepened. "Why are you dressed like a *whooaa*? No wonder the man was trying to rape you."

"I'm not dressed like a whore, and he wasn't trying to rape me. We were kissing. I'm old enough to kiss men if I want to." Sophia opened her mouth to protest, but Mary cut her off. "And don't tell me about that damn cow again. I refuse to listen."

"Your beautiful long hair is gone. And that dress . . ." She tsked her disapproval. "Indecent. A woman could catch cold with such a short dress."

She could also catch a man, Mary thought. Not that it would do her any good. Because once she caught him, her mother would barge in during a passionate kiss and throw cold water on them.

Who needed a chastity belt when you had Sophia?

"I like my new look and so does Dan."

"It's the Irish in him. They have lust in their loins. Look at the Kennedys. Clinton. Shameful, every last one. You don't see Mario Cuomo behaving like that.

"The reporter thinks you're easy."

Mary rolled her eyes. "Ma, I'm a thirty-three-year-old virgin. How easy can I be?"

"He'll never fit into the family."

Mary glanced into the kitchen and saw how well her father and Dan were getting along—they were laughing, talking sports like they'd known each other all their lives—but she didn't dispute her mother's assertion. "I'm not interested in marrying him, Ma. We're just dating, or were trying to, before you rushed in like the cavalry."

The barb rolled off Sophia's back. "You're going to bring him to my anniversary party, aren't you?"

"I was thinking about it." Actually, she hadn't been, but now that her mother mentioned it, looking so displeased at the prospect, it seemed a very good idea. Connie was dying to meet Dan, and Joe's opinion was always worth hearing. If she could convince Dan to go. And that was a big if. After tonight it was extremely unlikely.

"I won't be held responsible for the way he's treated by the family. Your uncle Alfredo will be there, you know."

"Are you afraid Dan might wake up one morning with a horse's head in his bed?" Mary laughed at the absurd notion.

Sophia turned the imaginary key to lock her lips. "I can say no more."

If only that were true! Mary thought, but knew it was extremely doubtful that she'd heard the last from her mother.

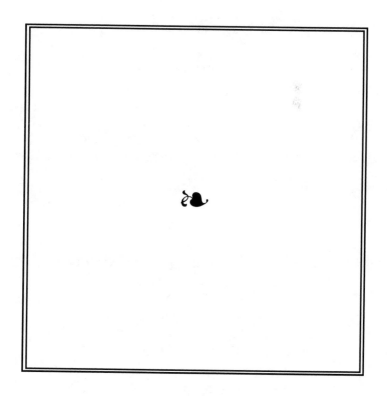

Annie's Meatball Sub

Meatballs

2 lbs. ground beef
2 eggs
1 cup Italian-style bread crumbs
4 cloves garlic, chopped
1 medium onion, chopped
oregano, basil, salt, and pepper to taste
$\frac{1}{4}$ cup chopped parsley
$\frac{1}{2}$ cup Parmesan cheese

In large bowl, mix above ingredients. Form into meatballs about 2 to 3 inches in diameter. Brown in hot olive oil. Drain on paper towels, then add to sauce.

Tomato Sauce

2 28-oz. cans crushed tomatoes with puree
2 28-oz. cans tomato puree
2 8-oz. cans tomato sauce
2 12-oz. cans tomato paste
garlic, onion (chopped)
basil, oregano, salt, and pepper to taste

Prepare sauce by sautéing garlic and onion in olive oil. Add tomato sauce, paste, puree, and whole tomatoes. Season with basil, oregano, salt, and pepper. Simmer 4–6 hours.

Slice 8-inch Italian-style roll in half, place several meatballs on roll, and cover with mozzarella and Parmesan cheese. Heat till cheese is melted.

CHAPTER
TWELVE

"I like the new fashion statement you're making, Mrs. Foragi. Very chic. Mind if I copy it?"

The landlady brushed several errant strands of salt-and pepper-hair away from her face, looked back over her shoulder, and shot Mary's friend a disgusted look, then went back to what she was doing. "You've got a fresh mouth on you, Annie Goldman. You should be more like your friend Mary here. She's quiet and polite to senior citizens."

Staring at the reddish-brown leather carpenter's belt slung around the woman's ample waist and hips, which was filled with every tool imaginable, Mary exchanged a grin with Annie. Mrs. Foragi was not your typical senior citizen, not by a long shot.

"Thanks for installing the new locks, Mrs. Foragi. I'll feel much safer knowing they're here."

The sounds of screaming children at play rolled up the stairwell to the top where they were standing, and the older woman covered her ears and made a face of disgust. "Little delinquents! Shouldn't they be in school?"

It was a Sunday, but no one was about to tell that to the landlady-turned-handywoman. Not when she had a hammer in her hand. Based on what Mrs. Foragi had said about her own grandchildren being ungrateful, spoiled brats, Mary had deduced that the woman was not overly fond of kids. Anyone's.

"I've put in a new gizmo, right beside the door on the

inside. It'll go off if anyone tries to get in again. And it's easy to use. Not fancy, like the security system you're installing in the restaurant. But it'll get people's attention. Just remember to set it before going out."

Holding up a white paper bag, Annie waved it back and forth like a flag of truce. "Here's a little something from the restaurant, Mrs. F. We thought you might be hungry." A safe bet, since Mrs. Foragi was always hungry. Annie compared her to a shark: a perfect eating machine.

The large woman's dark eyes lit with anticipation as she sniffed the air and gazed longingly at the bag dangling between Annie's fingers, then she licked her lips. "Calzone?"

Mary shook her head. "Meatball sub. Annie helped make the meatballs."

The woman scrunched up her face, giving the appearance of a pumpkin that had been left out in the sun two months too long. "Are you sure it's edible?"

"Hey, no need to be rude!" Annie tried to look offended, but didn't quite make it. It took a lot to offend Annie.

"Don't worry," Mary reassured her landlady. "Marco supervised. He's decided to teach Annie how to cook." Her chef claimed it went against his sensibilities to work with a woman who had no cooking talent. Apparently Annie had been giving off bad kitchen karma and didn't even know it. The fact that she'd agreed to the lessons had been nothing short of astonishing.

"Beggars can't be choosers," Annie pointed out.

Mary's landlady waved a screwdriver in Annie's direction. "No, but they can be dead if they eat food you prepare. Your mother should have done her duty and taught you how to cook. Young women these days don't know a thing about keeping house. It's disgraceful."

"I'm not married, so I don't need to know. That's what microwaves and fast food are for."

"You'll never get a man if you don't learn how to feed

him. Sex lasts only so long, but the stomach goes on forever." That was particularly true in Mrs. Foragi's case.

Annie's blue eyes sparkled mischievously. "You've been hanging around the wrong men, Mrs. F."

Listening to the two women bicker, Mary shook her head and smiled, because she knew for all their barb slinging and taunts, Annie and Mrs. Foragi actually liked each other. Hard to believe.

"I'm having an anniversary party for my parents on Saturday evening," Mary informed the older woman. "We're closing the restaurant for the occasion, and we'd love for you to join us."

Mrs. Foragi rolled up the sleeves of her blue-and-red plaid, cotton work shirt and smiled, pleased by the invitation. "I love a good party. Should I bring a date?"

"A date?" Mary repeated, shooting her friend a look of surprise and prompting the woman to respond, "You know, a man."

The idea that Mrs. Foragi might actually have a man in her life astounded Annie, whose brows shot up to her hairline. "We didn't know you were seeing anyone."

"Why would you? You think I share my sex life with children? Of course I'm seeing someone. Benny Buffano and I have been keeping company for six years, on and off. Sometimes he goes back with his wife, and then it's off for a while. But he usually comes back. Carmella is a putz. She moved back to New York to drive her children crazy. Better them than Benny."

Mary's jaw dropped. "Are you talking about Mr. Buffano the undertaker?" There'd been rumors that he and his wife were having marital problems, but she had no idea that Donatella Foragi was the "other woman." You didn't usually find many two-hundred-pound home-wreckers. Unless, of course, you worked for a demolition company.

"One and the same. We even did it once in the back of a hearse. Can you imagine? The casket with the dead body was inside and everything." Her voice filled with pride, and she actually looked quite pleased with herself.

While Mary stared horrified at the woman, Annie burst out laughing. "I like your style, Mrs. F. Who knew morticians could be so kinky and creative."

Donatella unhitched her tool belt and dropped it to the cement floor, where it landed with a thud and a clang. "You don't know the half of it. Benny's very talented. He'll probably do my makeup Saturday night. He's a whiz with foundation, blush, and eyeliner. After all, he's had a lot of practice, making all those dead people look good. He can give you girls some hints if you ask him."

Annie looked a bit too fascinated by the discussion for Mary's comfort zone, so she thanked the older woman again and dragged her friend into the apartment, shutting the door firmly behind her. "You're starting to scare me, Annie Goldman."

"*Oy vey!* Lighten up, will you? There's nothing wrong with a little experimentation." Dismissing her friend's concern with an airy wave, she looked about. "I see you cleaned up the place. After what you told me, I was expecting to find a mess."

"Dan was kind enough to help me straighten up before he left last night." Her parents had remained the whole time he was there, making the possibility of any more kisses between them hopeless.

"So, when are you and Dan going to do the deed? If you've got him doing domestic chores, slipping between the sheets can't be far behind, right?"

Looking deflated, Mary dropped to the sofa and sighed. "I told you—we'd just gotten to the good part when my parents crashed into the apartment."

"Tough break. Next time, lock your door. And don't forget, there's always a next time. Are you going to invite him to your parents' anniversary party?"

"Yes." She intended to pay Dan a visit this evening, in

fact. "Even after all the insults my mother threw at him, I've decided to ask him to come. I could be wrong, but I think he actually likes my parents. Can you believe it?" She couldn't.

"You're kidding!" Eyes wide, Annie looked suitably impressed by the news. It took quite a lot to impress Annie. "Brave man. This one could be a keeper, *cara*."

Mary had thought the very same thing, but she wasn't ready for a long-term commitment. And Dan had made it clear that he wasn't looking for one, either. Which was good, because he wanted a stay-at-home wife who would cook and clean and take care of the kids—a woman like her mother. She shuddered at the thought. And though being a housewife was honorable, marriage just wasn't something she felt ready for.

And even if she did want to get married, Dan wouldn't be the right choice. Sure, they were a good match in many ways—they liked the same movies and music, and he laughed at all her stupid jokes, and she at his—but his old-fashioned view on a woman's role was different from hers, as was his opinion of the church. Couple all that with the baggage he brought from his first marriage, and what she brought with all her hang-ups and insecurities . . . well, it was a wonder they were even friends.

She intended to make her position clear to Dan before anything happened between them. That would only be fair, and she had no doubt that he would be vastly relieved, judging from everything he'd already confided.

"That's odd, coming from Miss Love 'Em and Leave 'Em Goldman," Mary said finally.

Annie shrugged. "You're not me, Mary *mia*. I doubt you'll be able to have just a casual affair without getting involved up to your eyeballs." She ran crimson fingernails through cobalt-blue hair. Mr. Roy had obviously been having a bad hair day; Annie sure was.

Mary sighed at hearing her greatest fear voiced, for she had worried about the same thing. But she'd been reading

Cosmopolitan to give her inspiration, and she was determined and confident that she could remain detached.

Passionate, uncomplicated, no strings attached.

"Joe'll be at the party," she told her friend. "Just thought I'd warn you."

"I figured as much, seeing as how he's Sophia's pride and joy." Annie's smile grew teasing. "I'll try to wear something befitting the occasion."

Knowing exactly what that meant, Mary cringed inwardly, but opted not to say anything. It wouldn't do any good anyway. And it might serve to make the flamboyant woman choose something even more outlandish. "I haven't decided yet what I'm going to wear."

"The red dress. Definitely!"

Mary gasped. "I can't wear that to my mother's party. She'd faint dead away." The gown had slits up the side, making underpants a nonoption. You couldn't not wear underpants to your parents forty-third anniversary party. It wouldn't be right. It would create a scandal the Russos would never live down, not unlike the scandal Aunt Josie's Sally created by getting knocked up by Carmine Delvechio.

Because of Sally's weight it had taken months for her pregnancy to be detected. When it finally made itself known, all hell had broken loose, as well as a few of Carmine's front teeth, when Uncle Jimmy punched him in the mouth to avenge his daughter's honor. Of course, that animosity—bad blood, some called it—ended the moment Carmine and Sally got married.

"The way I see it, you have two choices: You can wear something conservative and dull and please Sophia, which will result in your maintaining the status quo, i.e.: virginity *intactus*; or you can wear the red dress, lose your inhibitions, and make love all night with Mr. Wonderful."

Mary sighed. "Tough choice."

"Yeah. That's what I thought, too."

* * *

Mary stared at the computer screen and shook her head, feeling utterly confused and totally frustrated. "I can't do it, Matt. I don't have a clue what you're talking about."

She had agreed to allow Matt to give her lessons on learning the computer—she hoped it would build his self-esteem, and at the same time help her modernize her business—but she just wasn't getting it. Not at all.

The kid had been talking about spreadsheets, bullets, columns, and keystrokes, and it was all Greek to her. She felt stupid and embarrassed.

"You just need to get the hang of using the computer, Mary," he said, astute enough to notice her frustration. "Even my dad's getting better on it." He made the statement as if it were nothing short of a miracle. "And you were pretty hopeless, right, Dad?"

Returning Mary's amused look with a halfhearted smile, his father replied, "That's right, son. I can almost open Windows 98 all by myself now." He winked at Mary, who just shook her head and pushed away from the desk.

"I appreciate your offering to teach me, Matt, but I don't think my mind's focused on it tonight. Maybe we can try another time, okay?" She was too nervous to think about modems and mouses. She still hadn't asked Dan about the party, though she'd been at his apartment for over an hour now. After last night's embarrassing episode with her parents, she was pretty sure he wouldn't want to come. Not that she could blame him.

The boy shrugged. "Sure. I gotta go to bed anyway. We're having a field trip tomorrow at school."

"Really? Where are you going? I always loved riding those big yellow buses and going on an adventure."

"Miss Osborne's taking us to see Fort McHenry. We're studying the flag, so it kinda fits in."

"I'll say it does, sport. Now get upstairs and get to bed, or you'll be too tired to admire the efforts of our founding fathers. I'll be up later to check on you."

" 'Night, Mary. 'Night, Dad." The child gave a little wave before disappearing up the stairs.

"Good night, sweetie," Mary said, and she suddenly realized how much a part of her life Dan's son had become in such a short time. Matt was a great kid, almost as wonderful as his father.

Gazing thoughtfully at Dan, she remembered the glorious kisses they'd shared and heaved a sigh. She'd thought of little else all day.

"That kid's got more energy. I don't know how he does it. I sure as heck can't keep up with him."

She grinned at Dan's woebegone expression. "I think it's called youth."

"Yeah. Thanks for the reminder that I'm getting old."

"There's something to be said for maturity."

His eyes darkened, and he stepped closer. "Ah. Now if you're talking about experience . . ."

Cheeks warm enough to toast bread, she put some distance between them by taking a seat on the sofa. Much to her chagrin, Dan followed, sitting down beside her.

"I'm glad you stopped by tonight. I just hope Matt's attempts at teaching you to use a computer didn't annoy you too much. He's really into that, you know."

"Not at all. I've got to make an effort to learn one of these days, or I'll be left behind in the Dark Ages. But learning how to use a computer isn't the reason I stopped over here tonight."

"Oh?" His eyes focused on her lips, as if remembering what they'd been doing last night before her parents had so rudely interrupted them.

Swallowing the grapefruit-sized lump in her throat, she said, "I'm giving my parents an anniversary party next Saturday night, and I was wondering if you'd like to attend . . . as my date." She took a deep breath, then released it when his face lit with a smile.

"Thanks! I'd love to!"

"Really?" She smiled happily, then gave him the particulars. "Well, I really should be going. I've got a lot to attend to before then, and—"

He reached for her hand. "Don't go yet, Mary. It's still early, and I'd like to finish what we started last night."

"I—" She didn't have the opportunity to protest, to even figure out if she wanted to protest—she was sure she didn't—because Dan leaned over, pulled her into his arms, and began to kiss her senseless.

With his clever tongue, he licked the seam of her mouth, then dove in to taste the pleasures inside, and Mary's blood began to heat. Tentatively, and then more aggressively, she responded in kind, and all thoughts of departure fled.

"God, Mary! I want you so badly. I haven't been with a woman in a long, long time, and you're making me crazy. You smell so good, feel so good." His hand went to her breast and he began to caress her nipple with his thumb; it beaded instantly. "You've got everything a man could possibly want."

When it finally registered through the haze of passion surrounding Mary what Dan actually wanted, she stiffened. She was on her back, her skirt hiked up past her thighs, and Dan's fingers were doing wonderful things to her nipples.

Relax! she told herself. This is what you've been wanting. But she couldn't. Even though Dan's *zinger* was working remarkably well—she could feel it pressed against her abdomen—she just couldn't make herself take the next step. Not tonight. The timing was all wrong. And Dan's son was asleep upstairs and could come down at any moment.

She pushed at his chest. "Dan, wait! Stop! I'm sorry, but I think we're both getting a bit carried away."

He pulled back instantly, trying to ignore the persistent throbbing between his legs, wiping perspiration from his forehead with the back of his sleeve. "I'm sorry. I thought you wanted to. I—"

She covered his mouth with her fingertips. "I do. I want

to very much," she admitted. "But not tonight. Not with Matt in the house."

He stared toward the stairs and looked as if he'd just been poleaxed. "Holy shit! I forgot." He shook his head. "You must really think I'm an ass."

She smiled softly and was tempted to kiss him again. "On the contrary, I think you're pretty wonderful. And it's because I do that I'd better go." She eased off the couch, but he latched on to her hand again.

"I'm looking forward to Saturday night, Mary."

She was, too. And probably for the very same reasons.

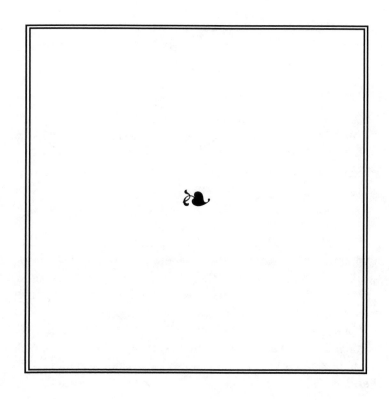

Anniversary Mushrooms Florentine

24–30 large stuffing mushrooms
1 10-oz. pkg. frozen chopped spinach
2 cloves garlic, minced fine
1 small onion, chopped
½ cup butter, melted
½ cup Italian-style bread crumbs
2 3-oz. pkgs. cream cheese, softened
⅛ tsp. black pepper
¾ tsp. dry mustard
¼ tsp. nutmeg
2 ½ tbsp. grated Parmesan cheese

Clean mushrooms and set on paper towels to dry. Remove stems, chop, and set aside to use later. Cook spinach without salt. Drain in collander. Mix in food processor or beat with electric mixer until smooth. Set aside.

Sauté garlic in butter, about 1 minute. Remove from heat. Dip mushroom caps in butter-and-garlic mixture, coating well, and place in a 13 × 9 × 2–inch baking dish. Stir the chopped mushroom stems and onion into the remaining butter-and-garlic mixture. Sauté until tender.

Combine spinach, cream cheese, bread crumbs, and seasonings in bowl; add mushroom mixture and mix well. Spoon spinach mixture into mushroom caps and sprinkle with Parmesan cheese. Bake at 375° for 15 minutes. Serves 8.

CHAPTER THIRTEEN

"So, you're the Irishman?"

Dan smiled at the short gentleman who barely reached his waist, and whose snow-white hair was in direct contrast to his deep-olive complexion. Trying not to feel insulted by the fact that everyone in Mary's family, with the exception of the woman herself, seemed to harbor a dislike of the Irish, he replied, "That's what they tell me." He stuck out his hand, which engulfed the man's smaller one. "Dan Gallagher. Pleased to meet you. And you are?"

"Uncle Jimmy. Josephine's husband. You've probably heard about my altercation with my son-in-law, Carmine. The bastard knocked up my baby girl, but things are fine now. They're married."

Apparently keeping one's dirty laundry hidden was not an Italian trait. Dan had already learned that Aunt Angie had had her bladder repaired six months ago—she'd been leaking like a sieve, or so she'd told him—and Mary's cousin Peter had just come out of the closet and admitted his homosexuality. Dan wasn't particularly homophobic, but he had set the man straight on his own sexual persuasion. You couldn't leave a thing like that hanging.

"No, I hadn't heard. Congratulations. Uh, by the way, do you know where Mary is? I'm supposed to meet her here." He glanced around the room again, then at his watch, a recent birthday present from his mother. Mary was late by almost twenty minutes, and he was starting to panic.

Having met a few of Mary's relatives, Dan already knew what they thought of him as a potential love interest, and it hadn't been a real boost to his ego. Cowardly though it might be, he'd been hoping she could run interference for him.

"Hard to say with women." Uncle Jimmy pulled a wooden toothpick out of his shirt pocket and poked it at his front teeth, trying to dislodge a dark green blob that looked suspiciously like spinach. The waiters had been passing around Mushrooms Florentine, and Dan guessed the old man had eaten his fill. Dan sure had. They'd been quite tasty, and he intended to ask Mary for the recipe.

"When my Josie's late it usually means she got a call from one of the kids. Mary doesn't have that problem. Yet.

"You'd better watch yourself," Mary's uncle added, a warning note in his voice. "I hear Sophia's going to get her brother, Alfredo, after you. He could be connected. No one knows for sure."

Dan's brow wrinkled. "Connected to what?" Probably the Sons of Italy organization, he decided. The close-knit group of Italian descendants boasted a huge membership nationwide.

Jimmy pressed his index finger to the side of his nose, as if that would explain everything. Either that, or the man had a severe sinus problem. "It's not right to speak of such things on such a happy occasion, but are you familiar with—" he pulled Dan down to his level and whispered, "—the Teflon don?"

"The Teflon . . ." Dan's eyes widened. "Are you talking about John Gotti?"

"Ssh!" Uncle Jimmy cautioned, looking over his shoulder to make certain no one had overheard them. "Gotti might be spending the rest of his life in prison, but he's still

got a following, if you know what I mean. These size-eights ain't going in cement any time soon, I can promise you that."

Just as Dan was starting to wonder if everyone in Mary's family was as certifiable as Uncle Jimmy, he spotted her manager walking in his direction and breathed a sigh of relief, despite the fact that he didn't think Annie was playing with a full deck, either.

Annie Goldman was a knockout in a red-beaded dress that dipped as low in the front as it did in the back, showing off a great deal of bosom. He suspected the eccentric woman didn't have a modest bone in her body. Although he didn't think she was an easy lay, either, making her quite the enigma. There was more to Annie Goldman than met the eye. He'd bet money on it.

"You don't mind if I steal Dan away for a minute, do you, Uncle Jimmy?" she said, smiling at the older man, whose eyes were fixed on her cleavage and glazing over. Not waiting for a response, she linked her arm through Dan's and whisked him away to the other side of the restaurant before Mary's uncle could protest.

Out of the corner of her eye, Annie caught sight of Mrs. Foragi and the undertaker. He'd obviously done her makeup, because the woman's face was so white she looked as if she'd been embalmed. It was apparent that Benny *the Stud* Buffano hadn't bothered to match skin tones.

"Mary's having a little problem with her dress," Annie explained at Dan's questioning look. "She asked me to come down and keep you company while she fixes it."

Frank Sinatra blared loudly from the music speakers, and Dan had to bend his head and raise his voice a few decibels to make himself heard. "Anything I can do to help? I'm pretty good with zippers." He grinned like a naughty schoolboy, and Annie laughed, before taking a sip of the wine she'd just filched from a passing waiter's tray.

"I just bet you are. The dress in question doesn't have a zipper, just two slits up the sides that proved too daring for her to wear once she put it on. Personally, I thought she looked dynamite in it, but Mary didn't want to upset her mother or offend her brother the priest, so she decided to change into something more sedate."

Dan wasn't surprised to hear Mary was being considerate of others, but he was rather disappointed that she hadn't worn the dress. He'd love to see her in it. Just imagining those slits, those fabulous legs . . .

"Mary's very thoughtful," he said, tossing back his beer in an attempt to cool off. "And she'd look great in just about anything, including a burlap sack."

"Sackcloth's more Sophia's style. Ah," Annie couldn't keep the pride out of her voice as she looked toward the doorway, her eyes filling with pleasure at the transformation she'd helped to create, "here she comes now."

As if on cue, the music ended and all heads turned to stare at the latecomer. Several of the men—Frank Russo being the most vocal after several bottles of *vino*—whistled and shouted their approval, bringing a bright blush to Mary's cheeks.

Dan choked on his beer as the image of her dressed in sexy black registered on his brain. Her gown was long-sleeved, high-necked, and thigh-high, and it hugged every one of her ample curves to perfection. The dress wasn't revealing at all, yet it revealed everything. She wore no jewelry, except for a pair of gold studs in her ears.

In a word, she looked orgasmic.

"Sorry I'm so late." Mary sidled up next to Dan, giving him a heated smile that almost reduced him to ashes. "I couldn't decide what to wear."

He took a deep, calming breath, wondering if he was doomed to spend the remainder of his life in permanent arousal. "You chose perfectly; you look absolutely beautiful."

Her cheeks filled with color again, and Annie laughed knowingly. "Guess I'll go find Father Joe and make nice for a while." She leaned over to kiss her friend's cheek, whispering, "You've made major points here tonight, *cara*. Keep it up. From what I've observed of Dan, that shouldn't be too difficult." With a throaty laugh at the man's obvious discomfort, she gave him a wink and departed.

Heat slithered up Dan's neck, but he tried to ignore it, hoping everyone at the party wasn't as perceptive as Ms. Goldman. "Annie's nice, though a bit unusual."

"Most people seem to think so, including my brother." She eyed the couple across the room. Joe was frowning as he took in Annie's low-cut gown, which, of course, made her friend laugh a little too loudly in response. "They've had their differences over the years."

Before she could elaborate, Grandma Flora approached, hauling Dan's son behind her and stealing their attention. She was dressed most becomingly in a black silk gown with a silver brooch at her throat, her white hair rolled so tightly by Mrs. Brucetti's nimble fingers, you could see her pink scalp.

Matt appeared to be quite smitten with the older woman, and Mary knew the feeling was mutual. She had seen them dancing together earlier.

"The *bambino* is hungry, Mary. When are we going to eat?"

It was still cocktail hour. Dinner wouldn't be served for a while yet, but Mary knew her grandmother—who ate promptly at five every night—didn't want to hear that. "Soon, *Nonna*, I promise. We'll eat very soon." The old lady grunted disapprovingly, but didn't argue.

"You sure do look pretty tonight, Mary," Matt said. "I bet my dad's going to get mushy again. He put smelly stuff all over his face and brushed his teeth three times tonight before leaving the condo. Weird, huh?"

Mary thought she could get used to that kind of "weird," and reached for Dan's hand, squeezing it gently. The gesture earned her a megawatt smile. "Your father looks very handsome tonight, and so do you, Matt."

Not bothering to hide the fact that he was uncomfortable dressed in a suit, the child yanked impatiently at his collar and tie. "Don't see why I had to wear one of these when my dad didn't."

"Don'ta be a fresh boy, Matthew," Grandma Flora scolded, wagging a bony finger at the child. "Itsa no good to speaka to your papa like that. You musta show more respect."

"Okay, Grandma," Matt replied obediently, hugging the old woman about her waist, and making his father's eyes widen in surprise and delight. "Let's go find something to eat. I see the waiters passing around those horse doovie things."

Mary and Dan couldn't help grinning at each other, and something undefinable passed between them—something that didn't go unnoticed.

Brown eyes sparkling, Grandma Flora smiled secretively to herself. "I will take Matthew home with me tonight, Daniel. I promised the *bambino* he could stay the night. Itsa okay, no?"

"Please, Dad! Me and Grandma got stuff to do, plans to make."

The old woman tugged the boy's ear to shut him up, and the gesture was observed by Mary, who'd been warned in similar fashion many times. She suspected her grandma was up to something, she just didn't know what.

"Ah . . . sure," Dan said, not about to pass up such a propitious offer. "If you're sure it's not too much trouble."

"Bah! Trouble? Whatta trouble? Children are a blessing from God. Mary will have lotsa them someday. I hope before I die I will hold her *bambina* in my arms."

Her grandmother was staring pointedly at Dan's crotch,

and Mary felt heat rise to her cheeks. What he must think of her family! She didn't even want to speculate. Because if he went by the old adage of the apple not falling far from the tree, she was pretty much doomed.

"Don't ask me why," Dan said after the pair had departed, "but for some reason your family makes me feel good. I like being around them. They're very likable people." With the possible exception of Sophia, and even she was starting to grow on him. He'd always had a thing for outspoken women.

Her mouth fell open. "They are? I mean—I know they're a little hard to take at first, but they're good-hearted. And they always mean well."

"I was an only child. A big family appeals to me. I always wanted brothers and sisters, aunts and uncles." He focused on Mary's sister and her doctor husband, who were wrapped in each other's arms as they danced, oblivious to everyone else in the room. He heaved a sigh of envy at the closeness of the Russos and their extended family.

"You don't know how lucky you are to have a family like yours. My dad was gone most of the time, and there wasn't much warmth in our house, even when he was there. My mom did her best to make up for his failings, but she was dealing with her own loneliness and unhappiness, and I think she kind of blamed me in a way for trapping her in an unhappy marriage." He'd never admitted that last part to himself until now.

This was the first time Dan had ever really opened up to her about his family, and Mary was glad he felt comfortable sharing things with her. "I'm sorry," she said, clasping his arm. "I didn't know. It must have been rough growing up like that.

"But you should know, Dan, that things aren't always what they seem. Yes, I have a loving family, and I'm grateful for them. But I was the middle child and was pretty much ignored. Joe was the apple of my mom's eye, while Connie, as the baby of the family, was doted on by my father. She was daddy's little girl. I was just sort of there, taking up space. At least that's how I felt.

"One of the reasons I think I stayed so long with my parents was that when Joe and Connie left I became the center of my parents' attention. I reveled in it, but then became trapped by it and couldn't break out on my own.

"So although things sometimes appear one way, they aren't always as rosy as you might imagine."

He squeezed her hand and kissed her cheek. "Thanks for sharing that. I needed to hear it." And it gave him better insight into Mary's need for independence.

"I'm sure everyone has issues with their parents and childhood, but I still consider myself very lucky. I love them, warts and all," Mary said.

There was a wealth of love in the room, and you didn't have to be Italian to feel it. Even an Irishman knew a good thing when he saw it. Dan gazed down at Mary again and his heart began pounding, the sound echoing in his ears. He hadn't expected to feel such a strong reaction, and swallowed with some difficulty.

"I bet you wouldn't trade your experiences for the world," he said.

"Good thing you didn't put chocolate on the bargaining table." Mary grinned, turning her attention to her parents, who had taken center stage on the dance floor and were twirling in each other's arms to the strains of "That's Amore." Dean Martin's voice filled the large room, and she sighed as she watched the anniversary couple.

Forty-three years Frank and Sophia Russo had been married. And for forty-three years they had loved, fought, borne children, fought, made each other miserable and deliriously happy.

Mary hoped she would be as lucky someday.

But she wasn't ready for that moon to hit her in the eye just yet.

Dan slid his arm around her waist, and she melted like warm chocolate. "Shall we dance?"

Okay, maybe not yet, but sooner is starting to look better than later.

On the other side of the restaurant, Annie and Joe were engaged in a heated discussion only volatile Italians wouldn't consider an argument.

"Why do you always have to flaunt yourself? What are you trying to prove?" Joe took in Annie's revealing dress, the large expanse of bosom, and shook his head disapprovingly. He disliked when Annie cheapened herself, like she was doing now.

Annie was a beautiful woman. She didn't need to draw attention to herself by wearing flamboyant costumes and crazy hair colors. She was perfect just the way she was.

Annie masked her hurt behind a wide smile. She and Joe couldn't be in the same room with each other for more than five minutes before they were at each other's throats. "I don't have to prove anything, especially to you, *Father* Joseph, so why don't you just butt out and leave me alone? I'm not your concern. I'm not a member of your parish. And, in case you don't remember, I'm not even Catholic."

Knowing he had handled things very badly, Joe heaved a sigh, running impatient fingers through his dark hair. He'd never been able to think clearly where Annie was concerned. "I'm just worried about you. I don't mean to lecture, but—"

Her mouth tightened into a grim line. "Your interest's about fourteen years too late, Joe. Save it for someone who cares. I don't." Without a backward glance, she strutted across the room, smiling widely at a muscular waiter and never noticing the hurt registered on the priest's face.

"Dammit all to hell!"

"Joseph Russo! Shame on you!"

He turned, sucked in his breath, and was relieved to find his sister, not his mother, standing next to him. If Sophia had heard him curse, he would have fallen right off that pedestal she'd placed him on all those years ago. Not an altogether bad thing, he decided. Being elevated to lofty heights definitely took its toll. You had nowhere else to go but down.

Thrusting aside his frustration, Joe pasted on a smile, unwilling to spoil Mary or his parents' evening. "Hey, peanut! Nice party. Mom and Dad are having a great time. How'd you talk Grandma into making a toast to the happy couple? Did you bribe her?"

Her brother's forced gaiety didn't fool Mary one bit. He and Annie had obviously just had another disagreement, one he didn't want to talk about. She wouldn't press him right now.

"It was *Nonna*'s idea. I guess she figured after forty-three years Ma and Pa weren't going to split up, so she might as well accept things as they are. It was a really lovely tribute, wasn't it? Ma bawled her eyes out." Something her mother rarely did in public, or in private, for that matter.

Joe glanced in Annie's direction once again, to find her flirting outrageously with three waiters now instead of one. From the trio's enraptured looks, he could see they didn't have any problem with her dress.

"Accepting things as they are is good advice for anyone."

Mary was about to say something, but Dan arrived with two glasses of champagne, and so she made the introductions. "Dan is the infamous reviewer I spoke to you about, Joe."

"Guess you actually learned a thing or two from my sermons on forgiveness, huh?" Joe smiled at the reporter and held out his hand. "You should feel good about that, Dan. Forgiveness doesn't come easy in this family."

Dan tossed Mary a wink. "So I've gathered."

"He likes the family." There was still a note of incredulity in Mary's voice, which made Dan smile as he sipped his drink.

"Even Uncle Alfredo?" Joe looked almost as surprised as his sister.

"Alfredo couldn't make it. He had to go into work at the last minute. Ma was terribly disappointed." Mary, on the other hand, had been relieved. She wasn't anxious for Dan to meet her flamboyant uncle.

"Ah. Well, maybe that's for the best. Alfredo's definitely an acquired taste. Nice guy, but he takes a bit of getting used to."

"So I gathered, but I was kinda looking forward to meeting someone so infamous, at least in Uncle Jimmy's eyes."

"You mustn't pay attention to anything Uncle Jimmy says," Mary cautioned. "He thinks his eighty-year-old butcher is harvesting animal organs to sell on the black market."

Dan threw back his head and laughed, then wrapped his arm about Mary's waist, pulling her tightly to him. The promise in his eyes spoke volumes, sending shivers all the way down to her toes. "I'm ready for another dance. No offense, Joe, but I'd like to have your sister all to myself for a while."

Heat consumed every inch of Mary's body, landing squarely on her cheeks. And other, less obvious, places.

Her brother laughed. "Go on, peanut. Have fun. You've worked hard on this party. Go enjoy yourself."

" 'Peanut'?" Dan's brow shot up.

"Never you mind about that." She kissed her brother's cheek. "Thanks, Joe. I'll see you later."

Watching his sister leave with Dan, Joe's heart lightened a bit. Whether or not the couple knew it, they were falling in love.

Mary had been a slow bloomer. She'd always hidden in

their mother's shadow, and then Annie's. But now she was standing alone out in the bright sunlight, and he was happy for her.

The peanut had finally blossomed into a rose.

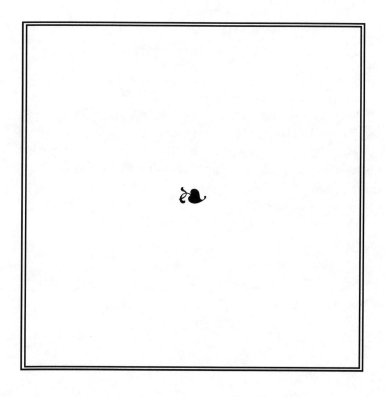

Pepper & Egg Frittata

2 large bell peppers, sliced
1 onion, chopped
4 eggs, beaten
2 tbsp. olive oil
salt and pepper to taste
provolone or mozzarella cheese (optional)

In a large frying pan, sauté sliced bell peppers and chopped onion in olive oil until cooked and almost transparent. Beat the eggs with a whisk and pour over peppers and onions. Move the frying pan back and forth over the flame until the egg is evenly distributed. Sprinkle with salt and pepper. Brown on one side and then the other. Add cheese, if desired, and melt.

Serve as an omelet, or as a sandwich on Italian bread.

CHAPTER FOURTEEN

Mary was feeling a bit woozy from the champagne she had consumed. Two glasses was her usual limit, but tonight's occasion had been special and she'd had three. Or was it four? She'd lost count. Though she strongly suspected the euphoric, walking-on-air feeling she entertained could be attributed to her companion, rather than the alcohol.

If there was a handsomer man alive she hadn't met him. She studied Dan's profile and heaved a sigh. He wasn't Brad Pitt pretty, but he was gorgeous. His eyelashes were outrageously long, and the small bump on the bridge of his nose only added character. And his lips . . . Ah, those lips pressed to hers made her feel and think things no unmarried woman should.

"You're a real hunk, Dan Gallagher. A stud extraordinaire!" When he threw back his head and laughed, she realized that what she'd been thinking had suddenly slipped from her mouth, and she slapped her hand over it, totally mortified. That'll teach you to drink too much champagne, she thought.

"Never been called a stud before." He braked for a red light, and his expression suddenly sobered. "Are you sure you're feeling up to going to my apartment tonight, Mary? You may have had a little too much to drink. And, well, Matt's not going to be there, and I don't want to take advantage of the situation."

Take advantage! Take advantage! she wanted to shout. At

least then she wouldn't have to make the decision that had been hounding her for days.

She leaned her head back and forced a confident smile, despite her nervousness. Tonight was the night. Tonight all the mystery, the yearning, the wondering would come to an end.

Mary had decided it was time to *zing!*

"Don't be silly. I'm fine. I'm looking forward to being alone with you, Dan. I've had a wonderful evening, and I don't want it to end."

He pulled the Explorer into the condo's driveway, cut the engine, and turned to gaze intently at her, looking as uncertain as she felt. "Are you sure?"

Mary wasn't sure about anything. It was a lot easier to think about having an affair, to imagine what it would be like making love with a caring, handsome man, than actually doing it.

Crossing her fingers, and praying for strength, she nodded.

The first thing Mary noticed when she entered Dan's condo was that it was as clean and tidy as the last time she'd visited, much cleaner than her own apartment could ever hope to be.

Sports Illustrated and *TV Guide* magazines were stacked neatly on the brass-and-glass coffee table. The thick-pile beige, wall-to-wall carpeting had been recently vacuumed, and even the cat's litter box was void of any unpleasantness.

Sheesh! Is the man obsessive or what?

"Would you like something to drink?" he asked when she turned to face him. "How about a glass of chardonnay? Or I've got champagne, if you're feeling reckless."

She smiled, wondering what her head would feel like in the morning. "The wine sounds great." Following him into the kitchen, she pulled up short.

You had to be suspicious of a man who claimed to be a gourmet cook and whose kitchen was spotless. The hunter-green tile countertops were eat-off-the-floor clean—ugh!—

and the towel hanging on the rack didn't have the usual gunk on it. Maybe he was a hands-on-shirt wiper like she was; it was almost a comforting thought.

Dan pulled a bottle of Kendall-Jackson out of the refrigerator, and she shook her head in disbelief upon discovering that his fridge was clean, too. With dread, because she knew with a certainty what she would find, she forced herself to face the stainless-steel stove, and nearly grew faint.

"Your stove's spotless!" It was more accusation than statement. Bending over, she peered through the glass door of the oven, her mouth falling open. You could actually see through the glass; it wasn't covered with grease and grime. "How's that possible?"

"I clean it?" He handed her the wineglass, clearly amused, and she took a sip, the fruity liquid tickling her palate.

"I realize that, but when do you have time? I mean, I hardly ever use my kitchen at the apartment and it's always a mess."

"I don't run my own business like you do," he said to be nice, letting her off the hook, but he probably thought she was a total slob. Compared to him, she felt like one.

Sophia would feel very self-righteous about this whole turn of events, if she knew. Mary would make certain she never did.

They settled themselves on the living room sofa in front of the brick fireplace. The gas log was unlit, due to the warm weather. "Your home is so lovely," she said with a sigh, admiring the framed sports photos on the wall and wondering if she'd ever own such a nice place.

"I'm totally envious of the view you have of the harbor." It was dark outside, so she couldn't see the water, but knew the water taxis would still be operating. Spring always brought an influx of visitors to Baltimore. The Inner Harbor, which sported everything from the National Aquarium to the Hard Rock Cafe, was a main attraction.

"My view's much better." He scooted closer, reaching out

to touch her hair. "Did I tell you how beautiful you look tonight?"

Her cheeks flushed, her throat clogged, making words impossible. She nodded.

"Kiss me, Mary. I've been thinking about kissing you all night. I don't think I can wait a moment longer."

"You have?" Her heart started racing, her nerve ends tingled. "A quivering mass" was how the romantic novels described what she was feeling. Well, she was already way past that point. Jello-O had nothing on her tonight!

Taking the glass she held, Dan set it on the coffee table. "I haven't been with a woman in a very long time. I wanted to wait, to find the right one. I'm glad I did." With that, he drew her into his embrace and pressed his lips to hers.

With a passion too long denied, Mary gave herself into the kiss, boldly thrusting her tongue in Dan's mouth, reaching out to caress the muscles of his chest, his thighs. He groaned, as if in agony, and her movements stilled.

"Let's go upstairs, sweet Mary. I want you, but not here. I want you in my bed."

His directness made her blink. Though Mary wanted the same thing, she was nervous at the prospect of making love with Dan and losing her virginity. What if she disappointed him? Did something wrong? After all, she wasn't experienced. All those niggling doubts, her fear of failure, rose up to choke her newly found confidence.

"I'd like to finish my wine first," she hedged, taking a fairly large gulp. "And . . . well, I think I should make a few things clear, so we don't have any misunderstanding between us."

Reaching out, he began toying with her hair again. "I always use protection, Mary, if that's what you're worried about. I wouldn't put you at risk."

Splotches of heat landed firmly on her cheeks. "That's not what I wanted to discuss, though I appreciate your thoughtfulness." Protection! She hadn't even thought of that. And didn't that make her feel stupid and even more inept?

Oh, God! What if he asked her to put a condom on him? She had no idea how to do it. She'd practiced once on a banana, but had managed to poke a hole through the damn thing.

"You're beautiful. A man could drown in the depths of those big brown eyes. Your eyes were one of the first things I noticed about you. Bedroom eyes, I've heard them called."

His words poured over her like hot fudge—sweet and comforting. She didn't have time to thank him, because he pulled her into his arms again and kissed her soundly, effectively shutting down all thought processes. Mary forgot momentarily what she was going to say. When they finally pulled apart and she could breathe again, it all came flooding back.

She took a deep breath, issued a cease and desist order to her pounding heart, and said, "I realize we're about to . . . to take our relationship to the next level, and I want to make certain you and I want the same thing."

Confusion glittered in his eyes, and he shook his head. "I don't—"

"I know we've talked about this before, but I'm still not ready to enter into a permanent relationship with anyone. I just wanted you to know that I hadn't changed my mind. I enjoy my life just the way it is, and I don't want that to change right now."

Dan forced a reassuring smile. "I'm not looking for anything permanent right now, either." Though he said the words she wanted to hear, he wasn't sure they were true anymore. Something had changed between them tonight. His feelings, certainly. And he'd hoped hers, too.

But maybe he'd been too premature in his thinking. Despite her success with the restaurant, Mary had never struck him as the career-minded sort. But that didn't mean she wasn't.

Could he deal with that again? He just didn't know.

Reaching for her hand, he rose to his feet and drew her with him. "Why don't we take one step at a time and see what develops?"

That one step became several, and Mary soon found herself upstairs in Dan's bedroom. A king-size bed covered with a navy-and-beige, geometric-patterned comforter dominated the large room. The furniture was light oak, as were the wooden blinds at the windows.

Pulling her into his arms, Dan kissed her tenderly, caressing her lips, her cheeks, then finally placing an affectionate peck on her forehead. "I've wanted you from the first moment I laid eyes on you, Mary Russo," he confessed. "Even when you were chewing me out over that review."

Smiling softly, she caressed his beard-stubbled cheek, her stomach knotting with apprehension. "I want you, too, Dan. I just hope . . ."

"What?"

"You won't be too disappointed. I'm not all that experienced." She couldn't bring herself to tell him she was a virgin. He'd think she was some sort of freak. There couldn't be that many thirty-three-year-old virgins still in existence.

"I'll take the lead, so you needn't worry about a thing. Just relax and enjoy it."

She swallowed at the intensity, the longing reflected in the depths of his green eyes, desire not unlike her own. "I didn't bring a nightgown." The excuse sounded lame, even to her own ears. But dammit! she was nervous.

He smiled tenderly. "What do you have on beneath that sexy dress?"

Remembering the scraps of red lace that supposedly passed for panties and bra she had donned earlier to wear with the other dress, Mary bit the inside of her cheek. "Just underwear."

"That'll do. Turn around and I'll unzip you." She complied and he had the zipper down in two seconds flat. She knew, because she'd been holding her breath the entire time. She wasn't sure if Dan's skill made her feel better or worse.

"Step out of your dress," he directed, nibbling the back of her neck, making the hairs stand on end. "I want to see all of you."

"Are you sure?" God, she was dreading this part. "Because, well, I'm not a supermodel or anything." Just your average cellulite-ridden woman, she wanted to add.

"Let me be the judge of that, okay?"

Taking another huge gulp of air, she stepped out of the dress and tossed it on a nearby chair. She heard Dan's sharp intake of breath, saw his eyes darken as he stared at her almost naked body, which made her feel a teensy bit better. He hadn't thrown up or anything. And wasn't she glad now that she'd ditched those white cotton briefs? She sincerely doubted they would have elicited the same reaction.

"You've got a great body."

Thank you, Wonderbra!

She wanted to cross her arms over her chest so badly it hurt, but she just stood there and allowed him to look his fill. "Now it's your turn," she said.

Grinning, and not showing the slightest bit of shyness or reticence—what was it about men that made them want to strip at the drop of a hat?—he removed his shirt and pants, leaving on only his briefs. And, boy, were they brief! Mary hadn't seen many men in their underwear—her father and brother wore boxers, but that didn't really count.

Raising her eyes to his chest, she swallowed. Ripples of hard muscle lightly sprinkled with hair awaited her exploration, making her fingers itch. "You're . . ." She paused, unsure of how one went about telling a man he was built like a brick outhouse. She licked her lips instead, not realizing what a provocative picture she made.

"Had your fill yet?" Dan asked, stepping toward her, the passion burning in his eyes making her swallow.

She shook her head, mesmerized by the sight. "I don't think so."

"Good, because neither have I." And then he led her to the bed.

Lying side by side with her, Dan could feel Mary tense beneath his hands. She was nervous, her eyes shut tight, and he wanted to reassure her that their coming together was right. Gently, he caressed her, gliding his hands down her arms, back, and thighs. "Relax. You're beautiful. I want to touch you. You're so soft, so incredibly perfect."

He toyed with the edge of her panties, making her stomach contract, then eased his hand beneath the fabric to cup her mound.

"Oh, my!" Mary's eyes flew open, then fluttered closed once again.

Capturing her soft sounds of pleasure with his mouth, his tongue mimicked the movement of his finger, creating an urgency she hadn't thought possible.

She knew the moment her panties were gone, then he released the clasp of her bra and removed that, too. Gazing down at her breasts, he teased her nipples with his tongue. "I'm developing a taste for Italian," he murmured, and heat consumed her entire body.

At the delicious sensations he was creating, Mary sought to keep herself from flying off the bed by gripping the sheets and trying to anchor herself.

"Relax, sweet Mary," he crooned again. "The ride's not over yet." He moved lower, trailing blistering hot kisses down her stomach, the inside of her thighs, until she wanted to scream out her frustration. When his tongue searched out *the* place, she couldn't hold back any longer, releasing a deep wanton sound of pleasure.

"Do you like this?"

"Yes, yes! Don't stop. Whatever you do, don't stop!" She thought she heard him chuckle, then his tongue delved deep inside, and she didn't hear anything more than her pounding heart echoing in her ears.

"Please! You're killing me." But what a way to die. Even better than chocolate!

Removing his underwear, Dan reached into the drawer of the bedside table for a condom and sheathed himself, then moved between her legs.

He kissed her again, slow and languorously, and the apprehension she felt was suddenly replaced by hunger, by an all-consuming need to have him deep inside her.

With one hard, powerful thrust, he entered, breaking through the barrier of her virginity, and she shut her eyes against the brief moment of pain.

Dan stopped, looked at her questioningly, then shook his head, his voice filling with concern. "Why didn't you tell me? God help me, but I can't stop now."

"I don't want you to stop." She moved her hips, urging him on, and he slid deeper, going slower this time, allowing her body to accommodate to his. Sweat beaded his forehead and upper lip as the effort to restrain himself took its toll. He was trying to be gentle, to spare her further discomfort, and joy replaced pain.

Her discomfort soon receded, and Mary was filled with a wonderment she had only dreamed about. His movements grew more frantic, and she met him stroke for stroke, eager to discover what the mystery was all about.

The tension built with every powerful thrust, mounting to a crescendo. She cried out, slipping over the edge and into a place she'd never known existed. Dan followed, reaching his climax soon after.

Breathing deeply, their sweat-slicked bodies locked together as one, they journeyed back to find the world hadn't really spun off its axis.

"You were wonderful!" Dan kissed Mary's brow, hugging her close. "But you should have told me you were a virgin. I would have handled things a bit differently had I known."

She smiled softly, kissing his chin. "I think you *handled* things just fine. And I was embarrassed to admit that at my age I still hadn't had sex. I didn't want you to think I was abnormal or anything."

Strands of damp hair clung to her face, and he pushed them away, knowing in that moment that he loved her. Loved her naïveté and honesty, her self-deprecating humor, the way she nibbled her lower lip when she was nervous and laughed from deep within her soul when she was happy.

He loved her. Every glorious inch of her.

"Being a virgin is . . . was . . . nothing to be ashamed of. I'm glad I was the first."

"You are?" she asked, surprised by the admission.

"It probably sounds sexist or macho to say so, but I think most men, whether or not they admit it, like knowing they were first. It's kind of that explorer/conqueror thing. It reverts back to 'Me, Tarzan, you, Jane.' "

"My mother said as much, but who knew she was right?" Her stomach growled just then, prompting her face to turn beet red, and Dan grinned. So much for alluring and sexy, Mary thought.

"Sounds like you're hungry."

"Sort of. I didn't have time to eat at the party. I was too busy supervising, and talking to people."

"Let's go downstairs, and I'll fix us something to eat." He made to rise, but she reached for his arm and pulled him back down.

"I was kinda hoping we could do this again. I'm just starting to get the hang of it."

Dan laughed and wrapped his arms about her, giving Mary what could only be described as a teddy-bear hug. "Do you know how absolutely adorable and kissable you are?" He kissed her just to make certain she did. "Of course we're going to do this again. Lots of times, if I have my way. But first, we're going to eat.

"I make a mean pepper-and-egg frittata, if I say so myself,

and it will give you the energy you need . . . for later." Her cheeks filled with color. "Besides, if we made love again right now, you'd be too sore to enjoy it."

Mary considered what he said, then replied, "Do you fry your peppers in extra virgin olive oil?" Her stomach grumbled again.

"Of course," he replied with a naughty grin. "I told you— I'm quite partial to virgins."

True to his word, she and Dan made love many more times during the night. And as predicted, Mary was starting to feel the effects of all that lovemaking. She was sated, but sore.

Gazing at his sleeping profile, she heaved a deep, contented sigh, admitting to herself that she'd done the one thing she'd promised herself she would never do: She'd fallen in love with Dan Gallagher. As hard as she'd tried to keep her heart out of the equation, she'd been unable to resist his tenderness, innate goodness, and heart-wrenching vulnerability. Not to mention that sexy smile!

She'd wanted to have an uncomplicated affair, put some "zing" into her life. She'd never counted on falling head-over-heels in love. "Damn!" she mouthed silently, and a single tear rolled down her cheek.

Well, it was just too bad if she was in love, she decided, because that didn't change anything. She had no intention of marrying him. He would ask more than she was willing to give—her business, her newfound identity as an independent woman.

Not that he was asking! Not that he'd made any declarations concerning how he felt about her!

Staring up at the ceiling fan whirring softly overhead, she wondered if she was now going to be damned to hell for surrendering herself before marriage, for committing a mortal sin. It seemed a likely possibility.

A little late to be thinking of that now. And a little late to be feeling guilty.

For a Catholic, guilt was inbred. For an Italian, it was a way of life. How could she not feel guilty?

Her eternal soul was in jeopardy of going up in flames, but she sure as hell wasn't going to confess this little transgression to Joe, even though she'd be unable to receive the sacraments again until she did. But Mary was fairly certain that reciting a few Hail Marys wasn't going to fix things this time.

Even with the danger of eternal damnation looming over her head, because she was unmarried and had engaged in illicit but delicious sex with someone who was not her husband— the Catholic church frowned on that sort of thing—she was not going to get married.

Not that he's asking!

"The trouble with you, Mary," Sophia would say, *"is that you're always asking for things you don't want. There's a lid for every pot and someday you're going to find one that fits."*

Yeah, it fit, all right. That lid fit so well it nearly made her pot boil right over.

But, she reminded herself, she could still cook without it, and that's just what she intended to do.

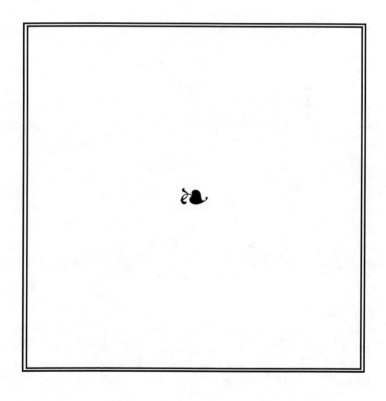

Chocolate Brownies

Chocolate Brownies

2 cups all-purpose flour
3 eggs
1 cup butter, softened
2 cups brown sugar, firmly packed
2 tsp. vanilla
1 ½ tsp. baking powder
½ tsp. salt
3 1-oz. squares unsweetened chocolate
1 cup chopped pecans or walnuts

Chocolate Frosting

¼ cup butter, melted
1 oz. unsweetened chocolate
1 ½ tsp. vanilla
2 cups confectioners' sugar
2–3 tbsp. milk

Preheat oven to 350°. Combine flour, baking powder, and salt. Set aside. In large bowl, combine butter, brown sugar, and vanilla extract. Add eggs. Melt squares of chocolate over low heat, cool, and add to mixture. Beating well, add flour mixture. Stir in chopped nuts. Spread batter into greased and floured 13 × 9 × 2–inch baking dish. Bake at 350° for 30 minutes. Cool on wire rack.

To prepare frosting: Melt 1 oz. square of chocolate over low heat. Melt butter, and combine with chocolate. Add vanilla. Mix well. Alternately blend milk with confectioners' sugar. Beat until smooth. Frost cooled brownies. Cut into squares. Makes 24 2-inch squares.

CHAPTER FIFTEEN

Dan awoke with a satisfied smile on his face, stretching his arms wide, only to find the woman he'd intended to embrace nowhere in sight. He glanced toward the chair where Mary had left her dress the night before, searched the bedclothes and floor for her underwear, but found nothing.

No shoes. No purse. No Mary.

Jumping out of bed, he grabbed his white terry-cloth robe from behind the bathroom door, knotted the belt, and hurried downstairs. Maybe she'd decided to make breakfast for him. A surprise of sorts.

He entered the kitchen. *Surprise! No Mary here, either.* "Well, hell!" he cursed, heading for the coffeepot. The automatic maker had brewed his special French roast; it was waiting for him, hot and chocked full of caffeine, just the way he liked it. He needed it now more than ever.

Filling a ceramic mug that read: START YOUR DAY WITH SUNSHINE: READ *THE BALTIMORE SUN*, he leaned against the counter and thought about last night. They'd been great together. Making love with Mary had been magic. He hadn't felt so all-powerful since he'd been a randy youth of eighteen.

I could climb Mount Everest barefooted, leap tall buildings in a single bound, prepare a Grand Marnier soufflé, and have it rise.

Love did that to a person, he thought. It made them feel invincible. From the moment he realized he loved Mary, the world had become a better place: The sun shone brighter, flowers smelled sweeter, and even the air seemed less polluted.

But what was he going to do with that love? Mary didn't want a committed relationship. She wanted her freedom, her business, her routine. She had no room in her life for a husband.

Bam! The thought hit him upside the head. *Husband!* Where had that come from?

Husband. Mary's husband. Mrs. Mary Gallagher. Mrs. Daniel Gallagher. Admittedly, it had a nice ring to it.

But was that what he really wanted? To open himself up to that kind of pain again? When he'd married Sharon he'd thought it would be forever; they were so much in love. But then things between them had disintegrated.

Would the same thing happen with Mary? Would his feelings for her, his love, die a slow, agonizing death?

Two career women in one lifetime? He didn't think so.

And yet . . .

Even if he decided that's what he wanted, Mary didn't want or need a husband. And he had no idea if she felt the same way about him. But she had allowed him to make love to her. And after waiting to make love for thirty-three years . . . well, that was saying something.

He paced the kitchen, trying to figure out what to do. The sun was streaming in through the window, people were hurrying to get to church, tourists were snapping photos. Life seemed normal. But it wasn't. Not anymore.

Mary Russo had entered his life, his heart, and nothing was ever going to be the same again.

He knew that just as surely as he knew that if he proposed anything less than marriage to Mary, he'd have the entire Russo clan down on his head. Uncle Alfredo might even pay him a visit, which probably wouldn't be half as bad as having to deal with Sophia. He'd much rather take his chances with the Mafia.

"Well, hell!" There was only one thing to do when you

didn't know what to do: Go back to bed. Which was exactly what Dan did.

Returning to her apartment, Mary let herself inside and disarmed the security device her landlady had installed. Her emotions were in turmoil, and all she could think about was a nice hot bath, a cold glass of milk, and about a dozen chocolate-frosted brownies. Chocolate had a way of putting everything into perspective.

Kicking off her heels, she headed toward the bedroom, and noticed her answering machine blinking furiously. The readout indicated three messages.

"Dan," she whispered, totally mesmerized by the little red light. Her stomach got all jumpy and her pulse started skittering. She loved him, but she didn't want to talk to him right now. She felt too vulnerable, too unsure of her emotions, and she might agree to just about anything he suggested, including giving up her restaurant and bearing sixteen of his children!

Chiding her foolishness, she pressed the button and the first voice she heard was Annie's. Breathing a sigh of relief, she listened. *"Hey, kiddo! So how was it? I'm assuming you and Dan did the dirty last night. Call me. I want all the pornographic details."* Mary couldn't help smiling. You just had to love Annie. She was so darn consistent.

"Mary!" Her mother's voice came blaring out, and Mary's smile quickly disappeared. *"Where are you? I called last night. You weren't in. It's nine o'clock in the morning. You should be home, not out gallivanting around town like a gypsy. Call me as soon as you get in. We've got trouble."* A pause, then as an afterthought. *"No deaths. The boy is fine."*

Well, isn't that encouraging? Mary thought.

After her mother's delightful communication, she hardly had the stamina to listen to the final message, but she braced herself, hoping it was good news instead of bad. No such luck.

"Hey, peanut, it's Joe. Look, there's something I need to

talk to you about. I've been doing some thinking, quite a lot of it, actually, and I'm . . . I'm thinking about leaving the church. Call me. And don't say anything to anyone just yet. Especially Mom."

"Holy shit!" Mary picked up the portable phone and headed into the bathroom.

She needed chocolate. Lots of chocolate. A dozen brownies would not be enough!

"Grandma Flora got arrested, and I got to ride in a squad car and go to the police station, just like in the movies. It was so cool!"

Matthew's face flushed with excitement as he regaled Mary with all the details. She smiled and stepped farther into the entry hall of her mother's house, shutting the door behind her. Dan had turned off the phone last night, or else they would have heard from the police directly. She was glad they hadn't.

"She got busted for shoplifting," he added, clearly impressed that he'd been an unwitting accomplice to Grandma Flora's crime.

Mary's gaze lifted from the child to her mother, who was now standing behind him, looking furious and embarrassed all at once. Sophia's mood had apparently not improved since their earlier telephone conversation, where she'd insisted, citing the probability of her immediate demise, that Mary drop everything and come right over.

"Well, Matt, it sounds as if you had a very interesting evening after you left the party," Mary said, trying to make light of the matter, though she doubted Dan was going to think it was too amusing that his son had been involved in a police matter. She dreaded having to tell him.

"Flora and the boy left the party early and walked to the drugstore," her mother explained. "I thought she wanted to refill her blood pressure medication, so I didn't think anything about it. But she didn't go for the medicine. The crazy old woman went to get Matthew a present. She shoplifted a water pistol. There was a cop in the store, and he caught her red-handed." Sophia looked toward the heavens and said a few choice epithets in Italian.

Grandma Flora's timing had never been great, Mary thought.

"It was so cool!" Matt's eyes and face lit up like a Christmas tree. "I've never seen a cop that close-up before. He had a gun, badge, and everything. 'Course, I didn't get to keep the water gun. I think it was impounded as evidence."

Too much *NYPD Blue*, Mary decided, ruffling the boy's hair. At least Matt didn't seem any the worse for the experience. "Where's *Nonna* now?" she asked her mother. "Is she all right?"

"Your grandmother's asleep. And she's the only person in this house who got any sleep after last night's escapade, I can tell you that. It was humiliating. I still get light-headed when I think about it. The police brought them home in a squad car." She threw her hands up in the air. "Now the whole neighborhood will know I'm harboring a criminal. *Madonna mia, disgrazia.* It's a disgrace."

After instructing Matt to go into the living room, where he could watch TV and not overhear their conversation, Mary followed her mother into the kitchen, taking a seat at the table. "I hardly think Grandma Flora is a criminal, Ma. She's an old woman who happens to think stealing isn't a crime. I doubt very much that Mr. Moressi is going to press charges. He knows what she's like. And it's not a good idea to say such things in front of Matt. He's very fond of Grandma."

"Moressi didn't press charges. But that's beside the point. I won't be able to hold my head up in this neighborhood any longer. Nina Santini will have a field day, especially now that you broke her son's heart. I told your father we would have to move."

Frank often talked about being buried in his backyard, he loved his house so much, so Mary thought it was highly unlikely that he had agreed with Sophia's histrionics. And Lou was dating a woman who worked at the dry cleaners, so he was definitely not pining over her.

"Where's Pa now?"

"Down at the police department. He plays bocci with one of the officers and thought he could have his mother's record expunged, whatever the hell that means."

Mary didn't think that would be necessary since charges weren't pressed. Grandma Flora had escaped the stigma of being Public Enemy Number One.

"I think you'd better forget about moving. Pa's never going to agree to that."

Shrugging her shoulders in defeat, her mother filled two cups with hot coffee, passing Mary one. "I know. That's why I told Frank he's going to have to commit Flora to a mental institution. She's nuts. We can't have her going around stealing. Besides, how would it look to the family? It's not normal behavior."

And pretending to be connected to a major crime family is?

Mary held her tongue. Sophia was very fond of her brother, much fonder than she was of her mother-in-law, glowing anniversary tribute or not.

"Grandma Flora is harmless. Just leave her be, Ma. You worry too much about what other people think."

"And you don't worry enough." Sophia scrutinized her daughter's face, looking for any telltale sign that she'd been corrupted. When she failed to find any evidence, she added, "You never mentioned where you were last night and this morning, Mary. I was starting to worry when I couldn't reach you."

The umbilical cord may have been cut thirty-three years ago, but the phone line was still very much attached. Ever since she'd moved into her own apartment, her mother called at least once a day, usually five times. She never had any specific reason for calling, she just wanted to know what Mary was doing, if she'd eaten breakfast, washed the dishes, brushed her teeth. That was fine before Mary had started dating Dan. Now she needed privacy.

Sipping her coffee, Mary pondered the possibility of telling her mother that she and Dan had spent the night together. Then she decided against it. Mary wasn't up to one of her mother's cow lectures, and Sophia might very well drop dead of shock when she discovered Mary had been dispensing milk like a dairy farmer.

"I went to the produce market this morning," she lied, hoping Sophia wouldn't ask about last night again and hoping that God wasn't listening. It really wasn't wise to pile venial sins upon mortal ones.

"On a Sunday? I didn't think they were open."

"I arranged ahead of time to meet with a few of my suppliers. I was pretty low on produce after your party." That, at least, was the truth.

Sophia glanced up at the vintage 1950's coffee-cup-shaped clock on the wall and slapped her forehead. "*Dio mio!* Your grandmother has me so upset I don't know where my head is. I almost forgot about mass. Father Joseph will be worried if I don't show up."

Mary had tried calling Joe, but she hadn't been able to reach him. She had no idea what his immediate plans were.

Relieved that her mother had something else to occupy her mind at the moment, she watched Sophia rise from the chair and hurry out of the room to get ready for church. Mass was just what the woman needed this morning to calm her down, providing Joe would be there to perform it. After the cryptic message he'd left on her machine, Mary couldn't be certain.

Gazing into the depths of her coffee and inhaling deeply of the strong aroma, she wondered what had prompted Joe's phone call. Something terrible must have happened for him to be thinking about leaving the church. And then she remembered his argument with Annie.

Alarm bells suddenly went off!

There could be only one reason Joe would consider leaving the church: He was still in love with Annie.

Good grief! She'd always suspected as much, but to think it might actually be true . . .

Mary didn't want to be around when her mother discovered the news. It was bad enough that Sophia's mother-in-law shoplifted, that her unmarried daughter was having an illicit affair and would likely burn in hell. Those were matters she could live with. She wouldn't like them, but she could deal with them.

But her only son, her precious Father Joseph, leaving the church? And for Annie Goldman? That was something Sophia could never countenance, would never understand. Not in a million years.

Sophia was going to go ballistic when that revelation came to light, and Mary didn't intend to be caught dead in the cross fire.

Dan strolled into his office, whistling an oldie but goody, and feeling on top of the world. Someone could make a fortune off his euphoria, if they could just figure out a way to bottle it.

"Morning, Linda." He paused before her desk, smiling widely.

"You're looking pleased with yourself this morning, Mr. Gallagher," his secretary commented, giving him the once-over. "You're not usually so jovial on a Monday morning."

He didn't usually have such a great Saturday night, Dan wanted to say, but didn't. "You're looking very nice yourself this morning. Is that a new sweater? Blue looks good on you. You should wear it more often. It brings out the color of your eyes."

Blushing, Linda nearly fell off her chair and had to reach for the edge of her desk to right herself. "Th—thank you! Yes, it's new. How nice of you to notice." And how very odd, her expression said.

"So, what's on the agenda? Any appointments I should know about before I tackle this week's feature: Pork butts we have known and loved?" Damn, but he was sick of editing the Food section. He couldn't wait for Rosemary to return, so he could get back to his old job. Pork butts didn't hold a candle to pigskin. Not by a long shot.

Despite the shock at her boss's unusual behavior, Linda couldn't help smiling. "I believe we decided on: 'Go Hog Wild with Pork.'"

"Right! Were we drunk when we came up with that idea? I forget."

"No, but I think you'd reached your maximum pork capacity that day."

Perching himself on the edge of his secretary's desk, Dan grew serious. "Are you still enjoying your job, Linda? Feeling challenged and useful? Because I want you to know, I appreciate all the help you've given me these past few months. I couldn't have managed that beef contest without you." A woman from Bethesda had won with her meatball stroganoff recipe. Dan had to admit it wasn't half-bad . . . for ground beef.

"Yes, I love it! And I appreciate your allowing me to contribute more to the section."

"That being the case, how would you like to write the pork feature this week? I've got a review to write that's going to be a challenge—what can one say about Mongolian food that hasn't been said before?—and I think it'll take most of the morning to write up."

Her eyes sparkled, her face glowing with excitement. "Thank you again, Mr. Gallagher! I can't believe you would place that much trust in me."

"You're undervalued here, Linda. I intend to talk to Walt— Mr. Beyerly about getting you a promotion before Rosemary comes back from maternity leave." It was something he'd been thinking about for some time. Linda's talents were being wasted as Rosemary's assistant.

"A promotion?" Linda's hand went to her throat, and she stared speechless at him. Dan feared she would burst into tears at any moment.

"Whoa! I'm not saying he'll do it, but I intend to try. And I will be editing your article, so be prepared to take constructive criticism." Editing someone else: the revenge of every writer.

"I will. And thank you! I don't know what you had for breakfast this morning, but I hope you get a daily dose of it from now on."

Chuckling, he replied, "Me, too!"

Entering his office, Dan kicked the door closed behind him. As soon as he reached his desk, he picked up the phone and dialed Mary's number while easing out of his sports coat.

She had left a message on his answering machine about Matt and her grandmother's police escapade. His son had filled him in on the rest when he'd picked him up at the Russos', and Dan didn't think he was any the worse for the experience. In fact, the kid had been so excited and enthusiastic after meeting Baltimore's finest, all he could talk about was becoming a policeman.

Dan couldn't wait to hear Mary's voice again. He missed her. But he'd purposely waited until this morning to return her call, because he hadn't wanted her to think that he was pressuring her in any way.

When she answered, the sound of her voice made his heart start to thump. "Hi! Glad I caught you before you left for the restaurant."

"It's only nine o'clock, Dan." There was amusement in her voice, and something else—happiness, maybe? "And it's Monday. I'm off on Monday, remember? Besides, I never go downstairs this early. Marco's still in his creative mode and hates it when I interfere."

"I miss you."

Her voice softened. "I miss you, too. Saturday night was very special to me."

"To me, too. So why did you leave before I woke up? It ruined my whole day." He and Matt had spent Sunday watching one televised ball game after another, but he hadn't been able to concentrate. And that wasn't like him, not when the Orioles were playing.

She was smiling, he was sure of it. "I thought if I didn't leave then, I'd spend the rest of the day in bed with you, and that just wouldn't have been a good idea."

"Says who?"

"Says me. Why don't you come over later? I'll fix us some lunch."

"Something Italian, no doubt." The only thing Italian he wanted was her.

"Seems to me I remember you saying you liked Italian. Or were you just caught up in the moment?"

Remembering what he'd been doing at the time he'd made the comment, he swallowed. "Are you naked in bed at this very moment? I need to form a mental picture while we're talking."

She laughed. "I don't want to encourage your voyeuristic tendencies, but no, I'm not naked. But I am wearing this positively indecent see-through black negligee."

"I don't suppose you'll have it on when I arrive for lunch?"

"Don't suppose I will."

"Damn! Foiled again."

"But I might consider donning that red dress you were asking me about."

"The one with the slits?" More than his interest was piqued, and he shifted in his seat, the Mongolian review forgotten for the time being.

"The very one."

"Can we eat lunch early, say around ten?"

His eagerness amused her, and she laughed again. The sexy sound had him reaching for his handkerchief to mop his sweating forehead.

"Well, maybe not lunch. But I think we can manage an appetizer."

Dan stiffened like a petrified tree trunk and glanced at his watch. "I'll be there in thirty minutes."

"And here I thought you were anxious to see me."

Mary hung up, and Dan shot from his chair, holding his briefcase in front of him as he bolted out the door.

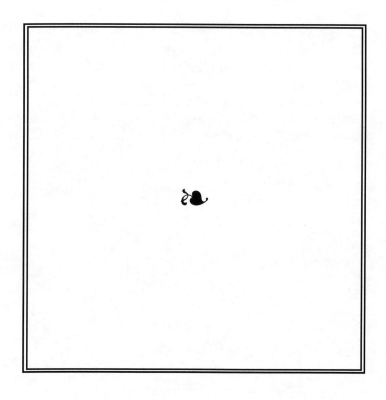

Baked Apricot Brie

1 6–8 oz. round of brie cheese
1 small jar apricot jam
sliced almonds or chopped pecans

Place brie cheese in an oven-proof dish and bake in a 350° oven for approximately 20 minutes, until softened. Remove from oven and frost with a small jar of apricot preserves, covering the entire top. Sprinkle with sliced almonds or chopped pecans. Return to oven and heat until warm.

Place on serving dish and garnish perimeter with slices of fresh or canned apricots. Serve with small pieces of Italian bread or French baguette.

CHAPTER SIXTEEN

"So how did your date with Dan go? Was he fabulous in bed? I want to hear all the sordid details, and don't leave anything out."

One thing about Annie, Mary thought, she always cut to the chase. Refilling their wineglasses with a full-bodied Bordeaux, she leaned back against the sofa, debating how much she should confide to her best friend.

"He was wonderful." She couldn't keep the happiness out of her voice. "Considerate, romantic, very sensitive to my needs. Both times."

"Both times!" Annie's eyes widened. "You mean you've been with Dan twice?"

Mary's grin was downright naughty. "We spent most of yesterday in bed, making love." The memory brought a soft blush to her cheeks.

Annie whistled, clearly impressed. "Well, I must say you surprise me, *cara*. After your thirty-three-year sex drought, you're sure making up for it in a hurry."

Reaching toward the plate of baked brie resting on the coffee table, Mary slathered a few pieces of Italian bread with the cheese/apricot mixture, and popped one in her mouth. "Sometimes I astound even myself."

Annie grinned. "Well, this certainly is reason to celebrate." She raised her glass in a toast. "I'm proud of you, *cara*. You're finally taking some risks, not playing it safe. That's good."

"Is it?" Mary sipped thoughtfully on her wine. "I hope

you're right." Because falling in love with Dan hadn't been in the original equation, and she feared one of them was going to get hurt.

"Of course I am. Dan's a great guy. And he's nuts about you."

A wistful sigh escaped her lips. "Dan's wonderful, there's no denying that. I'm just worried that we're not on the same wavelength about our relationship."

"What do you mean?"

"He's invited me to meet his mother. We're driving to Gaithersburg tomorrow." The three of them: she, Dan, and Matt. Just like a family. When he'd mentioned yesterday that Matt had the day off from school and wanted to see his grandmother, and asked if she would go along, she didn't have the heart to tell him no. But she was terrified at the prospect of what it could mean.

"Well, that sounds only fair, since it's my understanding that your mother's invited you and Dan over for dinner on Sunday." Annie's brow arched, and she couldn't help smiling at Mary's less-than-enthusiastic expression. "Has Sophia decided to welcome him into the family with open arms?"

"It was Pa's idea. He likes Dan. I tried to explain to him that we're not serious, but he's insisting that Dan and Matt come over and meet the rest of the family. Ma was not overly pleased." Neither was Mary, who already dreaded the ordeal. Dan, on the other hand, had been thrilled with the invitation. Go figure. The man was a glutton for punishment.

"Your relationship sounds serious, *cara*. I mean, if he's asking you to meet his mother, and you're parading him in front of the entire Russo clan . . ."

"Just because Dan and I are having an affair does not mean we intend to get married. I made my feelings on that subject very clear before going to bed with him."

Sipping her wine, Annie stared thoughtfully at her friend, her frown deepening. "First of all, Mary *mia*, one or two bouts of lovemaking does not constitute an affair. You have to do *it* a few more times to qualify for that status.

"And just because you made your feelings clear, does not mean you're not lying to yourself. You're in love with Dan Gallagher. I hear it in your voice every time you mention his name. Why deny it? Besides, Dan's a great guy. If you love him, you should marry him."

Annie was too perceptive for her own good. But then, she always had been, except when it came to her own relationships with men. "Okay, so I love Dan. So what? That doesn't mean a marriage between us would work. He thinks women belong in the home, and I don't want to become a carbon copy of my mother.

"I've worked hard to achieve my independence. I just can't see myself giving it up." And there were other factors she didn't want to get into with Annie, like Dan's aversion to religion, and the fact that he'd never once told her he loved her. And there was that pesky little detail—he'd never even come close to proposing.

Not that she wanted him to, she reminded herself.

Obviously, she was just a temporary amusement for Dan. So why not just enjoy their time together? It was what she wanted—no strings, no permanence. So why, then, did it hurt that he hadn't confessed any passionate feelings for her?

"Being independent's not all it's cracked up to be, *cara.* Trust me, I know what I'm talking about."

"That's because you've always had your independence, Annie. You've always known your own mind, did what you wanted. You're brave. You took risks. You didn't spend your life hiding from life, like I did. I'm just now starting to spread my wings, to get a sense of who I am, and to experience what you've taken for granted all these years."

"Cara," Annie said, patting her friend's hand, her brows pulled together in concern. "Your uniqueness is what makes you special. And the sum total of your life's experiences have made you who you are. Celebrate that, don't try to change it.

You could no more be like me than I could be like you. That's why we get along so well."

"But you were the one who encouraged me to 'go out and get laid,' I think is how you put it."

"It was time you lost your virginity, Mary. Cherries look good on trees and on top of ice cream sundaes, not on thirty-three-year-old women. And now that you've conquered your fear of intimacy—"

Mary's eyes widened. "Who says I have? Just because I'm no longer a virgin doesn't mean I'm ready to get married and risk failing at a lifelong committed relationship." She shook her head. "The idea terrifies me. I'm just not ready."

Annie sighed. "Life's a risk, Mary *mia*. There are no guarantees."

Mary knew Annie was right. That, however, was not reason enough for her to alter her thinking on the subject.

Lenore Gallagher was waiting on the front porch when Dan pulled into the driveway that Wednesday afternoon. The red-haired woman was dressed in navy slacks and a red sweater, waving and smiling at them, obviously excited at the prospect of seeing her son and grandson.

Mary wished she shared some of Mrs. Gallagher's enthusiasm. But she was nervous at the prospect of meeting Dan's mother.

"Grandma!" Matt yelled out the open window. "Where's Spanky?"

Suddenly a little black-and-white dog began barking furiously, jumping up and down like a circus dog, and Dan looked over at Mary and smiled. "Spanky's my mom's Boston terrier," he explained. "I got her the dog about three years ago, so she wouldn't be quite so lonely living here by herself."

"That was thoughtful of you."

He looked chagrined. "Yeah, well, the dog helps salve my

guilty conscience because I don't visit Mom as often as I should."

Once inside, Mrs. Gallagher enveloped Mary in a friendly embrace. "Dan's told me so much about you. I feel like I already know you. Come in and make yourself at home."

Dan had discussed her with his mother?

"Your house is lovely," she told the woman, surprised to find she liked Dan's mother. From the little he'd told her about his mother, Mary was expecting someone cold and aloof. But this woman with her kind eyes and warm smile was as friendly and welcoming as any of the Russo relatives.

"The house is old and needs remodeling, kind of like its owner." She laughed, displaying two dimples exactly like her son's. "But I don't want to spend the money. I keep thinking I'll move one of these days."

Wrapping his arms about his mom, Dan kissed her cheek. "You've aged like fine wine, Mom. You're still a beautiful woman."

"I hope you know Irishmen are fully of blarney, Mary," Dan's mother said, patting her son's cheek affectionately. "But we women love it, don't we?"

Apparently any problems the two might have had at one time were a thing of the past, and Mary felt relieved at the discovery. Knowing how unhappy Dan's childhood had been, she hadn't been sure what to expect between Dan and his mom.

"Come to Baltimore and live with us, Grandma," Matt said, hugging his grandmother around the waist. "It's not so bad once you get used to it. And I can introduce you to Mary's grandma. Grandma Flora's neat. She's got a criminal record."

Blushing to the tips of her toes, Mary darted Dan a threatening look when he began to chuckle.

Lenore smiled in amusement and ruffled the child's hair. "As tempting as that sounds, Matty, your father needs his privacy, and so do I. I've gotten used to living alone. Spanky and I do all right by ourselves. And I've been staying active, working at the church part-time, participating in my weekly book club."

Obviously Dan's mother didn't share her son's aversion to organized religion. "Do you belong to the Catholic church?" Mary asked once they were seated in the living room.

It was a pleasant room, with two overstuffed chairs, a large square coffee table laden with magazines and candles, and a comfortable sofa covered in a green-and-white-checked fabric. The house looked lived in, and Mary found that appealing.

Handing Mary a china cup filled with coffee, Mrs. Gallagher nodded. "Yes. My religion is very important to me. I only wish my stubborn son felt the same way."

Having had this conversation a time or two, Dan wasn't bothered by his mother's comments. He leaned back against the sofa, crossed his legs, and drummed his fingers on his shoe. "The church wasn't there for me . . . for us . . . when we needed it, Mom. I'd feel like a hypocrite embracing its doctrines now."

Lenore Gallagher heaved a dispirited sigh. "Your father's death was a long time ago, Daniel. You shouldn't blame God for taking Drew away. And maybe the congregation wasn't as supportive as it could have been. But we weren't attending mass regularly back then, so we shouldn't have expected more than we were willing to give.

"You really need to change your way of thinking, son. Your soul needs to be fed the same as your stomach."

He shrugged. "Too much pomp and circumstance, if you ask me. Too many rules and not enough compassion."

Annie had said something similar to Joe once, Mary recalled, during one of their heated arguments.

"What about you, Mary?" Dan's mother asked, clearly disappointed that her son hadn't come around to her way of thinking. "Do you attend church?"

Mary's gaze drifted between son and mother. No way was she getting into the middle of what appeared to be a long-standing disagreement. "Even though my brother's a priest,

I confess I don't attend mass every Sunday, Mrs. Gallagher. But religion has always been an important part of my life, and that of my family's."

The older woman nodded, seemingly pleased with the answer, while Dan appeared thoughtful, as if something he hadn't considered before had just occurred to him.

"Well, if you'll excuse me, I need to go check on dinner. I've made a traditional Italian meal in your honor, Mary."

Dan gasped, his face draining of all color. "Mom! I thought we agreed to grill hamburgers."

"I know we did, dear, but I just thought it would be nice if Mary sampled some of my cooking. And since she's Italian—"

"That's so nice of you, Mrs. Gallagher," Mary said quickly before Dan had a chance to say something rude that might hurt his mother's feelings. "I can never get enough of Italian food. It's my favorite, as you may have guessed."

"I was hoping," she said sweetly, before disappearing into the kitchen.

"Are you crazy, encouraging her like that?" Dan said in a low voice. "I didn't bring my Rolaids. And now we're going to eat my mom's Italian cooking?" He looked visibly ill. "I feel nauseous just thinking about it." He clutched his stomach dramatically.

"This is not the time to be a restaurant critic, Daniel Gallagher. I'm sure your mother has worked very hard to prepare a nice dinner for us. And even if it tastes like shoe leather, or worse, we'll just eat it anyway, and tell her it's wonderful. That's the polite thing to do."

"When did you get so sweet?" He pulled her into his arms and kissed her, leaving Mary slightly breathless and completely flustered.

"It's a good thing your son's outside with the dog and your mom's in the kitchen, because you shouldn't be kissing me like that in front of your family. It isn't right."

He looked around. "No one's here."

"You know what I mean. They might get the wrong idea."

His grin was teasing. "Oh, you mean they might think we've been together in the biblical sense? Well, that would fit in nicely with all this talk of religion, don't you think?"

"Shame on you! My mother would accuse you of blasphemy if she heard you say that." And then she'd drag out her rosary beads. No one could recite the rosary faster than Sophia Russo when she was in atonement mode.

"And what would be my penance?"

Mary thought for a moment. "Confession, definitely. And at least twenty-five Hail Marys. Maybe more."

Dan began to recite his own version of the prayer. "Pretty, Mary, fair of face, there's lust inside me . . ." He nibbled her lower lip. "Blessed are the fruits," he palmed her breasts, making her squeal in disapproval, "of thy sweet body."

"Stop it!" She slapped at his hands, making him laugh. "You're behaving very badly. Your mother could walk in at any moment."

"So? We're both consenting adults."

"That reasoning didn't exactly wash with my mother, if you recall," she reminded him, thinking back to the night Sophia had accused Dan of being a rapist. "And if you behave this outrageously on Sunday, you'll have the entire Russo and Graziano families on your back." A horrifying thought at best.

With a wink and a grin, he replied, "As long as it's you on my front, babe, I think I can handle it."

"Your friend Mary is nice, Dan. I like her very much." Lenore wiped perspiration off her forehead with the edge of her apron. "She seems to have a good head on her shoulders. She's settled, not flighty, like the other one."

Since his divorce Dan's mom always referred to Sharon as "the other one" or "the tramp," which pretty much summed up her feelings on his ex-wife. Though she was careful never to speak disparagingly of her in front of Matt.

"I'm glad you like Mary, because I do, too." He tried not

to gag as he watched the woman sprinkle cinnamon into her spaghetti sauce, then stir it in.

Wiping her hands on a paper towel, she turned to face him, a questioning look on her face. "Mary seems taken with Matt. I think she'd be good for him, don't you?"

His son had challenged Mary to a game of Scrabble, and the two were in the living room having a great time by the sound of it, laughing and giving high fives. "She's very patient. There's a real connection between them. And he's nuts about her family."

"This sounds serious," his mother said, seating herself at the kitchen table and inviting him to do the same, waiting expectantly for some type of announcement.

Dan heaved a sigh. "There's nothing definite yet. I'm not really sure how Mary feels, but I'm crazy about her."

Lenore's eyes widened. "But why aren't you sure of Mary's feelings? I've seen the way she looks at you. She looks like a woman in love to me."

"Mary doesn't want anything permanent. She's pretty caught up in making a success of her business right now."

She fiddled with the edge of the tablecloth. "I know it's none of my business, but . . . are you in love with her?"

"Yes, though I haven't told her as much. I think I'm as scared as she is about committing to a relationship. I didn't exactly make a go of the last one."

"You'll know when the time is right."

Wishing he had as much confidence as his mother, Dan reached out and clasped her hand. "I've missed you, Mom. I'm sorry I haven't visited more. I've just been busy with work, and taking custody of Matt has been a big adjustment for both of us."

She looked toward the living room, and her eyes brightened. "The boy's thriving. I can tell he likes it with you. Does he ask about . . . you know?"

"Not so much anymore. I think he's about given up on

Sharon ever coming back." Matt was finally learning to accept that his mother's leaving had not been his fault.

"I don't understand how a mother can desert her own child." Lenore shook her head. "I know we had our problems, Dan, before and after your father died, but I hope you always knew that I loved you."

Dan saw no point in dredging up any unpleasantness from the past. Like Matt, he'd learned to accept and forgive. "You've always been a good mother. Matt and I are lucky to have you, Mom."

Tears filled her eyes, and she patted his cheek. "I love you, Danny. Be happy. You deserve it."

"I'm trying, Mom. I'm really trying."

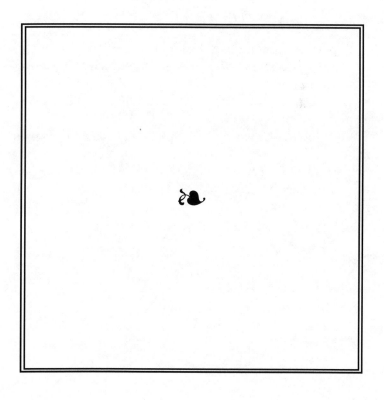

Pork Roast à la Russo

1 5–6-lb. pork tenderloin
3 garlic cloves, cut into slivers
salt and pepper to taste
2 cups apple wine, juice, or cider

Place pork in roasting pan. Insert slivers of garlic throughout roast. Season with salt and pepper. Pour apple wine over roast before putting into a 325° oven. Bake 25–30 minutes per pound. As the roast cooks, add additional apple wine to keep pork from drying out.

When the roast is cooked, remove from oven and place on platter. Make a gravy from the meat drippings/apple wine remnants, adding a small amount of flour to thicken. Use additional apple wine as necessary. Add canned or fresh sliced mushrooms to gravy.

Serve gravy over roasted pork and mashed potatoes.

CHAPTER
SEVENTEEN

In his gray felt fedora, black pin-striped suit, and dark wool overcoat draped over his shoulders, Alfredo Graziano looked every bit the made man he purported himself to be. As he waltzed into the living room of the Russos' house, he greeted everyone with a smile and a popelike wave.

In Mafia jargon, *a made man* meant someone who had killed for the mob and proven his loyalty. Mary's opinion of a made man was just a little bit different, as it pertained to her uncle. Alfredo was *made*, all right. He'd been *made* to embarrass the entire Russo clan, *made* to drive Mary nuts with his sly inferences that he was connected to the Gotti crime family, and he *made* Mary grit her teeth every time she introduced him to someone she knew.

Kissing the older man's flaccid cheek—Alfredo had never met a pasta he didn't like—she slapped on a smile. "Uncle Alfredo, I'd like you to meet my friend Dan Gallagher."

Dan stuck out his hand. "Nice to meet you. I've heard a lot about you."

A gross understatement, Mary thought, considering the many warnings she'd issued in advance about Alfredo's lack of sanity.

Did Dan actually have to look like he was enjoying himself? The man was grinning like a hyena.

Mary's uncle responded in kind, but not to shake Dan's hand. He held his out, waiting for the younger man to kiss it, to show him the proper respect. "You may call me *Don*

Alfredo," he said, the gold ring on his finger winking in the overhead light, as if finding the whole scenario as preposterous as Mary did.

If Dan had seen *The Godfather*, one, two, or three, he didn't allude to it, and merely shook the man's hand, omitting the self-imposed honor. Mary was fairly certain Mario Puzo was turning over in his grave at this very moment.

"We're sorry you missed the anniversary party, Uncle Alfredo." He wanted to be called Fredo, like in the movie, but she refused to humor him.

"There were business matters that had to be attended to. You know," he gave the five-finger shake, "when an offer is made, it cannot be refused." Marlon Brando would have been flattered. All that was missing from Alfredo's performance were marbles in his mouth.

Dan cast a sidelong glance at Mary, his eyes twinkling, and she groaned inwardly. "Did I happen to mention that Uncle Alfredo works for Lucky Louie's Auto World? He's quite the car salesman. Aren't you, Uncle?"

Purposely ignoring the question, the older man wrapped his arm about Dan's shoulders, saying in a conspiratorial whisper, "We don't tell the women everything, *capisce*?"

Before Dan could respond, Sophia appeared and took her brother's face in her hands, kissing him squarely on the mouth. There was genuine affection in her eyes. "Shame on you, Fredo, for missing my party! It's a good thing you came tonight to meet Mary's new friend. He's the one I've been telling you about."

"The Irishman?" Alfredo's eyes narrowed as he sized up the reporter again, as if seeing him for the very first time. "You want I should take him outside . . . to talk?"

Laughing, Sophia shook her head. "No. Mary's decided to keep company with Dan, so we're going to support her decision. Even though Dan's Irish, Frank thinks it's time Mary was married and settled down with children." The resigned expression she wore spoke volumes: she wasn't happy about the relationship, but she would accept it.

Heat erupted through every pore of Mary's body; her face felt like the inside of a pizza oven. There was no way she was going to look at Dan to gauge his response. She had no doubt he was as mortified as she. "Ma! Dan and I are friends. We are not 'keeping company,' as you so archaically put it. And we are not getting married. So stop! You're embarrassing me."

"What?" Her mother's wide-eyed innocence grated. "The man is here to meet your family. You like him, no? He likes you, too. What? What did I say?"

Wrapping his arm about Mary's shoulder, Dan squeezed gently and grinned. "You're absolutely right, Mrs. Russo. I like Mary very much."

Mary shot Dan a you-traitor! look.

"See?" her mother said. "The man isn't ashamed of his feelings. The trouble with Mary is that she likes to play hard to get," Sophia explained, as if she and Dan were accomplices in some grand scheme. "Sometimes that can backfire, as it did with Marc Forentini. The man was a good catch, but did my daughter want him?"

"Ma!" Having had her fill of her mother's opinions, and wishing the orange shag carpet would come to life and swallow her whole, Mary spun on her heel and stormed into the kitchen. There were pointy things in the kitchen, she thought, lots and lots of sharp objects.

"What? What did I say?" Sophia stared after her daughter, shaking her head. "I was only trying to help."

When Mary reached the safety of the kitchen, she headed straight for the pot of sauce simmering on the stove, lifted the lid, and began stirring. The aroma of oregano and basil wafted up, soothing her a bit.

Cooking helped ease her tensions, and, boy, was she ever tense. When Dan walked up behind her a few moments later and kissed the back of her neck, he created even more tension, but of a different kind.

"Your mother seems to have done a complete one-eighty. I think she likes me now," he said, sounding inordinately pleased by the turn of events, making Mary want to scream.

Why was it, she wondered, that everyone yearned for Sophia's approval? The woman went around dispensing blessings like the Pope. Even sophisticated men like Dan were not immune. "I noticed that," she said, not knowing quite what to make of it. Apparently her parents were now in cahoots to bring her and Dan together. The whole turn of events was very puzzling.

"Lucky you," she said finally.

He wrapped his arms about her waist. "You're the lucky one, Mary. Like I've said before, you've got a great family."

Eyes round as saucers, she turned to face him, setting the big wooden spoon down on the counter before she was tempted to crack him over the head with it and knock some sense into his thick skull. "How can you say that after meeting my uncle, the *Don*? And my mother—" *The Dolly Levi of Baltimore.*

"*Don* Alfredo? I like him. He's got panache. Most people don't have the guts to live out their fantasies. You gotta give him credit for that. And your mother's okay, too. Neither of them said anything that bothered me. I like colorful individuals."

"Then you're just as crazy as they are."

Dan grinned. "Crazy about you, maybe." He kissed her before she could protest, and she melted against him, surrendering to the heat of the moment.

The sauce wasn't the only thing about to boil over. Dan's emotions had gone from simmer to bubbling, and his need to confess how he felt couldn't wait a moment longer. "Mary, I—"

"Hey, what are you two lovebirds doing in the kitchen all by yourselves? As if I didn't know." Connie walked in, a smile as big as her hair, looking like a fashion model in black Versace. Her just-announced pregnancy hadn't made itself known as yet on her wafer-thin body.

Mary knew when, or if, she became pregnant she was going to look like a beached whale. Life wasn't fair.

"Ma won't like it that you've disappeared. This dinner is for your benefit."

Mary shot her sister a warning look that told Connie to shut up and mind her own business. "I'm stirring the sauce for the manicotti and keeping an eye on the pork roast."

Family dinners often included six or eight courses, starting with antipasto and working down through dessert and espresso, and could take anywhere from three to four hours to eat, if talk was held to a minimum, which it usually wasn't.

The only thing Italians liked better than eating was talking. And talk was definitely cheap. In the Russo household, words were not measured or held dear. Instead, they were spewed forth like an Uzi splaying bullets, hoping none wounded or injured too seriously once they hit their mark.

Connie chose not to take the hint. "It's nice you could join the family for dinner today, Dan. My daughter Jenny's already developed quite a crush on you. She thinks you look like David Duchovny. You know . . . from *The X-Files.*"

"My niece is quite a fan of the show," Mary explained at the man's puzzled look, wondering if Dan even knew about the popular series. He rarely watched TV other than sports programs on the cable channels.

"Yeah, she's ten going on thirty," Connie added with a laugh. "The other day she asked her father if she could have breast implant surgery. Can you imagine? Eddie told her that if she took after me, she wasn't going to need implants in a few more years."

"Connie!" Mary's face flamed in mortification. Again. Had her sister's fluctuating hormones addled her brain?

"Well, he did," Connie insisted. "Wasn't that sweet of Eddie?"

"Why don't you go rat your hair or something? It's beginning to look a little limp on top."

Reaching up, her sister patted the stiffly sprayed mass, which didn't move an inch, then reached for a long-handled fork and began lifting the strands with it. "What? Now we can't talk about breasts? You sure don't mind talking about butts." At the reminder, Mary's cheeks crimsoned, and Connie, now satisfied that her hair was sufficiently poofed, turned to Dan.

"You don't mind discussing breasts, do you, Dan?"

In typical male fashion, he shook his head and smiled— rather stupidly, in Mary's opinion. "Not at all. That's one of my favorite topics." She gritted her teeth, refusing to return his smile.

"Don't mind my sister," Connie told him. "She always gets a little touchy when she's around family. We drive her nuts, especially my mother."

Understatement alert!

Fists clenched, Mary looked as if she were ready to chew glass. Dan smiled inwardly. "I can't imagine why. I think your family's great."

"Come on, handsome." Connie linked her arm through his. "Let's leave Mary alone for a while. She'll be in a better mood during dinner. She's always happier after she eats."

Oh, I doubt that! I doubt that very much!

And Mary was right. Dinner proved to be an even bigger nightmare, only this time she couldn't escape. Her mother had boxed her in between Aunt Angie and Aunt Josephine, who kept leaning toward her and sniffing her silk blouse. Dan was directly across the table, buttressed on either side by Uncle Jimmy and Carmine Delvechio, the ultimate odd couple.

Uncle Jimmy told a few of his cornier jokes, his consumption of Chianti increasing as he went. Aunt Angie regaled everyone with all the gory details of her recent bunion surgery, while Sophia and Flora kept close watch on Dan's plate to gauge whether or not he was enjoying the meal, the review he'd penned on Mary's restaurant never far from their minds.

Between the antipasto and soup courses, Grandma Flora clanked her spoon against her glass to get everyone's attention. Anticipating the worst, Mary braced herself. She was not disappointed.

"We gotta some company with us today. Daniel and his *bambino*, Matthew. Daniel isa nicea man. He reminds me of my Salvatore. He'sa Irish, but also Catholic. We can't ask for more than that. He will make a good addition to the family.

"Now *mangia*. *Mangia*. Eat. Eat."

"You'll like being part of this family," Carmine whispered to Dan between bites of risotto, as if his being part of the family was a fait accompli. "They're a little weird, but life is never dull when you're around them."

Fascinated by the amount of hair gel in Carmine's hair, which resembled 30W motor oil, Dan nodded at the appropriate times, wondering what would happen if he and Mary didn't advance to the altar, as everyone expected. It was obvious they'd already given their stamp of approval.

Except, of course, Mary, who was having none of it, judging by her pursed lips and stiff posture. Even when she was annoyed, she was pretty. Her cheeks were flushed, her lips parted in anger—oh, he did like those lips!

"Do you like the food, Dan?" Sophia asked, drawing his attention. "I don't think you've had such good Italian food before, am I right? Not that Mary's not an excellent cook, because she is. After all, she learned from her mama." Sophia rested, waiting to take her due.

As if on cue, Angie said, "No one makes bracciole like my sister."

"I thought you told me the meat was tough," Josephine countered, and everyone at the table gasped. Sophia's lips thinned as she gave the evil eye to her sister.

The lull before the storm ensued. Sensing that matters would only get worse, Dan replied quickly, "It's excellent, Mrs. Russo. Some of the best manicotti and bracciole I've ever tasted."

The woman seemed pleased by the response and nodded, though she refused to glance at either of her sisters, who were apparently now on the outs. Not so Mary, who leveled a kick to Dan's shin under the table.

"Oww . . . I don't think I've ever had Mary's manicotti, however," he amended. "I'm sure it's just as good."

Mary smiled sweetly, and Dan felt her foot nudge its way under his pants leg, creating an immediate reaction in his groin area. He reached for his water glass, gulped the cold liquid, and glanced at his watch, wondering how many more hours he could survive.

The Russos were a tough bunch. And Mary was no slacker.

Much later, when everyone was sufficiently stuffed and taking their ease, Matt approached Mary and asked if she'd like to go outside for a while. Since Dan and the other men had gone down to her father's basement workshop to inspect his latest invention—an automatic toilet bowl cleaner made out of toothbrushes—she agreed.

"I'm not used to eating so much," the young boy admitted when they had seated themselves on the back-porch steps.

Car horns honked in the distance. A group of kids played ball in the nearby park and could be heard shouting obscenities at each other. All familiar sounds Mary had grown up with and associated with her neighborhood. It wasn't Beverly Hills, but it was home.

"How come you guys eat so much?" Matt wanted to know.

"Man, I've never had a dinner last so long. My butt was getting numb."

Mary hid a smile. "That's just the way things are done in Italian families, Matt. My mom loves to cook for her family, and she likes to make a little bit of everything, to please everyone." It should have been called a meal marathon rather than dinner.

His voice lowered. "Don't tell Mrs. Russo, 'cause I don't want her to be mad at me, but I think you cook better than she does."

My fortune for a tape recorder. "Why, thank you, sweetie. I'm glad you like my cooking."

"I was thinking . . ." he paused, scraping the toe of his shoe in the dirt, "you'd make a really good mom. You're pretty, smart, and you're really nice to kids."

"Thanks, Matt! It's really sweet of you to—"

"I wish you'd marry my dad," he blurted, his cheeks reddening. "Dad's lonely, and I know he likes you a lot. I sure would like to have another mom to take care of me. And Grandma Flora says it's time you got married and had lots of babies anyway."

Although startled by the child's declaration, Mary narrowed her eyes at her grandmother's comment. "Oh, she did, did she? And did Grandma Flora ask you to talk to me about this, by any chance?"

He shook his head. "Nah. Not really. It was my idea. But I know she'd be really happy if you and my dad were to get married. We talked about it a lot."

I just bet, Mary thought, knowing her grandmother's penchant for interfering was only slightly less than her mother's.

"So whatta ya think? Do you like my dad? Wanna marry him?"

"Of course I like your dad. I like him a lot." More than she wanted to. She loved him, totally and unequivocally.

And that scared her. It scared her witless. "But I'm not ready to get married right now."

His face fell. "Why not? It's not because of me, is it? I promise I'll be good. I won't be any trouble."

Heaving a sigh, Mary clasped the child's hand, unsure if she had the right words to explain how she felt. Matt was still vulnerable, and she didn't want to hurt him. "I love you, Matt. I think you're a great kid. And if I were to get married, I'd want a little boy just like you."

Hope lit his eyes. "Really?"

"But I'm just not sure I'm ready to make such a huge commitment. And my family pressuring me to get married isn't going to work." It was obvious that was what this whole family dinner was about, and she resented the heck out of them for it.

It was her life, her choice. She was finished letting other people decide for her. That was the old Mary, the one without a backbone. The new Mary stood her ground and took no prisoners.

A moot point at any rate, since Dan had never declared himself.

"I guess that's kinda like my mom deciding she didn't want to be a mom anymore."

His wounded expression tore at her heart. "There's no doubt in my mind that your mom loves you very much, Matt. I'm sure she agonized over her decision to leave. I'm not saying what she did was right. I don't think it was. But perhaps she had to leave to find herself. I'm sure when she gets it all worked out in her mind, she'll get in touch with you."

The fact that she hadn't didn't speak too highly of Sharon Gallagher. But Mary wouldn't criticize the woman to Matt, turn him against her. When all was said and done, Sharon was still his mother. Not that she deserved such a great kid!

"I don't miss her as much now that I have you, Dad, and

Grandma to love me. It was hard at first. I used to cry myself to sleep at night because I missed my mom. But now I'm getting used to her being gone."

"Oh, sweetie! I wish I could say something that would make it all better. I know how difficult this has been for you."

"Grandma Flora says that not all women should be moms. Maybe that's true. Maybe mine was forced into it, the way you're being forced into liking my dad. I wouldn't want you to leave, too." He clung to her, wrapping his arms about her neck. "Please don't leave, Mary."

She kissed the top of his head. He smelled like sunshine, soap, and sweat; he smelled like a little boy. "Don't be silly, Matt. I'm not going anywhere. I've got too much going on in my life right now to ever think about leaving."

He looked up, tears smudging his cheeks. "Like my dad?"

She kissed the tip of his nose. "Like your dad. And like you, sweetie. We'll always be friends, right?"

Matt nodded, then a worried look entered his eyes. "Unless my dad decides to marry someone else."

Bang! The shot to her heart was excruciatingly painful, and she clutched her chest, feeling physically ill at the idea that Dan might marry someone else. She didn't want him as a husband, but she didn't want someone else to have him, either. Selfish, she knew, but that's how she felt.

Besides, Mary thought, she was being silly. Dan had told her he was happy with things the way they were. He wasn't ready for a permanent commitment. That's what he said. But . . .

The back door slammed, interrupting Mary's disquieting thoughts.

"Hey, Father Joe! How come you're so late? You missed dinner."

Looking up, Mary was relieved to see that her brother had finally arrived. She'd been trying to reach him all week and hadn't been certain he would come today.

Joe ruffled the youngster's hair. "It's Sunday, Matt. A workday for me. I couldn't get away earlier.

"Hey, Mary." He smiled at his sister. "I understand from Mom that I missed a good meal."

"She saved you three platters' worth," Mary said, noting that her brother still wore his clerical collar. They still had a lot to talk about.

"Good, because I'm starving." He turned to the boy once again. "Matt, your dad's been looking for you. I think he wants you to go inside and watch the baseball game with him and the other men."

The boy's face lit. "Cool! I used to hate sports, but I'm liking them okay now." The child surprised Mary by kissing her cheek, then disappeared through the doorway.

"Cute kid. I like him."

She sighed. "Matt's great. I think he's finally learning to accept his mother's abandonment."

"Because he has you," Joe pointed out, seating himself beside her. "If you and Dan don't end up together, it's going to be hard on him."

"I've explained to Matt how it is, so don't try to pressure me. Everyone's been doing that all day, and they've been as subtle as steamrollers."

His eyes lit with understanding. No one knew better than Joe what family pressure could do. "I was hoping to catch you alone, Mary. I've been wanting to discuss that cryptic message I left on your phone. I'm sure you've wondered about it."

"I've been trying to reach you for a week. Where on earth have you been? You don't just leave a message like that and disappear. I was worried."

"I took a few days off and drove to the beach. I needed some time to think things through."

Glancing up to make sure the door and windows were shut, she lowered her voice anyway. Sophia had ears like radar dishes and could hone in on just about any conversation from just about any distance.

"I can't believe you're serious about this, Joe. You seem so devoted to the priesthood. And you're good at it. Why would you want to leave? I don't understand. You told me you were sure the church was what you wanted."

She knew at the time he'd made the decision to join the church it had been an agonizing one. She'd tried to talk him out of it, tried to counter her mother's enthusiasm that he was born to do the work of God. But once Joe had made up his mind, he'd refused to turn back.

"I'm not happy. I thought helping others would fill the void within me, but I'm still not content. I've grown disillusioned, not so much with the church, but more with myself and the lack of contribution I'm making."

She reached for his hand, knowing how difficult this next question would be for both of them. "Does your decision have anything to do with Annie? I know your relationship was . . . is muddled. And I know it's none of my business, but . . ." She swallowed. "Do you still love her?"

Joe didn't hesitate. "I've always loved Annie, and I always will. Nothing is ever going to change that." He was still in love with Annie Goldman, wanted her like a man wanted a woman, even after all these years, after everything they had been through. And his life would never be complete without her in it.

"Annie's only part of it." A big part, but he didn't want his sister to know that as yet. "I realize Annie doesn't feel the same way about me. Not anymore. And I've tried to accept that." Tried unsuccessfully, he should have said.

Joe shrugged. "It's just—I don't know. I'm confused, still sorting it all out. I thought maybe if you and I talked . . ."

"Promise me you won't make any rash decisions until you've thought everything over carefully. Leaving the church is going to be the most difficult decision you will ever make."

"No, Mary," he said, his eyes filling with pain, "it won't be. Joining the church and giving up the one thing I loved more than anything was the most difficult decision I ever made." And leaving Annie just when she needed him the most had been the most regrettable.

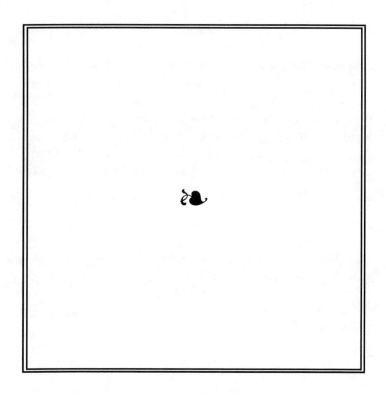

Better Than Sex Cream Puffs

Cream Puff Dough

1 cup water
¹/₂ cup butter
1 cup flour
4 eggs

Heat water to boiling. Add butter. Stir in, all at once, 1 cup of flour. Beat vigorously over low heat until the mixture leaves pan and forms ball (approximately 1 minute). Remove from heat. Beat in 4 eggs, one at a time, and continue beating mixture until smooth. Drop from large spoon onto ungreased baking sheet, and bake in 425° oven 45–50 minutes, or until browned and hollow-sounding.

Cream Puff Filling

In chilled bowl beat 3 cups whipping cream, ¼ cup confectioners' sugar, ¼ cup cocoa, and ¼ tsp. salt.

Split open cream puffs and fill with chocolate whipped-cream mixture. Sprinkle confectioners' sugar on top, and refrigerate. Serves 6.

CHAPTER EIGHTEEN

As soon as they reached her apartment, Mary headed straight to the kitchen, reached into the refrigerator, and pulled out a large platter of chocolate-filled cream puffs—a new dessert recipe she had baked that morning—placing them down on the table in front of her.

"You want to try one? I can personally vouch for how wonderful they are. Better than sex even," she said with a teasing smile.

Clutching his stomach, which was still full from the enormous dinner Sophia had prepared, Dan stared in amazement as Mary devoured first one, then another of the confections. "How can you eat those? You just ate a huge meal a couple hours ago. I know you can't be hungry."

"I'm not," she admitted, talking around the chocolate filling, then licking her lips. "I always eat when I'm upset. And I'm very upset. My family makes me nuts. I use food to make myself feel better. Especially chocolate. I always eat chocolate when I'm crazed."

Stepping toward the table, he pulled the plate out of her reach. "Believe me, these are not better than sex."

"Hey! I'm not done yet," she protested, trying to grab another.

"I can think of other ways to make you feel better." His eyes darkened with passion. "And I feel obligated to prove my point." Moving forward, he reached for her, and, with a deft hand, began pushing buttons through buttonholes to undo her blouse.

Her eyes widened, and she grasped his hand. "Stop! Are you crazy? We're in the kitchen." Sacred ground, she wanted to add, but knew if she did she'd sound stupid. Not many people would understand the sanctity of a kitchen, unless they were chefs or passionate about cooking, which Dan was. But judging by the prominent bulge in his pants, she didn't think he had food on his mind at the moment.

He flicked his tongue out to lick the chocolate off her lips, saying, "Mmmm. Tasty." Then, "So, we're in the kitchen? So what? I happen to like the kitchen."

"Uh." She looked down at the table, and her mouth and eyes both rounded into O's. "I don't think I'm the kitchen-table type. I mean—really. Look how long it took me just to try out the bed. And besides, a kitchen is for eating."

"My thoughts exactly," he replied, then began to unfasten her skirt, ignoring her shocked gasp. He pushed the blue silk from her shoulders and gazed admiringly at the teeny bra and underpants before sucking in his breath. Mary looked incredible—soft, silky, perfectly rounded.

"Remind me to buy stock in Victoria's Secret."

"I—"

He placed his finger over her lips. "Ssh! No more talking. There's a lot more you can do with that delectable mouth besides stuff it with cream puffs." Another gasp, louder this time. "Let's see if I'm correct." With one swoop of his arm, he cleared the table of the napkin holder and plastic salt and pepper shakers, lifting her onto it.

"Did I mention that I'm finding Italian absolutely delicious these days?"

"Please, Dan!" She could feel her cheeks glowing red. The overhead lights were still on, illuminating her mortification. Not to mention the fact that she was nearly naked and lying on her kitchen table like some sacrificial lamb chop.

This couldn't be normal behavior. Could it? Annie would

have said, "Yessss!" But Mary just wasn't as uninhibited. No matter how many pairs of sexy undergarments she bought, how many tight dresses hung in her closet, she would never think or be like her best friend. Annie had been right about that. "I can't! I'm—"

He swallowed her protestations with his mouth, his lips devouring, hot tongue searching, teasing, and tormenting, until Mary forgot her inhibitions. She moved to unbutton his shirt, unfastening his pants and helping to remove them.

When he placed his mouth over her breast, Mary decided that kitchens really had no business being sanctified.

"Did I happen to mention how crazy I am about you?" He unsnapped her bra, scooting her panties down to the floor, until she was naked beneath him. The table felt cold on her backside, but Dan was warm, and she was so hot she didn't much care.

"I need you, Mary. I need to be deep inside you. I've thought about nothing else all day."

Mary couldn't think at all. The feel of Dan's hands on her breasts, his lips on her nipples, had her breath coming in short gasps. "You don't play fair," she choked out between moans of pleasure. "I want you, too. And I shouldn't."

He gazed into the depths of her dark eyes and saw passion mingled with confusion. Dan had been confused at first, unsure of what he wanted from their relationship. But now he knew. He wanted Mary. He wanted to marry her.

"I love you," he whispered, kissing her brow, then her cheek. "I think I fell in love with you the first moment you stormed into my office, looking for blood."

Dan loved her! Mary played the words over and over in her head. Her heart raced, her blood heated, making her feel warm all over, like sunshine dappling a field of wildflowers. "Now you're really not playing fair."

"I don't intend to play fair, sweetheart. So be prepared." He drove into her then, capturing her mouth, absorbing her very essence into him, making her his, now and forever.

The pressure within Mary continued to build as they ascended higher and higher. Her breathing grew shallow; tiny lights, like silver fishes, began swimming before her eyes. She felt light-headed, and feared she would faint.

"Oh! Oh, my!" she cried, slipping over the edge and taking Dan with her in a free-falling, earth-shattering climax that seemed to go on forever.

When it finally ended, Dan kissed her forehead, nose, and lips. "Still think cream puffs are better?"

A dazed expression on her face, Mary shook her head.

"I love you, Mary. You're the best person I know. The kindest, sexiest woman on the face of this earth. I don't intend to ever let you go. And I sure as hell don't intend to play fair." He was determined to marry her, no matter what he had to do to convince her.

Finally regaining her breath and powers of speech, she smiled softly. "You don't know many people, then."

"I don't need anyone but you. And I'm going to make you love me back."

"Oh, Dan!" Tears filled her eyes, her voice clogging with emotion, and Dan knew a moment of fear until she said, "You don't have to make me love you. I already do." She hugged him closer. "I have for what seems like forever."

"You mean it?"

His happy smile filled her heart. "Of course I mean it. I hardly ever lie. Well, sometimes. But only when it's absolutely necessary."

"God! If you only knew how you make me feel."

"I know how you're making me feel," she replied, eyes twinkling. "But do you think we could have this conversation in bed? My back's starting to resemble a knotty pine board."

Grinning, he eased himself off the table, pulling her with him. "We'll go to bed, but not to sleep. Since Matt's staying with your parents tonight, and your dad's driving him to school in the morning, we've got the whole night ahead of us. I intend to make the most of it."

Mary gnawed her lower lip nervously. "We didn't use protection just now, Dan. We've got to be more careful in the future." It was her fault. She should have insisted, but . . . well, she'd gotten carried away by the moment.

Coming up from behind, he wrapped his arms around her, patting her flat stomach and nuzzling her neck. "I wouldn't mind if our lovemaking resulted in a baby, sweetheart, as long as he or she looks exactly like you."

For a moment she was held spellbound by his words, by the feel of his hands on her abdomen, by the image of a tiny version of Dan growing inside her, of holding their baby to her breast, and she heaved a sigh of pure contentment.

But then she remembered that the image didn't fit in with her plans. Not at all. "Are you crazy?" *Was she?* "I have no intention of getting pregnant and having a baby, yours or anyone else's. I have a business to run. I was honest with you from the beginning, Dan."

"But I love you. I want to marry you."

The words came as a shock, now that he'd finally said them. Mary was flattered, honored, and she didn't want to hurt him, so she tried desperately to find the right way to explain. "You might think that now, Dan, but you'd regret it eventually. I'm not willing to be just a homemaker. I don't want the kind of life my mother had. And you've said countless times that your first marriage failed because your ex-wife wanted a career."

"Yes, but—"

She shook her head. "I think you're just caught up in my family's overt attempts to bring us to the altar. My mother thinks everyone on the planet should be married. She doesn't understand relationships like ours."

Mary's words wounded, but Dan tried not to show it. Don't push, he told himself. Be patient. She's scared, not ready to commit. Their conversation at the party had told him that much. She needed more time.

"I saw condoms in the drawer of the nightstand last time I was here," he said, trying to lighten the moment. "Hope you bought stock in the company, because I've got a feeling we'll be using quite a few tonight."

Relief rushed through her, and she relaxed against him, then turned in his arms and caressed his cheek. "I love you, Dan," she whispered, the sentiment shining brightly in her eyes.

"Well, good. Now you can show me how much." Lifting her in his arms and accompanied by squeals of laughter, he carried her into the bedroom.

Walter Beyerly's tan had deepened since the last time Dan had seen him. The editor had just returned from a two-week vacation to Tahiti, which accounted for his relaxed look and glow of vitality. He actually looked younger. Or maybe it was the black hair dye he'd recently used to cover his gray. Walt might be aging, but he had no intention of succumbing without a fight.

At Dan's request, his boss had come to Dan's office to discuss the possibility of promoting Linda out of the Food section and into a more challenging position. It was time, and Dan intended to convince the man of that. Walt was a pretty reasonable guy, and Dan could be damn persuasive when he put his mind to it.

After all, he'd made Mary fall in love with him. The fact that she'd actually admitted it made him feel superhuman all over again. Now, if he could just convince her to marry him, life would be perfect.

"Damn stubborn woman," he muttered.

"Am I missing something here, Dan?" The street sounds below suddenly drew Walt's attention.

"Uh, no." Dan shook his head, hoping his face wasn't as red as it felt. "I'm hoping you'll agree, Walt, that Linda Fox is quite capable and needs to be promoted. Her talents are being wasted as Rosemary's assistant. Ten years is too long to be filing and typing when you've got Linda's abilities."

The editor of *The Sun* turned away from the window and the rush-hour traffic beyond to face Dan again, nodding approvingly as he did. "I'm glad you're taking the bull by the horns, Dan. It shows initiative, and it shows that you're taking your responsibilities to the department to heart. I like that."

"Just don't get any ideas about leaving me in the Food section, because the moment Rosemary returns from maternity leave, I'm outta here."

"As was our agreement. You don't know how happy I'll be when that day comes and I can finally get rid of Bradley. My nephew's a menace. He actually did a three-part series on player uniforms as a fashion statement. Did you see it?" Walt rolled his eyes. "The little bastard's running the section into the ground. No self-respecting, sports-minded male—or female, for that matter—wants to read crap like that."

Not bothering to hide his disdain, Dan said, "I read it," then popped a couple of Rolaids. Walt's visits always required increased antacid. "I just hope when things return to normal I won't be laughed out of every locker room on the East Coast." He shook his head.

"Even Mathilda's starting to see that the man's incapable, a real bozo," Walt said, looking somewhat relieved. "It shouldn't be too much longer before we can get rid of the little shit. My wife's family loyalty only goes so far. She keeps an eye on the bottom line."

"Before we get too far off track, Walt, I'd like to finish our discussion about Linda's promotion."

Perching himself on the edge of the metal desk, Walt rubbed his chin, usually a sign he was about to comply. Dan felt hopeful. "I'll see what I can do. If you feel that strongly about—"

A knock sounded on the door, then the present topic of discussion stuck her head in. "Excuse me, Mr. Gallagher,

Mr. Beyerly." Linda smiled apologetically at the two men, then said, "May I have a word with you, Mr. Gallagher?"

Damn! Talk about poor timing. "What is it, Linda? I'm in the middle of something here." He didn't bother to hide his frustration, but the woman merely rolled her eyes and shrugged.

"I've got two women out here by the name of Russo. They insist on seeing you at once. They claim it's urgent."

"One of them wouldn't happen to be named Mary, by any chance, would she?" Dan's heart swelled at the prospect of seeing Mary again. Last night had been incredible. Tonight, he vowed, would be even better.

Linda shook her head. "It's not the young lady from the restaurant. These women are older: a Mrs. Flora and Mrs. Sophia Russo."

Dan blanched. "Did they say what they wanted?" As if he didn't already know. Mary had warned him about the cow lecture. Holy hell! He was in for it now.

"No, sir. Only that it's very important they see you immediately. They don't look very happy. If I were you, I think I'd see them."

Casting his boss an awkward smile, Dan attempted to explain. "A little family problem to take care of. It shouldn't take but a minute."

Walt stood, nodding in empathy. "I know all about those, my boy. Go take care of it. I think I've got enough information to make a decision on what we've discussed. I'll get back to you soon with an answer." The older man smiled at Linda, mouthing "good luck" to Dan before departing.

I'm going to need it, the reporter told himself, reaching into his pocket for the Rolaids and popping a few more for good measure. Pasting on a welcoming smile, he greeted the two frowning women as they walked through the door.

Both Sophia and Flora were dressed entirely in black, and Dan had a sudden vision of what hell must look like. "Well, isn't this a nice surprise," he said smoothly, offering them the chairs in front of his desk. He tried to act nonchalant, as if their appearance hadn't totally floored him, but his stomach was grinding like a cement mixer, and he was pretty certain they could hear it.

"You shoulda try Bromo Seltzer," Grandma Flora pointed out, confirming his opinion. "Itsa good for the gas."

Lips thinned, chin jutting out, Sophia crossed her arms over her chest. Anyone who knew Sophia Russo knew this was not a good sign. "We prefer to stand," she told Dan, even though Flora was leaning heavily on her cane, looking as if she was about to collapse at any moment. "What we have to say won't take up much of your time, Mr. Gallagher."

Uh, oh. They were back to the mister part, Dan thought, deciding that a little buttering up was in order. "I really enjoyed the wonderful dinner you prepared yesterday, Mrs. Russo. Thanks again for inviting me." He flashed an engaging smile. "You know, I was just telling Mary the other day how much you remind me of Sophia Loren. I bet you get that a lot." Pleasure registered in her eyes, the corners of her mouth started to lift, but then flattened again. So much for flattery, he thought.

"You are in love with my granddaughter, no?" Flora questioned, pinning the man with a steely gaze, and making Dan squirm in his chair. It was "the look" Mary had warned him about. "Itsa time you two kids gotta married. We no can have Mary's reputation ruined. People will talk, call her a *puttana*. Itsa time."

Dan had a pretty good idea what a *puttana* was and his mouth fell open at the notion that anyone in their right mind would think of Mary in those terms. In fact, it pissed him off, though he did his best not to show it.

"My mother-in-law's right. Hanky-panky is against God's law. You're a Catholic. You know this. And don't try to pretend there's nothing going on between you and my daughter. A mother knows these things. I have a heaviness in my chest." She patted the space directly over her heart.

"I warned Mary about you," Sophia continued. "But would she listen? The Irish are known for this kind of behavior. It's in the blood."

Trying to regain his equilibrium, Dan said, "Please, won't you sit down?" There was nothing worse than looking up at two outraged women. Unless they were two outraged women holding a shotgun. Fortunately, these two were unarmed—unless you counted their verbal assault—and had decided to comply with his request.

"I do love Mary, and I'd like nothing better than to marry her."

The two women looked at each other and nodded, apparently taking full credit for his decision. "So, what's stopping you? My daughter's not getting any younger. Mary needs to have children before her eggs are no good. This is why I've decided to give my blessing to this union. I still don't like the idea of her marrying an Irishman, but we need to be practical. And my Frank thinks you're a good guy."

Sophia's stamp of approval, if you could call it that, felt like one of those purple brands butchers used on meat. He wasn't Prime or Grade A, merely passable. It was doubtful he'd make anyone in the family ill. Dan tried not to let such praise go to his head.

"Be quiet, Sophia! Let the man talk. He's gotta someting on his mind, I tink."

Dan was shocked when Mary's mother actually shut her mouth. He doubted anyone but Flora could get away with talking to the outspoken woman like that. It was Sophia's role in life to intimidate. She'd done a bang-up job of that with Mary, but Dan didn't intend to allow her to do the same to him. "I don't think I should be discussing something so personal with members of Mary's family."

"What? Personal?" Sophia threw up her hands. "I'm her mother. This is her grandmother. We have a right to know what's going on between you two."

Plowing agitated fingers through his hair, he released a

pent-up sigh and after a moment said, "Like I've already tried to explain, Mrs. Russo, Mary and I love each other. But Mary isn't interested in getting married right now."

"She told you this, Daniel? You asked Mary to marry you and she said no?" Grandma's questions brought splotches of color to the man's cheeks.

What the hell was he supposed to say? That she turned him down cold? That she blamed her family's interference for his proposal?

"Mary made it clear that she isn't ready for any kind of long-term commitment. I don't want to push her. I think she needs more time. She's uncertain, and—"

"Sometimes a woman needs to be pushed," Sophia explained, as if he were totally obtuse. "It's how they know men are really serious. The trouble with Mary is, she doesn't know her own mind. If she says she loves you, then she wants to marry you. But she's not going to make it easy. A woman needs to be courted. My daughters were not brought up to be easy. They're good Catholic girls."

Grandma pushed herself to her feet, leaning on her cane. "You're a good boy, Daniel. I know you will find a way to convince my granddaughter to marry you. I know you want a mother for your son. And in my heart I know you would never bring shame upon the Russo name."

"I wouldn't dream of it," he agreed, wondering how in hell he was going to please everyone, including himself. "I'm more than willing to marry her. I love Mary. But—"

"Good. Then it's settled." Sophia stood, as did Dan, who felt as if a Mack truck had just rolled over him. "Let me know when the deed is done, and I'll make the engagement party. We'll invite everyone, the whole family.

"Of course, you'll need to buy a ring first. Nothing too big. But big enough to make a statement. No woman wants to hide her head because her ring is too small. If the diamond is small and of poor quality, it shows that the man didn't think enough of her."

Flora's hand came up, and Dan, expecting the worst, sucked in his breath, then released it when she made the sign of the cross and shot her daughter-in-law a disgusted look. "Don't pay attention to her, Daniel. Sophia's like an old goat; she likes to butt, butt, butt. Itsa no wonder she doesn't get a headache. You take care of tings the way you want." The two women walked out, Sophia still mumbling under her breath about engagement rings.

Dan fell back into his chair, making sure his masculinity was still firmly in place. After that surreal episode, he couldn't be sure.

If Mary found out that her mother and grandmother had paid him a visit, she'd go ballistic, which is why he'd already decided he wouldn't tell her. Though he wasn't crazy about their interference, he didn't see the point in causing more family problems.

The Russos had plenty to contend with already.

But in fairness, he had to concede that Mary's mother and grandmother did have a point. Reputation was very important to the Russos. They were an old-fashioned, very traditional Italian family.

Mary had explained that in Italy a woman's virginity was a prized possession. After the wedding night it was often customary to hang the bride's sheets out the window to show proof that she'd been a virgin.

And despite her claims of independence and modern thinking, Mary was still an old-fashioned girl. She worried that her sheets weren't perfectly white, that she had sinned against the church and would probably end up in hell, despite Dan's assurances to the contrary.

Mary wasn't the type of woman to sleep around. She was a woman who needed to be married. Dan just needed to figure out the best way to convince her of that.

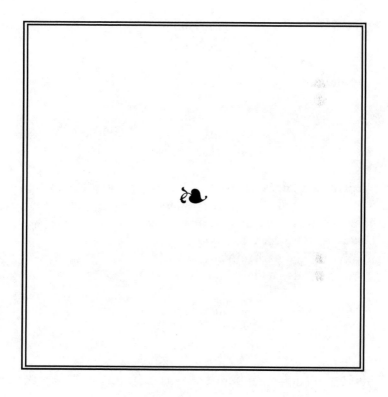

Antipasto à la Annie

On a large platter arrange:

> *thin slices of:*
> *salami*
> *prosciutto*
> *mortadella*

Add chunks or slices of:

> *provolone*
> *mozzarella*
> *or other cheeses*

Prepare thin slices of fresh mozzarella with slices of fresh tomatoes. Sprinkle with olive oil and fresh basil, and/or artichoke hearts that have been marinated in olive oil and garlic cloves, and/or green, red, and yellow sliced peppers sautèed in olive oil and garlic, then chilled.
 You may also add:

> *whole button mushrooms*
> *large black olives*
> *Italian bread, sliced*

Serve as an appetizer before the main meal.

CHAPTER
NINETEEN

Mary locked the door behind the last customer to leave and, heaving a sigh, leaned wearily against it. Her feet were killing her. They'd been two waiters short tonight and she'd had to fill in. Even her Reeboks and Sheer Energy support hose hadn't helped.

Next to cleaning, waitressing was her least favorite thing to do. She had a lot of respect for those who did it, but she didn't want to be included among their ranks, not on a regular basis anyway.

"We were busy tonight," Annie commented, running a total on the cash register and smiling in satisfaction. Mama Sophia's was finally starting to show a decent profit. Pulling the cash and credit card receipts out of the drawer, she placed them in a canvas bank bag, which she would later drop in the night deposit on her way home, as was her usual routine. "It's midweek and the gross receipts are hefty. You should be elated. I know I am."

"I'm very happy," Mary said, heading into the dining room, trying not to groan because her feet hurt so much. Annie followed close on her heels. "You want some coffee before you go?" she asked, hoping the caffeine would perk both of them up. Annie looked as dragged out as Mary felt.

"Okay."

Annie sat down at one of the tables, pushing the salt and pepper shakers back into place. Setting down the coffee cups, Mary eased herself into the chair across from her, thinking how wonderful it felt to finally get off her feet.

"You look troubled. Is something wrong?"

As usual, Annie was right on the money. Mary was worried. About Joe. About Dan. About what the future held in store for her. Worried, scared, and confused. "Do you ever wonder what your life's going to be like ten years from now? Twenty?"

The young woman shrugged, sipping slowly on the hot liquid. "I try not to think of those things. It's too depressing. But why are you worried? It's obvious you've got someone who's crazy in love with you. I think your future's set." Her voice held a wistfulness that Mary didn't pick up on.

"It's all going so fast," Mary said. "I feel like I'm on a freight train that's headed on a collision course. I . . ." Falling in love with Dan had happened too quickly, having him love her in return had been totally unexpected. It couldn't be real, it couldn't last, she told herself. Things like this happened to other women, not to Mary Russo.

Reaching out, Annie placed her hand over Mary's. "It's normal to be scared, *cara*. But you shouldn't be. Love is just part of life. And now that you've finally started to live yours, you should welcome all the new experiences coming your way. Be happy you have someone who really seems to care about you. You don't know how rare that is." The last was laced with bitterness. And regret. This time Mary heard both.

"I suppose you're right. But I'm still confused about so many things. I just wish I had all the answers, knew the best thing to do." Dan's marriage proposal had really thrown her for a loop, and it still continued to plague her, though he hadn't said another word about it since, for which she was grateful and vastly relieved.

"You think too much, Mary *mia*. You always have. You're going to analyze this relationship with Dan until you worry it into the ground. What happens happens. You can't worry about things that might never come to pass. Live for the moment. It's worked for me."

"Has it?" Mary stared intently at her friend and wasn't convinced. Annie's blue eyes were shadowed. She'd been distracted of late, not at all her usual bouncy self. And she'd dyed her hair back to its original color of dark brown. That in itself was very telling . . . of something. Mary just wasn't sure what, and it bothered her for some reason.

Annie's bizarre rainbow hair colors, though unusual and eccentric, were at least indicative of life, of her enthusiasm for living it to the fullest. This new and subdued version of her friend was cause for alarm.

"Did Joe show up at your mother's last Sunday?" her friend asked, trying not to seem as interested as she sounded.

"Yes, he was there, though he arrived late."

"So, how's he doing? Has he saved any souls lately?"

Though she usually shared everything with Annie, Mary had no intention of revealing what she knew. Joe had spoken to her in confidence. And at any rate, he was still with the church, so there was nothing dire to report.

Annie's animosity toward her brother made Mary unwilling to reveal his confession that he was still in love with the acrimonious young woman. It wouldn't be fair to Joe. And it certainly wouldn't be fair to Annie.

"Joe's fine. Still the same old Joe."

"Yeah? Well, that's nothing to brag about, in my opinion."

Mary frowned, but remained silent. Annie had to work out her own demons. Unfortunately, so did she.

The Rusty Rudder was packed for a Wednesday night, especially considering the lateness of the hour. Oldies music blared from the speakers—Otis Redding was still sitting on the dock of the bay—and Dan could hardly hear himself think as he sipped thoughtfully on his cold beer, waiting for Alan to put in an appearance.

The man had called an hour ago asking to meet him, but hadn't bothered to say what he wanted to talk to Dan about. Those damn investigative journalists were always so secretive.

Ten minutes later, Alan finally emerged through the throng of people, waving when he spotted Dan and making his way over to the corner booth Dan occupied to the left of the crowded dance floor.

Alan dressed in jeans and a lightweight blue pullover sweater should have been Dan's first clue that something was wrong. He looked casual, and Alan Grier was not a casual sort of guy. *GQ* was his bible, Brooks Brothers his religion. Dan used to tease him in college that fastidious Alan probably starched and ironed his underwear. Alan had admitted to the ironing, but not the starching.

"Hey, sport! How's it going?" Alan asked, sliding in across from Dan and pouring himself a beer from the frosty pitcher on the table. He took a large sip, wiping the foam from his mouth with the green linen napkin. Dan always used the back of his hand. "God, that's good! Thanks for meeting me." He seemed on edge, not at all the cool, collected, and composed Alan that Dan knew.

"I had to hire a baby-sitter before coming over here to meet you, so this better be good," Dan said, then wished he hadn't. Alan's smile faded instantly, his eyes filling with pain, and he felt like a shit for having brought up the baby-sitter. He'd never seen his friend look so distraught. Not even when he'd failed to break the Clinton/Lewinsky scandal.

"Helen's threatening to leave me."

"What? Shit! I'm sorry, man." Dan cursed beneath his breath. Alan and Helen had always seemed so solid, the perfect couple. This kinda crap couldn't be happening to them. If a couple like the Griers, who'd been happily married for years and had two great kids, were having marital trouble, what kind of chance did he and Mary have to make a marriage work? Dan didn't even want to think about that. Statistically, the odds were not in their favor.

"What's this about, Alan? Is this about Helen wanting to go back to work?" He'd had a sinking feeling the last time they'd talked that the topic of Helen's going back to work was going to prove an issue.

Alan hanged his head. "If I don't agree to allow Helen to start her own real estate business, she's going to leave me and take the kids with her. She claims I'm out of touch with the times, said I was archaic." Alan's look of disbelief would have been laughable, if Helen's assertion hadn't been so true. Of course, Dan wasn't exactly one to talk, since he'd felt pretty much the same way.

"Helen wants more out of life than just being a mother and housewife, as if there's something dishonorable in that. There used to be a time when a woman was proud to stay at home and take care of the family. Now it's not good enough." Alan refilled his beer glass and attempted to drown his sorrow.

Life was much easier back in college when all you had to worry about was how many beers you could drink before you passed out, or how to avoid breaking your neck at a Friday night frat party. Unfortunately, Alan wasn't saying anything that Dan hadn't already said to himself.

"Maybe Helen's just bluffing. You know how women get when they want their own way." He was glad Mary wasn't around to hear him say that. She'd probably dump the pitcher of beer over his head. But damn if it wasn't true!

There were some things men and women just didn't agree on, and emotional blackmail was one. Like acid eating into metal, women used tears to wear down a man. If there was one thing Dan couldn't take, it was watching a woman cry.

"I don't think so," Alan answered. "Helen seemed as serious as a heart attack. And I figured since you'd already gone through something similar, you might be able to give me some advice on what I should do."

Dan stared at his friend as if he hadn't heard him correctly. "Hello? You're asking me for advice?" He gulped his beer. "In case you've forgotten, Alan, ol' buddy, my wife left me for reasons that weren't all that different from yours. Sharon wanted her freedom, and she took it."

"Have you heard from her?"

Dan shook his head. "Not a word. And that pisses me off. Not for me, but for Matt. How can a woman who professes to love her child go off and just forget he ever existed? Matt doesn't ask about her as much anymore, but every day when the mail comes, his eyes fill with hope. I'm telling you, Alan, it just rips me apart. The bitch could have at least sent a postcard."

His friend nodded, sighing deeply, and, mired in his own misery, said, "What am I going to do, Dan? I love Helen. I can't lose her and the kids."

Dan took a moment before answering, unsure if Alan was going to like the advice he was about to give. "If you love your wife, Al, and you really want to keep your family together, then you've got to compromise. You've got to meet Helen halfway. Maybe she can work out of the house to start. Maybe you can offer to help get her business off the ground. You know a hell of a lot of people. Your connections would be invaluable to her."

Compromise, that's what it was all about. Dan realized that now.

Alan mulled over what Dan was saying. "I guess it's something to think about."

"Well, if it makes you feel any better, you're not alone. I'm having a similar problem."

"A problem between you and Mary? I thought you two were cozy."

"I want to marry her. Her family wants—no, make that *insists*—I marry her. But she's not going for it, despite the fact that she claims to love me." Dan knew she did. Mary wasn't that good a liar.

"Do you think it could have something to do with your boy? Some women don't want to raise another woman's child."

Dan shook his head. If there was one thing he was certain of, it was Mary's love for his son. He only wished he could say the same for his ex-wife. "Mary loves Matt. And he's crazy about her. I'm positive it's not that. Mary's just hung up on the independence thing. It has something to do with her childhood and her feelings of inadequacy."

"If I know you, Dan, you'll figure something out. You're one hell of a creative guy. Look to your talents for the answer. You'll come up with some way to convince the woman you love to marry you."

"Well, aren't you just Mr. Optimism all of a sudden."

Alan grinned, then tossed a twenty down on the table. "The beer and the baby-sitter's on me. I've got to get going. I've got a lot of thinking to do. Good luck with your problem, sport. I'm sure you'll figure it out. You're a pretty resourceful guy."

"Uh, huh. Sure. Whatever." Dan watched Alan walk away and wondered why, if that was true, he didn't have a clue about what to do.

The trouble with Mary was, she was damn perplexing.

Mary walked into the restaurant early Sunday morning and knew immediately something was wrong. Marco and Annie were standing shoulder to shoulder, reading the morning paper as if they were the best of friends. They actually looked happy to be in each other's company!

Well, if they were happy, she could be, too, she decided, pasting on a smile. "Good morning! How's everyone doing today?"

The duo peered over the newspaper and broke into excited grins. Marco rushed forward, hugging Mary around the waist, practically lifting her off the ground.

"Marco! For heaven's sake. Get hold of yourself." What on earth had come over the man? Was he drunk? Had he been dipping into the Chianti?

"Congratulations, Mary! I am so happy for you. Surprised, yes. But still, I am very happy." He waved his hand in the air, then squeezed his fingers together and kissed the ends. "Ah, *amore*. There's no telling the heart what to do."

She looked directly at Annie, who was grinning from ear to ear. "Would somebody mind telling me what's going on? I feel like I've just entered an episode of *The Twilight Zone*. Or maybe I'm on *Candid Camera*." She looked around, just to make sure that Funt guy wasn't lying in wait.

"I go. I have sauce simmering on the stove," the chef explained, then disappeared, but not before blowing Mary a kiss.

Mary stared after him as if he'd lost his mind. Something was very wrong. Had they received another hideous review? No, Marco had said something about love, and both he and Annie had been grinning like fools. Annie still was!

"Why didn't you tell me?" Annie interrupted her silent conversation. "And here you went on the other night about being confused, and all the time you had a wonderful secret. I should be mad at you for holding out on me. You really had me going, you know."

More confused than ever, Mary marched forward and ripped the newspaper out of the startled woman's hands, then looked for herself at what all the commotion was about.

"Oh, my God!" Her face paled, and she gasped. "Oh, my God! My God!" There, in black and white, for all the world to see, was a full-page ad that read simply:

> *Mary Russo, I can't live without you. I love you with all my heart and soul. Please marry me and put me out of my misery. Love, Dan.*

Despite everything she had told him, he still wanted to marry her.

"Oh . . . my . . . God!"

"Will you quit saying that? What?" Annie asked. "You don't look happy. Weren't you two planning this as a surprise for the rest of us?"

"Good grief! Whatever gave you that idea? I just spilled

my guts to you the other night, and you think I had something to do with this proposal of marriage? Get a grip, Annie. Don't you know what this means?"

The woman shrugged, then arched a brow. "That Dan
loves you and wants to marry you?"

"Yes, of course that's what it means. But I don't want to
get married. I told you that, and more importantly, I told
Dan that. I'm not ready. And now the whole damn city of
Baltimore will know it, too."

Annie's expression softened to one of sympathy. "I was
hoping you had changed your mind. No wonder you looked
so upset when Marco hugged you."

"Like you wouldn't be? The man hasn't said two nice
words to me since I hired him, and now he's throwing his
arms around me like we're bosom buddies? I don't think so!"

Mary began to pace. "What am I going to do, Annie?"

"I hope that's a rhetorical question, because I'm fresh out
of ideas. This is something you're going to have to figure out
all by your lonesome, kiddo."

"I don't want to hurt Dan. I love him." And Matt. What
about Matt? And she didn't even want to think about her
family.

"Oh, God! My mother. She's going to be beside herself."

Leaning against the bar, because all of Mary's pacing was
making her dizzy, Annie crossed her arms over her chest and
asked, "With grief or happiness?" When it came to Sophia,
you could never be certain.

"I don't really know for sure," Mary admitted. "My grandmother and father adore Dan, and they've made no bones
about welcoming him into the family. Ma's playing her cards
close to her chest. I don't know where she stands. She might
have been gracious enough to invite Dan to dinner, gone
along with my father to keep peace in the family, but—"

"Gracious? Sophia gracious?" Annie's eyes widened. "You
have just formed an oxymoron, kiddo."

Mary went on talking as if Annie hadn't spoken. "But an Irish son-in-law? She'd rather welcome Satan into the family."

"Hey! I thought I was Satan in your mother's eyes."

The phone rang and Mary cringed. "I'm not here."

"What if it's Dan?"

"Then I'm really not here." She wasn't ready to face him yet. Not until she figured out exactly what she was going to say. He obviously didn't believe her previous explanation.

Suddenly she had a feeling of déjà vu. The review, the newspaper, her first meeting with Dan. It all seemed eerily familiar, and she didn't have a doubt in her mind that he'd planned it that way. It was sweet. But also infuriating!

Annie answered on the fourth ring. "Oh, hi, Sophia. Uh, Mary's in the bathroom. Shall I have her call you? Okay, I'll give her the message." She hung up the phone. "Sophia wants you to come right over."

"Thanks, I think," Mary said, feeling slightly nauseated. She couldn't decide which was worse—facing Dan or her mother.

"Your reprieve is over, Mary *mia*. It's time to make a decision."

"I made my decision. I'm not going to marry Dan. He knows how I feel. Whatever possessed him to do such a thing?"

"I know you won't believe this, *cara,* but I think it's sweet that he's told the world how he feels. You don't know how lucky you are."

Mary's eyes widened. "Annie?" Of all the things she expected Annie to say, that wasn't it. She searched her friend's face for some sort of explanation, and found none. But then, Annie had always been good at hiding her emotions.

The woman waved her off. "I have to go. I promised Marco I'd help out in the kitchen. We're preparing Antipasto à la Annie." She forced a laugh. "Sid's going to freak when he sees how Italian I'm becoming. I guess now I'm going to have to learn to make matzo balls or some other Jewish delicacy to keep peace in the family. *Oy!*" She disappeared into the kitchen.

Mary gazed once again at the newspaper and her eyes filled with tears. "Oh, Dan! You're so wonderful. I love you so much. But I just can't marry you."

"What do you mean you don't want to marry Daniel?"

This was the question her grandmother posed two hours later when Mary finally got the gumption to go over to her parents' house and face the music. Now she was facing Grandma Flora across the kitchen table, and the old woman looked anything but pleased.

"I'm not ready to marry and settle down, *Nonna.* I love Dan, but—"

"You love him. Thatsa all I need to know. You will marry Daniel and be a good mother to Matthew. Itsa the right thing to do."

"Right for who? You? Ma? I just told you, *Nonna,* I don't want to marry anyone right now. I like running my restaurant. I like my life the way it is. And even if I wanted to marry Dan, which I don't, it would never work out."

"Why not? Tell me why not. He is a good man."

Mary sighed and tried to explain. "We have different views on things—on marriage, in particular. We wouldn't be compatible. I'm not willing to take a chance . . ." *That our marriage will fail and Dan will end up hating me.* There, she'd said it, at least to herself.

"Bah! I took your side against your mama the last time, but Sophia was right. Itsa time you had *bambini*, time you had a husband. Itsa good that you make a nicea restaurant, Mary, but now you musta make a nicea wife, too. *Capisce?*"

This conversation was going nowhere, and Mary was ready to end it. "Where's Ma? I didn't see her when I came in." Her mother's absence was quite curious, in fact. Why had she called, asking Mary to come over, then disappeared?

"She went to church. I'm not sure what she prays for."

Connie rushed in at that moment, all smiles and sporting a pair of diamond and sapphire earrings that must have cost Eddie a fortune. He would be cleaning out colons from now to kingdom come to pay for those baubles.

"I just read the newspaper. I'm so excited." Connie rushed forward and hugged Mary, kissing her cheek. "Congratulations. I'm thrilled for you. For both of us, actually. Now we can go shopping for baby clothes together, decorate our houses, and do—"

Mary held up her hand, effectively halting her sister's plans for a rosy future. "Your good wishes are a bit premature, Connie. I have no intention of accepting Dan's proposal. His second proposal, I might add."

"Stupida!"

Mary ignored her grandmother's unflattering assessment and was relieved a moment later when the old woman got up and walked out of the room. *Nonna* had never reacted quite so adamantly about anything before. Mary knew her grandmother liked Daniel, but until this moment had never realized to what extent. Of course, her love for Matt had no doubt colored her judgment where Mary's future was concerned, which is why, Mary was certain, her best ally had turned against her.

"But why not?" Connie asked, clearly disappointed. "Don't you love him? You two looked so adorable at the dinner party Ma gave in your honor. And Dan's such a nice guy, so handsome. He's a big improvement over Lou Santini. I bet he doesn't live with his mother."

"First of all, Connie, I had already refused Dan's offer of marriage, before he went behind my back and made the whole thing public." She threw her hands up in disgust. "What kind of behavior is that? Who wants to marry a man who can't take no for an answer? Who just ignores everything I say or feel?" She was desperate to find an argument that would bring family members to her side.

They were defecting one by one, and she didn't understand it. Whatever happened to *la famiglia*? To the ties that bind? She guessed in the Russo family they were made of thread, and not the heavy-duty kind.

"Daniel has declared his love to the world. It's so romantic. I can't believe you're upset about this. You should feel lucky. If my Eddie did something like that, I'd tie him to the bed and make love to him for a week."

Arms crossed over her chest, Mary stared back defiantly. "Well, I don't feel lucky. What I feel is angry. The man is too presumptuous by far. He didn't take my feelings into account at all."

"I'm sure Dan will explain everything when you see him again. Didn't you tell me on the phone last night that he's coming over to see you this evening?"

Mary blanched before breaking out in a cold sweat. When Dan had called yesterday and said it was very important that he see her tonight, she'd had no idea he was intending to make his declaration public, advertise it to the world.

Good grief! What on earth was she going to do now? And more importantly, what on earth was she going to say?

Matt's Minestrone

1 onion, chopped
4 cloves minced garlic
¼ cup olive oil
1 cup chopped zucchini
2 potatoes, diced
3 carrots, sliced
3 stalks celery, sliced
8 cups beef stock
3 cups chopped canned tomatoes
1 cup kidney beans, canned
1 cup garbonzo beans
2 cups water
basil, parsley, oregano to taste
salt and pepper to taste
½ pound small pasta shells

In large pot, sautè onion and garlic in olive oil, about 5 minutes. Add vegetables, beef stock, tomatoes, and remaining ingredients. Add seasonings, and simmer several hours. Add pasta about 15 minutes before end of cooking time. Serve with Parmesan cheese.

CHAPTER
TWENTY

"Dan, I've already told you, I can't marry you. I appreciate the offer, but . . ."

Sheesh! Mary rolled her eyes at her reflection as she practiced in front of the mirror. How could she say she appreciated the offer? She sounded like a used-car salesman, minus the white shoes. She presently wore fuzzy pink bedroom slippers.

"I'm really flattered, Daniel. Really. It's just that . . ."

What?

I'm a chicken shit? I don't know the first thing about being a wife and mother? I don't want to lose my identity? I don't want to be an extension of someone else? I don't want to fail?

All of the above.

How pathetic was it that she had to practice what she was going to say to the man she loved? How pathetic that she'd dressed in her dowdiest clothes and wore no makeup. Let Dan see who she really was, she'd decided. No doubt he'd forgotten. He wouldn't want to marry her. He wouldn't think she was such a bargain.

A knock sounded at the door. She took one last look at herself and cringed. No wonder she used to scare off suitors. Swallowing with a great deal of difficulty, she pasted on a tremulous smile, sucked in her breath, and opened the door . . . to find Mrs. Foragi waiting on the other side. Funny, but the sight of her landlady instead of Dan didn't make her feel at all relieved.

"I know it's late," the older woman said, looking not the least bit apologetic at the intrusion. "But I just heard the news and wanted to congratulate you. I'm not interrupting anything, am I?" She stood on tiptoe, trying to peer over Mary's shoulder into the living room. "Your fiancé isn't here?" She seemed quite disappointed that Dan wasn't reclining bare-ass-naked on the couch. Almost as disappointed as Mary.

Stop it! You have serious business to conduct. This is no time to be thinking about sex.

"Thanks, Mrs. Foragi. And no, Dan's not here yet. But he will be shortly." She couldn't bring herself to make another explanation about her marital decision, to disappoint yet another person.

"Will you be giving up the apartment, then? I need to advertise it. Even though top-quality rentals like this are always in demand, I still can't afford any vacancies."

Mary fought hard not to laugh. Mrs. Foragi had more money than God, despite her penchant for dressing like a pauper. Her dead husband had left her well-off. And the apartment wasn't exactly *Architectural Digest* material. It was quaint, and Mary liked it, but the faucets leaked, the bathtub had permanent rust stains, despite repeated scrubbings, and most of the windows had been painted shut, which didn't bode well for the upcoming summer months when the humidity would reach as high as the temperature.

"I've no plans to move in the immediate future, Mrs. Foragi. But if that changes, you'll be the first to know. I'd better go now." She started to shut the door. "I need to freshen up a bit. I'm sure you understand."

"I'll say," the woman replied, not bothering to hide her disdain as she stared at Mary's mismatched, threadbare sweats. "A little makeup couldn't hurt, either."

Deciding her opinionated landlady might have a point, Mary returned to the bathroom and reapplied her makeup. Just because Dan's marriage proposal had been downright unorthodox was no reason to punish the man. And seeing her without artificial enhancement was definitely punishment. Halloween ghouls were more attractive than she was without foundation, blush, and mascara.

"The trouble with Mary," her mother would say, *"is that she's no natural beauty. A little lipstick, a little padding never hurt anyone."*

Mary had eyelashes now and cheekbones, and she liked them. And her bosom wasn't half-bad, either, thanks to the miracle of underwires.

She had just set down her hairbrush when a series of short raps sounded. It was definitely Dan's decisive knock, and she took one last look in the mirror before hurrying to answer the door.

Better to get this over with cleanly and quickly.

But when she opened the door and saw the gleam in Dan's eye, the grin on his face, and the champagne and roses in his hands, she swallowed the lump in her throat and knew there wasn't going to be anything remotely quick or easy about what she had to do.

"God, I missed you!" he said, tossing the gifts on a chair and wrapping his arms about her. "Mmmm." He inhaled deeply. "You smell good. Is that a new scent? I like it."

Her deodorant must be working overtime, because she wasn't wearing any perfume. "I missed you, too."

"Guess you know why I'm here." He grinned sheepishly. "You saw the newspaper, right?" He tried to gauge her reaction, but her face remained expressionless, while his reflected disappointment.

"Uh, I think we'd better sit down."

Following her to the leather sofa, Dan sat beside her. "I'm sure you thought my proposal was very unromantic, but I thought since the newspaper had originally brought us together, it was kind of fitting. Sort of like coming full circle."

"I—I admit I was taken by surprise." *Understatement alert!* "I mean, I had already refused your proposal of marriage, Dan, and told you my reasons for it."

He reached for her hand. "I realize that. And I know you're not anxious to make a commitment, Mary, but I'm hoping to change your mind. I love you. I want to marry you. And I refuse to take no for an answer."

She sighed. "I love you, too, Dan. It's just . . ." Why did this have to be so difficult? Why couldn't things have remained the way they were? Whatever happened to *uncomplicated*?

The love Dan bore for her was shining in his eyes. He loved her. She loved him. And yet . . .

He slipped from the sofa to his knees and pulled a small velvet box from his coat pocket, handing it to her before she had a chance to protest. Her heart began thudding loudly, whirring like a tornado in her ears.

"I'm asking you to be my wife, Mary Russo. I promise to love, honor, and take care of you for the rest of our lives."

Opening the lid to find a perfect diamond solitaire perched on a band of gold, Mary sucked in her breath, tears filling her eyes. It was the most beautiful ring she had ever seen. And it looked horribly expensive, which made her feel even more guilty, if that was possible. At the moment, she didn't think it was. "It's gorgeous. Absolutely stunning."

Breathing a sigh of relief, he grinned, pleased and relieved by the praise. "I was hoping you'd like it. It's my understanding that the size of the diamond is very important to a woman. It has to be big enough to make a statement, but not too big as to be garish. I didn't want you to be embarrassed or think I didn't care enough because I didn't buy—"

"Where did you hear that from?" Mary grew immediately suspicious at the familiar-sounding diatribe. It sounded exactly like something her mother would—

"I think your mother might have mentioned it," he said, forgetting in all the excitement that Mary didn't know about Sophia and Flora's earlier visit to his office.

Her features froze. She looked at the ring once again, this time seeing her mother's smug reflection in the perfectly cut stone, and grew incensed. Snapping the velvet case shut and clutching it tightly in her hand, she asked, "Did my mother put you up to this, Dan? Is this whole marriage proposal business her idea?"

"No!" He shook his head adamantly. "I swear, Mary. I love you. I want to marry you. I'm willing to compromise about your working, and—"

Her eyes widened in disbelief. "Oh, now all of a sudden you're willing to compromise? Now you don't care that I have a business? Did you form those opinions before or after my mother talked to you?" As if she didn't already know.

"This is my idea," he insisted.

"And my mother had nothing to do with it?" She could see his mind working as he pondered his options, and her heart took a nosedive. He'd been pressured into it, just as she thought.

"I won't lie to you. Sophia and Flora visited me." She opened her mouth, but before she could say something, he blurted, "But that doesn't have anything to do with why I'm kneeling here now, asking you to be my wife."

Bright splotches of color landed on Mary's cheeks. Her mother! Why wasn't she surprised? The woman wasn't happy unless she was meddling. And Grandma Flora . . . her betrayal hurt most of all.

"Get up, Dan. I can't marry you."

"What?" Surprise replaced dismay. "What d'ya mean, you can't marry me?"

"First, I want you to know I'm very flattered that you asked me. Again. I love you. And if I were going to marry anyone, it would be you." His taut features started to relax, but then she added, "But I'm not!" and they froze again.

"But—"

"Secondly, the newspaper announcement, though sweet, was somewhat humiliating. It puts me in a terribly awkward position. I do have a business to run in this town, responsibilities to my employees.

"And last, but by no means least, if my mother so much as

hinted that you should propose, then I'm definitely not going to consent. The fact that she and my grandmother are involved in all this, well . . ." She bolted to her feet, leaving him to scramble to his.

"Mary, let me explain." He held out his hands beseechingly, but she would have none of it and shook her head fervently.

"My family's been trying to run my life for years. Sophia thinks she can manipulate and arrange things to suit herself. Why shouldn't she? She's been doing it all her life. And like fools, Connie, Joe, and I have let her get away with it. But no more. My mother will not win this time."

"Dammit, Mary!" Dan shoved his hands in his pockets, his face a mask of angry frustration. "Your mother has nothing to do with this. It's true, she suggested we get married. Okay, so it was more of a demand. But she was worried for your reputation."

"Ha! Sophia is more worried about not getting her hands on my children."

"Please believe me. Her opinions didn't sway me in the least. I'm a grown man. Don't you think I know my own mind? Don't you think I know when I'm in love, that I can't bear the thought of spending the rest of my life without you?"

Tears clogged her throat. "Oh, Dan, why do you have to make this so difficult?"

"Because it is difficult, Mary. It's our lives we're talking about. Our futures. I want to marry you, have babies with you, grow old with you. I love you more than life itself. Don't you know that?"

"But what if I don't want to have babies? What if I don't want you to take care of me? What if I'm capable of making my own decisions, running my own life, and taking care of myself?"

"I'm not suggesting you enter into slavery. Marriage is compromise, commitment, the sharing of ideas and opinions.

We would make decisions together. I'm not trying to control you."

When she tried to turn away, he forced her to look at him. "I'm not your mother, Mary."

She covered her ears. Dan was too persuasive. She was weak. And she needed to be strong. She would not be manipulated by anyone, especially someone she loved. Not again. "It wouldn't work, Dan. You said so yourself, that first time we discussed marriage. I can't take that risk. I'm a coward. I don't expect you to understand. If it didn't work out I'd . . ." She shook her head and turned away from him. "I'm confused. I can't think straight right now. I think you should go and leave me alone to think things through."

He came up behind her, wrapping his arms about her waist, resting his chin on the top of her head. "I don't want to leave you like this. You're upset."

She leaned back, releasing a sigh of great longing and even greater unhappiness. "I'll be fine. I just need to be alone for a while." Turning to face him, she opened her palm and held out the ring. "You'd better take this."

He shook his head. "No! Keep it. Look at it. And know every time you do that it's a symbol of my love for you."

"What's the matter? Don't you like the soup? I thought it turned out pretty good, considering."

Staring absently at the bowl of minestrone in front of him, Dan moved the spoon around and around, not paying much attention to what he was doing or what he was eating.

Since leaving Mary's apartment the previous evening, he had no appetite, no enthusiasm for anything. He just wanted to go off in a corner and lick his wounds like an injured animal, which is just how he felt. Hurt and abused. And somewhat numb.

But Matt was staring expectantly at him, waiting for an answer, looking for approval on his first attempt at making dinner. Unwilling to disappoint him, Dan forced a smile.

"It's good, Matt. Great job! And thanks for cooking dinner tonight. I didn't much feel like it."

Warmed by the praise, the boy's face brightened. "Grandma Flora helped me make it this afternoon, after school. She said every good Italian boy must know how to cook minestrone."

"You're not Italian, Matt. We're Irish."

"Yeah, I know. But Grandma thinks it's better to be Italian than Irish, and so do I. They've got better food and they have more fun than we do."

"Well, I hate to be the one to break the news, kid, but it doesn't look like we're going to be part of the Russo clan any time soon. Mary's refused my marriage proposal."

"Oh, man! That's the shits!" Matt blurted, then covered his mouth when his father's eyes widened, then narrowed in displeasure. "Sorry! I got carried away. Whatta ya mean? I thought you and her were gonna get married. That's what Grandma Flora told me."

"Yeah, well, everyone got a little ahead of themselves." He should never have brought up his first marriage to Mary, his stupid ideas on women in the workplace. And he should never have allowed Sophia and Flora to interfere in their relationship. He should have refused to . . . what? See them? Talk to them? That would have gone over real well.

Heaving a disappointed sigh, he explained, "Mary doesn't want to marry anyone."

"Is it because of me? She said it wasn't, but I kinda think it might be."

Dan set down his spoon and studied the apprehension on his son's face. Matt was still susceptible to rejection, still trying to make sense of why his mother hadn't wanted him. "It's not you, son. It's me. It's Mary's family. It's everything and nothing. I don't know. She's a woman. How in hell am I supposed to know what she's thinking?"

"Like you didn't know what Mom was thinking when she left?"

Dan pushed back his chair and held out his arms. Without

hesitating, Matt rushed into them and sat on his father's lap. Dan hugged him close. "I had no idea what was running through your mother's mind. I doubt if she knew herself. That's the trouble with women. They sometimes make rash decisions and go off half-cocked. Men, on the other hand, think things through rationally before doing them."

"Like you putting that marriage proposal in the paper? I'm not sure you thought that one through, Dad."

"Wise guy." Dan flicked the end of his son's nose and smiled ruefully. "No, I don't suppose I did. And see what happens when you don't think things through? They blow up in your face." And your heart explodes in a million pieces.

"So whatta we do now? How we gonna get Mary to change her mind? Because I really, really want her for my mom. I told her so."

Dan's eyes widened. He was surprised his son had been so bold as to discuss his feelings with Mary, and that made him feel even worse, for he knew how much Mary meant to Matt. Almost as much as she meant to *him*. "I'm sure she was flattered."

"That's what she said. But then she said she didn't want to get married."

"Yeah, that's the rub."

Matt thought for a minute. "The Italians might have better food, but the Irish aren't quitters, right? We just gotta put our heads together and figure this out. We're men. Men are good at figuring things out, right, Dad?"

Dan's heart lightened a bit, and he squeezed his son tighter. "I love you, Matt. I always have and I always will."

Matt gave his father a kiss. "I love you, too, Dad. Now, let's get to work. We've got a lot of figuring out to do."

When Mary arrived at her mother's house the following day, she was charged up like a stick of dynamite and ready to blow. It was time to have her say, she'd decided, time to get a few things off her chest. Her mother would rue the day she'd decided to butt into her relationship with Dan.

But when she entered the living room and saw the worried expression on her father's face, heard the utter quiet in the usually noisy house, her daughterly instincts kicked in and all thoughts of retaliation fled.

"What is it, Pa? What's wrong? You look as if someone died." He looked as if he were aging by the minute, so deep were the grooves around his mouth.

Pointing toward the back of the house, Frank shook his head. "It's your mother. She's lying down. She's not so good. I think it could be her heart."

Mary's eyes filled with fear. "Her heart?"

"Bah!" her grandmother said, swinging her rocker-recliner around to face Mary, ignoring her son's irate expression. "Sophia ate sausage and peppers for lunch. She's got heartburn. I gave her some Bromo Seltzer. She'll be fine in a little while."

"Did you call the doctor, Pa?"

"No. She wouldn't let me. You know how stubborn your mother can be. Sophia said if I called, she wouldn't go. She was very insistent."

Tossing her purse and sweater on the nearby end table, Mary landed a determined gaze squarely on the two older, but not necessarily wiser, people. "I think it's time Ma quit calling the shots around here, don't you?" Without giving them a chance to respond, or accuse her of being disrespectful, she marched into her parents' bedroom, steeling herself for battle of a different kind.

She entered to find her mother reclining against the pillows, her face as white as the embroidered slips covering them, her right hand draped across her chest. Tiny red roses entwined with green vines repeated on the cream-colored wallpaper behind her.

"Ma!" She rushed to the bed. "Why didn't you call the

doctor? You need to get up and go to the hospital right away. Hurry. I'll take you."

The older woman shook her head. "I'll be all right. The pain will go away." Then dramatically—because Sophia never did anything without being dramatic—she heaved a sigh and crossed herself. "If only I could have seen you married before I died, Mary."

Biting back the sharp retort teetering on the tip of her tongue, Mary grasped the bedcovers and pulled them off the startled woman, relieved to find her mother still dressed. "Get up. I'm taking you to the emergency room."

But Sophia didn't move. Instead, her eyes filled with tears, alarming her older daughter. "I'm scared. There might be something wrong with me. I don't want to find out."

Sitting down beside her, Mary felt her heart soften, and she took Sophia's hand. She'd never heard fear in her mother's voice before, never seen panic in her eyes. Sophia was always a rock for everyone, always the one in charge, the one to reassure.

Now that their roles were reversed, Mary wasn't sure how she felt about it. Seeing her mother weak and vulnerable made Sophia seem all too human. Mary had always been the one full of fear and insecurities. She never imagined her mother could feel the same way.

Well, one of them needed to put their fears aside and be strong, and it might as well be her. "Don't be silly, Ma. It's probably just heartburn, like *Nonna* says. But we need to be sure. I don't want to lose you."

"You're a good girl, Mary, even if you're stubborn, and a trial to an old woman." The younger woman opened her mouth to protest, but her mother didn't give her the chance. No surprise. Sophia was determined to have the last word. Even on her self-professed deathbed.

"All right." Her mother finally relented when it became clear that Mary wasn't giving an inch. "I'll get up and go with you to see Dr. Maggio. But no one else. I don't want those foreign doctors touching me. There's no telling what they've been eating, and I don't trust their education."

"Ma, they wouldn't be practicing medicine in the United States if they weren't board certified. But I'll call ahead and request that Dr. Maggio meet us at the emergency room."

It was the longest two hours Mary had ever spent.

Not just because of the one hour and forty-five minutes she'd wasted in the ER, reading old copies of *People* magazine—who knew Cher had had another face lift?— while waiting for the doctor to pronounce her mother fit as a horse. Dr. Maggio had declared that Sophia would survive to live another day to stuff her face with sausage and peppers. Grandma Flora had been right: Sophia had been diagnosed with acid indigestion and given a prescription for Prilosec. No, it was because for the last fifteen minutes, on the drive home, Sophia had pulled out all the stops to convince Mary how foolish she was in not accepting Dan's marriage proposal.

Suddenly the hated Irishman had turned into Saint Daniel. Go figure.

"I just don't understand you, Mary. For an intelligent woman, you're very thick. The man wants to marry you. He says he loves you. What's wrong that you don't want to marry him?" She lowered her voice to a whisper. "Is he no good in . . ." The pause was weighty. "You know what I mean? Sometimes men have a bit of difficulty with—"

"Ma!" Gasping aloud, Mary nearly rolled into the car in front of her before slamming on the brakes. "This is what I'm talking about. You should mind your own business. I'm a grown woman. I don't need to be told what to do or when to do it." And she sure didn't need to discuss her sex life with her mother!

Sophia clutched her chest. "You're making me have more acid. You shouldn't yell at your mother. I'm not fully recovered from my heart attack."

"Your mother's got a heart like a nineteen-year-old. She'll probably outlive the both of us." Thinking back to what Dr. Maggio had said, Mary rolled her eyes. "Let's drop it, then. I don't want to discuss Dan with you or anyone else. It's my problem. I'll handle it."

"Now it's a problem?"

Mary shot her mother a warning look. "Ma!"

"All right. All right. I won't say another word. So, tell me," she said, changing the subject, "have you spoken to your brother? He seems very quiet and depressed lately. I hope nothing's wrong."

From the frying pan into the fire, Mary thought with a sigh before answering. "I'm sure it's nothing, Ma." She pulled into the narrow driveway beside her parents' house, shifted into park, and set the brake. There was no way she would confide what she knew to her mother, so she hedged.

Hedging was perfectly acceptable in this instance. It couldn't really be considered lying, because someone's life was at stake. Mary knew if her mother found out what Joe was contemplating, she'd kill him. A mother's love only went so far.

"Joe's entitled to be quiet or depressed once in a while," she tried to explain. "Just because he's a priest doesn't mean he's not human, doesn't have the same needs as the rest of us."

Her narration went over like a two-ton bomb. Sophia turned in her seat, her face red. "Needs? What are you talking about? Priests are not like regular people. They are touched by the hand of God."

Mary fought the urge to roll her eyes at her mother's naïveté. Didn't the woman ever read the newspaper or see the television reports on corrupted priests? "Joe's a man, Ma, with needs and feelings."

"It's disgusting that you should say such a thing. Have you no shame? Your brother is a man of God. You don't under-stand him like I do."

"Well, if he's having problems with his work, then he'll have to go to his bishop and discuss them."

"Maybe I should talk to him."

"No!" Mary said the word so loudly her mother leaned back against the car door as if she were being attacked. "I mean, I don't think Joe would appreciate your interfering in his church business, Ma. You know, he's got all those privacy rules and such."

Her mother nodded. "People put their trust in your brother. That's what makes him so special. He's a wonderful priest. All right, I won't mention it. Unless he continues to look unhappy. Then I'll have no choice. He's a priest, but he's my son. I worry for all my children."

Mary forced a sick smile. "And we appreciate that, Ma, really we do." *Not!*

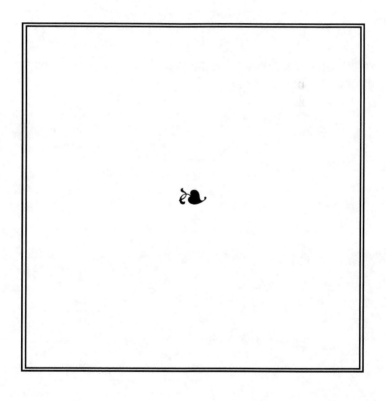

Frank's Favorite Leg of Lamb

1 4–5-lb. leg of lamb
garlic cloves, cut into slivers
salt and pepper to taste
oregano

Place lamb leg in roasting pan. With a sharp knife, make small cuts into skin of lamb and insert slivers of garlic throughout roast. Season with salt and pepper and oregano. Roast in a 325° oven, 25–30 minutes per pound.

Serve with apple sauce.

CHAPTER
TWENTY-ONE

This is a second look at the popular Italian eatery, Mama Sophia's. Though I may be accused of bias because of my ardent admiration for the owner, Mary Russo, I am here to set the record straight about this wonderful restaurant, located in the heart of Little Italy.

Mary could hardly believe her eyes as she read the glorious review in the morning edition of *The Sun*. In fact, she blinked twice, just to make sure she wasn't hallucinating.

Dan had done a complete about-face, apologizing for his *"short-sightedness, prejudice against Italian food,"* and *"total lack of culinary discernment,"* while referring to his previous review of Mama Sophia's.

Unable to read further because her eyes were filling with tears and the words before her were beginning to blur, she sniffed several times, wiping her runny nose on the sleeve of her Mickey Mouse nightshirt. She hadn't had the heart to don one of her sexy nighties; they reminded her too much of Dan, of what she and Dan had done. And were not doing at the moment!

"Oh, Dan, you sure don't make it easy. Damn you!"

Stuffing the last of the buttered toast into her mouth, she gulped down her coffee, pouring herself another cup to take into the bathroom with her.

As soon as she was showered, dressed, and suitably made-up, she intended to go down to the newspaper and thank Dan in person. She would let him know, maybe even show him, just how much his gesture had meant. Just because she'd rejected his marriage proposal didn't mean they couldn't remain good friends.

Or lovers.

Forty-five minutes later, Mary entered Dan's outer office, expecting to find his secretary seated at her desk, but the room was empty and the door to Dan's office was closed. Chastising herself for not having called first, she debated what to do, while pacing the length of the office and back. She decided to leave a note.

Perhaps she and Dan could meet for lunch. Or dinner. That would be even better. She would treat him to dinner to thank him for the wonderful review, she decided, then afterward . . . Well, anything was possible.

Searching the unlittered desktop for a pen and paper— Ms. Fox was apparently another neatnik—she heard Dan's booming laughter float through the closed door, followed by the sound of a woman's sultry voice. A woman who didn't sound at all like the staid Ms. Fox.

Mary's heart twisted, and her stomach tied itself in knots. Up till now jealousy had been an alien emotion, but she was feeling it in spades at the moment.

Straightening, she walked toward the sound, as if drawn like a magnet. She knew it was rude to eavesdrop, but she just couldn't help herself, not when, by the sounds of it, Dan and the mystery woman were having such a wonderful time.

As she leaned closer to hear what was being said, the door was suddenly thrust open, and she was greeted by Dan's startled expression, which she was sure mirrored her own exactly. She jumped back, with what had to be a guilty look on her face.

"Mary! What are you doing here?" he asked, looking over her shoulder into the outer office. "Where's Linda?" Then he glanced down at his watch and answered his own question. "Must be on break."

"I—I have no idea," she replied anyway, feeling ashamed for trying to listen to a conversation that was really none of her business. "I just got here." She looked into his office to spy an attractive, thirty-something blonde perched on the edge of Dan's desk. She had fabulous long legs that went on forever, and the rest of her wasn't bad, either.

Mary suddenly felt like a drab ugly duckling by comparison, and wished she'd worn something a bit sexier, tighter, newer. But she'd reverted back to wearing one of her baggy cotton jumpers, sacrificing sex appeal for comfort.

He smiled warmly at her. "Come in. I'd like you to meet one of my associates." He gestured toward the attractive blond goddess. "Valerie Tompkins, this is Mary Russo. Mary owns the restaurant I was telling you about. Valerie heads up our Lifestyles department, and does a first-rate job, I might add." The admiration in his voice made Mary nauseous.

The two women sized each other up, then Valerie flashed a hundred-watt smile that almost blinded Mary. Caps, she concluded. No one had teeth that straight or white, not even Annie. And she had great teeth!

"I've been hearing good things about your food. Dan's usually not so generous with his praise."

Chiding herself for her uncharitable thoughts, though she still felt like clawing the woman's pretty blue eyes out, Mary forced herself to relax. Jealousy gnawed at the pit of her stomach like a rabid dog in search of a blood donor. "Yes, well, Dan hasn't always been so generous," she replied, trying to smile just as brightly, but knowing she'd failed miserably. She'd managed maybe twenty-five watts, tops.

"You've seen the new review, I take it?" Dan asked with a lift of his brows, smiling, clearly pleased with himself.

Mary nodded. "That's why I'm here. I should have called first. I apologize for intruding on your business meeting." She wished she'd never come, never seen Dan's attractive coworker. There was something to be said for ignorance being bliss.

"Nonsense," Valerie said, sliding to stand, on her three-inch spiked heels. "We weren't conducting business. I was just sharing a morning cup of coffee with Dan. Old habits are hard to break. I need to be getting back to work anyway. Nice meeting you, Mary." With a seductive smile on her face, she said to Dan, "See you later, Daniel."

Later! Old habits!

What on earth was the woman talking about? Had Dan and Valerie Tompkins been romantically involved? They looked awfully cozy and comfortable with each other. And how dare she call him Daniel?

Mary didn't want to acknowledge the relief she felt when the woman's size-six body finally quit the room and the door closed behind her firm, cellulite-free fanny. Mary guessed it was uncharitable, even un-Christian-like, to hope that the woman got heel spurs from wearing such outrageous shoes.

There was much to dislike about Valerie Tompkins.

"I'm surprised to see you here," Dan said, drawing Mary's attention back from her spiteful thoughts. "After the other night I wasn't sure . . ." He shrugged, leaving the rest unsaid.

"I'm not that easy to get rid of. And it doesn't look like you lacked for company, at any rate."

The possessiveness Dan saw in her eyes made him smile. It was a good sign. A very good sign. "Valerie's an old friend."

"She didn't look that old to me." And just how friendly were they? she wanted to ask.

This time he laughed out loud. "Sounds like you might be a bit jealous."

She arched a brow, crossing her arms over her chest, and had to forcibly restrain herself from smacking the self-satisfied grin off the man's face. "Should I be?"

Suddenly Dan's smile melted and his expression grew serious. "You can't have it both ways, Mary. I love you. I want to marry you. But I'm not going to live like a monk for the rest of my life, if that's what you think. A man's got needs. And I don't want to have just a casual relationship with you. I love you too much for that.

"And as miserable as my first marriage turned out to be, I find that I want to be married again, to share my life with someone. With you."

Dark eyes flashing fire, she purposely ignored the latter and latched on to the former. "Men and their needs. Well, it certainly didn't take you long to transfer those needs to someone else, did it?"

"Like I said, Val and I are just good friends. There was a time when we considered pursuing a romance, but we decided against it. It's tough having a relationship while working together. Never works out."

Mary suddenly felt quite ill. Dan *had* been involved with the blond goddess. So what if they hadn't pursued it? (If that was really true.) He'd probably lusted after her gorgeous firm body anyway.

"I've got to go," she said quickly, feeling confused and miserable as she headed for the door. "I just wanted to thank you for the review. It was generous of you to do it."

"My pleasure. After all, since I publicly humiliated you, it was the least I could do."

"I—" She tried to say something more, but tears clogged her throat, and she merely shook her head and ran out.

Dan felt the acid of those tears ripping into his gut, and he heaved a sigh as he watched her go. "Dammit, Mary, why do you have to be so damn stubborn?" And they called the Irish hardheaded and difficult.

Obviously, whoever said that hadn't met any Italians.

Peering through the small-paned window to the left of Annie's front door, Mary gazed in to see her friend gyrating to the strains of Little Richard's "Long Tall Sally." Annie did forty-five minutes of exercise religiously every day, and she always worked out to the driving beat of Chuck Berry, Jerry Lee Lewis, or Little Richard.

Mary pounded on the door, but it was hopeless. Annie had the stereo up full-blast and couldn't hear her over the loud music.

Just as well, Mary thought with a sigh. She couldn't keep running to her best friend every time she had a problem. And Dan was one problem she was going to have to work out for herself.

Parking in a lot near the Inner Harbor, Mary decided to walk. Walking, as Annie liked to point out, was good exercise, and it also proved beneficial when you needed to do some serious thinking. And Mary definitely needed to think.

The restaurants around the harbor were crowded with tourists, as was the harbor itself, and she made her way through the throng of sun worshipers toward the water.

As she passed by The Cheesecake Factory, she was reminded of her date with Dan, how they'd laughed over the silliest things while stuffing their faces with turtle-praline cheesecake, and she smiled. It was probably the fact that he'd eaten as much as she had that night that had made her fall in love with him.

Plopping down on a bench, Mary looked out over the sun-dappled water. Water taxis made their way from one pier to the other, hauling passengers back and forth. Shielding her eyes, she stared off in the distance, trying to see Dan's condo, but it was too far away.

Maybe Valerie Tompkins was there with him now. Maybe Dan and the gorgeous blonde had decided to become more than just friends. The thought made her stomach clench and she reached into her purse for a candy bar—chocolate, of course. One couldn't contemplate life's problems and solutions without chocolate.

Seeing Dan with that blond bombshell had made Mary realize something: If she didn't put aside her fears and uncertainties, her stupid insecurities, and marry Dan, someone else—like Valerie Tompkins—would.

What was it Matt had told her once, when she'd said to him that they would always be friends? *"Unless my dad decides to marry someone else."*

Dan had made it pretty clear that he had no intention of waiting around for her much longer. *"A man's got needs,"* he'd said, which, roughly translated, meant Dan was going to be making love to another woman soon. Not only would he be making love to this other woman, but he'd be eating cheesecake with her, watching old black-and-white movies with her, and cooking roasted chicken for her!

And dammit! she liked his roasted chicken.

"Are you really going to allow that to happen, Mary?" she whispered to herself, feeling utterly miserable and alone. "Are you going to allow the best thing that ever happened to you to get away? Because if you do, then you're far more stupid and insane than I'd previously given you credit for."

It was time to grow up. Take the next step. Take a chance on a lifetime of happiness.

"You did it once, Mary, and your restaurant succeeded. There weren't any guarantees that time. Marrying Dan will be no different. Love conquers all, remember?"

Sophia's words suddenly echoed in her ears, and this time she listened: *"The trouble with you, Mary, is that you don't know a good thing when you see it. I knew your father was a piece of bread the first time I saw him, and I snatched him up, before Concetta Rosellini could get her hands on him."*

Having come to a momentous decision, Mary breathed a sigh of relief and smiled to herself. It was time to bite the bullet and have a little chat with her mother. She intended to let the woman know that she'd decided to marry Dan Gallagher.

When Mary was twelve her aunt Josie had gone to Disneyland and brought back an autograph book for her niece. Minnie Mouse graced the front of it, and between the covers were pretty sheets of colored paper. Mary had liked the pink sheets the best.

She had begged and bothered everyone to sign it, including her mother. And on the first page of the book, which happened to be pink, Sophia had written: *"When friends desert you, look to your own true friend, your mother."*

Mary wasn't quite sure why she was standing on the front porch of her parents' house thinking about that now, but it certainly seemed pertinent. Even prophetic.

She entered the house and followed her nose to the kitchen, where she knew she would find her mother this time of day. From the scent of it, Mary surmised that Sophia was making leg of lamb for dinner. It was Frank Russo's favorite meal, and it smelled delicious, making Mary's stomach grumble at the fact that she hadn't fed it since early that morning, unless you counted a candy bar, which didn't have a speck of nutritional value, so she didn't.

Mary subscribed to the theory that if you didn't count empty calories, they couldn't possibly make you gain weight.

"Hi, Ma!" she said, tossing her purse and keys down on the kitchen table, which was already set for the evening meal. "What's new?"

Her mother turned from the stove, her eyes narrowing as she stared suspiciously at her daughter, wiping her soiled hands on her apron. "Have you eaten? You look pale." She shoved a plate of freshly baked Italian bread in front of Mary, along with a small bowl of garlic-flavored olive oil. "You should eat. Men don't like bones."

Mary's mouth dropped open. Never before had her mother uttered that particular phrase to her. It was usually reserved for Connie. But she wasn't going to look a gift horse in the mouth and question her about it. "I had some toast this morning and a chocolate bar not long ago."

"A chocolate bar! What kind of food is that? Always with the chocolate, Mary." Sophia shook her head, then lowered her bulk onto the chair with a grunt. "What's wrong? I can tell something's bothering you. Did Marco upset you again? That man is such a little putz."

"No more than usual." Mary looked about to make certain they were alone. "Where's Pa and Grandma?"

"Your father took his crazy mother to the drugstore to make certain she didn't get any funny ideas in her head. I had to bribe him with the lamb to make him go. You know how crazy he is about my roast lamb."

Mary chewed her bread thoughtfully, unsure how to broach the subject uppermost on her mind. Her mother wasn't someone she usually sought advice from or asked opinions of. With Sophia, you didn't need to ask, because she usually offered both, whether or not you wanted to hear them.

"Ma, I'm going to marry Dan Gallagher. I love him, and he loves me."

Sophia stared intently at her daughter, a questioning look in her eyes. "But?"

Her mother was too perceptive for her own good. "But I intend to keep my restaurant. I don't want to stay at home and be just a housewife." She gnawed her lower lip. "I'm worried that Dan will change his mind about my working and insist that I stay at home after we're married." It was just a little doubt. She was entitled to a little doubt, Mary told herself. Being insecurity-free after thirty-three years wasn't all that easy.

"It's not such a bad thing to keep a home for a husband, Mary. I know young women don't think it's so exciting or fulfilling, but it is. I worked. But after I married your father and had kids, I stayed home to raise them. I was never sorry. And I'm proud of the way you all turned out. You, Connie, and Joe are my greatest accomplishments."

Though Mary was touched by the sentiment, her mother's words didn't change her mind. "Times are different now, Ma. A woman should be able to combine a career with marriage. I want children someday, but not right now."

A worried frown cracked Sophia's composure. "Dan has a child. Is Matthew going to be a problem?"

Mary shook her head. "No. Matt's a great kid. I'll have no problem being a mother to him. I love him. And anyway, he's in school most of the day, so I wouldn't have to change my schedule that much. But as for having a baby, that's a whole different ball game."

Sophia covered her daughter's hand. "Children are a blessing from God."

Yeah, well, so was birth control, and Mary intended to use it. Of course, she didn't intend to let her mother know that. "I'm going over to Dan's tonight to tell him my decision. I don't think I could stand living the rest of my life without him, Ma. I love him too much."

Her mother made the sign of the cross and looked heavenward, as if all her prayers had been answered. "The trouble with you, Mary, is that you worry too much. You imagine problems that may never happen.

"If you love the man, even though he's Irish, an unfortunate fact we cannot change"—though her sour expression clearly indicated she wanted to—"you must marry him. A man who is willing to humiliate himself in public is worth the risk. Everything will work out just fine, you'll see."

Smiling, she fluffed her hair. "Besides, he thinks I look like Sophia Loren. You know, people have been telling me that for years."

Mary realized then and there that Daniel had completely won over her mother. Her entire family, really. Frank had been given tickets for every major sporting event for the next year, and Grandma Flora had already told her to marry the man or risk being miserable.

"So, are you staying for dinner, or what?"

Mary had a feeling that for once her mother might be right. Everything was going to work out just fine. Mary would make sure of it.

"Yeah, Ma, I am. And thanks."

"For what?"

"For being you, I guess."

The doorbell rang, and Dan, who'd been getting Matthew ready for bed, handed his son the toothpaste-laden brush.

"Do a good job brushing your teeth, Matt, while I go see who that is." As he ran down the stairs, he wondered who could be calling at such a late hour.

He opened the front door to find Mary standing on his front porch, and his eyes widened. "Mary, what are you doing here?"

She smiled hesitantly, hoping Dan didn't have company. He looked awfully surprised to see her. "I need to talk to you. Are you busy?" She held her breath, half expecting Valerie Tompkins to come floating down the stairs at any moment, wearing a sexy negligee.

God! What if I've come too late?

"Come in. I'm glad you're here." He ushered her into the living room, and she released the breath she'd been holding. Then she began to pace.

"I want you to know, Dan, that I didn't come to this decision lightly. I've anguished over it for days, worried about whether or not it was right, wanted and needed to make sure it was the right thing for both of us. All of us," she amended, smiling at Matt. The boy, dressed in his *Star Wars* pajamas, had come to the foot of the stairs. He moved to sit on the sofa, next to his father, who was looking rather perplexed.

"I hate to appear dense, but do you mind telling me what it is you're talking about?" Dan said. Though he had a pretty good idea, and his heart began pounding loudly in his ears, he wanted to hear her say it. Needed to hear Mary say the words he'd been longing for. Because until she did, he wouldn't believe it.

Shaking his head, as if his father was the most obtuse man in the world, Matt elbowed Dan in the ribs. *"Daaad!"* he said impatiently. "Don't you get it? Mary's gonna marry you."

Dan gazed at Mary, and the smile on her face made his heart lodge in his throat. "Is Matt right? Are you going to put me out of my misery and finally accept my proposal?"

She nodded, flashing the engagement ring she now wore on her left hand. "Yes. But first we need to get a few things straight."

Leaning back against the sofa, he crossed his arms over his chest and bit back a grin. "Like what?" For some reason, with Mary you always got conditions.

"I won't give up the restaurant. I love it, and—"

"Whoa!" He held up his hands. "Who said anything about giving up Mama Sophia's? I don't recall asking that of you. I told you, I'm willing to compromise on your working."

"Heck, no!" Matt interjected, looking horrified. "Where would we have pizza? I love Mama Sophia's."

Mary's cheeks filled with color. "I know you said we would compromise, but I wasn't sure if that included me selling my restaurant. After you told me about the difficulties you had with your first marriage, your ex-wife's career, I just naturally—"

"Sharon and my problems went much deeper than her job, Mary. In fact, my career, not hers, was probably the greater cause of our marriage failing. I was on the road a great deal of the time and . . . well, we grew apart.

"Besides, why would I want you to sell the restaurant when I've got an idea about opening another one? I've been thinking it might be fun and profitable to open up a sports-theme type of restaurant. What d'ya think?"

Astounded by the suggestion, Mary could only nod her head while digesting everything. Finally, she blurted, "I don't want to have a baby right away!"

"Oh, shoot!" Matt looked very disappointed. "I was hoping for a brother."

Dan squeezed his son's shoulder. "That's fine with me,

sweetheart. I'd like to keep you to myself for a while. And Matt's going to need time to adjust to having both a mother and father again before we spring a brother or sister on him."

"Oh, Dad!"

Mary's smile lit up the entire room, and the love she bore for father and son shone brightly in her eyes. "I love you, Dan Gallagher. And I want to marry you. I love you, too, Matt, and I'd be proud to be your mother." She kissed both men on the cheek.

"You're not going to get all mushy now, are you?" Matt asked, wiping away her kiss with the back of his hand.

Mary laughed, sharing a seductive look with his father. "I guess not right now. Maybe later."

Exchanging a look of promise, Mary and Dan knew that from here on out they had a lot of "laters" to look forward to.

Mary & Dan's Chocolate Wedding Cake

Chocolate Layers

$^3\!/_4$ cup butter
1 $^3\!/_4$ cup sugar
2 eggs
1 tsp. vanilla
2 cups flour
$^3\!/_4$ cup cocoa
1 $^1\!/_4$ tsp. baking soda
$^1\!/_2$ tsp. salt
1$^1\!/_3$ cup water

Cream butter and sugar. Add eggs and vanilla. Beat 1 minute at medium speed. Combine flour, cocoa, baking soda, and salt and add to creamed butter and sugar mixture. Add water to the flour/cocoa mixture and mix well. Pour into 2 9-inch greased and floured cake pans. Bake at 350° for 30–35 minutes. To make additional layers, double or triple the recipe.

Cream Cheese Frosting

9 oz. cream cheese, softened
$^3\!/_4$ cup milk
6 cups confectioners' sugar
$^1\!/_4$ tsp. salt
2 tsp. vanilla

Mix all ingredients to desired consistency and spread on layers. A chocolate or cream filling can also be used between layers.

CHAPTER TWENTY-TWO

Dressed in a black Armani tux, Dan stood nervously at the candlelit, flower-adorned altar, wiping sweaty hands on the legs of his trousers, his gaze drawn down the long red-carpeted aisle of St. Francis of Assisi's Catholic Church.

In a few minutes Mary would join him at the altar and become his wife. His heart pounded in anticipation. And relief that she had finally consented to marry him. He loved her and Matt more than anything in the world, and he felt damn lucky to have them both in his life.

At the first strains of the wedding march, Dan's gaze riveted on the wide double doors at the back of the church, and his heart started pounding again.

Out of the corner of his eye he caught a glimpse of Sophia and Flora seated across the aisle. Dressed in a pink-floral satin dress, Sophia was weeping softly into her handkerchief, while Flora, in funeral black, was smiling widely, looking pleased as punch, as if she'd brought about the whole turn of events single-handedly.

Dan's mother, Lenore, radiant in royal-blue organza, was seated behind Dan in the second pew. Uncle Alfredo sat next to her—even though, according to tradition, he was on the wrong side of the church—not bothering to hide the fact that he was quite smitten with the widow.

Lenore smiled softly, tears of joy filling her bright green eyes when she gazed back at her son and mouthed the words "I love you." Dan winked and replied, "Me, too!"

The doors at the back of the church suddenly opened. Maid of honor Annie Goldman, dressed in deep-rose satin, with hair to match, clutched her bouquet of pink baby roses in a death grip and began the long walk down the aisle, a soft smile hovering about her lips as she stared straight ahead.

Dan heard Father Joseph's sharp intake of breath, but didn't turn to look at him. Following behind Annie marched Connie, dressed in similar fashion.

A collective gasp went up and all heads turned when Mary, clutching her father's arm, began her processional down the aisle. She was beautiful in yards of white satin, which had been encrusted with hundreds of tiny seed pearls. Her bouquet of white baby roses matched the satin roses on her gown and tulle headpiece.

Dan had never seen anything quite so glorious. Her blush veil obscured her expression somewhat, but he knew she was smiling behind it, and he loved her more in that moment than he'd ever loved anyone or anything.

When Father Joseph asked who was giving the bride away, Frank stood proudly erect, tears in his eyes, and said in a shaky voice, "Her mother and I."

Sophia was heard later to complain that her husband should have used her given name, not her title.

"Do you want some champagne?" Sophia asked her two sisters, who were admiring the four-foot-tall silver champagne fountain as it spewed forth the bubbly liquid.

"That's some fountain!" Angie said, suitably impressed, and Sophia preened under the compliment. "This reception must have cost Frank a pretty penny."

"And a sit-down dinner. Don't forget the sit-down," Josephine reminded her sister. "Filet mignon. Such a big spender, my sister is."

"The steaks were Prime, not Select," Sophia pointed out. "Marco catered the reception from Mary's restaurant, and Andrea Fiorelli made the wedding cake."

"It's got five tiers." Angie whistled. "It must have cost plenty."

At Mary's insistence, the cake layers had been made of chocolate, but Sophia wasn't going to spoil the surprise.

"Frank's got plenty of money to spend on his family. He just sold his heated-toilet-seat invention."

"The one that burned your ass?" Josephine's eyes widened in excitement, and she picked up a starched linen napkin off the table and began sniffing it.

"Yes, but he fixed that problem. My Frank's quite the electrician, you know. And a very smart man."

"A piece of bread. I always said Frank was a piece of bread," Angie stated.

"Like butter," Josie agreed.

The three sisters turned to look across the large banquet hall as the bride and groom emerged in their wedding finery. Later they would change into their traveling clothes before leaving for their honeymoon. "My son-in-law is taking my daughter to Italy for their honeymoon," Sophia said proudly. "Isn't that romantic?"

"They're a lovely couple," Josephine agreed. "And Mary made the most beautiful bride—next to my Sally, that is."

Sophia didn't voice the unpleasant thoughts racing through her head that her sister's comment elicited. Instead, she remarked, "Mary's like bones. I told her she needs to put on a few pounds, but will she listen to her mother? Well, I guess she's Dan's problem now."

Dan looked down at his new bride and smiled. "How long do we have to stay here? I'm anxious to get the honeymoon under way. I hear Venice is lovely this time of year."

"All I've heard for the past few weeks is how much everything is costing my father, so it's doubtful my mother is going to allow us to leave before the cutting of the cake."

"Why do I get the feeling that she's over there talking to your aunts about us?"

Mary gazed at the three women huddled together before the gaudy champagne fountain. "Because she is. She's probably telling them your sperm count and how soon it will be before I get pregnant."

He laughed, wrapping his arms about her. "I love you, Mrs. Gallagher."

"Love me, love my family."

"Oh, I do. No doubt about it. There's not a drab one in the bunch. Carmine told me once that if I married you there wouldn't be any dull moments in my life. I'm inclined to believe him."

Glancing across the room, Mary spied her brother in conversation with Donatella Foragi. The woman had arrived without an escort. Benny Buffano had decided to give his marriage one more try and had gone to New York to patch things up with his wife. Mrs. Foragi expected him to come crawling back at any moment.

"I'm so happy Joe performed our wedding ceremony. He did a beautiful job, don't you think?"

"Yes. I was quite moved by his words. Of course, the Latin stuff went right over my head, but I pretended I knew what he was talking about." Mary smiled indulgently. Dan hadn't batted an eyelash when she'd told him she wanted to get married in the church, with her brother officiating. He'd even taken classes to prepare for their nuptials.

Lowering his voice so no one else could hear, he added, "Has your brother said anything more about leaving the church?"

She shook her head. "No. Not a word. But I suspect that's because he didn't want to ruin my wedding day with any unpleasantness. And trust me, if the worst happens, and my mother finds out . . ." She shuddered, rubbing her arms.

"He seems quite taken with your maid of honor."

Mary heaved a sigh. "Annie despises the ground he walks on, so that's a dead end. Poor Joe, I hope he finds what he's looking for.

"I'm so deliriously happy. I want everyone I love to be just as happy."

Dan hugged her close and kissed her, then a round of applause ensued. "Whoops. I forgot we were in the middle of a crowd."

"Come on," she said, tugging his hand. "We've got to perform the traditional dances, then we'll cut the cake and be on our way."

"Who's making the toast to the bride and groom? Alan told me a little while ago that he's been relieved of the task and won't be giving the best-man toast. He was rather disappointed."

Mary's forehead wrinkled in confusion. "Who told him that?"

"I think it was your mother."

"Oh, God!"

"You see, Matthew. I told you we must be patient. All good tings come in time. But we must be patient and wait."

"I know, Grandma Flora. I prayed every night, just like you said, and I tried really hard not to make God mad at me."

The old woman grasped the child's face in her hands. "You're a good boy. Soon my granddaughter will have a baby and you will have a brother or sister."

Doubt filled his eyes, and he shook his head. "Oh, I don't think so, Grandma. I heard Mary tell my dad she wanted to wait a while before having any babies, and he said okay."

Flora Russo smiled secretively. "Don't you worry. You will have a new baby brother or sister by this time next year. I promise."

His eyes lit. "Really? That's so cool! But how do you know?"

"Because I am an old woman, and old women know about these tings. In the country of my birth, it is the old women who foretell the coming of the births and deaths. With age comes wisdom."

"Wow! Do you think you can tell if the Baltimore Orioles are going to win the World Series this year? My dad would be really happy if they did."

The old woman's eyes shone with laughter. "We shall see, Matthew. Maybe if you're good, and you keep praying to God, your Orioles will win. Stranger things have happened."

"Mind if I cut in, Dan? I haven't had the opportunity to dance with your lovely bride."

"Just as long as you don't try to sweet-talk her away from me, Walt, as you did with Linda Fox." Deciding that editing was not really her forte, Linda had accepted Walt's offer to become his executive assistant, at a huge increase in salary. Dan was happy for her.

Mary smiled at Dan's boss and held out her hand. "I'd be delighted, Mr. Beyerly. Dan's told me so much about you."

"Dan's a good man," he said, smoothly gliding her across the dance floor. "I'm happy as hell—pardon my French— I'm delighted to finally be able to offer him the Sports Editor position. He'll start as soon as you return from your honeymoon. My wife finally saw the light about getting rid of that little bas—weasel nephew of hers."

Knowing she might never have an opportunity like this again, Mary took the bull by the horns. "Have you ever given any thought to investing in the restaurant business, Mr. Beyerly? Dan thinks you'd be quite good at it."

"Really?" He seemed pleased by the notion as he spun her around. "No, can't say I've ever given it much thought."

"Well, you should talk to Dan. He's got some wonderful ideas that would tie in very nicely with the Sports section."

"I'll do that."

Mary could see Walt Beyerly's mind working, and she smiled to herself, wondering what kind of food one served in a sports restaurant.

* * *

Mary and Dan sat in the center of the long banquet table, flanked by Mary's sister and Annie, along with Dan's best man, Alan Grier. Sophia had also taken it upon herself to sit at the head table, and was preparing to address the room of well-wishers.

Dan squeezed Mary's hand under the table. "Here we go. Try to keep your cool and not get upset about anything your mother says," he whispered. "I'm sure she means well."

"Easy for you to say. She's not your mother."

His mother was at the moment drinking champagne with Uncle Alfredo and looking quite taken with the man. Dan feared he'd have his own set of headaches soon. "Just be happy your mother's already married."

Following his gaze, Mary's eyes widened. "I hadn't realized my uncle had put the moves on your mother. He's very slick with the ladies, you know. And he simply adores redheads." She smiled at her pretty mother-in-law, who grinned back and waved.

Sophia stood and moved to the microphone, and Mary's stomach tightened in anticipation and dread.

"Thank you all for coming to celebrate such a wonderful occasion. And didn't Father Joseph do a wonderful job with the mass?" She smiled proudly at her son, who gave a curt nod as the applause grew louder, thanks to his mother's encouragement, then sank lower in his chair.

"Even though it's traditional for the best man to give the toast to the bride and groom"—Sophia smiled apologetically at Alan—"I wanted to pay this honor to my daughter Mary and her new husband, Daniel.

"He's Irish, but what can I say? She loves him." Everyone laughed, then applauded.

Leaning over to Mary, Dan whispered, "If you ask me, it's a great day to be Irish!" and was rewarded with a wink.

"Frank and I thought we would never see the day when our daughter would finally get married."

Mary held her breath, squeezed Dan's hand, and counted to twenty.

"Because, well"—Sophia smiled down the table at her daughter—"the trouble with Mary is . . ."

Read on for a sneak peek at

WHAT TO DO ABOUT ANNIE

The next delicious romance by

Millie Criswell

Coming in Summer 2001

"An old maid who marries becomes a young wife."

CHAPTER ONE

Being a bridesmaid sucked!

Even if you were the maid of honor.

And weddings were totally overrated.

Annie Goldman knew this because she was presently in one—her best friend Mary's, to Dan Gallagher.

It wasn't bad enough she was dressed like a rose-tinted marshmallow, surrounded by other rose-tinted marshmallows. No, she had to endure wearing the hideous tulle headpiece—a headpiece even Queen Elizabeth would have objected to. And everyone knew Liz, who probably carried Prince Philip's family jewels in those frumpy purses she toted, had no taste.

Sophia Russo—Mary's mom and dictator extraordinaire—had insisted that her daughter could not be married without bridesmaids in tulle headpieces. Most likely tulle was some type of fertility material—Annie sure as heck hoped not!—because Sophia was planning on lots of grandkids.

Annie had never been a maid of honor before, and she had no intention of ever being one again. The reasons were numerous: The clothing was hideous; you had to hold the bridal bouquet, make sure you didn't fall on your face while marching up and down the aisle; and you were forced to wear a serene smile, which gave you the appearance of suffering from a serious case of gas.

Though on the latter she was covered, because her father, Sid, seated five pews back—and trying not to look too Jewish among all the Italian Catholics, despite the fact he wore a *kippah*—carried chewable Maalox with him wherever he went. Of course, if her father should happen to forget his antacids, one had only to search through Gina's purse to find a drug supply second only to old man Moressi's pharmaceuticals.

Her mother wasn't a drug addict, just a hypochondriac who believed in being prepared.

Gina Goldman was the Boy Scout of hypochondriacs. She had more ailments than Baskin-Robbins had flavors. What would be a headache to most people was a malignant brain tumor to her mother. Thirst translated into diabetes, a stomachache to ulcers, and on a particularly bad day a mild rash was usually construed as flesh-eating bacteria.

Dr. Mankin had given Gina a clean bill of health after her physical last week—her weekly physical—but she refused to believe she wasn't dying, which drove Annie's father crazy.

"*The woman's a nut! She's healthy as a horse and still she* kvetches*! She should go in good health.*" Which, in reality, meant quite the opposite.

Annie had been surprised—stunned, really!—when her mother had shown up at the church today, because this morning she'd been dying of food poisoning.

"*God forbid, but if I should die today, Annie, you'll take the Limoges china. I don't want the Goldman girls to get it.*"

Gina despised her sisters-in-law, who had never really accepted a *gentile* into their midst, but she was fond of Mary, liked and respected Mary's brother Joe, and so had made a special effort to overcome her latest fatal affliction.

Father Joseph Russo was performing the mass and the ceremony today. And he looked damn good in his vestments! The ladies of the parish called him Father What-a-Hunk! behind his back, and it was more than fitting.

The priest was well over six feet tall, dark-haired, brown-eyed, and had dimples in his cheeks that put Shirley Temple to shame. He'd been compared to everyone from Mel Gibson to Rupert Everett, though Rupert was purportedly gay—a major waste to womankind!—and Annie knew firsthand that Joe was not.

Joe would be mortified if he knew what was being said about him. Unlike Annie, he didn't draw attention to himself, so she thought it might be prudent and very amusing to enlighten him. After all, what were friends for?

There was no doubt that his holiness was a hotty. Under those vestments lurked the body of a man who worked out on a regular basis. Sinewy forearms, bulging biceps, muscular chest, and . . .

Well, it wouldn't be prudent to venture below the waist while in church. She didn't want to be struck down, smited a mighty blow, turned into a pillar of salt— No, wait! That was Lot's nosy wife.

The man should have been called Father What-a-Waste, in Annie's opinion, because celibacy and Father Joseph Russo just didn't go hand in hand.

"I, Mary Russo, take you, Daniel Gallagher, to be my husband, to have and to hold from this day forward, for better or for worse . . ."

As his younger sister recited in a whisper-soft, dreamy voice the vows that would bind her to Daniel Gallagher forever, Joe's gaze slipped from the lovely bride before him to the woman standing solemnly next to her.

Or as solemn as a maid of honor could look sporting hair the same rose color as her form-fitting satin gown.

The beautiful woman was anything but maidenly. And she certainly wasn't demure. She was outspoken, outlandish, and quite unorthodox, a free spirit who was totally unconventional.

Annie Goldman had captivated him from the first moment he laid eyes on her: she was six and as scrawny as a gangly filly; he was nine, just as scrawny, and had no use for girls.

Not then, anyway.

For an instant their eyes locked. Hers widened in appreciation, then narrowed slightly before she hurriedly looked down at the pink baby roses in her hands, while his filled with regret.

If only . . .

His soon-to-be brother-in-law cleared his throat loudly, drawing Joe's attention back to the bridal couple and the matter at hand. They looked confused and a little bit dismayed. Not that he could blame them.

Smiling apologetically, he continued on with the ceremony. His sister's wedding would be his last official duty as parish priest of St. Francis of Assisi's Catholic Church, though nobody knew it as yet.

Joe was hanging up his rosary beads after today and quitting the church.

It hadn't been an easy decision, but it had been one a long time in coming. He'd grown disillusioned with the church—or more, his lack of contribution to it. And though he wasn't one-hundred percent certain quitting was the right thing to do, he intended to go through with it.

He had feelings that needed to be sorted out and dealt with. Feelings no man of God should possess within the confines of a church, or outside of it, for that matter. And questions that needed answers, like: *What to do about Annie?*

"You made an absolutely gorgeous bride, *cara*," Annie told Mary later at the reception. The music of the Paisans, the band that comprised five Russo male relatives of various ages, from fifty to eighty, blared loudly from the overhead speakers.

They weren't the Beastie Boys, but they weren't exactly Guy Lombardo, either.

"Uncle Tony's version of 'That's Amore' is going to make Dean Martin turn over in his grave," Mary said, looking uncertain and apologetic at the same time. "But they came cheap. My father's brother practically begged for the gig. Or so I was told." Her expression remained skeptical.

"Meaning they were free, right?" Annie knew Mary's mother was big on bargains and saving a buck. Sophia had finagled a deal with the VFW, so the reception could be held at their large banquet hall. Nevermind that a Sherman tank sat in front of the building.

"So what if there's a tank?" Sophia had told her daughter when Mary expressed concern. *"The trouble with you, Mary, is that you're not patriotic. Those old geezers risked their lives to save us from the Nazis, so you could get married in this hall."*

Sophia had a thing about Nazis. Especially now that she couldn't voice her sentiments about the Irish. At least not aloud. Mary's new husband was of Irish descent, and Sophia had been forced to rein in her tongue. A blessing for everyone concerned, Annie decided.

"We have to feed them, that's about it," Mary said. "Thank goodness Marco agreed to cater the event. At least I know the food will be good."

Marco Valenti was head chef at Mary's restaurant, Mama Sophia's. He was temperamental as hell, had the disposition of Attila the Hun, but was an excellent cook. If you had a thing for the Pillsbury Dough Boy, Marco was your man.

The irritating little chef was presently teaching Annie how to cook, and she was driving him nuts in the process, which seemed a fair exchange. Paybacks were tough. And Marco had annoyed the heck out of her on more than one occasion, with his bossy ways and air of superiority.

Mary shook her head and winced when Uncle Tony hit a high note only a dog could appreciate. "The way they sound, I guess it's good we didn't have to pay them."

"Such a deal!" Annie mimicked her father perfectly. "What more do you want? Gabriel coming down from heaven and blowing horns? Free is good."

"Mary!" Sophia Russo shouted from the other side of the

room, waving frantically at her daughter, an impatient look on her face. "Come on. The photographer is waiting."

Dan was trapped between Sophia and Mary's aunt Josephine, who was sniffing his coat sleeve and looking altogether too blissful. (Admittedly, Aunt Josie had a few problems.) He, on the other hand, wore the pathetic look of an abused, neglected puppy.

"You'd better go, kiddo. Dan's in need of rescue, and I don't want your mom accusing me of ruining your wedding by monopolizing all of your time."

"Will we get a chance to talk again before I leave for the honeymoon?" Mary asked.

Annie shook her head, feeling sad at the thought that life as they knew it would be forever changed. "Not unless Dan wants to engage in a little ménage à trois tonight." She smiled wickedly. "On second thought—"

"Annie Goldman, shame on you! This is my wedding day!" The bride did her best to look indignant, but she was laughing and couldn't quite carry it off.

"*Oy vey!* I was only kidding. Now, go. Be happy." Hugging her around the waist, Annie kissed Mary's cheek, surprised by the tears suddenly flooding her eyes. She wasn't a woman normally prone to tears. Annie had made a career out of hiding her vulnerability.

"Have a wonderful time in Venice, and a wonderful life with Dan. And call me when you get back. I want to hear all the pornographic details."

From the other side of the room, where he stood next to the garish four-foot-tall silver champagne fountain that was spewing forth bubbly like an out-of-control geyser, and that his mother had insisted they needed so his father wouldn't come off looking cheap in front of the relatives—a major factor in any Italian social gathering—Joe observed Annie.

She was guiding Dan's son, Matthew, onto the dance floor.

The eight-year-old boy had been looking somewhat lost and left out during the festivities, and it was so like Annie to come to the child's rescue.

Bending over, she bussed him on the cheek, and the kid's face reddened before he wiped her kiss away with the back of his hand, making Joe grin. He could distinctly remember doing the very same thing when his mother's sisters came to call. Aunt Josephine and Aunt Angie were big on kissing, pinching cheeks, and patting bottoms. They majored in mortification.

For all her tough exterior, Annie Goldman was a tender-hearted woman, a real soft touch. Though she'd be horrified to learn anyone thought so. She was also a woman who professed indifference, who liked playing it cool and detached.

But Joe knew otherwise. From the moment he'd taken Annie to her homecoming as a favor to Mrs. Goldman, who didn't approve of the boys her daughter associated with, he realized she was someone special.

But that hadn't always been the case.

Joe had been in his junior year of college and not at all thrilled by the idea of dating his little sister's best friend, who was still in high school. He'd never really paid much attention to Annie Goldman while she was growing up, though she'd been at the house almost every day, hanging out with Mary and making his mother crazed.

She'd always been a little wild and unconventional, her clothing over the top. After all, how many teenagers dressed up as Rita Hayworth's Gilda to go to homecoming?

Annie Goldman just wasn't his type at all.

Or so he'd thought.

But Joe learned soon enough that there was substance beneath Annie's flash and flamboyance. She was smart, funny, and could talk intelligently on any number of topics. And she was much more mature than the other girls her age.

He'd been drawn to her wit, infectious laugh, and very ample charms.

Annie had a body made for sin. And Joe, at twenty-one, had been ready and willing to break a few commandments.

There was a bit of the forbidden about Annie. Like Adam to Eve, he'd been lured by her blatant sexuality and had quickly developed a healthy appetite for . . . *apples.*

Annie laughed at something the child was saying, and the husky, sensual sound drew Joe's attention back to the present, skittering down his spine like a feather on bare skin.

Filling a glass with champagne, he took a sip, then gulped a great deal more when the woman began moving across the crowded floor, in his direction. Undulating, was more like it. Annie moved like a tidal wave, and he felt like a man going under for the very last time.

"Well, well, if it isn't Father What-a-Hunk," Annie said, arching a brow at the champagne glass in his hand. "Are you trying to drown your sorrows? That's so unpriestlike. I'm actually quite shocked that you're imbibing like the rest of us mere mortals, your holiness."

"Father what?" Joe asked, and she shook her head and moved to fill a glass for herself.

Though he was tempted to tell Annie of his decision to quit the church, he wouldn't. Sophia was likely to go ballistic when she heard the news that her precious son, the priest, was turning in his clerical collar, and he wouldn't let anything ruin his sister's special day.

Mary's decision to marry Dan Gallagher, the sportswriter-turned-restaurant-critic—the very man who had trashed her restaurant—had been an agonizing one.

Thanks to his mother's overwhelming, controlling personality, all three of the Russo children had had issues to deal with while growing up. Mary's was a fear of commitment and failure, and it had taken a great deal of persuading and patience on Dan's part to bring the stubborn woman around to his way of thinking.

Of course, now that she was married and had taken over the role of mother to Dan's son, Mary said she couldn't think of a time when she'd ever objected to becoming the journalist's wife.

And wasn't it just like a woman to forget the important things in a relationship?

Flashing a smile in Annie's direction to cover his discomfort, Joe said finally, "I drink communion wine all the time, so I guess you can't call me a teetotaler."

She shrugged. "Whatever. You did a nice job on the ceremony today. I was impressed with all the Latin you spewed forth, not that I understood a word of it."

Her compliment took him by surprise. Annie had very little good to say about him these days. "It comes with the territory."

Joe's gaze drifted to the dance floor where his parents were dancing, as was his sister Connie and her proctologist husband, Eddie Falcone, who took a great deal of ribbing from the Russo clan because of his medical specialty. Mary ungraciously referred to the poor guy as "the butt doctor."

He didn't miss the wistful smile crossing Annie's lips as she watched the laughing couples. She loved to dance, to participate in anything having to do with music. "Would you like to join them?" he asked. "I'm a bit rusty, but I think I can manage without doing you serious injury."

Blue eyes widened at the invitation, then her cheeks warmed as she sipped more of the bubbly liquid while contemplating her answer. Finally, she said, "Might as well. Even though the band sucks big-time, I'd hate for all that music to go to waste."

"It won't ruin your reputation to be seen dancing with a priest?" he asked while leading her onto the dance floor, a teasing smile hovering about his lips.

"I don't give a f—a fig about my reputation. Or haven't I made that clear over the years, Father Joseph? And since you're dressed in a nice suit instead of your holier-than-thou garments, I guess I'll take my chances."

They began moving about the floor to the romantic strains of a Frank Sinatra standard, and it didn't take Annie long to become *bewitched, bothered, and bewildered* by Joe's nearness. Though she hated to admit it, even to herself, it felt wonderful to be held in his arms again. It had been a long time.

Fourteen years was a very long time.

The nostalgic thoughts bothered Annie, so she decided that when the song ended she would make her excuses and drift off to the other side of the room, away from the man's charms. The sexual attraction that had always existed between them was still as potent as ever, and she had no intention of repeating past mistakes.

"I was watching you when the bridal bouquet was tossed," Joe said. "It was nice of you to pretend to miss it so our cousin Rosemary could catch it." Tipping the scales at over two hundred and fifty pounds, poor Rosie needed all the help she could get. The overweight, unmarried woman hadn't met a cannoli she didn't like.

"I'm not looking to get hitched, so it wasn't that great a sacrifice."

"You're a lot nicer than you give yourself credit for, Annie. I watched you with Dan's boy earlier. You're a natural as a mother."

His compliment surprised and pleased her, but she tried not letting it show. "I'd better go. Your mother's been giving me the evil eye, and I can't afford to have any curses put on my head."

Before she could make good her escape, the Paisans began playing a tarantella, and Joe latched on to her hand, dragging her into the circle of energetic Italians, who were clapping their hands above their heads and singing loud enough to raise the dead as they cavorted to the lively folk dance.

"Let me worry about my mother," he told her when she started to protest again.

Someone thrust a tambourine at Annie, and she was soon banging it and singing as loudly as the rest of them, forgetting all about where she was, and whom she was with, as the magic of the music took hold.

"I am totally out of breath," Annie admitted with a smile after the dance ended, clasping an open palm to her breast. "I can't dance another step right now. But it was so much fun."

Joe's grin widened as she sucked in huge gulps of air. "And here I thought you were in shape from all those aerobic exercises you're always doing." Her tight, compact body gave testimony to that.

Concentrate on something else, he told himself, lifting his gaze to her mouth, to the fullness of her lush rose-petal lips, which proved to be an even bigger mistake. Annie had a mouth that fueled erotic dreams even a priest wasn't immune to.

Pausing midbreath, Annie shot him a look that would have withered lesser men. "I am in shape. And I haven't heard any complaints from the other men here tonight."

"And you'll get none from me," Joe said quickly, hoping to avoid an argument. "Come on, let's go sing some karaoke. I've always wanted to try it." There were a great many things he'd missed out on these past years, and he intended to rectify that, starting tonight.

Tonight was for new beginnings. He'd worry about the consequences tomorrow.

She looked at him as if he had suddenly become possessed. "What? Have you lost your mind? A priest singing karaoke? Your mother will faint dead away."

Smiling in conspiratorial fashion, he winked. "That's too good to pass up, don't you think?" With a sigh of misgiving, she relented, allowing herself to be led up to the bandstand.

"I'm not singing, just as long as you know that."

"I never took you for a chicken, Annie Goldman."

"And I never took you for a jackass, Joseph Russo."

Swallowing his smile, he settled her down onto a chair, told her to wait, and moved to talk to the guy in charge of the equipment.

A few moments later, Annie watched nervously as Joe grabbed the microphone and the screen before him lit. She had a bad feeling about this whole stupid idea. Then the music started playing, Joe began to sing, and she almost fell out of her chair.

"You fill up my senses . . ."

"Annie's Song." She sucked in her breath at the familiar strains of the John Denver classic. It was her song. The song Joe used to sing to her when they were dating—the song he had sung the first time they'd made love. A large lump lodged in her throat at the memories it conjured up.

Then cursing herself for her moment of weakness, she quickly regained control of her emotions.

"Come let me love you. Come love me again."

In a pig's eye! Annie thought, knowing *that* was never going to happen. Not again.

How could Joe do this to her? Didn't he realize what that song meant to her? He was obviously more callous than she'd given him credit for.

Noting that several curious onlookers had gathered in front of the stage and were now staring at her with stupid smiles on their faces, as if she were the "luckiest girl in the whole USA," to borrow a line from one of those hillbilly songs she detested, she felt trapped and angry.

Squirming restlessly in her seat, Annie wanted nothing more than to bolt. Except, that is, to kill Joseph Russo. That she wanted in the worst way.

Forcing a smile that was really more of a smirk, she kept her rage carefully hidden when he came to kneel down before her, and silently enumerated all the hideous things she was going to do to Joe when she got the chance.

Out of the corner of her eye, Annie caught Sophia Russo's hateful glare. She was obviously furious at her son's public display toward a woman she detested.

The woman's anger almost made Annie's pain bearable.

Almost.

But not quite.

AFTER TWILIGHT

by Dee Davis

It was the perfect place to disappear. . .

When Kacy Macgrath's life crumbled two years ago, she changed her name and escaped to her grandmother's cottage in Ireland. After her husband's awful death, Kacy uncovered secrets about him she was better off not knowing, so she ran away. Now someone is watching her.

Braedon Roche has traveled across an ocean looking for justice—to expose Kacy Macgrath as a master forger who had nearly destroyed his career as an art dealer. What Braedon doesn't expect is his undeniable attraction to the fragile widow hiding behind a web of deception. But Braedon isn't the only man following Kacy. A savage killer stalks from the shadows, chipping away at her sanity, and trapping her in an unspeakable nightmare. . . .

Published by Ballantine Books.
Available in bookstores everywhere.

Look for these page-turning novels

by Suzanne Brockmann

THE UNSUNG HERO

After a head injury, navy SEAL lieutenant Tom Paoletti catches a terrifying glimpse of an international terrorist in his New England hometown. When the navy dismisses the danger, Tom creates his own makeshift counterterrorist team, assembling his most loyal officers, two elderly war veterans, a couple of misfit teenagers, and Dr. Kelly Ashton-the sweet "girl next door" who has grown into a remarkable woman. The town's infamous bad boy, Tom has always longed for Kelly. Now he has one final chance for happiness, one last chance to win her heart, and one desperate chance to save the day . . .

HEARTTHROB

Once voted the "Sexiest Man Alive," Jericho Beaumont had dominated the box office before his fall from grace. Now poised for a comeback, he wants the role of Laramie bad enough to sign an outrageous contract with top producer Kate O'Laughlin—one that gives her authority to supervise JB's every move, twenty-four hours a day, seven days a week.

BODYGUARD

Threatened by underworld boss Michael Trotta, Alessandra Lamont is nearly blown to pieces in a mob hit. The last thing she wants is to put what's left of her life in the hands of the sexy, loose-cannon federal agent who seems to look right through her yet won't let her out of his sight. But the explosive attraction that threatens to consume them both puts them into the greatest danger of all. . . falling in love.

Published by Ballantine Books.
Available in bookstores everywhere.

THE DUKE

by Gaelen Foley

Driven to uncover the truth about the mysterious death of his ladylove, the Duke of Hawkscliffe will go to any lengths to unmask a murderer. Even if it means jeopardizing his reputation by engaging in a scandalous affair with London's most provocative courtesan—the desirable but aloof Belinda Hamilton. He asks nothing of her body, but seeks her help in snaring the same man who shattered her virtue. Together they tempt the unforgiving wrath of society—until their risky charade turns into a dangerous attraction, and Bel must make a devastating decision that could ruin her last chance at love. . . .

Published by Ballantine Books.
Available in bookstores everywhere.

National bestselling author **Millie Criswell** didn't start out to be a writer. Instead, she had aspirations of joining the Rockettes as a toe-tapping member of their dance troop, or tapping her heart away in one of those big, corny MGM musicals. Of course, she was only ten at the time, had absolutely no talent as a dancer, and cannot be blamed for her failure to succeed.

To date, Ms. Criswell has written eighteen historical, category, and contemporary romances. She has won numerous awards, including the *Romantic Times* Career Achievement Award and Reviewers' Choice Award, and the coveted MAGGIE Award from the Georgia Romance Writers.

Ms. Criswell resides in Virginia with her husband of thirty-one years. She has two grown children, both lawyers, and one neurotic Boston terrier.

Printed in the United States
by Baker & Taylor Publisher Services